· HONEY MOUNTAIN SERIES ·

SIMPLY Mine

· HONEY MOUNTAIN SERIES ·

SIMPLY *Mine*

USA TODAY BESTSELLING AUTHOR

LAURA PAVLOV

Entangled Publishing, LLC
644 Shrewsbury Commons Ave., STE 181
Shrewsbury, PA 17361
rights@entangledpublishing.com

Amara is an imprint of Entangled Publishing, LLC.

Visit our website at www.entangledpublishing.com.

Edited by Sue Grimshaw
Cover design by LJ Anderson, Mayhem Cover Creations
Edge design by LJ Anderson, Mayhem Cover Creations
Stock art by Galyna Andrushko/Shutterstock, jcarroll-images/GettyImages,
and Olga Grigorevykh/GettyImages
Interior design by Britt Marczak

ISBN 978-1-64937-868-2

Manufactured in China

First Edition April 2025

10 9 8 7 6 5 4 3 2 1

ALSO BY LAURA PAVLOV

HONEY MOUNTAIN

Always Mine
Ever Mine
Make You Mine
Simply Mine
Only Mine

MAGNOLIA FALLS

Loving Romeo
Wild River
Forbidden King
Beating Heart
Finding Hayes

COTTONWOOD COVE

Into the Tide
Under the Stars
On the Shore
Before the Sunset
After the Storm

Gregory Christopher Leon Dimitri Pavlov,
You are the man behind every great hero that I write. Thank
you for believing in me and encouraging me to chase my
dreams.

Our love story is truly my favorite.

Love you forever!
xo ~ Laura

Simply Mine is a sweet and sexy small-town romance with all the feels. However, the story includes elements that might not be suitable for all readers, including the loss of a parent in the novel's backstory. Readers who may be sensitive to this, please take note.

Chapter 1
Charlotte

The last two weeks of school were always exhausting. Summer was calling our name, and everyone was ready to be out in the sunshine, spending time at the lake—especially the kindergarteners, who were finishing up their first year of full-day school. My students would be moving on to first grade soon, and I was going to miss them so much. I thought about all of the changes to come as I took my seat at the front of the classroom, just as I did every morning when the first bell rang. All twenty-two of my kiddos were sitting on the floor in front of me, the same seats on the carpet that they'd had for the last two months—aside from the fact that Darwin had the same spot the entire school year, as it was the one that allowed him to be the least disruptive.

"You said we had ten days left of school when we left on Friday, but I counted this morning, and we only need to wake up nine more times before it's summer break," Darwin blurted, and all the kids looked between him and me to see if I was going to remind him to raise his hand and wait his turn.

Of course, I would. I was a kindergarten teacher after all. It was a part of my vocabulary, especially after spending the last ten and a half months with Darwin Deerborne. I was warned by his pre-k teacher that he would be a handful. Warned by his mother that she had yet to find a strategy to figure out how to get him to listen. Warned by more than half of the students in my class that Darwin would be changing cards often, just as he had the year before in preschool.

Card changes in kindergarten were like parking tickets for adults.

Like being grounded as a teenager.

Or getting cut off on drinks at a bar when you were in your twenties.

Darwin's card changes were the hottest gossip in our classroom, and I was proud to say that he didn't get them all that often anymore. We just kind of got one another.

I sucked in a breath, making a tiny gasping sound that got his attention, and I held one finger to my lips before holding up the other hand to remind him what he needed to do, as my gaze locked with his.

He made two little fists with his hands and grunted as if he were angry with himself for forgetting to do this on his own. His big brown eyes pinched together as he processed what I wanted him to do. Seconds later, his hand shot up high in the air, and he waited.

It had taken us months to get to this point.

"Yes, Darwin," I said with a smile on my face because I

was damn proud of the progress that he'd made.

He repeated the question, and I nodded. "Right. It's the morning, so we still have to count today. But you're correct, we have nine more sleeps until summer break. I sure am going to miss you all, but I'm excited for you to move on to first grade and see how you all shine."

I loved my students, even on the days when I wanted to pull my hair out.

Bella raised her hand, and I nodded for her to speak. "I hope I see you at the lake this summer, Miss Thomas."

"Oh, I hope so, too. That'll be so fun." I nodded.

"I have three—" Darwin started to speak before making a squeaking noise and raising his hand. I covered my mouth with my hand to keep from laughing, before motioning for him to speak. "Three questions for you."

"Go ahead," I said.

"Do you like the lake? Are you a good swimmer? Do you know I'm going to marry you someday?"

All the kids giggled, aside from Marcy Waters. Darwin's presence just seemed to annoy her.

"You can't marry your teacher, Darwin," Marcy hissed, and her bright red curls bounced on her shoulders.

"You can't talk without raising your hand," Darwin insisted as he looked over his shoulder to face her before turning back to smile at me.

"All right. Let's settle down. Marcy is correct, but I think our delivery could be a little kinder." I raised a brow at the little girl who was endlessly sassy to her classmates. "I love the lake, and I am a pretty strong swimmer, as I grew up spending my summers in the water. You're going to marry someone real special someday, Darwin. But you're a little young to be thinking about that right now. And I'm flattered by the offer, but I'm a little old for you, sweetheart. Now, let's get back to business, because we've got field day today, and we need to get our work done early."

All the kids cheered, and we started our morning routine.

An hour later, the kids were at their desks working on their phonics packets as my aide, Kell Anders, walked from table to table to check on the kids. I was inputting some grades into my computer when the door opened. Principal Peters walked in first with Dan Garfer, the superintendent of our school district. My shoulders squared, and I pushed to my feet just as Ledger Dane stepped into the classroom behind them. My stomach dipped, my hands fisted, and I swear my inner thermometer shot up. I could feel the sweat gathering at my temple, and I cleared my throat as all the kids turned around to see the three men walking my way.

What the hell was this? Ledger's brown eyes locked with mine, and flashbacks of every teen fantasy I ever had hit me hard. You know how most teens fangirl over a famous singer or actor? All of my daydreams back in the day revolved around this boy—who was no longer a boy. I'd seen him over the last few years when he'd come home, but I always managed to keep it short and sweet. After all, we had a history. One no one aside from my baby sister, Ashlan, knew about.

"Miss Thomas," Principal Peters said as he stopped in front of me. "I hope we aren't interrupting."

He always said that when he came into my classroom. He was an amazing man to work for, and he'd always treated me with kindness.

"Of course not," I said, pulling my gaze from Ledger's. "What can I do for you?"

"Well, I'm hoping you can help us convince this man here to grace us with his talent for the future plans we have here in Honey Mountain for the new middle school. Apparently, Mr. Dane says you're an old friend." Dan Garfer raised a brow at me.

Ledger Dane was my best friend's older brother. He was the guy every girl swooned over in high school. He was now a successful architect in San Francisco.

And yes, he was also my first crush.

My first kiss.

My first—I digress.

"Yes. Ledger is Jilly's brother," I said, trying to keep my tone even as it felt like my heart might burst from my chest. His presence always did that to me.

"Oh, come on. Don't embarrass me. I'm slightly more than your best friend's older brother." Ledger waggled his brows, and I felt my face flush. He wrapped an arm around my shoulder. "I'd say we're friends, too."

I let out a long breath, afraid that he was going to *out me* in front of my boss. But for what? Making out with him when I was fifteen? Doing even more with him when I was seventeen? Fantasizing about him my entire adolescence?

No. He wouldn't do that.

"Yes. Of course, we're friends."

Both of the older men chuckled before Principal Peters smiled at me. "Great. Well, we just took him out to the field behind the school to show him where we plan to build the new middle school. We're hoping he'll consider designing it for us.

Being from Honey Mountain means he's a little invested in the project, too."

"So, you'll get back to us when you know more?" Mr. Garfer asked.

"I will. I'll talk to my boss and run it by him."

"Sounds good. You've got my number, and I'll look forward to hearing from you."

Ledger nodded. His chocolate brown waves were cut a little shorter than they used to be, and scruff peppered his jaw. He wore a pair of dark jeans and a white button-up. He'd always towered over me as he was well over six feet tall, slender, with just the right amount of muscle that strained against his dress shirt when he removed his arm from my shoulder and extended his hand to both men.

The recess bell rang just then, and all the kids hurried to line up at the door as Kell moved to the front of the line. She stood behind Ledger and raised a brow at me with her typical mischievous look. She was in her mid-thirties, always laughing, and never missed pointing out a good-looking man, even though she'd been married to her amazing husband for the last ten years. She was always trying to fix me up with someone.

"Would you like to walk out with us?" asked Principal Peters, and Ledger glanced at me with a knowing smirk on his handsome face.

"I'm going to stay for a minute and catch up with Miss Thomas, if that's all right?"

"Of course, it is. Thanks again." They both left the classroom, and Kell pushed the door open and hustled the kids out to the playground. When she closed the door behind her, the air in the room shifted.

It was suddenly silent, and his eyes locked with mine.

"How're you doing, Ladybug?" My stomach dipped at the nickname he'd always called me. So maybe I had a thing for rescuing ladybugs when I was young. What can I say? My favorite color is red, and polka dots are my jam.

I moved behind my desk, needing to put a little space between us. I wasn't the same girl I was all those years ago. Ledger Dane had toyed with me enough over the years. I would not be affected by this man now.

"I'm good. How about you?"

He nodded as he moved closer to the desk, and his eyes did a slow perusal of my body before he cocked his head to the side and smiled. "I'm doing well. I wanted to stop by and see you. Jilly Bean told me you were teaching here."

"Yep. And to say I'm ready for summer break would be a massive understatement." A nervous laugh escaped, and I wished I could channel my twin sister Dylan's coolness when I was in these types of situations.

"I'll bet. You always loved spending time out at the lake." He smiled, and I squeezed my thighs together because he was ridiculously handsome, and I couldn't stop my body from reacting to him.

Not today, hormones. I'm an adult now… or at least I can pretend to be.

"I remember that day we went down the circular slide together. You were so scared, and you howled all the way down." He chuckled.

"I spent so many summers watching everyone else go down, and I was determined. But then I froze at the top, and you just happened to be right behind me." I shook my head and laughed at the memory.

"I always was good at being in the right place at the right time."

This was what I was talking about. He was a wicked flirt.

"I can't believe you remember that."

"Are you kidding? You had on that cute red-and-black polka-dot bikini. Damn, Ladybug, you had every teenage boy checking you out." His tongue swiped out to wet his bottom lip, and he crossed his arms over his chest and smiled.

Did I mention that the man was sinfully charming?

And why did he always have to look at me like that?

"Well, I don't quite remember it that way, and I always had Dilly there to protect me."

He whistled. "Dilly would cut a dude if he looked at you wrong. That girl was badass from the minute she took her first breath. I'm looking forward to seeing all your sisters while I'm home for a few weeks. That's what I wanted to talk to you about. I was hoping you could meet me for dinner tonight so we could discuss a few things for the wedding?"

I reached for my water bottle, taking a long sip in hopes of calming my nerves.

Relax. He was your childhood crush. You're a grownup now.

You can do this.

"Oh, okay. Are Jilly and Garrett going?"

His lips turned up in the corners. "No. Just you and me. The best man and the maid of honor. Do you have a problem being alone with me?"

Um... the few times that actually happened over the years,

it always led to something.

Something I never could get enough of.

Something that never lasted beyond the moment.

Something he didn't want to take further.

"Of course not. Where should we meet?"

"Why don't I pick you up at six? I heard you bought Vivi's old house on the lake."

Small spaces and Ledger Dane were never a good thing. But I couldn't exactly tell him that. And I was fairly certain he had a girlfriend. And things were different now.

I was different.

Older and wiser.

"Sure. That sounds great."

The door from the playground flew open, and Darwin was the first one to step into the classroom, as he hurried toward me. He stopped in front of Ledger, hands on his hips as he narrowed his gaze. His head tipped completely back, and he looked up at him. "Who are you?"

"Darwin. Use your manners, please," I said, walking around my desk as we'd be starting math class now.

"Hello, mister. Who are you?"

Ledger chuckled and bent down to Darwin's eye level. "I'm Ledger Dane, little man. Who are you?"

"I'm Darwin Deerborne, and I'm going to marry Miss Thomas one day. Even though Meanie Marcy says that I can't." He stomped his little foot, and Ledger's head tipped back as laughter bellowed around the room.

"Darwin. We don't speak about our classmates that way. Please go to your seat." I raised a brow, and he shrugged.

Ledger pushed to stand and rumpled Darwin's hair. "I get

it, little dude. But you're going to have to get in line for Miss Thomas."

I could feel my cheeks heat. "You're not helping, Ledger. Take your seat," I said to Darwin before turning my attention back to the man who was causing me to lose my mind in front of my class as they all filed in quietly. "I'll see you tonight."

He knocked on the desk twice and winked. "See you later, Ladybug."

This was not how I saw the day going. My mind was reeling with how I'd survive having dinner with him.

But this was a test. And I was ready for it. I'd moved on from my silly crush.

Tonight, I'd have the opportunity to show myself and Ledger that.

"Billy cut me in line!" Daniel shouted, and I was brought back to reality.

Ledger couldn't just come to town and turn my world upside down. Besides, he'd be leaving as quickly as he came.

Just like he always did.

Chapter 2

Ledger

When I arrived in Honey Mountain today, I'd gone straight to the elementary school to meet Dan Garfer to discuss the middle school project. The man had been relentless, leaving me messages at the office about meeting with him, and he'd reached out to my grandmother, who insisted I call him immediately. This was the thing about small towns... everyone knew Jilly and Garrett were getting married in two weeks, which meant he knew I'd be coming home.

Jilly Bean was the closest person in my life, next to my mom and Nan. I loved my three girls fiercely. The fact that Jilly had agreed to let our father walk her down the aisle pissed me the hell off, but I wouldn't interfere with her special day. Of course, the man wanted to have the honor of giving her away and put on the big show—yet he wouldn't drop a penny to help give her the dream wedding she'd always wanted.

He was a piece of shit husband and an even worse father.

God only knew what young piece of ass he'd be bringing with him to the wedding. The man had been divorced several times since he blew up our family.

He was a selfish asshole who only thought with his dick.

I let out a long breath as I pulled into the driveway.

Mom and Jilly would be at work for a little while longer, but Nan was expecting me, and I was fairly certain she'd cooked up a storm as she always liked to feed me.

I took a second to think about Charlotte Thomas. The girl was good to the core. Always had been. Kind and sweet and smart. A little bit shy, which I'd always found attractive.

Damn, she looked good.

She definitely had her guard up with me, and I understood it.

Our history was—complicated.

I'd always been drawn to her. But she'd always been off limits for a multitude of reasons. For starters, fucking Lucy Blocker, who'd been best friends with Jilly and Charlie when they were kids, had all but attacked me when she kissed me at a party my freshman year in high school, and she was only in seventh grade. I quickly stopped it when the girl tried to climb me like a motherfucking oak tree. She didn't take the rejection well, and she'd had a complete meltdown, refusing to be friends with Jilly because, apparently, I was the devil for turning her down. And somehow, I was the dick in the situation. Jilly didn't speak to me for weeks and made me promise that all friends moving forward were off-limits.

No problem.

I did just fine where girls were concerned and certainly

wasn't seeking out her friends.

Until my junior year when Ladybug had her first cocktail with my sister. I'd picked them both up from a party. Jilly had passed out, so Charlotte and I had stayed up for hours talking. She cried about her mama, who'd passed away from cancer a few years earlier, and I opened up about my father. I was fairly certain I was her first kiss. She wasn't mine, but she sure as hell was the most memorable.

I could still remember how those lips felt against mine.

How she tasted like beer and cherry lip gloss.

And I fucking loved it.

Wasn't that just the way it goes? You always wanted the one you couldn't have.

But it was for the best. I'd been going through a rebellious stage after my father destroyed our family, devastating both my mother and my sister. I did what I could to be the man of the house—but I was drinking and messing around with girls back then. Charlotte Thomas could do a whole lot better than me.

The door flew open to the guest house that sat behind the home I'd grown up in. We moved in when I was five years old, and my mother had wanted this house because it came with a guest cottage for my grandmother. Nan stood there, waving her hands at me. I laughed and jumped out of the car.

"I could die before you finally make your way over here!" she shouted. "I'm an old lady. I can't be waiting on you all day. I'm not like the young girls you run around with."

I rolled my eyes as I made my way to the front door and scooped her off her feet and spun her around. "You know you're the only girl for me, Nan."

I loved this woman in a way I couldn't even begin to describe. She and I had always been close, and I made sure I came home at least once a month to see her, Jilly, and Mom. Sometimes, I only had time to stay for one night because I worked insane hours most of the time, but I always made sure I was here.

I was not my father.

I didn't abandon the people that I loved just because I couldn't keep my dick in my pants.

"Mmmhmmm... you smell like success." She giggled when I set her down on her feet.

"And you smell like bacon."

"Pork is the way to a man's heart, right?" She had gray hair that was short and curled close to her head. The woman had had the same hairstyle since the day I was born. She wore a floral dress with a ruffled apron tied over it. Nan always wore aprons. I bought her a new one every year for her birthday and Christmas, and Nan Day. Yes. We had a Nan Day. It was the day after Valentine's Day because she hated Valentine's Day after Papa passed away when I was only five years old, and she moved into the guest house behind our home. So, I came up with Nan Day. And she'd allow herself a good cry on Valentine's Day and then partied it up on Nan Day.

"It sure is. And I haven't had a home-cooked meal in far too long."

"Oh, let me guess," she said as she set a plate down on the white, round table in her kitchen, and she gestured for me to sit. "Jessica doesn't cook?"

"Ah, not really her thing, and we broke up, actually."

She set down her plate and took the chair across from me.

Peach roses sat in a crystal vase in the center of the table. My grandmother's passion was gardening. Well, that and dirty talk. The woman was a self-proclaimed dirty bird, and I loved everything about her.

"I spoke to you several times last week, and you never said a word."

I took a bite of my BLT that only Nan made taste this good and moaned, my mouth already watering as I took in the homemade potato salad on my plate. "Damn, I missed your cooking."

"You are looking a little thin." She said this every time she saw me. I was probably down a few pounds right now because I'd been working like crazy. I'd known I'd be taking a few weeks off to be here for the wedding, and I hoped to avoid endless calls from my boss—so I'd been putting in long hours. "Tell me about Jessica."

"It wasn't all that serious. She wanted it to be, and I didn't."

"And how does that play out, seeing as she's your boss's daughter?" She raised a brow.

I finished chewing. "I think we can handle it like adults. He pushed hard for me to ask her out, and I gave it a shot. But she was ready to plan our wedding, and I was going through the motions. We only dated for a few weeks, and it just didn't go all that deep, you know? I think she's just looking for a husband who makes a good living and doesn't care if there's anything more there."

I had tried hard to avoid my boss, Harold's, insistence that I meet his youngest daughter. Jessica had come on strong, and I'd taken her out a few times over the last two months. She was beautiful and smart, but there just wasn't any spark or connection. The girl wouldn't know a joke if it bitch-slapped her in the face. We never once laughed together, and that was a deal breaker for me, not that I was even looking for something serious.

I wasn't.

"How was the sex?" She rubbed her hands together, and I barked out a laugh.

"It was fine, you dirty old bird."

"I'm eighty-seven years young, and don't you forget it. Let me tell you the secret to happiness." She was such an anomaly. She wore floral dresses and had cute granny hair. But she cussed like a sailor and always wanted the dirty details.

"Do tell." I took a bite of potato salad and closed my eyes because it was so fucking good.

"Your partner should be your best friend and your lover. And the sex, well, it needs to be mind-blowing. No pun intended." She cackled and then pulled herself together. "You want to be coming back for more year after year. You just keep meeting these women, but you don't have the connection. And without the connection, I'm sorry, but the orgasms are shallow." She shrugged and reached for her glass of orange juice.

I barked out a laugh and shook my head. "I do just fine, Nan. But I appreciate the concern."

"You aren't your father, Ledger." Her tone turned serious.

"I know that. I still can't believe that fucker is going to be at the wedding."

"Well, your sister wants to make amends with that *jackass*." She raised her brow, reminding me that she didn't care for the F-word. It was the one and only word she didn't like, as far as I knew. "So, we need to respect her wishes. But you are nothing like him, my boy. Even all those years ago, when your mama brought him home to meet me, I wasn't a fan. I noticed the way he always looked at other women. But I accepted him after they got married and had the two most beautiful babies in the world. I think his dad running out on them when he was a little boy, and then his mother becoming a raging alcoholic, damaged him in a lot of ways. But willing someone to be something they aren't just doesn't work. He's a cad, or what is it you young people call it these days? A player."

"I've dated quite a bit in my lifetime, so I'm sure some would call me a player." I'd never met my father's father. He never returned after he'd run off, and I'd only met his mother twice. She didn't keep in touch with any of us, and my father didn't want us to have a relationship with her. Jilly and I never missed them because we didn't really know much about them. I wasn't jumping on ancestry dot com anytime soon, that was for sure.

"You're not a player, Ledger." She smiled up at me and reached across the table. "You aren't pretending to be someone you aren't. You date, and you're faithful to those women while you're with them. You're honest from the start about what you want. You know, I think you have a fear of commitment after all you've been through with your dad and then losing Colt so suddenly. But you don't cheat on anyone, and that's the difference. You aren't lying about who you are. You embrace it."

The mention of my best friend being gone still sat heavy on my shoulders. And did I mention that my grandmother was a therapist for thirty years? The woman loved to dissect people and their thoughts, and I thought I was her favorite to analyze.

"Thanks, Nan. Losing Colt was the worst thing I've ever been through. But I can't bring him back, and I know that. As far as Dad goes, I'd never want to treat anyone the way that he treated Mom. But who knows, maybe if I were married and unhappy, I'd be an asshole, too. Maybe the asshole gene runs in our family?" I raised a brow, half-joking, half-serious.

She squeezed my hand. "You didn't get the asshole gene, my boy."

"How do you know?"

"Because an asshole doesn't work as hard as you do. An asshole doesn't come home every month to see his girls. An asshole doesn't pay for his sister's dream wedding when her father refuses to contribute. An asshole doesn't step up as a teenage boy and force his mom to get out of bed and get in the shower because she's so devastated. Your heart is far too big to be in the body of a selfish man. It's not who you are. But you're the only one who doesn't see it."

I pushed to my feet. This conversation always made me uncomfortable. I hated talking about the man who I worshipped for the first thirteen years of my life. The first time I caught him with another woman. The first time he asked me not to tell anyone what I'd seen. The first time I lied to my mother.

It had changed me in a way.

My perfect world had shattered that day.

"Don't be too concerned. I think I'm pretty amazing," I teased as I walked to the sink to wash my hands because I couldn't look at her. "I'm just content being a bachelor for the rest of my life. Since when is being a wealthy, single dude such a bad thing?"

"It's not a bad thing if it's truly what you want. Now get back over here, my boy. You don't get to hide from me. You can pull that shit with everyone else, but I know it bothers you. What he asked you to do for him. He's a selfish man."

I sat down in my chair and looked at her. "Can we just focus on the wedding and make this a great time for Jilly Bean? I don't want to go deep, Nan. Not right now."

"There's never a good time to dig up the painful stuff, but I promise, Ledger, it will be waiting for you. And I'll be right here with open arms when it all boils to the surface."

"Let's not boil anything to the surface, you crazy old bird."

"That's dirty bird to you," she said with a laugh. "Tell me how it went at the school. Principal Peters sure is easy on the eyes, am I right?"

"Um, that's a hard no from me. The man is in his late sixties and has no respect for manscaping those bushy eyebrows of his."

"I like a hairy fella," she said, and we both laughed. "Did you see my Charlie girl?"

Nan and Charlotte had always been close. She used to come over when she was young and spend her Saturdays gardening with my grandmother while my sister was out riding her bike. And after her mother passed, she looked for that warmth from Nan even more. Maybe it was the way my grandmother listened because she knew how to get people to talk—but they had a connection that was important to both of them.

"I did. We're going to have dinner tonight to talk about what we need to do for the wedding." I picked up my juice so I wouldn't have to look at her.

"Oh, really? You can't work that out via laptop or cellular device or whatever you young people do today?" She smirked.

"No. I want to have a real conversation. This is my only sister's wedding, after all. She's been cutting out magazine photos for her special day since she was a kid, for Christ's sake."

"Don't be bringing the Lord into your rant." She chuckled. "She and Charlie always did like to talk about their future wedding day when they were young. I think Charlie's single right now. She was just over last weekend, helping me prune my roses. She and the bug guy had been dating for a little bit, but she said she didn't see a future with him, and they were better off as friends."

"The bug guy? What the hell is that about?"

"He was an exterminator, you know. They take care of the bugs."

"Yeah, I got it. She can do much better."

"You don't even know him." She quirked a brow.

"I know enough." Isn't that how I've always felt about her? Maybe I was just being protective. She was my little sister's best friend, after all.

"Oh, yes. You sure do. Didn't you scare the living crap out of poor Rand Carson his junior year in high school when you came back from college that weekend? Even today, when I run into that little brat, he can't even look at me."

"He's a fuc—dickless creep. He took her to a dance, and then she caught him making out with Wendy Hamble behind the trees at the bonfire. The asshole realized that she wasn't going to put out, and he moved on while they were still at the dance. That piece of shit should run if he sees me."

"So you did give him that black eye back then. I remember hearing he tripped and ran into a tree."

"Well, let's just say he tripped and ran into my fist. We'll leave it at that. He humiliated her."

"Yes. That was the night Jilly lied and said she was sleeping over at the Thomases' house, and you picked up Charlie, knowing all along that Jilly was out with Garrett. It's all coming back to me."

Nan could deliver a guilt blow whenever they were available; I didn't think she'd ever let me forget that night. Let's just say she was none too pleased that I helped cover for my sister. "Well, she was seventeen years old, and she's marrying him in a few weeks, so I think it worked out fine."

Nan rolled her eyes. "And you took Charlie home that night, didn't you? After your fist had a run-in with Rand's face. You were always so mysterious about that night." Because it was the night that I'd crossed the line. Lost control.

"I was in college. I didn't have a curfew. A man needs to have some secrets, right?"

"Sure. I love a mysterious man." She waggled her brows as she ran her fingers over one of the roses in the vase. "Just remember that sometimes, everything you want is right in front of you."

"So wise, Nan. Are you talking about the fact that I saw that peach cobbler over there on the counter? That is everything I want right now."

She howled in laughter. "Fine. Let's have some pie and go

sit out in the garden. I want to show you the daisies and the peonies that bloomed."

"Oh, I love it when you talk pie and flowers with me. You know I'm all about the blooms." I groaned as I pushed to my feet and cleared both of our plates.

I spent the next two hours smelling flowers, listening to stories about the ladies of her bridge club, and how Loretta Barns was sleeping with the tennis pro, Frankie Freel, from the Honey Mountain Country Club. I nearly choked on my cobbler because we'd gone to school together, and the thought that he was banging a woman in her mid-eighties was something I would rather not know. Nan had insisted that Loretta's face-lift made her look like she wasn't a day over seventy. As if that made it so much better.

But I wasn't a judger, unless we were talking about my father, who deserved all the judgment in the world, at this point. Otherwise, I preferred not to know everything that went on in this town.

I glanced down at my watch and pushed to my feet. "All right, I'm going to go see if Mom and Jilly are home. Then I need to take a quick shower and head to dinner."

She whistled. "I'll bet you do. I know I've told you this, but Papa and I met when we were in middle school, and he showed me no interest the first time he spoke to me. And then he was nearly panting over me every time he saw me in high school. He said I was the one who almost got away, because it took him a long time to win me over after ignoring me for so long."

She followed me back inside toward the front door, rambling on, making a point about something that I had no idea where she was going with it. There was always a life lesson hidden beneath her chatter.

"Well, you were worth the wait, Nan. Best lady I know." I kissed the top of her head.

"Oh, don't get all mushy on me now. I was making a point."

I pulled open the door and laughed. "And that is?"

"Maybe there's someone special that almost got away from you."

"You been dipping in the booze early, Nan?" I asked as I walked backward down the driveway toward my mom's house.

"Open your eyes, you stubborn ass. I know you better than you know yourself."

"I love you. I'll call you later."

"You know... maybe I will take a dip in the sauce a little early today. You've made me nostalgic."

I turned around, waved my hand over my head, and pushed open the front door to the home I'd grown up in. The home I had a love-hate relationship with. So many good memories here, and some I wish I could forget.

"Anyone home?"

Jilly came charging around the corner and lunged into my arms. "Hey, brother dearest. I'm so happy you're here."

Garrett came over next, and I set my sister down and did that half-handshake-half-hug thing that dudes always did.

"Are you guys ready for the big day?"

Garrett shrugged and glanced at my sister before turning back to look at me. "It's all in the boss's hands now. She's got it all under control."

"Oh, I like that name. Yes. Let's go with that. Call me Boss Lady." Jilly leaned her head on my shoulder, and I wrapped an arm around her, and we walked into the kitchen.

"There's my handsome boy," my mom said, as she set the bag of groceries down on the counter and hurried over to hug me as Jilly moved to unpack the groceries. My mother was one of the most amazing women I'd ever known. She worked her ass off as an ER nurse, tolerating years of my father's get-rich-quick schemes, where he used all that they had in their savings account to start up whatever new business he was feeling at the moment. The man was a complete scam artist, and he'd buried his wife in debt in the process. He'd also been cheating on her for years, as well. God knows he pulled that shit for much longer than anyone should have had to endure. She managed to save our home, and she never complained about the hand that she was dealt.

"Hi, Mama," I said, pulling her into my arms and hugging her.

"Did Nan feed you?" she asked.

"Of course, she did. You know how she is when I come home."

"Well, I thought I could make pasta for dinner. Will anyone be around?"

"You know we won't miss a home-cooked meal," Jilly said as she winked at Garrett. My sister lived with my mother, and she'd just graduated from college a few months ago. Garrett had his own condo that she'd move into after the wedding, but the two of them were looking for a home of their own, as well.

"I'm actually going to dinner with Charlie to go over some of our duties as maid of honor and best man. I saw her over at the school today when I met with Dan Garfer."

"Oh, good. She's the best planner. She's been working on

her speech for weeks and won't tell me anything that's in it."
Jilly shrugged. Garrett was studying me with a smirk on his
face, like the bastard was in on a secret that no one else knew.
"Speaking of weddings, look at this floral arrangement that
Mrs. Winthrop sent me today." She grabbed her phone, and
she and my mother stood huddled over it as she showed her
endless photos of what looked like the exact same arrangement
in each picture, yet they gasped as if each one was better than
the last. I moved to the fridge to grab a bottle of water, and
Garrett came up behind me.

"You and Charlie are going to dinner, huh?" he whispered,
glancing over his shoulder to make sure no one was listening.

"Yes. She is the maid of honor, right?"

"Sure, she is." He chuckled. "You know how everyone
calls me the silent observer?"

"No. I thought everyone called you Jilly's bitch." I barked
out a laugh because he'd sent me a text about running into
endless people while he was at the store picking up tampons
for my sister last week.

"That's just you, dicklicker." He raised a brow. "Remember,
I've been around a long time."

"I have no idea what you're talking about." I took a long
pull from my water bottle.

"Sure, you don't. Smartest dude I know. Have fun at your
work dinner."

"I will. You have fun eating pasta and looking at
three hundred fucking pictures of the same exact floral
arrangement." I clapped him on the shoulder. "I'm going to
go grab a shower before I leave."

"Oh, I'll bet you are," Garrett said as he waggled his brows, and I flipped him the bird as I headed to my room. Our home was a little dated, but my mother had a knack for making it feel warm and comfortable. The master bedroom sat on one end of the house, and my room and Jilly's room were connected by one bathroom. We used to have some knockdown, drag-out fights over this bathroom. Mostly because she spent more time than any human should ever spend getting ready.

I stripped down and climbed into the shower, letting the hot water beat down on my back. I thought about how fucking good Charlotte looked today in that pink-fitted dress. It hugged her curves in all the right places. I gripped my dick and squeezed my eyes closed.

I wasn't proud that it wasn't my first time slapping the salami to my sister's best friend.

Hell, it wasn't even the first time this week.

She's always been the girl I fantasized about.

The one I thought about.

Maybe Nan was right.

Maybe Charlotte Thomas was the one who got away.

Chapter 3

Charlotte

I texted my sisters as soon as I got home from work, because this is just what you do when you have four sisters and you're all close.

Me: I'm having dinner with Ledger to discuss our responsibilities as best man and maid of honor. What should I wear? I mean, I don't care, but I just want to dress appropriately.

Dylan: My ass, you don't care. I'd start by saying that his responsibilities include you sitting on his face. It's the least he can do as best man.

I swear my twin sister said things just to get a rise out of people. And it normally worked, which it most definitely would here.

Everly: Why must you be so crude?

Dylan: Have you ever sat on a sexy man's face before, Sissy?

Everly: Oh my gosh. I'm nursing your nephew right now. I will not answer that.

Dylan: I'm guessing that's a yes, seeing as you got knocked up so quickly after getting married.

Vivian: I'm not getting involved in that conversation. I vote for shorts, blouse, flats.

Dylan: I'm sorry. I just fell asleep because that is maybe the most boring outfit ever. This is Ledger freaking Dane. Whether you claim you're still attracted to him or not, you crushed hard on him when you were young. Let him see what he's been missing.

Ashlan: White sundress, sandals, hair in loose waves.

Dylan: Must I be everything to everyone? That is not going to get his attention.

Everly: Why don't you just tell her what to wear, then, instead of insulting everyone?

Dylan: Go eat some protein, Ever. Nursing is making you grumpy.

Everly: <middle finger emoji>

Dylan: But, yes. Happy to help. White silk tank, dark skinny jeans, nude heels, and let's put a lacy black bra under that tank and really torture the bastard.

Vivian: I never like when I see a colored bra under a white blouse.

Everly: Agreed. It's a little trashy.

Dylan: Hey, Mother Teresa called. She asked that you return to the convent for Bible study.

Ashlan: <laughing face emoji> <praying hands emoji>

Vivian: I like everything you said, but I'd wear a nude bra and bring your cute floral clutch.

Dylan: Slip a few condoms in that wholesome clutch. <winky face emoji>

Me: OMG! Stop. This is Ledger. Jilly's brother. We're friends. We've hardly spoken over the last few years.

Dylan: Good. Maybe you're out of the friend zone. And you dumped the beetle, so you're single.

Ashlan: His name is Lyle. He's an exterminator. What is your obsession with the bug guy?

Dylan: Snooze fest. I didn't care for him.

Me: I'm proud to say that I saw Ledger today, and I'm no longer affected by him. Plus, I'm pretty sure he has a girlfriend, anyway. And he doesn't live here. You're reaching.

Dylan: So you're just asking what to wear to dinner because it doesn't matter?

Me: Because I'm indecisive and tired. I teach five-year-olds for a living. I can't think straight by the end of the school year. And, FYI, the P.E. teacher, Tobias, asked me out today.

Dylan: No. I saw that dude at the diner last week, and he kept scratching his balls. That's a big red flag. Maybe he should call the bug guy and get that taken care of? <laughing face emoji>

Ashlan: <eye roll emoji>

Dylan: Just go and have a little fun tonight. Don't overthink it.

Everly: I agree. Have fun. Don't stress. Although I saw Ledger a few weeks ago when he was home, and he somehow managed to get even better looking.

Vivian: Don't worry about it, Charlie. Just go have dinner. We love you.

Ashlan: Text us after.

Dylan: Or don't. If you're getting down and dirty. <winky face emoji> <panting face emoji>

The group messages were completely normal with my sisters. This went on all day, every day. We talked about Everly's nipples being sore from my nephew, Jackson, who was four months old now. And Vivian updated us constantly on the color of Baby Bee's poop. My little niece had just turned a year old, so I wasn't sure why we needed to know the color of her poops every single day. Ashlan liked to send us screenshots of the drawings that Paisley and Hadley, her future stepdaughters, made for her. And Dylan liked to share her road rage stories or tell us about the hot men that she would see who quickly annoyed her by the next text.

So, it was always entertaining in the Thomas girls' family group chat. I took one last glance in the mirror and dabbed on a little pink lip gloss. I'd gone with the white silk tank, dark skinny jeans, nude heels, and much to Dilly's disappointment— I'd worn the nude bra underneath.

There was a knock on the door, and I hurried to grab my keys and purse. Like I said, I didn't trust myself in small spaces with Ledger Dane. I was older now. Wiser. And I wouldn't be panting over this man anymore. I'd wasted enough years doing that. We were going to talk about Jilly's wedding.

That was all this was.

I pulled open the door and tried to keep my mouth from gaping. He wore a black button-up and dark jeans. He was tan, and his muscles strained just a little against his dress shirt. He was tall and lean and impossible not to stare at.

"Hey, Ladybug. You look gorgeous."

"Oh. Thanks. Are you ready?" I asked nervously, nearly tripping and falling into his chest as I tried to get out the door. He reached for my shoulders and helped me find my footing.

"I take it you aren't inviting me in?" He raised a brow, and I pulled the door closed behind me and hurried past him.

"I didn't think you'd care to see it."

"No problem. I'll see it when I drop you off." He moved in

front of me and pulled open the passenger door.

I sucked in a breath. Great. Now he wanted to come over after I had a glass of wine in me.

Liquor and Ledger Dane definitely didn't mesh.

I learned that the first time I was ever intoxicated.

"So how's work?" I asked as we drove the short distance to the restaurant.

"It's great. My boss keeps dangling this partnership over my head, so I've been working a lot. But I wanted to take this time off to be here for Jilly," he said as he pulled the car into the parking lot behind my favorite steakhouse.

"That's amazing. You always wanted to own your own firm, right? So, becoming a partner would make you a partial owner, wouldn't it?"

He jumped out of the car and opened my door as I stepped out. Ledger's mom and Nan were sticklers for manners, and even though the boy left a lot of broken hearts in his trail, he was always a gentleman.

"Well, it wouldn't quite be like being an owner because I wouldn't have enough of the pie to ever have a say in what projects we'd do, but it would be better money than I'm making now." He pulled open the door to the restaurant, and I stepped inside.

The hostess took her time drinking him in, making no attempt to hide her slow perusal, and I rolled my eyes. He ignored it, or at least pretended not to notice, as she led us to the table. Classical music played lightly in the background, and the room was dimly lit. We didn't need to come here to chat about the wedding, as it was more of a fine dining restaurant, but I wasn't complaining because I lived on a teaching salary, and I didn't eat here often. Once we sat down and ordered a glass of wine, I focused my attention back on the conversation.

"You already make an insane amount of money, don't you?" I knew this because Jilly told me he owned a gorgeous condo in San Francisco, and he'd offered to pay for her wedding, and she'd spared no expense.

"I do okay." He shrugged as he paused when the server brought over our wine.

We placed our dinner order, and I took a sip of wine. The fruity flavors burst on my tongue, and I moaned. "Nothing is better than a glass of wine after a day of trying to get five-year-olds to listen to you."

He chuckled. "Well, that little dude, Darwin, seemed like he'd do just about anything you asked him to."

I smiled at the thought of that little angel. "He's come a long way. Everyone warned me about him, but he's the highlight of my day most days."

"That doesn't surprise me," he said, his tongue dipping out to wet his bottom lip. "You always had a thing for lost causes. You wanted to fix everyone."

I raised a brow. "I did not. Who are you referring to?"

"Abandoned ladybugs, that injured pigeon that Tommy Rubello's dad shot with a pellet gun." He shook his head at the memory. "Remember, you made that citizen's arrest, and he promised to never shoot an animal again."

I let out a long breath. The man was such an asshole. "Well, Dilly egged his truck a few months later, and I reported him to animal control when I saw him mistreating his dog, so I think he retired his evil ways and currently lives animal-free."

"And me," he said, surprising me. "You were the only

person I confided in about my dad. You were the one who confronted me about how much I was drinking before I finally told my mom what had happened. It wasn't just the bugs and the birds, Ladybug. It's who you are."

I looked away for a minute. I think I loved this boy long before I even knew what it meant. There'd always just been something about him. The way he demanded the attention of everyone in the room. The way he cared for his mom and sister and grandmother. The way he watched out for me from the first day Jilly and I became friends. And I hated that I felt so much for him. Hated how much time I'd wasted loving this boy who'd never reciprocated those feelings. Feelings I'd kept from my best friend all these years and buried deep inside me.

"Fine. You caught me. I'm a bleeding heart." I waved my hands around and chuckled. I needed to change the subject because taking a trip down memory lane would bring it all back. The feeling of want and desire. He never saw me the way that I saw him. "So let's talk about the wedding."

"Nice subject change. You never liked when someone showered you with attention, did you?"

I've always liked when you showered me in attention, though.

"No, I'm more of a blend in type of girl." I shrugged as our server set our plates down.

"But you never blended in very well, did you? You were born to shine, Ladybug. Even if you don't know it." He raised a brow at me before cutting into his T-bone steak.

The smell of honey and butter wafted around the restaurant, and my stomach growled as I cut a bite of my filet.

"And you've always been a giant flirt and tease." I popped

the steak in my mouth and took my time chewing. There. I said it. It was time to stop this cycle. We hadn't spent much time together over the last few years since he moved away. I'd always make an excuse that I had to be somewhere when I'd see him. We'd certainly never gone to dinner, just the two of us. But this pattern, him pulling me in whenever we were alone—it was time to break it.

He smirked as if he liked being called out. "And you were also the only one to call me out on my shit. Aside from Jilly reaming my ass every time one of her friends crushed on me, or I threatened a dude for looking at you or her wrong."

"I mean, you are the reason we aren't friends with Lucy Blocker anymore."

He threw his hands up and gaped at me. "Are you serious right now? She kissed me. She was in seventh fucking grade, and I shut it down, and then she went all stalker-crazy-town on me. I mean, she did everything but boil a bunny on my stovetop or kidnap me and tie me to her bed and have her way with me."

Ledger was right. Lucy had acted absolutely insane. She'd crushed on him for a long time, and she took her shot. When he didn't return the feelings, she literally lost her shit. She cut Jilly and me off and told Jilly she was trash just like her brother. It was a whole thing back then, but now it was almost laughable.

"She did not handle that well." I shrugged and tried not to laugh.

"She prank called our house for a year. She used to come to the classes I was in my junior year in high school and pretend to be in them. She was a fucking freshman. You two should be thanking me that she stopped being friends with you. The girl was not stable." He shivered like he was still traumatized.

"I will give you that—she was definitely crazed when it came to you. But, it hardly slowed you down. You were freaking homecoming king junior year and prom king senior year. You did just fine, didn't you?"

He leaned forward, his face inches from mine. "Are you keeping tabs on me, Ladybug?"

"Hardly. You were hard to miss." I chuckled.

"So were you." He leaned back. "But you were too good for everyone in this town. You still are."

He'd always said that. It annoyed me back then, because I always wondered if it was just a way of letting me know there could never be anything between us. Not that Jilly would have been okay with it, anyway, but also because he didn't feel that way about me.

"I think that's just what you say when you don't want someone the way they want you." I reached for my glass and polished off my last sip. I couldn't believe that I'd actually just said that. I wasn't a timid teen who was all tongue-twisted over her best friend's older brother anymore.

"Trust me. I don't say shit that I don't mean. You can even ask Lucy Blocker how fucking honest I am, and I'm sure she'd vouch for me. I don't lie—you know I hate liars."

Ledger resented his father for all he'd done to his family and for asking Ledger to lie for him. I knew how he felt about dishonesty. But I also knew that he loved me like a little sister, and he'd never want to hurt me. So, I'd always been confused by his mixed signals.

"Fine. I'm too good for everyone. Just good enough to kiss

and do whatever it is we did in that car that night—but nothing more." I looked away. We never talked about it. The few times we shared those secret moments, we pretended they never happened afterward.

His face dropped. He looked like I'd slapped him. "Fuck, Charlie. You know I only stopped it both times because I didn't want to hurt you. You deserved better. I did the right thing, and I stand by that."

"Were you drunk when that happened? I know the first time we kissed, I was tipsy. Were you?"

"Not even a little bit. I was clearheaded." He took another bite of his steak and chewed as he studied me.

"But then you regretted it?"

"Never. I just—" He looked away.

"It was just something to do, I guess? Knowing that I crushed on you, and you didn't feel the same? It was probably fun to tease me that way, huh? Knowing I couldn't talk to my best friend about it. I had to just accept that my feelings weren't reciprocated and pretend it didn't hurt." Well, I certainly wasn't holding back anymore, was I? I waited for him to look at me and raised a brow when his gaze locked with mine. I didn't know where this courage had come from. I wasn't upset with Ledger; I guess I just wondered all these years later why it even happened. Why he even went there if he didn't see me that way? Why I still thought about it all these years later?

"You couldn't be more wrong." He shook his head and sucked in a breath before looking away. I just waited. I'd never asked before, but maybe I was channeling my inner Dylan the older I got. "You'd lost your mama, and you were heartbroken.

I wanted to comfort you. I always worried about you. And that time I picked you up after you drank for the first time, mind you, I think you had two sips of beer." He chuckled at the memory. "Jilly was a hot mess, and I'd taken her home. And you and I had stayed up late talking, and you opened up to me. And fuck, I just wanted to be there for you."

"I get it. I was your little sister's best friend, and that's how you saw me. It was probably me who wanted that to happen. You were my first kiss, and I don't regret it."

"I don't either, Ladybug. You don't get to leave here thinking that I didn't see you the way that you saw me. I wanted you more than you wanted me back then."

My eyes widened, and I shook my head. "Don't lie to me, Ledger. I'm not the same little girl I was all those years ago. It doesn't even matter anymore, so don't make this something that it's not."

"Jesus, you really don't get it." He shrugged. "I was fucking crazy about you. I'd thought about kissing you for months before that first time I kissed you."

"Yet you pulled away when things started to get heated."

"Exactly. My father had just married wife number two that year. My mom was like a robot back then, just working and existing. Jilly was heartbroken about our family breaking up, and our father was completely ignoring us, which was why she'd gotten plastered that night. And I was angry. I saw him with his secretary, Suzette, years earlier, and I kept that a secret from everyone but you. I felt like a piece of shit when I finally told my mom everything that had happened. So yeah, I didn't think it was a good idea to mess around with the girl I'd always kept on a pedestal. The girl I knew deserved better.

And you did, Ladybug. You deserved a guy who wasn't fucked-up about what was happening with his family. You deserved a guy who knew he could give you what you needed, and I wasn't that guy. I was just surviving back then. Jilly needed you, and I couldn't risk fucking that up either."

My mouth fell open as I listened. I hadn't expected him to say that. Not even close. I figured he'd apologize for leading me on back then. For keeping the attraction a secret. For keeping the depth of our friendship a secret. Because Ledger had been the one that I'd opened up to about my mother more times than I could count. I couldn't talk to my sisters back then because we were all struggling. And Jilly was falling apart about her dad leaving her mom. So, the few times I let it out, it was with this boy who was now a man sitting in front of me.

We'd come this far. I wanted to know everything. I had nothing to lose. I wasn't a girl with a crush anymore. That ship had sailed. Even if he was a beautiful man, I was in control of my feelings now.

"What about my junior year when you came home from college, and you punched Rand Carson in the face and then drove me home? Do you remember what happened in that car?" I let out a long breath because I'd held all this in for so long. I'd talked to my baby sister, Ashlan, about it because she took secrets to the grave. But I told her I didn't ever want to bring it up again after I'd had a good cry when he'd gone back to school and we both pretended like nothing had happened.

"Do I remember what happened? I fucking fantasize about it every day, Charlie. The way I kissed you until we were both delirious. The way you came apart for me when I slipped my fingers beneath your panties. The way it took every bit of restraint to stop there. Yeah. I fucking remember."

Oh. Apparently, he does remember.

My breaths were coming hard and fast as I leaned closer and let anger take over. "The way I begged you to take my virginity, and you turned me down."

"I don't regret that. You would have hated me. Hell, I hated myself for not having the strength to drop you off without touching you. I hated myself for being happy that douchedick Rand had fucked things up because I was seething with jealousy that night when I watched you with him at the photos before the dance. I was happy when Jilly called me and said you were upset and that you needed me. That's what a selfish prick I am."

"Well, not enough to actually do anything about it. I wasn't worth the fight, was I?"

He cursed under his breath. "It was never fucking like that."

I shook my head. "What was it like, then, Ledger?"

"Well, let's see. I was a freshman in college, and I'd just lost my best friend a few months before, and then I had to pack my bags and go to school without him. I'd just found out that my father had left my mother in serious debt, and she was broke. I was trying to wrap my head around the fact that if I hadn't received that football scholarship, I wouldn't be going away to school at all. I was doing my best to process how fucked-up my dad was, trying to figure out what that would mean for Jilly and for me, and grieving my best friend all at the same time."

My chest heaved as memories flooded my head. I tried to

be there for Ledger back then, but he shut me and everyone else out before leaving for school. I remembered how the whole town had mourned the death of Colt Moretti, who'd been Ledger's best friend since they were in elementary school. They were going off to the same college to play football together. Colt had been out at the lake with his brother one night, and he jumped off the boat, insisting he could swim across the lake in the dark, and they don't know how it happened, but he drowned before anyone could get to him. It was a horrific accident that left everyone in Honey Mountain grieving terribly.

"I'd been drinking a lot myself that first year away at school. Colt and I had always planned to play college ball together, and I couldn't wrap my head around the fact that he was gone. I tried like hell to numb some of that pain away, even while knowing that wasn't going to be the way to get through it. So, I came home because I missed my family. Missed you. And then I'd gone and punched that asshole Rand in the face, and you and I had gotten together. I was sure I'd fucked things up between us. I didn't have my head on straight at that time, so I hauled ass back to school and started getting my shit together."

"I would have been there for you."

"I didn't want to bring you down, Ladybug. You deserved better than me back then, and every day since. I may be a selfish man in a lot of ways, but never when it comes to you. I've always wanted the best for you, and I stand by that. You're the best person I know."

A tear ran down my cheek, and I shook my head. Because Ledger Dane was the best person I knew, even when I desperately wanted to hate him.

And he didn't see himself the way that I did.

But I knew in that moment that I'd love him until I took my last breath.

I always had.

But nothing could ever happen between us.

I learned that lesson the hard way.

And I wouldn't make the same mistake twice.

Chapter 4

Ledger

The way her hazel eyes locked with mine, wet with emotion. I knew I'd done the right thing by finally telling her the truth about why I'd been the way I had all those years ago. After my family had blown up, I'd felt like nothing could be worse. And then Colt was gone. It made no sense to me. He was a tremendous athlete. Hell, we spent summers swimming in that lake. But he'd always been a stubborn ass in the best way when we were growing up. The dude would take any dare. He'd always been invincible to me, and then he had this fluke accident, and there was no bringing him back.

And then what did I do to complicate matters even more? I came home and hooked up with Charlotte Thomas. She begged me that night to take things further—and that had been my chance at redemption. Because I knew that was something I didn't deserve. Hell, I had nothing to offer her

back then. I was just surviving. So, I'd done the right thing
and shut it down.

I knew it couldn't go anywhere, and she moved on after
that. Rightfully so. But after everything I'd been through with
my father, I knew how important the truth was. And she was
asking, so I wouldn't lie.

"Well, I appreciate you telling me all of this." She
shook her head. "I'm glad to know that my feelings weren't
completely one-sided."

"I didn't know you ever doubted mine. I know I didn't
bring up what happened between us back then, but neither did
you. I always wondered if you regretted it."

"Never." She shrugged. So fucking honest and genuine.
I'd always been so drawn to all her goodness. But I could tell
she still didn't fully believe me.

"I know I fucked things up, and I hate how everything
changed after that." I folded my hands on the table. Maybe it
was being back home that brought back so many memories.

"Me, too." She ran her fingers around the rim of her
wineglass. The move had my dick going hard immediately.
What the fuck was wrong with me? Here I was confessing to
hurting her back in the day, and the truth was, I wanted her
just as much today as I had back then, even when I knew it
was wrong.

Attraction wasn't something you could control. Sure,
I could not give into it—but it didn't mean it wasn't there.
Stronger than ever.

"When I'd come home for Jilly's graduation from high
school—and as long as we're admitting the truth, I came home
for yours just as much as for hers—I'd pulled my shit together

by then, but you were more standoffish with me because of what had happened the year before." I raised a brow.

"That was the first time anyone had ever touched me," she whispered. "And then I asked for more, and you rejected me. At least that was how it had felt." Turning down Charlotte Thomas when she asked me to take her virginity was the single hardest decision of my life. And I was proud of myself for doing it. I knew I didn't deserve it. My father always took what he could from anyone who offered him anything. I didn't want to be that guy. I wanted to earn my way. Be worthy. And I wasn't back then. At least I didn't think I was.

"I texted you when I got back to school several times, but you didn't respond."

"You texted, and I quote, '*Have a nice summer break, Ladybug.*' And then the next few texts just said, '*Hey.*'" She rolled her eyes. "So I decided in that moment that I needed to move on. Let my silly crush go. I certainly didn't want to be desperate like Lucy Blocker."

"There was nothing between Lucy and me, and you know it. You know what you and I shared was different. How could you not? Fuck. Back then, I couldn't handle all that was happening. I had intense football training all summer at school, I was grieving the loss of my best friend, and I had so much anger toward my father I didn't know how to handle all of it. And I sure as shit didn't know what to say to you because you jumped out of the car and slammed the door. You'd never been angry at me before that night, and I didn't know what to do. So, I just tried playing it cool, and you never responded. And then when I came home the next time, you were short with me. I thought you regretted what happened. I saw you at your graduation, and you barely looked at me."

"I was moving on." She shrugged. "A girl can only take so much rejection, Ledger."

"It was never about rejecting you. It was about protecting you. Doing the right thing. And trust me when I tell you, it hurt like hell that we weren't talking."

"Well, you certainly had plenty of girls you dated over the years. You didn't seem to be hurting that badly."

I nodded. She was right. I never hurt for female attention. But the only one I ever wanted it from was the one girl I knew I couldn't have. The only real connection I'd ever felt with a woman happened to be the one that I met when I was a kid. What are the fucking chances you'd ever find that again? But it was okay. Connections were overrated as far as I was concerned.

"I'd say we both moved on and did just fine. But I hate this distance I feel between us. I'm not saying I did everything right. I admit that I was young and immature and a little bit fucked-up for a couple of years—but hurting you was the last thing I ever wanted to do. And I miss being friends. I miss talking about everything with you. You were the only one I ever felt comfortable enough to share how bad things were. I trusted you. Hell, I still do. And I guess I miss that." Damn, I was laying my heart on the line here. It wasn't something that came easily to me, but I wanted to fix this.

"I'm still your friend, Ledger. You know I'd always be there for you if you needed me."

"What do you say about a fresh start, Ladybug?" I fucking missed everything about her. I'd been with my fair share of women, had a few serious relationships over the years, yet no one ever flooded my thoughts the way Charlotte Thomas did.

"Sure. I guess we have a lot of catching up to do. So, fill me in. I heard you're dating your boss's daughter?" She raised a brow, which made me laugh.

"Nope. Not anymore. It didn't work out. How about you? I heard you broke up with the bug guy," I said as our server approached, and we ordered dessert, because she's always had a sweet tooth, and I insisted.

"Oh my gosh." Her head fell back in laughter. "His name is Lyle. Why does everyone call him the bug guy?"

"Was it serious?" I asked, suddenly desperate to know. "Did you love the bug guy?"

She rolled her eyes and chuckled. "You are quite possibly the most confusing man on the planet. This is supposed to be our fresh start at renewing our friendship, and you're already being weird."

"Hey! Not fair. This is what friends talk about. Answer the question, Charlie."

"No. I didn't. How about you? Did you love *the boss's daughter*?" I didn't miss the sarcasm or the hint of jealousy she tried hard to hide.

"I did not."

"Well, this is a good start. I'm glad we're doing this. It's closure for both of us. So, friends, again?" She extended her hand, and I reached for it.

"Yes. Here's to friendship." I squeezed her hand, but she pulled it away quickly. She didn't fully trust me yet, and I understood her hesitation. Trust never came easy for me, but it killed me that she didn't think she could trust me. There isn't one moment in my memory that I wouldn't walk through fire for this girl. Including right now. I held up my spoon and waited for her to do the same as the server set down the brownie sundae between us.

"Should we talk about the wedding?" she asked.

"Yeah. Are you bringing a date to the wedding?" I inquired, because that was all I really cared about.

"I don't know. The P.E. teacher at work asked me out. I'll have to see how that goes." She smirked as she said it, and even in the dim lighting, I could see her cheeks flush every time our gazes locked. But she dipped her spoon in the ice cream and then slipped it between her lips as her gaze locked with mine. Had there ever been a sexier woman?

"Really? So you're into sweaty dudes that like to play with balls that aren't their own?" I said as I knocked her spoon out of the way and took the bite she was going for.

"I don't know what I'm into these days." She laughed as she knocked my spoon out of the way next. "I guess I'm looking for a man who knows what he wants."

"Well, your last boyfriend was into bugs, so don't get too cocky."

Her head fell back in laughter, and it reminded me of every happy memory I ever had growing up. Her eyes were focused on my mouth, and I took advantage of the moment, leaning forward as my tongue swiped out slowly. "You still hungry, Ladybug?"

"I'm not as easily teased as I was when we were young, Ledger. Your sexy ways do not affect me anymore."

I glanced down at her white blouse to see her nipples poking against the fabric, and I raised a brow.

"I don't know about that." I scooped some ice cream onto

my spoon and leaned forward. "Here, let me help you with that hunger, bestie."

She blinked up at me and smiled before leaning forward and opening her mouth. My dick strained so hard against my zipper I feared it would break through. I moved the spoon forward and then pulled back, teasing her just because I loved seeing how she reacted to me. But this time, she surprised me by lunging forward and covering her sweet mouth over the spoon as she groaned.

I closed my eyes because I nearly came undone right there.

"Two can play that game, buddy," she said with a chuckle.

"I see you're pretty good at it."

She leaned back in her chair. "Are you bringing a date to the wedding?"

I wasn't. But I wasn't going to admit that just yet. "I'm playing it by ear. How about we make a deal?"

"What kind of deal?"

"If we both go alone to the wedding, we can be one another's dates. I mean, we are friends, right?"

"Sure. Friends can go to weddings together. But I do need to see where things go with the P.E. teacher." She waggled her brows, knowing she was getting under my skin.

"What's interesting to me is that you have yet to call him by name. So you can't be that into the dude. It would be like him saying that he asked out the kindergarten teacher. It's weird, Ladybug."

She shook her head and chuckled. "His name is Tobias."

"Tobias Blackstone?" I groaned. "I can't stand that dude. He was a grade older than me, and he was a total bully."

"You do realize that you had a problem with every guy

I ever went out with, right? Is every single guy in Honey Mountain a bully?"

"Hey, I'm just looking out for you. It's what friends do. Plus, Tobias used to brag about shaving his balls in high school, so you might want to be careful there. The fact that his testicles are super hairy is very alarming."

She fell back in her chair, laughing. "What am I going to do with you, Ledger Dane?"

"I don't know, Charlotte Thomas. What do you want to do with me?"

Her chest was rising and falling as she studied me, and then her shoulders squared, and she pursed her lips. "Well, I think we're supposed to talk about the wedding. Not who we're taking, but our responsibilities with being the maid of honor and the best man."

"Ah, yes." I did a dramatic fake yawn. "But it's awfully late to dive into that conversation now. We have a lot to go over. How about I bring lunch by the school tomorrow, and we can talk about it over your lunch break?"

"I don't think Darwin will be too pleased if you come back again."

"I'm more afraid of Meanie Marcy," I said.

She laughed, and her teeth found her bottom lip, and she held them there for a moment as she thought over my offer.

"Obviously, I don't want to slack on my responsibility as the maid of honor."

"Obviously."

"And we're working on this friendship, so I guess it can't hurt," she said.

"Agreed. Man, it's good to see you, Ladybug. I'm glad we

cleared the air."

She smiled. "I'm glad you're home, Ledger Dane. I think I've missed you a lot."

"Me, too. I'm here for two weeks, so I plan on repairing our friendship while I'm home. And with you being out of school soon, you'll have plenty of time to help me with that."

"I mean, that's all pending me and Tobias don't run off into the sunset together." She shrugged.

"You don't strike me as a girl who likes hairy balls."

She covered her face with her hands, but I could still see her shoulders shaking with laughter. "Is this how you repair our friendship? I mean, Dilly would love this conversation."

I smiled. "Yeah. I'm looking forward to seeing everyone."

The server came over, and I handed her my card to pay the bill.

Charlotte grabbed her purse, and I reached across the table and wrapped my fingers around her wrist. "Do not even think about it."

"Fine. This place is a little pricey for my wallet, anyway. I'll get lunch tomorrow."

"You won't. I've got you, Ladybug."

And I always would.

Chapter 5

Charlotte

I practically floated into work today. I didn't know what that was between Ledger and me last night, but I enjoyed every second of it. We continued our flirtation on the drive home when he walked me to the door and asked to come in and see the place. I refused him, telling him it was a little late for a friend to stop by. He laughed on my doorstep when I pushed him back and shut the door in his face.

I knew I was playing with fire.

I'd always wanted him, and I knew without a shadow of a doubt that he wanted me, too. At least physically. But he didn't live here, and I highly doubted he ever wanted to come back. Nor did I think Ledger was the settling down type. Hell, Jilly said his boss's daughter was really pretty and very wealthy, and he hadn't made an effort to make that work.

So, a flirty friendship wasn't a bad thing.

I enjoyed spending time with him, and I was happy that we didn't have this weirdness between us anymore. He'd been such a big part of my life for so long, and I missed him.

So, I may or may not have worn my favorite white shift dress to work today and curled my hair, which I rarely did.

I sat down in my chair while the kids settled on the carpet, and Darwin's hand shot up in the air. I motioned for him to speak.

"Why is your hair bouncy? It's not the first day of school or the winter program. You only wear bouncy hair for special days."

Marcy's hand shot up, and she waved it frantically, so I nodded for her to speak. "A woman can wear bouncy hair whenever she wants, Darwin. She doesn't need a reason. Right, Miss Thomas?"

Marcy had probably been marching for women's rights from the moment she took her first steps. I couldn't help but chuckle about the fact that they not only noticed my hair being different, but were also willing to argue about it.

"I just felt like wearing bouncy hair today, I guess."

Jayden's hand went up, and I motioned for him to speak. "Do elephants have babies?"

Welcome to my life—where anything goes.

"They do," I said, completely unfazed by the random question. "How about we get our morning started so we can get to centers because I have the Play-Doh out, and I know how much you love that." Centers in kindergarten were like gold to five-year-olds. The kids moved from building with magnets to water painting to working with Play-Doh in their small groups. It was a creative time, and they loved it.

They cheered, and I started our routine. The morning flew by in a blur, and Kell spent the last few hours in the copy room before she came back to get the kids ready to take to lunch and recess.

"Are you going to tell me why you've got bouncy hair today?" she teased. "And this dress is something. You are looking good, Miss Thomas."

I shook my head and laughed. "It's summer, and I'm just in a good mood, I guess."

"Does it have anything to do with that beautiful man who dropped by yesterday? Damn." She whistled. "If I were ten years younger and not married to my ball and chain and tied down with those two needy mini-mes, I'd be all over that guy."

Kell was all talk.

She and Ray were one of the cutest couples I'd ever met, and she was crazy about him and their kids. But this was her shtick.

The door opened, and Jenna, who ran our front office, walked in with Ledger behind her. Her cheeks were pink, and when her gaze locked with mine, she smirked and raised her eyebrows at me. Jenna and Kell were the two people I worked with who made me laugh endlessly.

"Miss Thomas," she purred. "You have a visitor."

"Oh, man. He's here again. Is he your boyfriend?" Darwin grumped, folding his arms over his chest, and all the kids, aside from Marcy, giggled.

"You can't say that to a big person, Darwin." Marcy over-accentuated her words when she spoke, and I couldn't remember a time this year that she spoke to Darwin without having her hands on her hips as she huffed.

"Yes, I can. It's called speaking your brain." He ran toward me in frustration, and I couldn't help but laugh as I wrapped an arm around him.

"You mean speaking your mind," I said, patting him on the head.

"Enough of that. In line, kiddos. Time for lunch." Kell winked at me and walked toward the door.

Ledger wore a pair of jeans, a white tee, and sneakers. His dark waves were tousled, and he looked effortlessly sexy. He strolled by the kids and paused in front of Darwin and held up his fist.

Darwin beamed and pounded it with his own, and Ledger smirked. "May the best man win, little dude."

Marcy's mouth gaped open as if she were stunned that he was acknowledging Darwin.

Ledger had his back to Kell, and she mouthed, *Oh my god,* and fanned her face.

"See you later, Miss Thomas!" she shouted before marching the kids out of the classroom.

Ledger walked toward me and paused as he blatantly ran his eyes down my body and back up until his gaze locked with mine. "You always were the prettiest girl I'd ever seen."

I took the Honey Bee's Bakery bag from his hands and turned away quickly, because his flirt game always got to me, and I needed to keep myself in check. I was proud of myself for staying in control where he was concerned, because it had never been easy for me.

The kids left the room, and I led him to the back reading table, where I often ate when I stayed in my classroom for lunch. I had two adult chairs in the room, and I'd wheeled them back here so we wouldn't be sitting in the tiny chairs.

"You went to Honey Bee's?" I asked, smiling at the fact that I knew that meant Vivian would pack my favorite chicken salad sandwich because she knew it was what I'd want. My sister's bakery was a popular hot spot in Honey Mountain.

"Yep. I got to see Vivi, and the Tasmanian devil, Dilly, also happened to be there. So I got the third degree about where I was going, so prepare yourself for some intense questioning." He dropped to his seat, and this time, when my gaze locked with his, I saw something there. He was trying hard to hide it—but there was something. I'd always been an expert at knowing when he was off. He was so used to charming everyone that he hid his emotions well, but not from me, aside from the fact that I'd never known he felt as strongly about me as he claimed to last night. Even if I still wasn't sure I believed him fully.

I handed him his sandwich and a napkin. "Thank you so much for this. I owe you the next meal."

"Don't be silly. I'm just glad you agreed to let me come by."

I tilted my head. "What's happening here? You're upset."

His eyes widened in surprise. "What? No. I'm fine."

"I thought we were trying to work on our friendship?" I took a bite of my sandwich, taking my time chewing as I watched him.

"We are. What are you talking about?"

"Don't lie to me, Ledger. I know you better than that. Plus, you hate liars," I said, raising a brow in challenge. "Something's up, and if you want this friendship to get back on track, you should talk to me about it. That's what we used to do, right?"

He reached for his water bottle and took a long pull before speaking. "My dad was at Honey Bee's with his new girlfriend, Bambi. I didn't know they were in town already."

Dean Dane had moved out of Honey Mountain after his divorce years ago, claiming that he wanted a fresh start. It had been very hard on both Ledger and Jilly, but at least they hadn't had to see him with his girlfriends over the years.

"I thought Jilly said her name was Brenda?" I asked as I studied him.

"Brenda, Bambi, I can't keep them straight. She's practically a teenager," he hissed.

I chuckled. "Your sister told me that she's thirty-eight years old. You're being dramatic."

"Is this how you rekindle our friendship, by insulting me?"

"I'm not insulting you. I'm talking to you like a friend. You don't have a problem with Brenda or her age. You have a problem with your father. So let's talk about that. How was seeing him?"

"Weird as fuck. We act like we're business acquaintances. He's got spiky hair, his teeth are too white, and he dresses like a fifty-year-old man trying to look like he's in his twenties."

"So you have a problem with his hair and teeth and clothes?" I asked after I finished chewing. He needed to deal with his dad issues, because they weren't going to go away until he did.

"I do. He looks like an actor from a cheesy eighties porno. He's ridiculous. Flashing his Cartier watch while he isn't paying one penny for his only daughter's wedding. Who even knows if she is his only daughter, anyway? The dude probably has kids all over the place. He takes no responsibility for anything."

"Have you ever considered confronting him? Of getting it all off your chest?"

"What good would that do? He's never going to change, Ladybug."

"But it might do you some good. You know, to let it out. Instead of being passive-aggressive with him." I shrugged before taking another bite.

"How am I being passive-aggressive?" He didn't hide his irritation.

"Well, by definition, being passive-aggressive means that you are displaying negative feelings, resentment, and aggression in an unassertive way. Like, you aren't confronting him. You're being short and cold with him instead. Which means he just continues what he's doing because you aren't calling him out."

"Why do you know the definition of passive-aggressive?" He raised a brow and smiled, as if he were impressed.

"Because Dilly always tells me I'm passive-aggressive, so I'm working on it. Working on confronting people when something bothers me."

"Like you confronted me last night?" he asked.

"Yeah. I guess I did." I laughed. "But you aren't a passive-aggressive person, Ledger. Only with your father. Maybe you're afraid to confront him because it means facing a time in your life that you didn't enjoy. A time in your life that was difficult."

"Fuck that dude for making me weak, even for a second. I always like to think I'm just not giving him my energy, but maybe you're right. Maybe I should tell him what a dick I think he is. I mean, I rarely ever speak to him, not that he calls often. I don't need a relationship with him."

"But you need to let this anger go. It's holding you back."

"How the fuck do you know me so goddamn well?" He popped the last bit of his sandwich in his mouth and studied me.

"I don't know. I guess it's a gift," I said, and he barked out a laugh.

"It sure is, Ladybug."

"Oh, I hope I'm not interrupting." Tobias opened my classroom door and peeked his head in, startling us both.

"No. We're just having lunch. You remember Ledger, right?" I said, dabbing at my mouth with my napkin.

"Of course. Yes. You're the older brother, right?"

"Not *her* older brother," Ledger hissed. "I'm Jilly's older brother."

"Oh, right. Tomato, tomahto. Just keeping it real, dude. I was just dropping by to see if you were available for dinner tonight, *Miss Thomas?*" I think he was attempting to make my name sound sexy, but it didn't work at all. In fact, it was completely cringy the way he deepened his voice and then waggled his brows.

"She's not. She's on wedding duty. That's why I'm here. We're having dinner tonight with Jilly and Garrett to discuss our duties. She's going to be very busy for the next couple of weeks." Ledger balled the paper that his sandwich was wrapped in and shot it at the trash can across the room, and somehow, managed to dunk it.

I gave him a warning look. First off, I knew nothing of

said dinner with Jilly and Garrett. Second, I didn't need him to answer for me. But the truth was, I was relieved, because I had no desire to go to dinner with Tobias tonight or anytime soon. I think I liked telling Ledger that he'd asked me out more than the idea of actually going out with him.

"I can speak for myself, Ledger. But yes, I have plans tonight, and the next two weeks are pretty packed with tasks for the wedding. Sorry about that."

I reached for my water bottle, taking a sip, before my eyes flashed as Tobias moved a hand to his crotch and literally gave it a blatant, long scratch before moving it to his hair and slicking it back. I spewed water all over the table and started coughing as I quickly looked away and tried to play it off.

Ledger barked out a laugh and was on his feet, patting my back dramatically.

"I'm fine," I said over my laughter. "It just went down the wrong tube."

"All right, Miss Thomas. Well, it'll be better this summer, anyway. Maybe we can take a picnic out to the lake and spend the day there?"

"Apparently, you have no regard for skin cancer and the risks of being out in the sun all day," Ledger said, squaring his shoulders and staring at Tobias, who still stood in the doorway. Ledger was acting as crazy as the P.E. teacher was.

"She's tan. And I'm sure she looks mighty fine in a bikini." His tongue swiped out to wet his lips, and I fought back the urge to roll my eyes and vomit at the same time.

"Listen, this isn't really the time or place to discuss this. I'll speak to you later, Tobias. Thanks for dropping by." I pushed to my feet and raised a brow at him, letting him know this conversation was finished.

I'd most definitely be making it clear that we wouldn't be going out or spending the day at the lake this summer—but I wasn't about to do it in front of an audience. The guy was giving me creeper vibes today, but I wasn't going to be cruel.

He just smirked and knocked on the door frame. "See you later. Take care, *big brother.*"

What the hell was that about?

He closed the door, and I turned to gape at Ledger, who was stewing and pacing in little circles. "I'd love to kick that dude's ass, but I think the fact that he clearly has razor burn on his balls is punishment enough. He has no shame. He just goes right in and scratches that itch. Who does that? And what's with the big brother shit? He's older than me. And he's looking at you in a way that is highly unprofessional."

I crossed my arms over my chest. "Unprofessional, huh?"

"Yeah. We're friends. It's my duty to protect you."

My stomach dipped at his words. There were so many memories with Ledger. Some that I'd tried hard not to think about over the last few years.

"Does that include you answering for me when someone asks me out?" I quirked a brow. He was standing so close to me, and the smell of mint and sage flooded my senses.

"When he's grabbing a fist full of his balls and talking about you in a bikini—I answer for you." He took a step forward, crowding me even more.

"You're ridiculous."

"I thought I was passive-aggressive?" He smirked.

The back door opened, and the kids filed into the classroom, and I let out a long breath. "Great. We never even discussed the wedding. Again."

"Bummer." He didn't hide his sarcasm as a wide grin spread across his handsome face. "We really do have dinner tonight with Jilly and Garrett. They want to discuss the schedule. I'll pick you up at six."

"Why do I feel like you're completely fine with the fact that, once again, we didn't discuss what we were supposed to?" I smiled as Darwin walked over to me and looked between me and Ledger.

Ledger held up his hands and walked backward toward the door. "Hey, I can't help it if you wanted to take a deep dive into my emotional state today. But thank you. I'm feeling much better, Ladybug."

"Whatever, bestie. I'll see you later." I turned away, unable to stop smiling.

Because I was happy that he was back.

Even though I knew it would hurt like hell when he left again.

And I knew he would.

But this time, I'd be prepared for it.

Chapter 6

Ledger

Charlotte and I arrived at the restaurant, and Jilly had a notebook out with a pack of markers beside her on the table, and Garrett was just smiling at her.

"She knows it's dinner and not a PTA meeting, right?" I whispered, my lips grazing the shell of Charlotte's ear, and she shivered just enough for me to notice.

"It's her wedding. Your job is to make it as easy as possible for her."

"She has a wedding planner. Isn't that *her* job?"

Charlotte elbowed me in the side, and I couldn't help but laugh. I'd seen my father today, and normally I would have buried my sorrows in a bottle of booze and found a woman to get lost in. But instead, I was fine. Lunch had turned my mood around, even with a visit from itchy-balls Tobias. The dude was shady as fuck, and I knew he was up to no good with her.

I'd make sure she knew it because I didn't want her anywhere near him.

Call me protective. Call me a hypocrite.

I didn't give a shit.

Not when it came to Charlotte Thomas.

I never could see straight around this girl. And that hadn't changed.

"Why are there notebooks and handouts?" I asked, as I observed the stapled packets on each of our place settings.

"Because I wanted you to have the itinerary. There are a ton of events coming up, and I wanted to make sure you two had the schedule."

"How very thoughtful," I said, my tone oozing sarcasm as I pulled out Charlotte's chair, and she sat down, and I took the seat beside her.

Garrett chuckled. "That was awfully nice of you to pick Charlie up on the way."

That little shit was messing with me again. Two could play that game.

"Of course. It wasn't a problem. I figured with the leash my sister has on you being so tight, it might be hard for you to make another stop. Plus, you probably had to get to the print shop to pick up the orientation packets for our dinner, and then maybe grab her a couple boxes of tampons. Unless you're menstruating, too?"

Garrett barked out a laugh, and Charlotte fell forward in a fit of giggles. I glanced over at my sister, who was highlighting her notes like she was preparing to take an exam. So focused on what she was doing, she didn't even notice. I couldn't make this shit up.

"Baby." Garrett tapped her on the shoulder. "Let's visit for a bit."

I chuckled at how sweet he was with her. I fucking loved it. Garrett Jones was a salt of the earth dude, and I couldn't ask for a better brother-in-law.

"Hey, bridezilla, let's order some food before you give us our instructions." I quirked a brow at my baby sister, who looked so grown up lately that it caused a lump to form in my throat. I'd worried about her most of my life. Hated that my father had been her male role model and did my best to compensate for that. To protect her the way a parent should.

She smiled and shook her head. "I'm sorry, guys. I guess I'm just so excited about the big day that I got distracted." She pushed her notebook away, and we ordered a bottle of wine for the table.

"Of course, you're excited. We've been talking about this day our entire lives," Charlotte said, looking at my sister with the most empathetic eyes. I'd always been thankful that Jilly had a friend like Charlie. A ride-or-die, loyal-to-the-fucking-core friend. That was what Colt and I had always been to one another, and there wasn't a day that went by that I didn't miss him.

Jilly had needed that, too. When Charlotte had gone away to college and Jilly had decided to stay living at home with our mom and attend community college for the first two years, I'd worried they'd drift apart, which I knew would devastate my sister. But Charlotte came home once a month, and they continued speaking daily, even when they were apart.

Like I said, this girl was all goodness.

Our server brought over the wine, and I sampled it,

because I considered myself somewhat of a wine expert these days. We ordered dinner, and the conversation flowed.

"Dad said he ran into you today," Jilly said, looking at me over the rim of her glass. "He said you guys had a great conversation."

"He talked about himself. Classic Dean Dane move. I listened. I didn't want to embarrass him in front of Bambi."

Garrett chuckled. "You hate when people know you're kind, don't you?"

"Yeah, every time I tell anyone you're paying for the wedding, you rip my head off," Jilly said.

I shrugged. "I don't do shit for credit. I do it because I want to. Because I work hard to be able to do things for the people I love."

"You're a kind man, Ledger. You're the only one who doesn't know it." Charlotte reached for her glass and smiled at me, and my fucking chest squeezed.

Women didn't make my chest squeeze.

Sure, my dick often had a mind of his own.

But Charlotte Thomas had every part of me reacting.

And that shit pissed me off. I was not a hormonal teenage boy anymore.

Buck the fuck up, man.

I let out a long breath. "Enough about that. Let's talk about the wedding."

"Ledger." Jilly's voice shook. "I don't want to stop talking about it. Thank you for giving me my dream wedding. And thank you for paying off Mama's house. She told me this morning."

I'd made one request to my mother.

Not to tell anyone.

I was fucking happy to do it. She worked her whole damn life to support us, to give us everything we ever wanted or needed. She never complained, even when her deadbeat husband left her high and dry.

And I was doing well financially. I started studying the stock market a few years back and had a lot of luck on my investments. I was working at the hottest architect firm in San Francisco, and I bought a few rental homes over the years when the market was down, and they were proving to be a very lucrative investment as well.

Bottom line. I could afford to help my mother and my sister—and that was what I worked for.

"You paid off your mother's house?" Charlotte said as she shook her head in disbelief.

"She didn't owe that much. She's paid for that house with hard work and persistence. Her telling everyone that I paid it off is taking away from that." I raised a brow at my sister, because this was exactly why I didn't want my mother to tell anyone. "Now she can stop working so damn hard."

"Dude. She's proud of you. That's why she told us." Garrett shrugged, and then I felt like an asshole.

"Listen, I have a career that does well. I don't work any harder than any of you. I just got lucky." I took another long pull from my glass. I wasn't normally such a humble guy—but when it came to these three, I was different.

"Sometimes I worry that you aren't chasing your own dreams, though," Jilly said, as she reached across the table and squeezed my hand. "You always wanted to own your own firm. Choose your own projects. But instead, you're just making the big bucks working for some bougie guy in the city who gets to cash in on *your* talent. And who pressures you to date his daughter. I don't like it."

I chuckled. "Yeah, Harold Cartwright is not cashing in on my talent. The dude is famous for his design. He's responsible for more than a dozen iconic buildings in the city. And sometimes you don't chase the original dream because the dream has changed."

And that was the truth. I wouldn't be living this lifestyle if I were working for myself. I wouldn't be able to provide for my family the way I had been able to these last few years if I'd taken a different path. I'd gotten a break when I'd been given an internship at Cartwright Designs, and the man had believed in me. We didn't always see eye-to-eye, but he respected my craft. He said he liked tapping into the younger ideas because he'd grown tired of studying architecture after all these years. So I brought a fresh perspective. I didn't get to choose the projects that we did, and he wasn't big on doing things that weren't lucrative, even if they were for a good cause—but he did let me take the lead when it came to the design.

"I love you, Ledger. And I am so grateful that you helped Mama and that you've done so much for me. And Garrett and I... we couldn't begin to thank you enough for giving us this special day. But I want you to start focusing on *you*, moving forward. When was the last time you stopped to think about what you wanted? Dated someone because you actually wanted to? Thought about starting a family?"

I choked on my wine, and Charlotte's hand immediately found my back as she gently patted it until the cough passed.

"Jesus, Jilly Bean. I'm doing pretty damn good for myself.

I have everything I want. And having a family has never been something that I've been interested in. I have you and Mom and Nan, and that's enough for me. As far as women go—I do just fine. Don't you worry about that."

Charlotte's hand moved away, and her shoulders stiffened beside me, as if my words were offensive. Good. I wanted her to be glad that I hadn't let things go further when we were young. Because she'd probably hate me now. And we were getting our friendship back on track.

Did that mean I wasn't attracted to her?

Hell no.

But I would not go there with Charlotte Thomas.

Because there'd be no turning back if I did.

She'd want the whole package. The dude on the white horse. The fairy tale.

I didn't even believe in fairy tales.

I knew all too well how they ended.

"Well, if you were into shallow relationships like you claim, I think you'd still be dating Jessica. So you can pretend you don't want more, if that makes you feel cool or something, but I know you better than you know yourself," my sister said, as she raised one brow, just begging me to challenge her.

"Then you know that I'm starving right now, correct?" I teased as the server set our food down. I was in no mood for this conversation.

I glanced down at my phone and saw a text from Harold, my boss. I'd sent him all the information for the middle school project. I told him it was a job I'd happily oversee because it was personal to me.

Harold: It's a no on the small-town middle school.

> The numbers don't work for the time involved, and
> it won't do anything to build our portfolio. No one
> cares about a little school in a small town. Let them
> know we've declined the project.

Fuck. That pissed me off. In all my years there, I'd never asked for a personal favor. To take on a project that meant something to me.

> **Me:** That's extremely disappointing.

> **Harold:** When you own your own company, you can
> call the shots.

Interesting, since he kept saying he was going to make me a partner soon. He'd been saying it for the last year and a half, and I was starting to wonder if it was just a way of keeping me on the hook.

He must have realized what he said, because he responded again quickly.

> **Harold:** When you're partner, you will have a lot
> more of a say in what we do. However, I will always
> be the ultimate decision maker as I won't give up
> a large stake in this company. And I'm sorry to tell
> you, Ledger, but a middle school in Honey Mountain
> serves no purpose to us.

Right. Because the purpose would be to provide a place for kids in the community to learn. What the fuck was he talking about? We bumped heads often on things like this, but this time, being here—it felt different. It stung more.

> **Me:** The purpose of art is not always self-serving. I
> will leave it at that.

Harold: And this is why I knew I needed you on my team. You're a good man. A better man than me, which isn't always good for our bottom line. Anyway, I wanted to invite you on the yacht when you return. Me, you, Maureen, and Jessica for a week in Mexico. How does that sound?

It sounded awkward as fuck, considering I wasn't dating his daughter any longer. When he heard we broke up, he just didn't acknowledge it. It didn't bother me because it hadn't been serious, so I assumed he was fine with it. But this was definitely throwing me for a loop.

Me: After taking off for two weeks, I'm guessing I better hold down the fort when you leave.

"Hey, phones away. Let's eat," Jilly said.

I turned my ringer off and set my phone beside me. But an uneasy feeling settled in my gut.

And I always trusted my gut.

The rest of the dinner was light and fun. We talked, and we laughed, and my sister gave us strict instructions for the bachelor and bachelorette parties, which would be on the same night, and both would end at Beer Mountain.

"Like I said. It's a tight leash, buddy. But I'm glad it's you on the other end." I clapped Garrett on the shoulder, and my sister just laughed as she walked with Charlotte in front of us. The girls had had several glasses of wine, and Garrett and I had stopped at one because we were both driving.

We hugged goodbye, and I opened the passenger door for Charlotte. She paused and smiled at me, and her cheeks were flushed, eyes a little glossy. The girl never could handle her booze.

But she was so fucking cute, it was hard to look away.

"Let me help you," I said after she settled into the passenger seat and hiccuped. I leaned over her and pulled her seat belt across her body. My fingers accidentally grazed her tits as I moved the strap to the other side and clicked it in its place. "Sorry about that."

"I'm not," she whispered as I pulled back, our gazes locked.

Fuck me.

Pops of amber and gold sparkled in her hazel eyes as the moonlight shone through the windshield. Her plump lips were calling to me, and I quickly pulled back and closed the door. I adjusted myself as I walked around the car because my dick was raging against my zipper.

I couldn't wait to get home and give him a little relief.

That was what I needed. A cold shower and a little time with my own hand.

Being home. Being close to Charlotte Thomas. It was more difficult than I'd expected.

Yet, I craved more.

I craved her.

This wasn't what I was here for. I was here for my sister's wedding. I wanted to make amends with her best friend. Hell, Charlotte was the best friend I'd ever had, as well, aside from Colt.

I wanted to make things better, not complicate them.

We drove home in silence until she turned to me at the light just a block from her house.

Her cheek was resting on my car seat, and she smiled up at me.

"You're a good man, Ledger. Stop trying to pretend you aren't."

My hand found her cheek. "Not pretending, Ladybug. Just being honest about who I am."

The light changed colors, and I pulled my hand away and drove forward.

"Will you be here a lot more if your company takes on the middle school project? Would you be overseeing that?"

I cleared my throat. "My boss doesn't want to do it. It's not financially a very good move. It doesn't really serve a purpose for him."

She chuckled. "Wow. I can't imagine building a school that thousands upon thousands of children will attend over the next hundred years and thinking that it doesn't serve a purpose. How about the purpose of giving back?"

"Sometimes business doesn't work that way. That's not how you make the big bucks." There was a tease in my voice, but it didn't feel genuine because I didn't agree with what I was saying.

I was all about making money. But I was also about giving back.

What the hell was it all for if you didn't?

"Well, I doubt your boss would think it was good business that you paid off your mama's house and you're paying for your sister's wedding, either, right?"

I pulled into her driveway. "You're probably right. But he doesn't call the shots on my personal life."

I put the car in park and turned to face her.

"But he convinced you to date his daughter, didn't he? Sounds like he wants to call the shots on both your personal and your professional life, if you ask me."

I processed her words, and that uneasiness I felt at the restaurant was there—stronger than ever.

I'd felt it when he continued nagging me about asking out Jessica. The man was my mentor. He'd given me my career. Helped me make a name for myself.

"Don't worry about me, Ladybug. I'll be just fine."

I unbuckled and stepped out of the car, then made my way to the passenger door and helped her out. Her cheeks were still a little pink, but she appeared to have sobered up fairly quickly.

"Thanks for the ride." She walked ahead of me and put the key in the door.

Turn around, motherfucker.

Go home.

I moved up the three steps to her front door, standing right behind her. She spun around. "So you really don't want a family someday? That makes me sad for you."

I let out a long breath, running my fingers through my hair. "I have a family. I don't need to risk fucking up anyone else's life."

She cocked her head to the side and studied me. I was so close; all I'd have to do was move forward just a little, and my lips would graze hers. "There's always risk, Ledger. But those risks are worth it. Look at how much you love your mom, Nan, and Jilly. Don't you want a family of your own?"

"I take risks in my business life, but not in my personal life. I know what I want and what I'm willing to give. And my relationships suit me."

Her hand moved to the side of my face, and her fingers

grazed the scruff that peppered my jaw. Her warm breath tickled my cheek.

I wanted her.

Just a taste.

Just one more time.

My tongue swiped out and wet my bottom lip, and her eyes zoned in on the movement.

"It sounds lonely to me," she whispered.

"You worried about me, Charlie?"

"Always," she said, and her voice cracked. Fuck. I hadn't even kissed her, and I was already hurting her. But the thought of walking completely away just wasn't an option. So instead, I stepped back, putting just a little distance between us.

"Now that we have our itinerary, how about I bring takeout over tomorrow, and we can go over the plan for the bachelor and bachelorette parties?"

"That sounds good to me. But I'll pick up dinner for us this time."

"Fine. I'll see you tomorrow night," I said, walking backward down the stairs as she pushed her door open.

"You know she wants the parties to end over at Beer Mountain. I might not be able to protect you from Lucy Blocker. She's quite a bit taller than me." Her head fell back in laughter, and I couldn't peel my eyes away.

"Don't you worry about me, Ladybug. I can take care of myself."

I've been doing it most of my life.

She chuckled and stepped inside, shutting the door.

I climbed in my car and groaned at my throbbing erection.

It was going to be a long two weeks at home. I glanced

down at my phone and saw a text from Jessica. We hadn't spoken in several weeks, so I was surprised to be hearing from her now.

> **Jessica:** Please don't turn Daddy down on the Mexico trip. I miss you. It would give us a chance to rekindle things. I'm game if you are.

Fuck. This would complicate things. I thought we'd ended amicably, but the fact that Harold was pushing this trip meant Jessica was pressing him to make it happen. Because in all my years of working for the man, we'd never once vacationed together.

> **Me:** I don't think that's a good idea. I wish you nothing but the best. But I think it's best if we both move on.

> **Jessica:** What if I don't want to?

This had been a problem for me in the short time we'd spent together. She didn't like being told no, and I'd seen a few mild tantrums when I didn't go along with what she wanted to do. She was spoiled. Entitled. And I wasn't attracted to that. I'd been straight with her from the beginning that I wasn't looking for anything serious. She'd insisted that she wasn't either.

> **Me:** I'm sorry. But I don't feel that way. I hope there will come a time when we can be friends.

I couldn't get much more direct than that.

And oddly, I wasn't stressed about it. Normally, the fact that my boss's daughter was not handling our breakup would stress me out.

But all I could think of was Charlotte Thomas.
And the way she'd just looked at me.
The way her lips had parted for me.
And how fucking bad I wanted her.

Chapter 7

Charlotte

The next morning, when I rolled into work, I couldn't stop thinking about Ledger, but that didn't stop me from running right into Tobias when I came around the corner to head to my classroom.

"Miss Thomas, good morning," he said, but he did that creepy voice thing again. I didn't know what that was about. He hadn't worked here all that long. Our P.E. teacher, Mrs. Holiday, had left on maternity leave, and he'd be subbing for her until the end of the school year.

"Hey. Good morning. You're here early," I said, as he fell into stride beside me and followed me to my classroom.

"Early bird gets the worm, right?"

"Sure." I chuckled awkwardly as I set my purse on my desk and turned to face him.

"I got lit at Beer Mountain last night. Man, it was wild

over there. You should meet me there sometime."

That was his idea of a date? Meet him at Beer Mountain when he was drunk?

"Maybe I'll run into you sometime." I took my seat and turned on my computer, hoping he'd take the hint.

"Are you seeing someone? Is that why you keep brushing me off?" He licked his lips as his gaze locked with mine.

"Something like that," I said, because I didn't want to be mean, but this was not going anywhere.

"Well, you let me know when you're single, and if you're lucky, no one will have snatched me up yet. The competition is fierce." He laughed ridiculously loud and then winked before walking out the door.

Dear God, please do not let this be a sign of what's to come today.

I pulled out my journal and wrote a quick entry. I kept my journal in my desk at work and usually wrote in it during my prep time. It was something that my mother had started with my sisters and me when we were young, but I'd never stopped the habit. My mother taught us to start the day with gratitude. I'd write three things that I was grateful for every single day. Often, they were the same several days in a row, but today's entry was definitely different.

1. I'm grateful that Ledger is back in my life. I missed him.

2. I'm grateful that I got closure with my past. And a part of me is extra grateful to learn that it wasn't a one-sided crush.

3. I'm grateful for my family and Jilly and my amazing job.

I closed my journal and tucked it back in the drawer as my phone vibrated.

Ledger: Don't mention Harold not wanting to do the middle school project to anyone. I'm going to try to make that happen. Not sure I can, but it's worth a shot.

Me: See, there is a decent man beneath that good-looking exterior.

I chewed on my thumbnail as I waited for him to respond. I loved that we had this secret flirty relationship. I worried Jilly would notice, but she definitely didn't appear to because she'd talked about setting me up with Robby, Garrett's cousin, who was flying in from New York for the wedding.

I swear I felt Ledger stiffen beside me as she talked about it at dinner last night, but maybe I was just imagining it. Maybe a little part of me still carried a torch for my childhood crush. God knows I was ridiculously attracted to him, but I also knew that it could never go anywhere.

We wanted different things.

We lived in different cities.

He never fought for me back in the day, and he certainly wouldn't now.

I shook it off, hating that my mind always went there with him. He'd offered me a friendship, and I was still daydreaming about the guy.

I silently cursed myself out before the bell rang and the kids filed into the classroom. Kell and I got the centers set up while they had free time before the morning bell rang. Darwin followed me around, just like he always did before class started. When I moved to the chair at the front of the room, waiting for the bell to ring, he stepped closer. Darwin didn't have great social skills when it came to personal space and boundaries. We were working on that.

But Rome wasn't built in a day, and Darwin wasn't going to accomplish every single goal that I had for him during kindergarten.

"Remember what I told you about moving too close to people?" I asked, as his nose nearly bumped mine and his hands moved to my cheeks.

"I know, Miss Thomas. But I just want to see what you had for breakfast." He sniffed a few times and then smiled. "Yogurt and fruit again?"

I snorted because this boy was unbelievable when it came to scents. He'd called out Marcy Waters many times for her salami breath. And seeing as Marcy was easily triggered—that never went over well. However, he was usually very accurate.

"Yes. Yogurt and fruit. But remember, people don't like when you smell their breath. Some people think it's rude."

"Do you think I'm rude?" he asked, his brown eyes big as saucers.

"I don't, Darwin. Because I know your heart. But there still are rules to follow that people appreciate from others. So, it's something I really want you to practice, okay?"

"Okay. Miss Thomas, are you going to marry Mr. Dane? I think he wants to marry you."

I chuckled. "He definitely does not want to marry me. We're just friends."

"Phew," he said dramatically and swiped at his forehead. "Then I can still marry you someday."

I squeezed his hand and smiled because the boy was sweet as sugar. I motioned for him to take his seat on the carpet just as the bell rang.

The countdown was on, and we were running out of days together. I let them have more time than usual on the carpet to share and ask questions today.

"Yes, Raymond," I said, giving him a nod to speak.

"I'm worried about my mama," he said, his voice shaky.

"What's wrong with your mom, honey? Is she not feeling well?" I realized in that moment that I hadn't seen her this week. His grandmother had been picking him up.

"She got new boobies. They're real big, but we can't see them yet under the bandages. She said she's going to get her a new husband with them. But they hurt, Miss Thomas. She's been sleeping a lot."

Welcome to my life.

Kell was working at the back table and her head fell back in hysterical laughter before she covered her mouth and corrected herself. I took a minute to compose myself, as well, and Marcy could not contain her anger.

"He said *boobies*. You can't say boobies in school. And my mother said that it doesn't matter if your boobies are big or small. They're all beautiful." Marcy burst into tears because it was hard to be five and want to control the world.

I get it.

"Honey, go get a drink of water, please." I raised a brow at Marcy and then turned to Raymond. "I promise your mama will be good as new in no time. Don't you worry."

Probably better than new.

I couldn't help but glance down at my chest and wonder what it would be like to have some big girls staring back at me. I looked up to meet Kell's gaze, and we both shook our heads and tried hard not to laugh.

Thankfully, the rest of the day went by quickly, aside from the fact that Marcy ended up projectile vomiting all over the reading table and was sent home sick. Kindergarten was an unpredictable place to spend your days—but I loved it all the same.

I stopped by to grab a large pizza from Honey Mountain Pie Company, only the best pizza in town. The Crawford family owned the place, and little Creek Crawford was in my class, so they were always so sweet when I popped in. I dropped the pizza box onto the passenger seat of my car and ran into Honey Bee's to see Vivian and grab a few pastries for tonight, as well.

The bakery was dead as she was about to lock up. Baby Bee was home with Niko as he was off today, and Jilly had left for the day already.

Vivi packed up a box of goodies and handed it to me. "So, you've been busy. The wedding plans are coming along well? Jilly said you all had dinner last night to go over everything. She told me she wants to set you up with Garrett's cousin, Robby?"

"Yeah. It sounds promising." I shrugged. "Although, he lives in New York, so not really sure how that would work."

She chuckled. "How's it going with Ledger?"

"Fine. We're meeting tonight to plan the bachelor and bachelorette parties."

She came around the counter and studied me. "Seems like you've been meeting up a lot since he's been back."

"You know, we kind of fell out of touch over the years. So,

we agreed to work on our friendship all while getting things ready for the wedding."

She smiled and reached forward to tuck a loose strand of hair behind my ear. "Good. I know he means a lot to you. I think that's great. You know... I don't think Jilly would be bothered by it all these years later if something happened between you two."

I shook my head, my eyes finding the ceiling. "That's not happening. First off, he doesn't even live here."

"Well, he lives a lot closer than the cousin in New York." She chuckled.

"Ledger isn't like that. He dates casually. He doesn't do serious. We couldn't be more different that way. I want a family. He doesn't. I'm happy being friends with him, but it's nothing more than that."

"He was awfully concerned about your sandwich yesterday. But when his father came into the bakery, he went ice cold. There is not a lot of love there, is there?"

"I think there's been a lot of damage. He has a lot of anger."

"I think that's what you and he bonded over so much when you were teenagers," she said, her eyes wet with emotion.

"What?"

"You were sad about Mama passing. We were all hurting too much to be much help to the other back then. But after Ledger and Jilly's dad left, it seemed like Jilly went a little wild for a bit, and Ledger took on the weight of the world. I just remember seeing you two talking all the time. Way too deep of a conversation for teenagers. But now I get it. You were both grieving different things. You lost your mother, and his family split up."

I nodded. "You're wiser than your years, Vivian West." I kissed her cheek. "He was a really good friend to me back then. I didn't talk to many people about it, but I always felt safe with him."

"He must have felt safe with you, too, because he was goofy with everyone else. The charming, funny guy at school. He never showed the other side of himself that he showed you."

"I guess we were lucky we had one another back then."

"Definitely. I wouldn't have survived without Niko."

"I know. He was a good friend to you before he became your hubby." I kissed her cheek. "I need to get going. Give Niko and Baby Bee my love. I'll come by this weekend to see her."

"Love you, Charlie."

"Love you," I said as I strolled out the door and hopped into my car.

When I pulled into my driveway, I hurried inside and changed into a pair of jean shorts and a white tank top. I pulled my hair into a ponytail and walked out to the backyard to water my plants. I loved this little house so much. It was tiny, but it was all mine. It sat right up on the lake, and every day, I had my coffee outside as I looked at the gorgeous turquoise water.

This had been Vivi's first home, and I'd scored because she'd redone the bathroom and the kitchen. But she and Niko had bought a large home on the lake not too far from here, and I bought this from her.

I was saving up for a canoe of my own, but for now, I

usually just went over to Vivian's or Everly's homes as they both had houses on the lake with canoes and jet skis and every other water sport toy you could think of. But I looked forward to the day I had my own and could take it out on the water. Dylan lived in Everly's guest house, but she planned on getting her own place once she knew where she'd be living. She was currently studying for the bar exam as she'd just graduated law school, and she'd accepted a clerkship here in town for the next few months to get some experience under her belt.

There was a knock on the door, and I turned off the hose and hurried inside. When I opened the door, Ledger stood there holding a bottle of wine and a bouquet of flowers. Pink peonies. My favorite. He wore a white tee and a pair of khaki shorts, and he managed to make it look ridiculously sexy. His dark waves were tousled on his head, and his dark eyes locked with mine.

His eyes had always been intoxicating to me. I'd never seen another set of eyes that were as unique as his. Sometimes they were brown, with hints of gold and pops of amber, and other times, they would darken and almost appear black. But they were always expressive when they met mine.

"I told you I was taking care of everything tonight," I said as I stepped back and let him inside.

He whistled. "This place is so... you. And I'm not an asshole. I don't go to someone's house empty-handed. Nan sent these from her garden."

He handed me the flowers, and I took a moment to smell them, closing my eyes and breathing them in. These particular blooms brought back so many memories for me. I'd first smelled peonies in Ledger's grandmother's garden when I was a little girl. And then my mama and I planted them in our backyard, and they were still blooming today. And every year on the anniversary of my mother's death, I put a bouquet of pink peonies at her grave. They were her favorite flower, too. Every year on February 13—the day my mother had passed—I received a bouquet of pink peonies. They came to our home because no matter what we were doing, we all always came home so we could visit her grave together. There was never a card attached, but I had a hunch it was from my sister, Dylan. She'd never admit to being that thoughtful, but she was. She'd also never want to hurt our sisters if she was only sending them to me, and she knew that our mother and I shared a love for this particular flower. I always tried to get Mrs. Winthrop to tell me who sent them all these years, but she insisted it would be a breach of her customer's confidentiality. I always chuckled, because Dilly could be intimidating, and I had no doubt she'd sworn the woman to secrecy. My twin sister could be as scary as a mob boss if she was protecting someone.

I made my way to the kitchen and pulled down a vase, filling it with water and trimming the stems to fit just right.

"Is this how you woo all the ladies back in the city? Pretty flowers and expensive wine?" I eyed the bottle that he set down on the counter.

"You sure are concerned about me and the ladies, huh?"

"Not concerned, just observant."

He chuckled and turned around, slowly taking in the place. I led him out back and showed him the view.

"This is beautiful. You always said you were going to live on the lake someday."

"I did. And when you were ten years old, you said you

were going to build a castle for your dad, your mom, Nan, Jilly, and me to live in. And I believe you also said you'd be moving in all your girlfriends. You were a player even back then."

He barked out a laugh. "Well, I won't be building a castle for my father, that's for sure."

I led him back inside and poured us each a glass of wine, and we moved to sit at the cute white, round table. "Does it bother you that your dad is walking Jilly down the aisle?"

He thought about it and took a sip of wine before setting down his glass. "I want her to do whatever she wants. This is her day. But I don't understand it, why she'd set herself up to be let down by him again. He's shown her who he is. He ditched our mother and didn't help financially after he remarried a second time or a third. He never called. He just completely checked out. So yeah, I think it's strange to invite him back into her life after all that."

I opened the pizza box and set two slices on his plate before taking a slice for myself.

"Jilly is in a happy place. She's made peace with it. She wants to forgive because sometimes holding on to all that anger just holds you back." I picked up my slice and took a bite, and he did the same, but he nearly ate half the slice in one bite, which made me laugh.

"How about you? Are you in a happy place?" He changed the subject.

"I am. I mean, there are things I want. Things I'm working toward. But yeah, I'm in a good place. How about you?"

"Well, my father's a dick, and I can't change that. But I have a killer condo in the city. I like my job, but I also hate not being independent, and I'd prefer to choose the projects that I work on. So I'd say I'm in a decent place, but things could improve."

"Maybe you should talk to your dad while you're both in town. It might help. I'm not saying you have to forgive him, but you could make peace with it."

"You worried about me, Ladybug?"

I smiled. "Stop trying to turn this on me. We're talking about you."

"Fine. I'll talk to him. He texted me earlier and asked me to meet him for lunch this week. Let's just hope he doesn't try to bail on walking Jilly down the aisle now that she's counting on it. Plus, I'm looking forward to walking you down the aisle."

My stomach dipped at his words. Because I was looking forward to it, too.

But I didn't want the wedding to come too quickly.

Because that meant he'd be leaving right after. And I was enjoying this time with him right now. Jilly was too busy wedding planning to notice that I wasn't around much.

"Eat up, Dane. We're working tonight. I will not be distracted. Not even by the beautiful peonies."

His hand rested on the table beside mine, and he glanced down at his phone, picking it up as his gaze pinched together and he read the text before setting it down.

"Everything okay?"

"Yeah. Just trying to negotiate that middle school deal with my boss, but he's stubborn, so it's not going very well." His pinky finger brushed against mine, and he lifted it just a little and intertwined ours together. "I'll keep trying."

"That's all you can do, right?" I whispered, and his gaze

focused on my mouth.

My breath nearly hitched in my throat at the contact.

Warning bells were going off in my head.

I was getting in too deep.

Just our fingers touching had my body reacting.

I pulled my hand away and pushed to my feet. "Let me get some paper, and we can get to work."

And that was exactly what we did.

We planned the bachelor and bachelorette parties, we ate pizza, we reminisced, and we laughed.

I kept my distance when he said goodbye and made his way to the door. I held my hand up and waved because hugging him right now wouldn't be wise.

But when his heated gaze locked with mine, my stomach flipped.

"See you soon, Ladybug."

I nodded and shut the door behind him.

I leaned my back against the door and thought about what I'd write in my gratitude journal in the morning.

And I knew that Ledger Dane would be at the top of the list again.

Chapter 8
Ledger

I spent the morning working at Nan's house while she was out in the garden. I was sending over some numbers for Harold, as he'd finally agreed to take a deeper look at the middle school project. Dan Garfer had been blowing up my phone for days, and I'd called him this morning to let him know I was still working on it, but I couldn't make any promises.

I knew that there were other architects that he could use.

But I grew up in Honey Mountain.

My family lived here.

Hell, Charlotte worked for the school district.

I wanted to make this happen.

"Okay, it's time," Nan said, as she came in and dropped her sun hat on the table and smiled at me. She wore baggy linen shorts and a long-sleeved white linen shirt to cover her arms from the sun. It was a warm one today. She pulled off her garden gloves and walked toward the laundry room to drop them in the wash. "I've got my swimsuit on already. Go get your suit on. You promised."

I groaned. Nan was a member of the Honey Mountain Seniors Association. They had a clubhouse, a pool, and a workout room. She played cards and bridge and spent her summers walking laps in the pool to keep in shape. But I had no desire to go hang out at a seniors' day club in the pool.

"You sure I won't be infringing on your time with your friends?" I asked as a last-ditch effort to get out of it.

"No chance, Ledger. The ladies are all excited to see a hot young man with ripped muscles at the pool. I promised to bring you today, and even Miranda Highwater is coming just to see if you live up to the hype. That one's got a big ole stick up her behind, and I can't wait to show you off."

"My god. You're whoring me out to the elderly?" I grumped as I pushed to my feet.

"Hey. Don't be so dramatic. Us elderly still have eyeballs, you know. It would be nice to see a man in the pool who wasn't wrinkly and could hear without us standing so close we were bumping privates. Obviously, bringing you doesn't really do anything for me. I certainly can't grope my grandson. But I promised the ladies."

"Grope your grandson? What the hell, Nan? They better not touch me. What did you sign me up for?" I laughed as I moved to the bathroom and pulled on my swim trunks. I couldn't even believe I had to do this today. And then I'd get to follow it up with lunch with my dad. Lucky me. I hadn't seen Charlotte in two days. We'd been spending a lot of time together, and the lines were getting blurred. We'd gotten everything ordered for the bachelor and bachelorette parties, and we'd had dinner the next night to discuss our speeches, so there wasn't much more I could make up to meet about. And I didn't like that I woke up thinking about her and fell asleep thinking about her, as well. Things were getting complicated.

I didn't do complicated.

So I said I had to do some family things yesterday, and she claimed she had plans, too. But tonight, I figured I'd see her at Beer Mountain because Everly's husband, Hawk, had texted me to meet him, Niko, and Jace there for a quick drink. The bachelor party was tomorrow night, so it wouldn't be a late one. Garrett told me he and Jilly were going to stop by, as well, so I assumed Charlotte would be there, too. I was looking forward to seeing everyone, and I was tempted to text Charlotte to make sure she was going, but I didn't want to look like a needy bastard.

But when it came to Charlotte Thomas—I was a needy bastard.

Nan got into the passenger seat and fiddled with my radio until she found some sort of elevator music on XM Radio. I rolled my eyes when the song "Piña Colada" came on, and she clapped along.

"One hour, all right? I have to meet Dad for lunch, as much as that pains me to say."

"That's very big of you," she said, eyeing me suspiciously when we pulled into the parking lot at what I called the *Blue Hair Club*. "Did Jilly ask you to meet with him?"

"Nah. She's so caught up in wedding planning, I haven't even told her I'm going."

"So you just decided to do this all on your own? You hate

the man. That's very out of character." She gathered up her beach bag, and I climbed out of the car and moved around to help her out.

"Do you always have to be a therapist when you talk to me?"

"Old habits die hard. So, what made you decide to meet with him?" I fell in stride beside her as we made our way through the parking lot.

"Well, no sense carrying all that anger around, right? It's just holding me back."

Her head fell back, and she chuckled. "Who are you, and what have you done with my bitter grandson, Ledger?"

I rolled my eyes. "Fine. Charlie suggested I meet with him, and he had texted about grabbing lunch today, so I agreed. She thinks I should just make peace with him. Stop carrying this around with me."

"She's always been wise for her years."

I nodded in agreement as I held the door open, and we stepped inside, pausing at the desk to sign in.

A woman who had to be in her mid-eighties smiled up at me. She had just a few sparse white hairs that were tied in an elastic on her head with a big pink flower tucked behind her ear, bright orange lipstick that was drawn well outside of her lip line, and the sweetest blue eyes. "You must be the famous Ledger Dane. Your nan, here, says that you're a real lady killer."

For fuck's sake. Was my grandmother pimping me out to her girlfriends?

"It's nice to meet you." I extended my hand and ignored the lady killer comment, because it was just wrong for a multitude of reasons.

"I'm Bernadette." She giggled before taking my hand to her lips and planting a kiss there.

I glanced down to see a bright orange pucker on the backside of my hand, and I just smiled at her.

"What did you tell these people?" I leaned close to Nan and hissed in her ear as she led me outside.

"Oh, relax. Let the ladies have a little look-see. Hey, maybe you'll make some cash tips."

"What the fu—" I was cut off when she pushed the door open, and there stood about fifteen elderly women in a long line. It looked like a *Golden Girls* reunion on steroids.

"Look at the turnout," Nan gasped and clapped her hands together because she was so excited.

"Is he going to take his shirt off?" one of them shouted.

"Take it off, Handsome!" another one shouted.

What the actual fuck was happening?

Nan turned me away from the ladies and pushed up on her tiptoes to speak close to my ear. "Listen to me. We took a field trip to that *Thunder Down Under* a while back. The girls loved it. I showed them a few pictures of you, and they made me promise to bring you by the club when you were home. How about you put on a little show?"

"I am literally going to put dish soap in that blueberry pie you made when we get home," I snarled. "And I'm not watching *Jeopardy* with you tonight, either."

"Hey, I can live with that. Let's go take a dip in the pool. Lose the shirt," she said over her laughter.

I glared at Nan and reached over my head and yanked off my shirt. I'd never felt so dirty, the way they all gasped and whistled.

I was fit. I worked out. But you'd think I was a goddamn rock star the way they were carrying on.

Nan totally ditched me and hurried off to join the groupies that she sicced on me.

"Ledger, Loretta said she's got some oil in her beach bag if you need it!" Nan shouted, and they all clapped and giggled. Loretta waved at me, and I knew it was her because she wore a hot pink visor with her name painted across the front of it. Loretta was also far too tan for her own good, and her skin resembled that of a raisin. It was probably all that time she spent outside with her young tennis pro.

I drew the line at oil.

I was naturally tan.

That was a hard no for me.

"I already moisturized today, Loretta. How about we mosey on into the water, ladies?" I purred when I moved to the pool.

Hey, if you can't beat 'em, join 'em, I guess. Nan was having the time of her life, and I sure as fuck wouldn't do anything to ruin it for her. But she would pay for this later.

I spent the next hour being pawed on, propositioned, and offered to date several of the women's granddaughters. The woman that Nan had mentioned, Miranda Highwater, ran her long red nails down my abdomen while I was chatting with the ladies. She gave zero fucks that she did not have permission to touch me, nor that I happened to have extremely sensitive skin. She was lucky she didn't break the skin with those claws of hers because I would have no problem pressing charges. She then climbed out of the pool, no shame at all, and dropped on a lawn chair and lit up a cigarette.

I didn't even think people still smoked in this day and age.

When I told Nan we needed to get going, as I was due to have lunch with my father and I still had to stop by the house to change, she told me she'd get a ride with Loretta.

I kissed her cheek, and she pulled me down so she could speak into my ear. "You were a good sport today. I love you. Go make peace with the devil at lunch. But don't go putting soap in that pie, all right? I'm looking forward to eating that when we watch *Jeopardy* tonight."

"You're very lucky I love you, dirty bird."

"I sure am," she said.

I waved goodbye to her friends, and as I climbed out of the pool, someone smacked my ass unusually hard, and I whipped around. A tiny woman with a yellow bathing cap and gigantic sunglasses laughed. "That's a nice derriere you have there, sonny boy."

My god. If a woman got manhandled at an elderly home like this by males, I'd tell her to press charges. But these ladies just acted like we were shooting the shit about the weather, not that they were pawing all over me and treating me like a piece of meat.

"Um, thanks. Take care."

I couldn't get out of that place quick enough.

I needed a long shower after that shit show.

When I got to my car, I couldn't help but laugh and feel a sense of relief that I was free. But I almost wondered if I'd rather stay in that pool getting groped than have lunch with my father.

I started up the car and glanced down at my phone before pulling out. There was a text from Charlotte.

Ladybug: Good luck at lunch. Just say what you need to say and make peace with it. You'll feel much better after.

Me: Fine. I just left Nan's old ladies club, and I've never felt so dirty. Those are some horny old birds over there.

Ladybug: OMG! Was Loretta Barnes there? Niko calls her Mrs. Robinson. She likes the young fellas.

Me: Well, Nan had no problem pimping me out. And don't even get me started on Miranda Highwater. The woman raked her sharp nails down my stomach, and I'm not happy about it. Who the fuck does that?

Ladybug: An eighty-three-year-old rich woman who is used to getting what she wants. <laughing face emoji> And she clearly wanted you. <fire emoji>

Me: That is not hot, Ladybug. I happen to bruise like a peach, and this one is going to leave a mark. And please don't use the fire emoji when describing me and Miranda.

Ladybug: So, only use the fire emoji when describing YOU? <winky face emoji>

Me: Careful, Ladybug. I'm not the guy you want to flirt with, remember?

Ladybug: Friends can flirt.

Me: So you think I'm hot…

Ladybug: That's no secret.

Me: I think you're fucking hot, too, bestie.

Ladybug: It's a mutual respect.

Me: It definitely is. Are you going to Beer Mountain tonight?

Ladybug: Yep. For a little bit. I'm down to the last few days of school, so a little fun sounds good.

Me: I'll see you there.

Ladybug: You will. Don't be a baby. Go to lunch and face this.

Me: A hot baby, though, right?

Ladybug: I'm going to regret saying that, aren't I?

Me: You have to speak the truth, hot Ladybug.

Ladybug: LOL. The bell rang. Kids are coming in now. See you later.

Me: Give Darwin a fist pump for me.

Ladybug: <thumbs up emoji>

I pulled out of the parking lot, and once again, I was in a good mood because just talking to this girl had a way of turning things around for me. I drove home to change really quick and then made my way to the Honey Mountain Café. I let out a long breath before stepping out of my car.

Stop being a pussy. You can do this.

My father and I hadn't had many conversations over the last decade. There'd been a huge fight when I finally couldn't hold in my anger anymore. And the fucker had blamed me for our family blowing up. Saying that my confession to my mom about what I saw was the reason we weren't a family anymore. I'd caught him a second time with another woman, and I told my mother. I couldn't carry that secret any longer.

And I hated him for that, because for the longest time, I blamed myself for what happened. But after years of Nan talking things through with me—sometimes ad nauseum—I'd come to realize that I'd been punishing myself for many years for a crime that I didn't commit. My father was to blame for what happened between him and my mother.

I learned a long time ago that you have very little control over things that happened to the people you love. Colt was a big reminder of that. Losing a guy who'd been more like a brother to me my entire life made me realize just how precious life was. I kept my circle small, which was a conscious decision on my part. It was important to me to stay in control of the relationships that I had. Protect the people that I loved and not let too many people in. There was too much room for things to go wrong.

When I stepped inside the busy café, my father waved me over immediately. I was glad that he hadn't brought Bambi, or whatever the hell her name was, because I wouldn't be able to have a conversation with him if we had an audience.

He gave me an awkward half-bro type of hug, and I quickly took my seat across from him in the booth.

"Thanks for meeting me for lunch, son." He cleared his throat. I hated when he called me that. Because it inferred that he had been a father to me, and over the last decade, nothing could be less true.

"Yep. I guess it's time we clear the air, huh?"

"I think so," he said, pausing when the server appeared. We both quickly ordered our drinks and lunch all at once, as I think we both wanted to get this over with.

"I hate that we're distant." He put it out there the minute she walked away.

Here we go.

"Well, I don't like it either. But it's the reason that we're distant that's the real problem."

"I hurt your mama, and you hate me for it. I get it. I guess I deserve it." He shrugged.

This was typical Dean Dane behavior. He had a way of making light of his actions. Taking years of bad behavior and rolling it into one single action and making himself the victim.

"So let's unpack this, shall we?" I said, pausing when our drinks were set in front of us.

Don't be a baby. Face this.

Charlotte's words echoed in my mind as I took a long sip of my iced tea before setting it down.

"Sure. I can't take back the past, so I'm a believer in moving forward."

"Of course, you are. Because all the shit you did is inexcusable, so it's easier to just move forward. But that's not how life works. Maybe when you own some of that shit, we'll be able to move forward."

"That sounds like a lot of therapy mumbo-jumbo talk from your grandmother, but if it makes you feel better to tell me I fucked up, then so be it."

Jesus. This man was such a dick it was hard for me to wrap my mind around the fact that I actually worshipped him at one point in my life.

"In life, there are consequences for our actions. Trust me. I'm not a perfect man. But I accept the consequences of my actions."

Thoughts of Charlotte and how I fucked up all those years ago flooded my mind. But I knew I didn't deserve her back then, and I accepted it. This man wanted everything but gave nothing back.

"I lost my family." He shrugged.

"You left your family," I hissed, leaning forward as my gaze locked with his. "You didn't fight for anything. You asked me to lie for you when I was a fucking kid. Do you have any idea how fucked up that was? How bad I felt about lying to Mom? Promising it would never happen again and then doing it over and over."

"I still stand by the fact that we'd still be together if you never told her. That hadn't been my first affair, Ledger. But until you actually spilled the beans, there'd never been a problem. She didn't like that you knew. For whatever reason, that was her breaking point. So, you need to own your part."

My head fell back, and I closed my eyes and counted down from ten to one. It was a technique that Nan had taught me years ago, and it kept me from putting my fist through his fucking face. I looked back at him, and I saw the apprehension there.

"Your actions are the reason you and Mom aren't together. Your actions are the reason we have no relationship. Your actions are the reason you're always broke. Your. Actions."

"Mom kicking me out of the house followed you telling her about my affair. So that's also a little bit on you and a little bit on her." He smiled when the server set our plates down in front of him, and my hands fisted at my sides. I waited for the older woman to walk away.

"You're un-fucking-believable. The fact that you can blame me and Mom for you having multiple affairs, dragging your young son into your bullshit, turning your back on your daughter both emotionally and financially—and you take no ownership. What the fuck is wrong with you?"

My father looked around to make sure no one was looking. Hell, everyone in this town knew his story. He conned money out of a ton of people in Honey Mountain for his bullshit business ideas that never panned out. That was why he was constantly moving. His lies and deceit followed him everywhere he went.

"Ledger, listen to me. I know what I asked of you was wrong. I'm sorry I put you in that position. I didn't mean to take away from that. I just meant that I wish she'd never found out. I wish I'd kept our family together."

"I wish you'd kept your dick in your pants. There's the problem. Instead of blaming everyone for who told who and who found out… if you'd been faithful… if you'd been true to your word, none of that would have happened."

"You want the truth? Is that what you want?" His tone was harsh, and his dark red face did not hide his anger.

"I know the truth. You're the one who won't own it."

"How about this? I wasn't in love with your mother. I only married her because I knocked her up. With you. You're the reason I married her. She's an amazing lady, no doubt about it. But she just didn't do it for me. So, I tried, and I failed. I deserved to be happy, too. But I'd still have stayed with my family, because life was better for all of us when we were together."

Anger built, and I couldn't think straight. His words were starting to get mumbled, and I needed to get out of there. *He'd only married her because she was pregnant with me*? Did my mother know that?

"You might be the biggest piece of shit I've ever met." A maniacal laugh escaped me. "It's funny, you know? All this time, I thought I'd lost this great man. The man I looked up to. But the truth is, I was just a naïve kid. You were never that man. You were never really around all that much, but I romanticized it. The idea of what a father should be. I didn't lose my father all those years ago—I got introduced to him. This is who you are, isn't it?"

He stared at me, unsure how to answer. I just took him in. His ridiculous spiky hair. His Cartier watch that he continued to make sure everyone saw as he flicked his wrist around. But for the first time in my life, I saw him. He was just not a good guy. He hadn't changed. He was who he was, and he made no apologies. He took what he needed from people and then threw them away. It all came together now.

"If that's how you see it. But that doesn't mean I don't want a relationship with you." He shrugged. "I think you're extremely talented. That's why Brenda and I wanted to see if you would design a home for us. Her last husband was a wealthy man, and she's got the funds for us to build our dream house. We're getting married. She's pregnant."

Motherfucker.

He hadn't invited me here to make amends.

He wanted me to design his fucking house.

I pushed to my feet. I came. I talked. And I actually made peace with it.

I didn't want a relationship with this man who disrespected my mother and my sister. Who blamed *me* for having to get married in the first place.

To think I always feared that I was just like him.

But we were nothing alike. He didn't have a loyal bone in his body.

"That's not happening. We're done." I leaned down, my face in his. "But you're not going to say a fucking word to Jilly now or on her wedding day. Don't mention your marriage. Your new baby. Or your new house. For once in your godforsaken, selfish life, put her first. Walk her down the aisle and act like you fucking care."

He held his hands up and shook his head. "Well, I don't know that I can convince Brenda to stick around here if you're not willing to help us with the new house. There's no reason to stay."

"How about the fact that your only daughter asked you to fucking give her away?" I said, spewing venom as the words left my mouth.

"Well, I guess you'll decide if you want to ruin your sister's wedding by turning us down, all because you're angry that your childhood didn't turn out the way you wanted. You've done quite well for yourself, Ledger. Maybe it's time to man up."

Hello pot, I'm kettle.

"Are you fucking blackmailing me? Holding my sister—

your daughter's wedding over my head? You've reached an all-new low."

"Some people don't have a rock bottom, son. I'm willing to do what I need to in order to make my fiancée happy. She wants you to design our home. You've made quite a name for yourself. So how about you scratch my back and I scratch yours?"

There were times in your life when you faced obstacles you didn't see coming. My father's first affair rocked my world. His departure that came so easily for him rocked it again. But this... this was a new low. Even for him.

"Tell her I'll think about it." And I stormed out of there.

I'd come for closure, but that sure as shit hadn't happened.

Chapter 9

Charlotte

I texted Ledger a few times to see how lunch went, but I hadn't heard back. I knew this was important for him to deal with, because whether he wanted to admit it or not, he was carrying so much anger about his father.

My door flew open, and Dylan strolled in. She was wearing jean shorts and a black tank, her hair tied up on her head in a messy knot, and, of course, she looked like a freaking supermodel.

"Hey, you ready?" she asked.

"Yep. You look gorgeous as always," I said, grabbing my keys and heading toward the door. Beer Mountain was only a few blocks away, so we could walk there.

"You look gorgeous yourself." She walked out the door and waited for me to lock up. "I need a drink. Studying for the bar is killing me."

"You've got this. You're going to do amazing. Have you thought about what you want to do once you pass?"

"I don't know. I have this clerkship that starts next week, which will look really good on my résumé, so I'm going to do that for three months. And Hawk and Ever were telling me about how the Lions have a chief legal for the team, and it sounds super interesting."

"You hate sports," I said with a laugh.

"I like the law. And negotiating contracts. And I don't mind professional athletes, so I'm sure I could get on board with sports."

My head fell back in laughter. My twin sister was like no one I'd ever met. Unique and special. Loyal and hilarious. Fierce and protective. "If anyone could do it—it would be you."

"Hawk said there aren't a ton of females in the industry, so of course, that makes me want to do it even more. I'm going to put my feelers out and see what I'd need to pursue that path. But I'm open to all the possibilities."

"Of course, you are. And you have a good in because you happen to know the GOAT of the NHL." I laughed. Our brother-in-law, Hawk Madden, was a famous hockey player, and my sister Everly worked for the Lions as a sports psychologist.

"That's true. So, what's happening with you and Ledger? Will he be there tonight?"

"Nothing. Just wedding planning." I shrugged as we approached the bar. "He's supposed to be there tonight, but he had lunch with his dad, and I haven't heard from him since."

"Ewww. That man is such a piece of work. I can't believe

Jilly's letting him walk her down the aisle."

"Yeah. She wants to have a relationship with him. I just hope she doesn't get hurt again."

Dylan yanked the bar door open, and I stepped inside. My eyes scanned the crowd.

There was no sign of Ledger, Jilly, or Garrett. I checked my phone again, and there was a text from my best friend.

> **Jilly:** Hey, girl. We're not going to come tonight. We ate too many tacos for dinner, and we're exhausted. I'm putting on my stretchy pants, and we're going to watch a movie. My brother isn't answering his phone, so will you let him know that we're sorry we aren't making it? I love you forever.

It's something we always said when we texted.

> **Me:** Of course. I haven't seen him yet, but I'll let him know. Call me tomorrow. Love you forever.

I nodded. "I'm sure he'll be here."

I made my way over to Hawk, and he handed me and Dylan a beer. "Have you heard from Ledger? He said he'd be here."

"I'm sure he'll be here soon."

Hawk and Jace each hugged me and said they were only staying for a few drinks with Ledger before they had to get home. There were a few firefighters here, and they were playing pool. Tomorrow night was the bachelor and bachelorette party, so I highly doubted anyone would drink much tonight.

I turned to see Lucy Blocker behind the bar, and she waved. We always acted like we hadn't had a fallout all those years ago—even though she'd behaved like a crazy person. I waved back, and then my gaze moved to the door to see Ledger walk in. His eyes locked with mine, and I knew something was off.

He made his way over to me and gave me a quick hug and kissed my cheek, before moving through the group. All the guys were loud and boisterous as they hadn't seen one another in a while. He hugged Dylan, but his eyes never left mine as he forced a smile and acted like his charming self.

But I knew something was wrong.

He made his way back to me. "How was school?"

"It was good. How did lunch go?"

He opened his mouth to speak, but a loud voice shouted, "Ledger fucking Dane. Say it isn't so!"

He glanced behind the bar and then looked back at me before moving close to whisper in my ear. "You have got to be fucking kidding me. I've been groped by the golden girls, horrified by my father, and now my childhood stalker is my bartender. The hits just keep coming."

"Hello, Lucy." His tone was serious, and he crossed his arms over his chest.

"Wow. You look good, Dane. Are you single?" she asked, leaning over the bar and flipping her long red hair over one shoulder.

"I am not. I'm very much with someone," he said, making no attempt to hide his irritation. I could tell that he'd been pushed today and was at the end of his rope.

"Damn. Well, I'm not looking for anything serious anyway, but I'm also open to something casual." She winked, and I cringed at how awkward this interaction was. Was she seriously hitting on him after all that happened?

"For fuck's sake. I'm in a relationship. Not everyone is

a fucking cheater, okay?" he snapped, catching us both off guard, although she smirked and waggled her brows as if she enjoyed seeing him angry. I reached for his hand and squeezed it, hoping to calm him down.

"Down, boy. Yes, I can work with that. Let's get a drink in you, and we'll talk after my shift," Lucy said.

He shook his head and looked at me, his hand still in mine and our fingers now intertwined. I glanced around to make sure no one was looking, and my gaze locked with Dylan's. Of course, she was watching like a hawk. She raised a brow and smiled before turning away to grab her beer.

"How about a beer?" I asked him, and he nodded.

"Don't open the bottle," he said, as he glanced at Lucy, and she chuckled.

"You got it, hottie."

"Don't open the bottle?" I laughed after Lucy walked away.

"Listen. After the day I've had, I wouldn't be surprised if the woman drugged me and took me home and made me her sex slave."

"How about I agree to keep an eye on you? You can relax."

"You going to stay by my side, Ladybug?"

"If you need me to, yes." I pulled my hand away from his when Lucy set the beer down.

"Here's an opener. But I dig that you're concerned. You get me, Ledger Dane."

When she walked away, he opened the bottle and took a long pull, nearly finishing the entire thing in one shot. He set the opener back down on the bar.

"Wow. That bad of a day, huh?"

"You have no fucking idea. I didn't want to text you after, because I didn't want to put my shit on you."

"We're friends. That's what friends do. Which, by the way, Jilly asked me to tell you she wasn't coming tonight. She's tired and ate too many tacos." I chuckled. "She said you weren't answering her texts."

"I can't tell her what happened today. She doesn't know I met with him, and I can't bother her with this shit when her wedding is in a week. You want another beer?"

I held mine up and shook my head. "Nope. I'm just sipping this one."

"I'll take one more," Ledger said when Lucy strolled back over. She came back with a beer and a bottle of tequila and a shot glass.

"I figured you didn't trust me to pour you a shot on the house. So have at it, big guy."

"You know I'm not going home with you, right?" he asked as he popped the top off his next beer.

"That's your story, and you're sticking to it, huh?" She chuckled, and even I had to laugh because she sure was persistent. Hawk, Niko, and Jace appeared beside him, making jokes about how they were going to torture Garrett tomorrow night. Of course, Dylan bellied right up to the bar and joined in. Ledger offered me a shot, but I declined. I didn't trust myself to get too drunk when I was with him. I knew he was upset about something, and I needed to look out for him.

The music boomed, and we danced, and we sang, and we laughed.

Dylan had to get home because she needed to be up early to study, so she caught a ride home with Hawk, Niko, and

Jace, who all left at the same time.

But Ledger and I stayed. We ran into a few old friends and were having a good time.

It was one of those nights where I didn't have big expectations, and it ended up being a lot of fun.

Ledger was drinking pretty heavily and appeared to relax, but he kept making sure I was right there next to him. I snuck away to use the restroom while everyone in the bar was singing along to Billy Joel's, "Only the Good Die Young".

I hurried into the stall when a voice startled me.

"Ladybug? Are you in here?"

"Ledger! Get out. Let a girl pee."

"Besties pee together, don't they?" he purred, and I flushed the toilet and hurried out.

I pulled the faucet handle up and held my hands under the running water, scrubbing them with soap and shaking my head at him. "This is the women's restroom. You can't be in here."

"Says who? You think Lucy Cockblocker is going to kick me out? We both know that's not going to happen."

I barked out a laugh. "I don't think Lucy cockblocked you. You did just fine after you broke her heart."

"She cockblocked me from you. Made you off limits." He ran a hand down his face, and I moved to stand in front of him.

"You made me off limits. Not Lucy. But we're past that. We've done a damn good job of getting our friendship back on track, haven't we?"

"You're so fucking beautiful." My breath caught in my throat, but before I could respond, he ran to the stall and vomited. He heaved three or four times, and I'd never seen someone throw up quite this much.

I rubbed his back until he stopped, and I flushed the toilet.

"Come on, Dane. Let's get you home."

"That was such a fucking rookie move. Tell a girl she's beautiful and then puke multiple times. Damn. I'm reliving my college years." His laughter bellowed around me.

We made our way back out to the bar and said our goodbyes. No one paid us much attention as the party was still going strong.

Lucy made her way around the bar just as we pushed open the door. "Ledger. Take this. I'm available anytime." She tucked a piece of paper into his hand.

When we stepped outside, he laughed so loud it startled me. "Those are some balls on the cockblocker, am I right?"

"She's definitely not afraid to put herself out there." We started walking toward his house, which was in the same direction as mine.

"What about you, Ladybug? Do you put yourself out there?"

I chuckled. "Not like Lucy, no."

I paused as we stood across the street from his mom's house.

"Can I stay the night at your place? I don't want to see Jilly like this, because I don't want her to know what happened today. I need to sober up so I can put on a good front."

I sighed. "Of course. How about you tell me what happened? Maybe if you get it off your chest, it'll help."

Ledger unloaded all of the happenings from his lunch, and my jaw hung open at how unbelievably awful his father was. Telling him that he never loved his mom. That he only married her because she was pregnant with Ledger. What kind of man puts that on his son? He'd also made no apologies for his affairs or for asking Ledger to lie for him. And how he was pressuring him to design his new home, or he'd break Jilly's heart and not show up to the wedding.

"He's such an asshole. I'm so sorry you had to deal with that. I feel bad that I told you to go. I thought you'd get some much-needed closure."

"I actually did. I realized that I've romanticized him in my head. I've always thought that he was this great man who lost himself. But the truth is, I was just a kid who saw what I wanted to see. He's always been selfish. He truly doesn't care about anyone but himself. But for the first time in a long time, I know I'm nothing like him. And that's the one good thing that came out of today. I'm ready to move on. I just don't want to hurt Jilly in the process."

When we got to my house, I had him sit on the couch, and I grabbed some Tylenol and a glass of water. "Take these. Do you think you should tell Jilly what he said? Maybe she'd get closure where he's concerned, too?"

"Fuck. Do I tell her before her big day? This wedding is so important to her. I want her to have everything she wants."

"So you'd design a house for a man you despise just to save Jilly from being hurt?"

"Yeah. I think I would. Although, I have the potential to make the house really ugly." He smirked at me.

"You really are nothing like that man, Ledger."

"Thank you. And thank you for letting me stay here. I appreciate it."

"What are friends for?"

He studied me, his brown eyes heavy and tired. "You were always the best part of my day when we were young. You know that?"

I smiled. Even though his words were still slurring, I knew he was being genuine. "I feel the same way. How about I sleep on the couch, and you take my bed?"

"No. I'll take the couch. Don't be ridonkulous. Ridonkulous?" He barked a laugh.

"Ridiculous," I said, shaking my head. "This couch is small. You won't be able to stretch out."

He turned to look beside him and chuckled. "It is awfully tiny. But I'm not putting you on the couch. We used to camp out together when we were kids. I'm sure we could share a bed. Have you ever slept with Jilly?"

I snorted. "More times than I can count. She's my best friend."

"Well, you're my best friend, Charlotte Thomas. I give you my word that I won't touch you. Unless you request a little friends-with-benefits action." He waggled his brows.

My stomach dipped at the thought of sharing a bed with Ledger. I tried to keep my cool. He was right. I'd slept with Jilly hundreds of times. We were two adults. We were friends. This was not a big deal.

So why was I sweating?

"Fine, you can sleep in the bed. But no touching. Come on, bestie. Let's get some sleep."

He followed me to the bedroom and into the master bathroom, where he sat on the toilet and watched as I washed my face and tied my long hair up in a bun on top of my head. I was grateful that it was Friday night, and I didn't need to be up early.

"Go," I said, pointing to my room. "I need to get my jammies on."

"Why am I so excited to see what you sleep in?" he asked as his knuckles grazed my cheek before he stumbled into my bedroom, and I shut the door. I changed into my tank top and sleep shorts and shouted through the door.

"Because you're drunk."

"I'm not that drunk, Ladybug."

I made my way out of the bathroom and found Ledger sitting on the bed in nothing but a pair of black boxer briefs. His stomach was tan and chiseled. You could literally count the abs on him, they were so distinct. His arms were bent as his hands were interlocked behind his head. I nearly dropped to my knees at the sight of him.

"Do you see this here? These horrific scratches?" He motioned to his stomach. "This is from that freaking animal, Miranda Highwater. The woman completely violated me."

I moved closer and saw the light scratches that barely left a mark. "You know you're being a huge baby."

He reached for my wrist and tugged me across him onto the bed. I was on my back, and he propped himself above me. His fingers wrapped around both of my wrists now as he held them above my head, his eyes on my mouth, my chest rising and falling rapidly.

Desire and want pulsed between my thighs.

An ache I'd never experienced throbbed, and I couldn't speak.

"You think I'm a baby, Ladybug?"

I shook my head. His mouth moved closer, his lips grazing

mine. I didn't know if I was even breathing anymore. He leaned down and nipped at my bottom lip before pulling away. His gaze locked on mine. A phone vibrated on the nightstand, and he jumped back and reached for it.

I moved to sit before crawling over to the opposite side of the bed. What just happened?

I thought he was going to kiss me, and I'm fairly certain that I wouldn't have stopped him.

"Fuck," he hissed, before dropping his phone onto the nightstand.

"Everything okay?"

"It's just this day. The hits keep coming. That was Jessica, and she's suddenly consumed with getting back together. I don't know why the fuck this is happening."

Well, that will bring a girl back to reality. He was about to kiss me while his ex was texting him to get back together.

His boss's daughter.

He'd be going back there in a week.

Probably back to her.

I pushed to my feet and flipped the lights off before climbing under the covers and rolling on my side, with my back to him.

I needed to get myself under control.

Fool me once. Shame on you.

Fool me twice. Shame on me.

"Good night, Ladybug."

"Good night, Ledger," I whispered, my heart still racing from having him in my bed.

"Thanks for being there tonight. You know I'd do anything for you, don't you?"

"Sure."

"I know I haven't shown it enough. But that's why I send the peonies. Because I know they're your favorite. Every year, Ladybug. February 13. I'm thinking of you. And every other day, I'm thinking of you," he said, his voice sounding sleepy, and I froze at his words.

"You send the peonies to me every year?"

"Always. I never wanted you to feel like you were alone."

I remained completely still and heard his breathing fall into a rhythmic sound. He was asleep.

But now I was wide awake.

Ledger Dane had been sending me flowers all these years.

Maybe he cared just as much as I did.

Chapter 10

Ledger

What the fuck was that noise? Was someone jackhammering my head?

I reached for my pillow to cover my face, but my fingers tangled in something silky.

My eyes flew open just as the warm body beside me jumped to her feet.

"Oh my god. It's Jilly. Get in the closet." Charlotte looked manic. Her long hair was wild and falling all around her shoulders, and she nearly tripped as she ran to the closet to get a robe.

My head was pounding, my mouth dry, but I couldn't look away from the gorgeous woman in front of me.

More loud jackhammering, which I now realized was her front door. Someone was banging on it like they were planning to knock it down.

"Charlie. Open up." Now I understood the panic. My sister was at the door. But the way Charlotte was behaving, you'd think I had a wife who was at the door.

"Did we... do something?" I paused, because if I touched her when I was drunk, I'd be fucking pissed at myself because I couldn't remember a goddamn thing from last night at the moment.

"Oh my gosh," she hissed. "No. Get in the closet, Ledger," she whisper-hissed.

"Why?" I pushed to my feet, my hangover rearing its ugly head right now. "We didn't do anything wrong."

"Oh, really?" She shoved me in the direction of her closet, and when I opened the door, she pushed me inside. "You're in my bed. How will that look? She's getting married in a few days. She does not need drama."

"Why am I drama?" I groaned as I fell back beneath a bunch of long dresses, and she shut the door.

"Coming!" she yelled. I wished she were saying that to me for different reasons, but apparently, she'd just taken care of my drunk ass last night, and I'd slept beside her.

I closed my eyes and tried to remember all that had happened yesterday. I'd been violated by Nan's friends, had lunch with Satan himself... ah, yes. My fucked-up father had caused me to spiral a bit. It didn't help that Harold Cartwright had refused my proposal for the middle school project *again*, and his daughter was blowing up my phone daily now.

This breakup was definitely going to complicate my relationship with my boss. This was the reason I'd fought it for so long. I knew it wasn't a good idea.

Hell, I hadn't even agreed. He'd just brought her to a

dinner, and then they'd invited me to an event, which he'd said was mandatory for my job, and the next thing I knew, we were dating. I wasn't saying that Jessica wasn't a beautiful woman. I wasn't saying that my time with her was terrible.

But we had nothing in common, and I knew it immediately.

So I was fucked in a million ways at the moment.

But the only thing that mattered right now was making sure Jilly got her dream wedding. That was what I was here for, right?

I heard vibrating on the other side of the closet door, and I realized my phone was still out there.

Fuck.

Well, hopefully, she wouldn't come into the bedroom.

"What took you so long? Do you have a man in here?" my sister said once she was inside, and I heard the door close behind her.

"No. I was sleeping in. It is Saturday," Charlotte said, and she sounded a little rattled. But maybe I was reading into it because I knew she was flustered.

"Charlie," my sister said, and I leaned close to the door because it sounded like she was crying now.

"Oh my gosh. What happened?" Charlie said, and I heard a lot of sniffling and sobbing, and my chest squeezed. Why the fuck was I hiding in the closet?

Oh, yes, apparently, I was the drama. I wasn't the one out there crying.

"I'm sorry," my sister cried, and it sounded like she was gasping for air. "I couldn't talk to Garrett because he'll get protective of me. I didn't want to tell Mom because she has her reasons for despising my father, and I don't want to make things worse. And God knows I can't tell Ledger. He'll lose his shit. But I have no choice."

Well, someone was being a bit judgmental.

"Tell me what's wrong." Damn, Charlotte was kind to her core.

"My dad doesn't know if he can stay for the wedding. He said he may have to leave for an emergency back home. Brenda's mom is sick. He's waiting to talk to Ledger. He told me to have him call him." She sobbed some more.

And damn it if my sister didn't know me well—I did feel like I was about to lose my shit.

"Why does he need you to tell Ledger to call him? What does your brother have to do with this?"

Charlie was being a fabulous actress because I had a quick flashback of me spilling everything that had happened with my father to her last night. But that still didn't explain why he didn't just call me.

"He said that Ledger never calls him back, and he thought if I asked him to call, he'd do it. He wants to ask Ledger if he'll walk me down the aisle if my father can't. I mean, he's still so worried about me, but he said Brenda's mom is really sick."

That fucker.

He's laying it on strong. Twisting everything to make himself the good guy. My disdain for him just reached new heights, if that was even possible.

Making Jilly come to me, knowing I'd do whatever he wanted me to do if it meant she'd be happy.

"The wedding is still a few days away. There's time to get everything figured out. You know Ledger will be happy to walk you down the aisle."

More sniffling.

"I know. But I just wanted to feel like I had a normal family for one day, you know? Everyone in Honey Mountain knows our story. It's embarrassing, Charlie." Jilly broke down again. "I just wanted a traditional wedding where the dad walks his little girl down the aisle. But I knew it wouldn't happen in the end."

"Your father doesn't decide if your family is normal. I mean, my mom passed away, Jilly. That doesn't make us abnormal. It just means that we had to find our new dynamic." Charlotte's voice was even. Soothing. Hell, she was making me feel better, and my fists started to relax. "You have a mother and a brother and a grandmother who adore you. You're marrying a man who's crazy about you. That's a family. That's all you need. It's just about love, right? And you've got lots of it. And you know I love you endlessly. Don't let him get to you."

I assumed it was my sister who hiccuped. "You're right. I'm not expecting a miracle from the man. It's just that Garrett's family is so great, and they keep asking when they're going to meet my dad. I just can't imagine what they'll think if he doesn't even bother to show up for my wedding. I've just never been important to him. I've tried so hard, Charlie."

I dropped down to sit on the floor because I was queasy as hell, and my head was pounding—but most of all, I was fucking pissed. Jilly doesn't deserve this shit.

"I know you have. But it has nothing to do with you." Charlotte comforted my sister. "He's got problems, Jilly. He's just a selfish man who got really lucky having two great kids."

Fuck, yeah. I couldn't agree more.

"You're right. And maybe he'll still come. But I need to find Ledger and see if he can talk to Dad. Maybe he can convince him to let Brenda go be with her mom, and he can stay here until after the wedding." My sister was still trying to make the bastard stay. Still trying to get him to do the right fucking thing. And she didn't even know the worst of it. Brenda's mom wasn't even sick. He wanted me to do him a favor, or he was going to punish my sister.

"It'll be perfect no matter what happens."

"Okay. I'm just going to use your bathroom and clean up my face. I need to go meet Garrett for breakfast at his mom's house. And then I'll try to convince Ledger to call our dad and talk some sense into him. Thanks for making me feel better."

"Of course. You know I'm always here for you." Charlotte sounded closer, and the footsteps appeared to be right outside the closet door. I heard the sink turn on against the opposite wall, and I stayed perfectly still.

"Wow, you really rumpled up the bed, didn't you? How was last night?" Jilly asked, and my heart nearly stopped when I realized my clothes were on the other side of the bed. My phone was on the nightstand. And I had no fucking idea why I was shoved into a closet because I didn't even get the girl.

"It was fun," Charlotte said, and she cleared her throat. "Let me make us a quick cup of coffee before you go, and I'll tell you all about it."

They must have left the room because their voices were farther away again. I sat cooped up in her little closet and listened as Charlotte proceeded to make Jilly laugh hysterically when she told her about Lucy Blocker being at

Beer Mountain. She told her how crazy I acted by refusing to let her open my beer bottles.

I stand by that decision, by the way.

I've had too many experiences with the young Lucy, and I can only imagine what she'd be like as an adult.

Not happening.

I nearly dozed off when I finally heard them say goodbye, and the door closed. But I didn't move until the closet doors flew open, and Charlotte's wild hazel eyes found mine.

"You okay in there?"

I pushed to my feet. "No. I'm hungover, and now I've got leg cramps. Did you really need to go on and on about Lucy fucking Blocker?"

"I panicked. I thought she saw your clothes and your phone. I needed to get her out of the bedroom." She offered me a hand, and I made my way out of the closet.

But I didn't let go of her hand. I was standing there in my boxers, and she was in these tiny little pajamas, and I didn't miss the way her nipples hardened when I glanced at her.

"Cute jammies." Was my voice gruff now? I was hungover, so maybe it was all the cocktails. Not the fact that the hottest girl I'd ever seen was standing in front of me in tiny shorts and a thin tank top.

She looked down, and I followed her gaze to see my morning wood on full display. My erection was standing proud and tall, pointing right at her like he was picking her out of a lineup.

"Um, you've got a little situation going on." Her teeth bit down on her juicy bottom lip to try to keep from laughing.

I squeezed her hand. "Hey, nothing little about it. It's

morning. He's got a mind of his own. And no offense, but you could turn the headlights down yourself."

She looked down at her chest and smirked. "It's cold in here."

"It's June. It's not cold enough to explain that." Our fingers were intertwined now. "So, nothing happened last night?"

"I hope I'd be a bit more memorable than that." She pulled her hand away.

"I just meant that I was drunk, and I wanted to make sure I didn't make an ass of myself."

She moved to the bathroom, and I followed. I closed the toilet seat and sat down beside the clawfoot bathtub while she moved to the sink and brushed her teeth. She bent over and the bottom of her ass was on full display, and I didn't see any panties in sight. My mouth watered at how badly I wanted her right now. We were painfully close. Barely any fabric between us.

"Well, you definitely made an ass of yourself. I can't help you out there."

"Good to know."

My eyes trailed from her ass down to her ankles before looking up to meet her gaze in the mirror as she watched me. She handed me a spare toothbrush that had never been opened, and I pushed to my feet and brushed my teeth right alongside her.

She wiped her mouth with a washcloth, her gaze locking with mine in the mirror. "What are you thinking? You look like you're up to no good."

I'm thinking that I want to touch you.

Taste you.

I'm guessing that might be a bit too much.

So instead, I set the toothbrush down and stepped back and turned her to face me. My hands moved beside her waist and landed on each side of the vanity, caging her in. My mouth was so close to hers, her warm breath tickled my cheek.

"I'm just grateful that you took care of me last night." I leaned forward and kissed her forehead before pulling back to look at her.

She chuckled now. "It was my pleasure."

She leaned forward and kissed my cheek, but this time, I turned my face so her lips met mine. It was a fast kiss, and we both studied the other with wide eyes.

"Friends kiss sometimes, right?" I asked, my hand moving to her hair.

"I mean, we've kissed before. So it wouldn't even be new."

"That's very true. It would be a thank you kiss." I tucked her hair behind her ear, and my tongue swiped out to wet my lips.

Fuck, I wanted her so badly.

Even if just in this moment. Right now.

I didn't live here, and I'd be leaving soon, so it was a dick move. A selfish move.

And the only way I'd stop it was if she asked me not to.

"What are you thanking me for?" she whispered.

"Being so good to my sister. To me. Just for being you. Being amazing. And being fucking beautiful."

"Well, then, it seems like the least you could do."

My mouth crashed into hers, and I lifted her up and set her on the sink as I moved to stand between her legs. Her lips parted, letting my tongue in. Her little moans were driving me fucking crazy, and my hand found the back of her head, tipping it back so I could take the kiss deeper.

My cock was so hard, I was certain it was going to tear through the thin fabric holding him back. But she started grinding up against my erection, and it was the sexiest thing that anyone had ever done. Hell, we were both clothed, just kissing, yet it was so much more.

Years of need.

Years of desire.

Years of want.

My fingers moved to the thin strap of fabric on her shoulder, moving it down her arm as my hand cupped her perfect tit. My lips moved against hers as her head fell back, leaning against the mirror, and I kissed my way down her neck. I covered her hard peak with my lips, sucking before I grazed my teeth against her nipple, and she groaned, the sound so erotic, I nearly came right there. Like a teenage boy who had no experience. Not a man who was always in control when it came to the women he spent time with.

"Please, Ledger," she whispered, and I knew exactly what she needed.

My mouth continued lavishing her as I tugged the strap on the other side of her shoulder down and moved from one breast to the other, taking turns with one and then the other. I couldn't get enough. My fingers moved between her legs, and I startled when I realized that she wasn't wearing panties. Her slick heat was waiting for me.

"So wet, Ladybug. Tell me what you want," I demanded. I wouldn't take anything from this girl that she didn't ask for.

"I want you to make me feel good. Please."

With those words, my finger found her entrance and slipped inside slowly, and her entire body started to shake. My mouth moved back to hers, and I kissed her like my life depended on it. Another finger slipped in, and I moved in and out, just the way I knew she needed. My thumb found her clit, and she nearly bucked off the counter when I moved it around, slowly applying just the right amount of pressure.

I just kept kissing her. Pumping my fingers in and out and loving all the sounds she was making. If I died right now. Right here.

I'd go a happy man.

I could stay right here forever.

She was grinding against my hand, her fingers clawing at my hair. I'd take her to the edge and then back down, again and again, wanting to make this last as long as I could.

"Ledger," she groaned, and I couldn't deny her. I moved faster, knowing just what she needed.

"Come for me, Charlie," I whispered against her ear, and her head fell back again, but this time, she cried out my name as her body quaked beneath me. Her pussy convulsed around my fingers, and it was the hottest thing I'd ever seen. She rode out every last bit of pleasure, and I savored every second of it. Memorizing every line and every curve of her face. The way her lips parted and her cheeks pinked when she fell apart for me.

The way her chest rose and fell.

The way her breaths came hard and fast.

I couldn't get enough.

But I knew I'd taken more than I deserved.

I pulled my hand away when her gaze locked with mine.

I slipped my fingers in my mouth, and her eyes widened. I groaned. "So fucking sweet."

"Wow. That was something."

"It sure as fuck was. There's nothing better than seeing you come apart beneath me. Are you okay?"

"I've never been better." She glanced at her tank top that had one torn strap.

"Sorry about that."

"I'm sorry about *that*," she said, her gaze moving down to my bulging erection. "Should we do something about it? I mean, was this a mistake? Because if you want to pretend that it didn't happen like we did all those years ago, I don't think we should take this any further. Not with the wedding being next week."

What the fuck did that mean?

"Why does the wedding matter?" I asked, using my finger to tip her chin up to meet my gaze.

"Because you're leaving right after, Ledger. So, all of this will come to an end, right? We're playing with fire."

Maybe I liked playing with fire.

In a simpler world, this girl would be mine.

Simply mine.

But the world wasn't that simple. At least not the one I came from.

Chapter 11
Charlotte

Panic coursed through my veins. This was happening all over again. I wanted him. I was fairly certain that he wanted me just as badly. But then he'd be gone. He was leaving soon.

His ex-girlfriend was still calling him.

He was going back to work for her father.

But then I thought about the flowers and what he said last night.

Everything was jumbled.

"What do you want this to be?" he asked, moving closer, his lips grazing my ear.

I couldn't think straight.

I pushed him back. I needed space in order to have a normal conversation with him.

"Let's go get breakfast. We can discuss our options there." I hurried to the bedroom. I couldn't have this conversation alone with Ledger half-naked in my bathroom moments after giving me the best orgasm of my life, only second to the one he'd given me all those years ago.

He and his massive erection would have to wait until after breakfast to decide what we'd do about it.

"So, I'm going to breakfast with a bad case of blue balls?" He chuckled as he walked around the bed and picked up his jeans and pulled them on.

I scanned his torso one last time before he tugged his T-shirt over his head and I pulled on a sundress before grabbing my sandals and tying my hair in a messy knot on top of my head. When I glanced in the mirror, I smiled.

My face was completely sated.

I did feel bad about the fact that he was walking to breakfast with a raging erection.

I dabbed on some lip gloss and put on some mascara and led him out the door.

"I'm sorry you're, um—uncomfortable." I peeked up at him, and he slipped his sunglasses on his face and smiled.

"Normally, this would be a bummer. But I've got to say, Ladybug, I actually enjoy getting you off more than getting myself off."

I sucked in a breath and squeezed my thighs together at his words.

Was it possible for me to be turned on again already?

"Well, then, you'd be the first guy I've been with that felt that way."

"Oh, this I've got to hear. Let me guess, the bug guy didn't deliver all the orgasms, did he?" He chuckled, and I rolled my eyes as we walked into the café. It was unusually quiet for a Saturday in Honey Mountain, and I was thankful. Although, everyone already knew Ledger and I were friends, so it wouldn't be weird for us to have breakfast together. Even if we ran into Jilly, I could just say we were meeting about the wedding.

Sleeping in the same bed would be a different story.

And that brought me back to my conversation with my best friend.

When we took our seats, we both glanced at the menu before placing our order when the server walked over.

"We should talk about what happened with Jilly this morning before we discuss our current situation." I raised a brow.

"Our current situation? You're so formal, Ladybug. Okay, let's do it."

"How do you feel about what she said about your father? He's just the worst. I mean, that's the reason you got drunk last night, right?"

"Yep. But for whatever reason—maybe because I just made you come with only my fingers, so it has me imagining seeing you come apart with my tongue and my cock—oddly, my father's bullshit isn't bothering me today." He smirked at me like this was perfectly normal to talk like this over breakfast.

I could feel my cheeks flush, and I fanned my face. "Do you talk like this to all your ladies?"

He snorted. "You make me sound so dirty. I don't sleep around all that much anymore. Not since college. I date casually. A few weeks or a few months here and there. Nothing serious. So, no. We don't discuss how much I like pleasing them, because even though I always make sure my partner finds their release first, I don't give a shit about anyone else's pleasure the way I do yours."

My stomach flipped around, and I took a minute to process his words.

"Back to your dad, please. Let's close that door first."

"He's a fucker. I got a front-row seat to how shitty he still is yesterday. Today, I'm over it. He holds the cards, so I'll give him what he wants."

"You're going to agree to design their home?"

"Yep. If it means he gives Jilly what she wants on her wedding day—even if I don't think he should have the honor—I respect her wishes. And chances are the house won't ever happen, anyway. I'm guessing at some point, Bambi will wisen up and cut him loose. Who knows if their wedding will even happen? And if it does, then I'll design them a fucking house. It won't be my best work, but I'll do it." He shrugged like it was no big deal.

"Just like that?"

"Just like that. What do you have next? Tell me I'm the best you've ever had, even before you've had me. Because you ain't seen nothing yet." He leaned forward and tucked my hair behind my ear.

"You're acting completely crazy. Are you forgetting several things?"

"Such as?"

"Such as… we're working on our friendship."

"Fuck that. I was all for it, but now that I've kissed you, I want to do it again."

"So, you want to be friends with benefits?"

He studied me. "That's not your thing, is it?"

"Not so much. Plus, we live in different cities. So, this would just be a one-and-done?" I asked, pausing as the waitress stopped by and set down our coffees and orange juice before walking away.

"It wouldn't be a one-and-done, because once would never be enough for me." His tongue swiped out to wet his lips, and I couldn't look away from his mouth.

"What does that mean, Ledger? We need to think this out. I don't want you to leave and us to not speak again for years."

"I don't either."

"No. We need some new rules, and we need to stick to them this time."

"Ah... I am here for a teachable moment, Miss Thomas. Tell me the rules. And then I'll do everything in my power to break them so you have to punish me." He smiled, and his eyes never left mine as our server set our plates down and refreshed our coffee.

I thought about our situation.

Thought about how he made me feel this morning.

Made me feel a way no one else ever had.

And I'd be lying if I said I didn't want more.

But I also needed to be realistic.

It could never work.

Once we were alone again, he picked up a piece of bacon and raised a brow, waiting for me to respond.

"We don't cross the line again. That was a moment of weakness. It's all part of the closure we've been getting over the last week. We want different things. There's no sense crossing a line when we know it can't go anywhere. I highly doubt Jilly would be okay with this. I mean, we've kept our history a secret; why would we risk upsetting her now?"

The more I thought about it, the more I knew it needed to stop.

"For the orgasms," he teased and reached for his coffee and took a sip. "Listen. I know I'm not the kind of guy who deserves you. I've always known it. It's the reason I've stayed away. But that doesn't make me want you any fucking less."

I hated that he felt that way. But I loved hearing that he wanted me as badly as I wanted him.

"So, we should call it done for those reasons alone. We have the bachelor and bachelorette parties tonight. We don't want to make it awkward, so it's probably best to stick to the friendship plan, and we'll pretend this morning never happened."

"All right. If that's what you want. I think you coming apart for me this morning will get me through the next decade because it's all I'll see every time I close my eyes." He shrugged.

"You can't talk like that, Ledger."

"I speak the truth, Ladybug." He looked smug, like he wasn't really on board with the new plan.

"Today never happened. Friends?" I offered him my hand, but being this close to him was making it difficult not to think about his mouth on mine. About the way his hands explored my body. The way his fingers worked their magic.

He took my hand in his and smiled. "You're a little flushed, bestie."

"I'll be fine," I said, pulling my hand away. This was called self-preservation. Maturity. I could spot heartbreak a mile away, and allowing this to continue would be a huge disaster for me and my heart.

He chuckled, and we continued eating breakfast and discussed the plans for tonight.

He didn't bring up what happened this morning again, and he walked me home and didn't come inside. We agreed to meet at Beer Mountain after our two groups had some fun grabbing dinner and visiting a few other bars in town.

I went home and cleaned up my place before taking a shower and getting ready. Dylan was coming to my house, and everyone else would meet at the barbecue place where Jilly had chosen to have dinner.

My sister arrived and looked me up and down once she was inside. I could tell she approved of my black leather skirt and my silk camisole with the nude heels. So maybe this was sexier than usual for me. I knew I'd be seeing Ledger tonight, and even though we agreed that nothing could happen, it didn't mean that I didn't want him to think I looked good.

"Damn. You look hot," she said, dropping her purse onto the counter.

She wore a black strapless dress and a pair of red stilettos.

"Um… right back at you. I'm loving this outfit."

She smiled. "Okay, we have thirty minutes before we have to leave and go decorate the table at the restaurant. Fill me in. You said something happened with Tobias?"

In the midst of my Ledger haze, I'd missed the six texts that had come through in the middle of the night. The P.E. teacher had been drunk texting me while I was in bed with my best friend's brother. Just sleeping, of course.

I showed her my phone, and she gasped as she read the texts.

"He's such a perv. That little fucker scratches his balls blatantly all the time, which should have been enough of a red flag. But now the dude is drunk texting you at all hours of the night? And the asshat clearly doesn't know you if he thinks you'd be interested in his dirty ass texts," Dylan hissed.

Yes, he mentioned that he thought I had perfect tits. His words, not mine. He also texted that he liked my *tight ass*. And this is a man I worked with. We'd never gone out. We'd never spoken on the phone. He obviously got my phone number from the school directory.

"Yeah. The good news is that I have a perfect out now, and it won't be awkward to turn him down. He definitely crossed the line with these texts. And with the school year ending, when we see one another after the summer, this mess will be long forgotten."

"One can hope. I wish you'd let me go to school Monday and give him a piece of my mind."

"You're starting your internship Monday; this is the last thing you need to be worrying about," I said as I poured us each a glass of wine and handed one to her.

"Okay, well, I want to hear about what's going on with Ledger. You've literally spent every day with him since he's come back. And you looked awfully cozy last night, so spill. No more secrets, Charlie."

I let out a long breath. "It's going well. We kind of lost our friendship over the years, and he wants us to work on that again. I missed him, and it's good to see him."

"Charlotte Thomas. I shared a womb with you. I saw the

way you looked at one another last night," she purred, because Dilly loved getting to the bottom of things. She was born to be an attorney.

I laughed. "There's an attraction. Of course, there is."

"What are you not telling me? Ohhhhhh. Did something happen last night?" Her mouth hung open, and her eyes were wide.

"You can't tell anyone, Dilly. Jilly is getting married in a few days. I don't want anything to take away from that."

"I promise, I will not say a word. Start talking."

I was struggling with it all. Our history. Our current situation. What happened this morning. That a part of me wanted it to happen again, but I was also terrified of getting hurt.

And I spilled it all right there in my kitchen as my twin sister just listened and sipped her wine.

"I knew something happened all those years ago."

I shook my head. "I just never wanted to talk about it. I told Ash and made her promise never to speak of it. But all those feelings are coming back. And I know they shouldn't be. I feel so guilty about Jilly. I can't believe I let that happen this morning, but I can't help myself when I'm around him."

Dylan leaned forward and swiped the tear running down my cheek. "Wow. They aren't kidding when they say that there is one sweet twin and one naughty twin. I'd be all over that man. I don't understand the guilt. But I know you, and I know you think about how every single decision affects everyone around you." She reached for my hands as we sat on the two barstools at the kitchen counter.

"You're sweeter than people think. You're also the

strongest person I know, and I wish I could channel some of that strength," I said.

"You're wrong, Charlie. You're so much stronger than you know. I'd have just gone for it with Ledger. Knowing how you felt about him all those years and not allowing yourself to talk about it or feel any of it... You're selfless. But there's a cost to that. And at some point, you're going to need to take something for yourself."

"Who are you, and what have you done with my sister, who hates to talk about feelings?"

Her head fell back, and she chuckled. "Remember when Mama died? You just shut down and helped everyone where you could. I acted out. Through temper tantrums. And you sat with me the first time that I drank my feelings away as a teenager. You held my hair back when I puked. And you lectured me when I acted like a jerk. You're such a caretaker, Charlie. But you need to take care of you, too. Jilly will not be upset as long as no one gets hurt. She's a grown woman. She got her happily ever after. Shouldn't you be allowed to get yours?"

My head reared back. "Dilly, he doesn't want anything like that with me. Sure, we're attracted to one another. But he doesn't want a family. He doesn't want a serious relationship. That's who I am. I don't do casual."

"So enjoy a few days of bliss, and then go find your boring husband afterward. At least you'll have experienced that kind of passion. You've had two boyfriends in your life, Charlie. So what if you have a little bit of fun with the boy you've loved your whole life? Maybe every relationship doesn't have to go the whole distance. Different people come in and out of your life for a reason. Ledger has always been such a presence in your life. And he's hot as hell. You're painfully attracted to him. Let yourself have this. Don't overthink it."

"What about Jilly?" I whispered as I shook my head.

"If it's just a fling for a few days; you don't even have to tell her. But if it turns into more, you can talk to her then. She loves you. She would understand, I promise. You and Ledger are grown-ups. You can make decisions for yourself."

"What if he breaks my heart?" There it was. The real reason I was terrified to let anything happen between us. Because he would leave and move on. And I'd spend the next decade looking for someone to make me feel the way he did, just like I'd spent the last decade.

"You're strong, Charlie. Don't *not* take risks because you're afraid of getting hurt. I mean, do you think Dad would have not married Mom if he knew he wouldn't have gotten forever with her? Hell, no. When someone makes you feel alive, grab that shit and run with it. I'm still waiting for someone to make me feel that way. You've had it. It's always been him. So just be in the moment. Stop thinking about the future. Let yourself have some fun. You're twenty-five years old. Grab that bull by the horns, girl. *Literally and figuratively.* And don't even get me started on the damn peonies he's been sending all these years. The guy loves you, regardless of what he can give you in the long game. Just enjoy the right now for once in your life. Be selfish."

I nodded. What she said about my mother and my father struck me. I've always wanted that kind of love. They set the bar high. And Dylan was right. My father would do it all over again, even knowing that he'd lose her way too soon.

Maybe a fling would be fun. If I were going to do it with anyone, Ledger would be the guy I'd want to do it with.

He made me feel safe.

Loved.

Wanted.

And I wanted him.

But could I do this? Take this for myself even knowing it would hurt like hell after?

"So how exactly does having a fling work?" I asked my sister, who burst out in laughter.

"It's easy. He's already told you he wants you. There's no risk. He leaves in a few days, so you just enjoy this week and have all the fun and all the orgasms. It's a win-win. No one has to know anything. This could just be for you. I know that doesn't come naturally to you, but it feels damn good to do what you want. And I know for a fact that you want Ledger Dane."

I fanned my face and glanced down at my phone before pushing to my feet. "Okay. Today is not about that. Today is about Jilly and Garrett. We need to go."

"Let's give it a name. I know you do better with a plan. Let's call it plan ATO."

"Do I even want to know?"

"All. The. Orgasms." She waggled her brows, and I handed her the bag of party décor, and she

reached inside and pulled out a handful of rubber penises. "I'm guessing it's going to be hard not to think of Ledger when you're going to be surrounded by rubber dicks everywhere you turn."

I rolled my eyes. "Of course, you took it there. Not another word about Ledger today, okay?"

We walked out the door and made our way the two blocks to the restaurant, where we were meeting everyone.

"Tell me about that lawyer that asked you to dinner." I needed a subject change. My mind was racing with what we'd talked about.

"He's a well-known attorney in the city, and he's here on vacation. Early forties. I'm totally down with the older man vibe right now. He's a silver fox. He doesn't want to take me to Beer Mountain because he's beyond that immature bullshit. He wants to take me in his helicopter to San Francisco for freaking dinner."

"What if he's a serial killer? You can't go in a helicopter with a guy you barely know."

"Listen, does anyone have better radar than me? My special gift is reading people. This man does not have murderer vibes. He's got sexy, let me wine and dine you with my deep voice and experienced tongue and magic penis—"

"Dilly!" I shouted, coming to a stop. "I cannot talk about sex with you anymore. Let's focus on the party."

"Ohhhh... someone is hot and bothered, and I am so here for it."

I groaned, but in reality, she was right.

She really did have a gift for reading people.

Chapter 12

Ledger

I've attended my fair share of bachelor parties, and I had to say that I didn't mind that the tamest one I'd been to was my brother-in-law's. I never understood a dude about to commit to a woman for the rest of his life—yet you put a stripper in front of him, and he turns into a college frat boy on spring break.

My father was probably that dude.

He probably fucked around on my mother on their wedding night. I mean, he already admitted he didn't want to marry her. He cheated throughout their marriage, of course, he was cheating before it.

While she was pregnant with me.

We finished dinner and had made it to another bar. The drinks were flowing, and we were heading to meet the girls at Beer Mountain in a little bit.

I couldn't stop thinking about this morning.

Charlotte's mouth. Her perfect tits. The sounds she made as she fell apart for me.

I adjusted myself beneath the table because even after two cold showers, I was rock hard again.

I'd respect her wishes that we wouldn't let that happen again, but a part of me knew that it would. The draw was too strong. It always has been.

I wasn't drinking much because I wanted to make sure Garrett was all right, as he was several shots deep and already slurring and telling everyone how much he loved my sister. Plus, I knew I'd be seeing Charlie tonight, and I had already made an ass of myself last night. I didn't trust myself to be drunk around her and behave. If anything further happened between us, it would be because she wanted it to.

The ball was in her court.

"I hope you won't be pissed, but your dad called me a little while ago and said he wanted to stop by and buy me a drink." Garrett leaned against me and patted my cheek.

My father wasn't coming to buy him a drink.

He called me a few times today, and I hadn't returned his call.

I knew I was going to do what he wanted, and I hadn't felt like talking to him just yet. But I told Jilly that I would, so I knew it was inevitable.

I glanced up to see my father heading my way.

"You fucking owe me one, brother," I said to Garrett, and he sat forward and faced my dad.

"Mr. Dane. Nice to see you. Thanks for stopping by." The dude was trying to sound straight, even though he was three shades to drunkville. What he didn't understand was that it didn't matter. My father didn't give two shits about the man that his daughter was about to marry.

"No problem. Is it an open bar?" my father teased, and I blew out a breath because I couldn't stand the guy.

"Ledger is picking up the tab," Garrett said proudly as he stumbled to his feet and announced that he was going to take a piss. I glared at my father when he moved to sit on the barstool beside me.

"Nice of you to pick up the tab. Business must be good, huh?"

"It's called holding a steady job and working your ass off. I'm sure the concept is foreign to you."

He chuckled as if we were just two dudes giving one another a hard time. Not the fact that I was the spawn of the devil, and I despised this man, more now than ever.

"Did Jilly speak to you?" he asked, holding his hand up and ordering a bourbon, straight up.

"She did. Way to upset the bride a week before her wedding." I reached for the dish full of nuts and popped a few into my mouth.

"It's your choice, Ledger. You want your sister to be happy, and so do I. But I also want Brenda to be happy. Happy wife, happy life."

I barked out a laugh. "Says the dude who's been divorced four times and has never put anyone before himself. Are you going to leave her with a huge mortgage and strap her down with the kids while you run off and find a younger version?"

"I'm not here to discuss what kind of man you think I am. I'm here to find out if Brenda and I are hitting the road before the wedding or staying put until the big day. You think you're so morally superior, let's see what you do when you're forced to do something for someone that you don't care for."

I stared at him in disbelief. Was he referring to my mother? To me and Jilly?

His family?

Of course, that was what the fucker was talking about; need I remind myself he told me he'd rather I hadn't been born? That I was the reason he *had* to marry my mother?

"I'm glad to know that you just didn't care for us. That you married a woman that you didn't love because she was pregnant with me. Thanks for clearing that up, asshole. That makes things easier."

The bartender set the glass down, and my father tipped his head back and slammed it in one long pull. "What's your answer, son?"

My hands fisted at my sides, but when I saw Garrett out of my peripheral, I made sure to stay composed. "I'll do it. You better be at that wedding and be on your best behavior. Make her think you actually give a fuck about her."

"Looks like I did a pretty damn good job of raising you, after all. And please don't think I'm a dick, but I'm going to need something in writing saying you'll do this before the wedding day. I don't fully trust you, son." The way he said *son* was evil and only made me hate this man all the more.

"Too late for that. I think you're a complete dick. I'll have the office email the contract over." Harold wouldn't care about this because I could do this project in my sleep, and it wouldn't take any man hours from anyone on our team.

"I look forward to working with you." He held his hand

out and when Garrett moved beside us, I took his hand and shook it so he wouldn't know anything was going on.

"Are you leaving already?" Garrett asked. "We're just heading over to meet the girls. I know Jilly would love to see you."

Garrett's cheeks were pink, and he had a sappy look on his face when he spoke of my sister.

"I might meet you over there. Brenda's waiting for me back at the hotel, so I need to go check in with the boss, if you know what I mean." He always laughed too loud at his own jokes, and Garrett chuckled, but looked completely confused as to why he was leaving so soon.

Niko came up beside me as I paid the tab, and Hawk and Jace were getting all of Garrett's friends together to finish off their drinks so we could head to Beer Mountain.

"Are you all right?" Niko asked.

"Yeah. Just some shit with my dad, you know?" I scrubbed the back of my neck. We grew up together, and he and I both had shitty fathers, so we bonded over beers and bad memories more times than I could count.

"He's not worth it, dude. Thank God Jilly has you looking out for her, because that guy has never looked out for anyone but himself."

"Damn straight. But my sister is still holding out hope for a relationship with the asshole, so I've got to play along."

"I get it. You're a good man, my friend." He finished his beer and set the mug down on the bar. "Wish you'd consider moving back here. We've missed having you around."

I missed it, too. It had surprised me what a good time I'd had since I'd been home. Even with my father being here, it had been a good trip. I was usually in and out of town in a day or two, so this was the most time I'd spent back home in years.

"Yeah, it's actually been great being back."

"I told you about that house-flipping business we've been doing, and you know if you ever want in, just say the word. We're buying up homes and businesses, and it's been great."

"Jace told me you guys bought the vet space that Hunter Hall abandoned, and you've got Emilia Langford in there now."

He chuckled. "Travis, Jace's brother, had a lot to do with that. They've been dating for a while, and I'm glad we could get her in there."

I thought about it. I liked the idea of getting involved with them. I invested in real estate all the time—I just hadn't considered doing it back here in Honey Mountain.

"I'm definitely interested."

"All right. Let's set up a meeting, and we'll show you what we're up to. Who knows, maybe we'll get you back here full time someday."

I laughed. "I don't know about that, but I don't need to live here to invest."

He nodded, and we made our way out the door. The short walk to Beer Mountain was entertaining as hell, because Garrett started reciting his vows to my sister, and he got all emotional and hugged me no less than a dozen times.

When we stepped inside, the girls were dancing in the center of the bar and having a good time. It didn't take me long to find her.

Charlotte Thomas.

My gaze locked with hers, and she smiled.

Jilly charged me and kissed my cheek. Her face was flushed, so I knew she'd had plenty to drink, as well. "Thanks for taking care of him."

"Not a problem, but I'm not sure how much longer he's going to last."

"Yeah, I can tell." She chuckled. "He said that Dad came to the party. Did you speak to him?"

"Yeah. I did. I told him I'd walk you down the aisle but that I knew you wanted him to do it, so he actually agreed to stay. I guess Bambi's mom is doing better today." The pit in my stomach twisted every time I lied to her.

"What? Really?" Her entire face lit up. "He's going to stay?"

"Yep. Looks like it's all going to work out."

"I'm so happy, Ledger. And you and Dad are talking. Maybe we can be a family again someday; it'll just be a different dynamic."

"Sure. Maybe you're right." I cringed. When I looked up, I found Charlotte watching me. She knew exactly what I was doing. The empathy I saw in her gaze nearly brought me to my knees. This girl knew me better than anyone ever had. Her lips turned up in the corners before Dylan tugged at her arm, and they started dancing to the song "Jump Around" by House of Pain.

I talked with Hawk for the next hour about his upcoming hockey season and teased him about the fact that he had extended his contract another year. Every year, he swore it was the last. I tried to go to as many home games as I could to support him, seeing as their home games were in the city that I lived in.

"You guys are spending more and more time here in Honey Mountain these days, huh?" I asked, because he and Everly had a home on the lake here and a condo in the city that they stayed at during the season. Everly worked for the San Francisco Lions, as well.

"Yep. It works for us. We like raising Jackson here, and Ever wants to leave when I retire. She'll still work, but she'd like to help out at the high school here so she can be home with the kids and close to family. We're taking it one season at a time. But we want to have another kid, and it's going to get to be too much when Jackson gets older. So I figure, one or two more seasons and we'll call it done, and live here full time. It's a peaceful life, you know?"

I nodded. It was. I couldn't agree more. My stress level was high in the city. My job was fast-paced, and there was no sign of that slowing down.

"That does not sound bad, my friend."

"Well, we've worked hard, right? You and I both have had our hustle on for years. What's the purpose if you can't enjoy it at some point?" He clapped me on the shoulder and laughed at Charlotte as she tried to help Jilly walk my way.

"Looks like someone's had enough to drink," I said as I took my baby sister in.

"Yeah. Niko and Vivi are going to give me and Garrett a ride home," Jilly slurred.

Everly moved in our direction and wrapped an arm around Hawk.

"Looks like we're all heading out," Hawk called out. "You coming with us, Dilly?"

Dylan lived in the guest house on their property.

"Yep. We closed the place down. They're locking up. The party is over, my friends," Dylan said over a fit of laughter as she high-fived me.

The whole group made their way toward the door as I tried to pay the tab, only to find out that Niko, Jace, and Hawk had already paid it.

"You didn't need to do that." I shot them a look.

"You got dinner and the bar; I think it's the least we could do," Jace said, elbowing me in the side as Ashlan settled beneath his other arm.

Jilly stumbled back and turned around to face me. "Wait. Will you make sure Charlie gets home safely?"

"Of course, I will." I nodded, and I looked up to see Dylan wink at me.

The girl was nothing but trouble, and I fucking loved it.

Everyone hugged and said their goodbyes. Some hopped in Ubers. Some walked. And I was left standing there with Charlotte.

"Do you want me to call a car or walk?" I asked.

"Let's walk." She led the way and told me all about the dinner and the fake penises and all the fun they'd had. Her words weren't slurring, and she seemed to be fine.

"You didn't drink much tonight?" I asked.

"No. I wanted to be clearheaded."

"You're a good fucking friend, Ladybug." My hand swung beside me and grazed hers, and I linked my finger with hers.

"Don't give me too much credit," she said with a laugh. "Of course, I wanted Jilly to have a great night. But that's not why I wanted to be clearheaded."

Our fingers remained linked.

"You going to tell me what you're talking about? Is this because you don't want to be drunk around me because you're afraid we'll cross the line again?"

We walked up her driveway, and she pulled her keys out before unlocking the door and pushing it open. She turned to face me.

"Nope. It's because I wanted to be thinking clearly when I propositioned you."

I raised a brow. She definitely had my attention. "Propositioned me for what?"

"I know what we discussed this morning, but I've re-thought my previous plan."

I moved closer, backing her up against her door. "Oh, yeah? Tell me."

She let out a long breath. "Remember when I said I hadn't been with a guy who put my needs first before?"

"Yeah. What did you mean by that?"

"We're friends, right?" she asked, and I could tell she was nervous.

I placed my finger and my thumb beneath her chin and tipped it up, forcing her gaze to meet mine. The light on the porch allowed me to see her beautiful face.

"Of course, we are. Always."

"Well, I've had sex with two men in my life, Ledger. You were my first orgasm back in the day and my second this morning, so that tells you how that went. And... I'm not going to lie, I liked it."

"You've never come with a man before?"

She gasped at my words and shook her head. "No. It's always been a bit of a chore. Not a lot of fun. I've never understood the hype until this morning."

A nervous laugh escaped her sweet mouth.

"What about when they went down on you?" I asked. I wanted—no, *needed* to know.

"I've never done any of that. I've just had boring sex, I guess."

I narrowed my gaze. How the fuck had she gone this long with no one tasting her? Pleasing her?

She tried to turn away, embarrassment covering her cheeks.

"Hey, don't turn away from me. There's no shame in that. I'm happy you haven't done any of that."

"Why?"

"Because I'd fucking love to be the first man to taste you. To make you come apart from my lips and tongue."

"Ledger," she whispered, and she covered her eyes with her hand.

"You don't need to be shy with me. Tell me what you want, Ladybug." I pulled her hands away from her pretty face.

"I know we want different things. I know what this is, and I'm okay with it." She shrugged. "I know you're leaving, and I know it's a little selfish to do to Jilly because she wouldn't be happy. But I want this for me. For us. A few days to keep with me forever."

I studied her. She was so certain that I'd be able to walk away from her easily, and I knew it would be the hardest fucking thing I'd ever do. But she was right. We wanted different things. We lived in different cities. I couldn't even wrap my head around the things that she wanted.

The impossible dream.

I was a realist. I lived my life that way.

"You're wrong about Jilly. She doesn't have anything to do with this. This is about you and me. Hell, it's always been about you and me, hasn't it?"

"It has. No one's ever made me feel the way you do. So, selfishly, I want that. I want you to show me what I've been missing. Make me feel alive, even if just for a few days. I don't want to feel guilty about feeling good and taking something for myself. And then we'll go on with our lives and hopefully be all the better for it."

That was all I needed to hear. My fingers were in her hair. My body closed the space between us as my mouth crashed into hers. The breeze blew around us, cooling my heated skin. Crickets chirped in the background, and I took the kiss deeper.

I backed her inside the house and closed the door, pushing her up against the door. I kissed her like I was taking my last breath.

My tongue slipped in to find hers, tasting and exploring her sweet mouth with a need I'd never experienced before.

My cock was so hard, and the way she was grinding up against me had me losing my fucking mind. She reached down between us, and her hand stroked my erection. I wrapped my fingers around her wrist and pulled back.

"I'm taking my time with you tonight. I've waited my whole fucking life for this. So, if you're giving me a few days, I'm going to enjoy every last minute. I'm going to taste every inch of you. I'm going to make you come so many times that we'll both close our eyes and remember it for years to come. Does that sound all right with you?"

She nodded, her hazel eyes wild and filled with need. I pushed her dark brown hair back from her face and tucked it behind her ears.

And then I dropped to my knees, the hard wood clunking beneath me. The light was flooding from the back windows, illuminating around her like some kind of angel.

My mouth watered at the thought of tasting her.

How many years had I fantasized about this very moment?

She gasped when I pushed her black leather skirt slowly up her legs, and I reached for the hem of her lace panties and tore them off. I wasn't willing to wait another second by pulling them down her legs.

I wanted her now.

Needed her now.

"Now, spread those pretty little thighs for me, Ladybug."

Chapter 13

Charlotte

Oh. My. Gosh.

My hands were tangled in his hair, my back up against the door and my skirt hiked all the way up. My stilettos were struggling to hold me in place, but Ledger settled himself between my thighs, one hand on each of my hips, holding me still.

He tore my lace panties from my body as if he couldn't wait a second longer.

I gasped as his tongue swiped out along my seam. The sensation of his scruff rubbing against the inside of my thighs was in great contrast to his silky tongue moving along my most sensitive area.

My eyes nearly rolled back in my head as his tongue started working back and forth, his mouth taking turns sucking on my clit and teasing my entrance.

My breaths filled the air around us, and I glanced down to see him looking up at me as he groaned.

I couldn't think straight.

Nothing had ever felt better.

I tugged at his hair, wanting more, and I lost all sense of myself in that moment.

I wasn't shy. I wasn't embarrassed. I wasn't questioning what we were doing.

I was lost in the moment.

Lost in this man.

His hand moved from my hip, and he pulled my leg over his shoulder to get better access, and my back arched off the door, my knees nearly buckling. But he was there to steady me as his tongue pressed inside.

The sensation was too much.

And not enough.

How was that possible?

His tongue moved in and out, and I was no longer able to control myself.

The euphoric build took over in my body.

My hands and arms and legs tingled.

The feeling was so overwhelming I couldn't hold my eyes open any longer as my head fell back against the door, and I reveled in the moment. My fingers sliding through his silky curls, moving his head just where I needed him.

How had I survived for so long without experiencing this?

I couldn't feel my legs and had no idea if I was supporting myself anymore.

And I didn't care.

I was floating on air.

Grinding against his mouth. His lips. His tongue.

Desperate for relief.

I couldn't stop it.

"Ledger, please," I said. My voice was completely unrecognizable.

His tongue pulled out, his fingers slipped in, and his mouth moved back to my clit just as the most powerful orgasm of my life ripped through my body with force.

Lights blasted behind my eyelids.

I gasped and cried out his name.

My entire body shook, and he stayed right there, riding out every last minute of pleasure. My fingers ached from yanking on his hair.

My breathing finally slowed.

I knew if he pulled away, I'd fall to the floor, as I had no feeling in my legs.

My eyes slowly opened, and I peeked down at him just as he looked up.

His lips were slick with my pleasure. His tongue swiped out, and he smiled.

"You're so fucking beautiful, Charlie."

I just stared at him in awe of what he'd just done to me.

"I don't think I can stand up," I whispered.

"I've got you." He pushed to his feet, his hands firm on my hips as he studied me.

"Thank you," I finally said.

"I should be thanking you."

"For what?" I searched his brown eyes.

"For letting me be lucky enough to be the first man to taste you."

I shook my head and covered my eyes with my hand because I couldn't believe what had just happened, nor what he was saying to me.

"Nope." He wrapped his fingers around my wrist. "We're not doing that. When we're together, your eyes are on me. You don't ever need to hide from me, Ladybug."

I nodded, and my hand moved down to find his erection straining hard against his jeans. I knew it had to be painful, so I stroked him a few times over the denim and then cocked my head to the side.

"Now it's your turn."

I adjusted my skirt, and before I could drop to my knees, he was reaching for my wrist.

"Not tonight. Tonight is about you. We have plenty of time for that. But right now, I want to be inside you. I've thought about it for so fucking long."

"Me, too," I whispered.

Before I even knew what was happening, he scooped me up in his arms and carried me to my bedroom. He dropped me onto the bed and just stared at me.

"I love seeing you all sexy and sated."

I pushed to sit up and reached for the button on his jeans as he stood between my legs.

"It's what you do to me."

"And this is what you do to me," he said, as I unzipped his pants and pushed them, along with his boxer briefs, down his legs.

His cock sprung free. Full and thick and pointing right at me.

"Wow," I whispered.

"Arms up," he said, and he pulled my camisole over my head before reaching over his shoulder and yanking his shirt off as well. He bent down, and his mouth found mine as his fingers moved behind my back and unsnapped my bra. The lace slipped off my shoulders, and he reached between us and tossed it on the floor, his lips never losing contact with mine as he helped me to lie back.

His tongue had my head spinning again.

My body was still humming from the last orgasm I'd had just minutes ago. He pulled back and kissed his way down my jaw and neck, taking his time on my throat, licking and sucking between kisses. His hand palmed my breast, and I arched into his touch. He looked down at me, his dark, wavy hair wild and disheveled from where I'd tugged at it.

"Your tits are works of art, Ladybug. So fucking perfect." His mouth came down, covering one hard peak, and I groaned. The sensation was overwhelming. His tongue circled my nipple, and then his mouth covered my breast. He took turns going back and forth from one to the other, kissing and licking until I was writhing beneath him. A layer of sweat covered my hairline.

My body hummed. Tingling with anticipation.

"I need you now," I whispered, my voice filled with desire.

He pulled back and reached down for his jeans. I scooched back on the bed and watched as he tore the edge of the condom off with his teeth, dropping the wrapper to the floor. My eyes widened, and I couldn't look away as he rolled the latex over his engorged cock.

"What if it doesn't fit?" I asked, suddenly nervous about his size.

He chuckled and climbed over me, hovering as he propped himself on his forearms.

"If it hurts—we stop. We'll just see how you feel as we go, okay?" He stroked the hair away from my face, and I nodded.

"I want it to fit. I want this to happen."

"So eager, Ladybug." He smiled this wickedly sexy grin, and my lady bits went into overdrive. I bucked up against him, anxious to try.

He kissed me, slowly this time. His hands found mine and pulled them both above my head, where our fingers were intertwined. He just kept kissing me. My hips bucked against him.

Eager.

Needy.

And a little scared, but I found that to be thrilling, as well.

He pulled one hand away, the other still above my head, as he reached between us and gripped his erection, teasing my entrance, before pushing in just a little bit.

I sucked in a breath, and so did he.

He pulled back to look at me. "Should I stop?"

I shook my head. "No. Please don't stop."

His other hand reached for my breast and tweaked my nipple, and I groaned as he moved forward, inch by glorious inch, his eyes never leaving mine.

"You're so wet and so fucking tight; you're driving me out of my mind."

That was all it took. I arched nearly off the bed, and my free hand found his hair, tangling in his thick waves. I pulled his mouth down to mine just as he thrust all the way inside me, and the mix of pleasure and pain nearly had me crying out.

My lips parted, and his tongue slipped in, and he kissed me as his hips moved out slowly, before thrusting back in.

Oh. My. God.

Nothing had ever felt better.

He continued moving in and out until we found our perfect rhythm. I met him with every thrust. My body moving of its own volition.

Floating.

Flying.

Free falling.

Our breaths the only audible sound in the room.

The build was so powerful, I didn't feel in control of my own body. He knew exactly what I needed, and his hand moved between us and found my clit, rubbing little circles there and driving me out of my mind.

I couldn't think.

I couldn't breathe.

I could only feel.

My back arched, and he pulled back just as I cried out his name.

Little stars lit up the darkness behind my eyes. Tremors racked my body, and he continued to pump in and out of me until he shouted my name and went right over the edge with me. We both kept moving—riding out every last bit of pleasure.

I'd never experienced anything like this in my life.

I finally understood the hype.

I wished this moment would never end.

Because I knew nothing after my time with Ledger would ever compare.

So I was going to enjoy this time and soak up every last bit of joy.

His breathing evened out, and he rolled to his side, taking me with him, so he wouldn't crush me. He pushed the hair out of my face as he studied me in the little bit of moonlight coming through the windows.

"Are you okay?"

"I'm better than okay. I've never felt better." I shook my head and smiled.

He planted a kiss on my forehead before slowly pulling out and making his way to the bathroom. I assumed he was disposing of the condom, and I just stayed in that spot, because my body was so relaxed I didn't think I could move if I wanted to. I hoped he'd come back, but I knew what this was. It was temporary. So if he walked out that door right now, I would be okay. I wasn't going to overthink this. It felt too damn good.

I'd waited way too long to feel this way.

But he strolled back in the room, buck naked, and climbed back into the bed beside me.

"Hey," I whispered.

"Hey." His teeth bit down onto his plump bottom lip, and I swear desire pooled between my legs again.

Maybe I had a problem?

I was a greedy, sex-crazed woman when it came to Ledger Dane.

"What are you thinking? I can tell those wheels are spinning." His fingers intertwined with mine between us.

Well, that was a loaded question.

"Not sure you really want to ask that, but here goes." I chuckled. "I'm wondering if you regret what just happened.

I'm wondering how this will work. What will everyone think? Do we keep this a secret? Will it happen again? We've got one week. Or do you think we should call it done and not mess with fire? I'm wondering if I'll ever feel this way with someone else, now that I know how good it could be. And I'm wondering if we can do it again before we call it done."

He barked out a ridiculously loud laugh. "There's a lot to unpack there. But here's the thing, Charlie. We're two consenting adults. We make the rules. This has nothing to do with anyone but us. I have nothing to hide. If you want the world to know that we're together, it's your call, and that's fine by me."

"I don't want to tell anyone when it's just temporary. Especially Jilly. She'll stress out that I'm going to be hurt. Everyone will make it into a big deal, and I want this just to be our thing. And I'm fine with our little—" I sighed. "Sexy arrangement."

"You're so fucking cute, Ladybug. I regret nothing about what just happened. I think we've both wondered for a long time what it would be like, and it blew my expectations right out of the fucking water."

"Really?" I asked, and the word came out all breathily. I wanted it to feel as good for him as it had for me.

"Abso-fucking-lutely. And I want it to happen again. As many times as possible." He smirked, and I laughed. "I have one more week here. And I want to spend it with you."

"Me, too. It's been fun having you back home." I closed my eyes for a minute to get myself under control. I didn't want to get needy or sappy when I knew what this was. I was the one who'd initiated it.

"This last week has been fucking amazing, and that's because of you. And now you add in your gorgeous fucking body and our little—what did you call it... sexy arrangement—it only makes it better."

"So let's lay down some ground rules," I said, needing to make sure we kept things realistic. That way, no one would get hurt.

Well, so I wouldn't get hurt. I was the one who was at risk here.

He chuckled. "All right. There's only one rule for me."

"What's that?"

"You can have me anytime you want. Day or night. You say the word, Ladybug."

My lips turned up in the corners, and I was certain I had a ridiculous smile on my face, but I couldn't turn it off. "Same. But it's for one week, and then when you leave, we go back to being friends, and we never speak of this again."

His gaze narrowed. "We just pretend it never happened?"

"Yeah. I mean, it's a fling, right? No one talks about those later. We'll have a week of unlimited orgasms, and then you'll go back to your crazy single life in the city, and I'll probably find some great guy who's a boring lover but a fabulous husband, and I'll fantasize about my one wild fling for the rest of my life."

He shook his head in disbelief. "Wow. All right, then. You've got it all figured out."

"That's the only way that no one gets hurt. Everything's out in the open, and we both know what this is."

"And you don't want anyone to know? So I'm your dirty little secret?" He waggled his brows.

"Well, Dilly will be the tough one to keep it from. I swear that girl can read my mind. So keep your hands to yourself when we're in public, and hopefully, she won't be sniffing around for details."

He laughed again. "How are you feeling now? Are you sore?"

"Why? You want to go again already?" I asked, my words coming out breathy, because I was ready, too.

"We've got one week together. I want to go every chance we get. But I think we should probably have you soak in a tub for a little bit, and we can get some sleep. Tomorrow's another day."

"You're staying here?"

"You're naked, Charlie. I'm not going anywhere."

At least, not right now.

I had one week.

And I was going to enjoy every moment.

Chapter 14

Ledger

"I can't believe you're making me get in this thing with you. I'm more of a shower guy," I groaned, as I slipped into her clawfoot tub first. I yelped because the water was so hot, and she just stood there, laughing.

Charlotte Thomas was standing naked in front of me, smiling, tits bouncing, and sexy as shit.

I swear this could easily be one of the many hot fantasies I've had about this girl—but it was actually happening.

And it had been the best fucking sex of my life, and unlike Charlie, I'd had good sex before. Hell, I thought I'd had great sex before—but this… this was next level. This was blow-your-mind, intoxicating, addicting sex. Normally, I was anxious for space after spending time with a woman, but I just wanted more.

I mean, here I was, climbing into some sort of fancy bathtub just to please this girl.

"Stop being a baby; it's not that hot." She waited for me to get settled, and then she climbed in to sit between my legs. Her hair was tied up on top of her head in a messy knot, and my chin settled on her shoulder.

If you'd have asked me even yesterday if I'd ever consider bathing with a woman, I would have laughed. But here I was—and I wasn't complaining about it. I wanted to be here. Liked being close to her. Enjoyed her naked body resting against mine.

"See, this isn't so bad, is it?" she asked, and her hand found mine on her hip, and she intertwined our fingers.

Thoughts of the way she'd looked when she came undone, as she cried out my name and shook beneath me, flooded my thoughts. Fuck. I couldn't wait to make her come apart again and again. I'd always been a believer in pleasing a woman first. I never understood a dude who could chase his own pleasure. But the way I felt about pleasing Charlotte was different. I actually got off more on pleasing her than pleasing myself. Hearing her little moans. The way her body responded to my touch. To my kisses.

To my cock.

Like she was fucking made for me.

"Nope. Not bad at all. I don't care for baths, but it's a little different, seeing as you're lying in here with me naked. Kind of changes my perspective." I chuckled.

She rolled over, her hazel eyes looking a little greener in the light from the crystal chandelier hanging above the tub, her chest resting against mine, as my dick hardened instantly.

"Thanks for being my first, you know... the first one to go downtown."

I barked out a laugh. "That's shocking to me, but I'm fucking happy I got to be the first one to make you fall apart against my tongue."

"Oh my gosh, Ledger." She buried her head in my neck. "You can't talk like that."

I chuckled. She was too sweet for her own good. "Why? Are you embarrassed that I think you have the sweetest pussy?"

Her head flew back, eyes wide and cheeks pink. She kissed me hard, and I knew it was to silence me. And then she pulled back and raised a brow. "Never met a dirty-talking architect."

"Then you've been missing out, Ladybug. Because I'll never tire of telling you how sweet you are."

She rolled over, her back against my chest again. and sighed. "Well, I've got one week to get used to it."

She was really hung up on the timeline aspect of this arrangement. I'd never gone into anything with so many rules. I just found that most relationships I'd been in ran their course quickly. The conversation tired, and the excitement of sex would die down. I wouldn't consider myself a relationship-phobe, but I also wasn't a big-picture guy. I wasn't looking for the long game. Never had. I didn't believe in it, if I was being honest—and had good reason.

I was happy my sister found it, and I hoped like hell that it would work out. But I didn't think it was in my DNA. I enjoyed women and always tried to be respectful, but I never wanted to take things further.

Charlotte was all about the big picture, so this was a stretch for her. I got it. And she was protecting her heart, which was wise. She knew who I was, and she wanted rules to be in place so no one would get hurt.

So she *wouldn't get hurt.*

I understood it. She was the last person on the planet I would ever want to hurt. And a part of me knew this wasn't wise—but I couldn't stop myself. Because I'd never wanted anyone or anything the way I wanted Charlotte Thomas. So, she was right… If that meant we had this one week of fucking amazing memories, I'd take it. Then she'd go off and marry some lucky bastard, and I'd continue having meaningless relationships and be just fine with it.

"If you want out any time before, you know you just say the word."

"Same with you," she whispered.

I never would. I may not be a guy who could give her forever—but I was a guy who could give her right now. It was my specialty.

But there was something that I'd never told her that she deserved to know. Something about the way she spoke still made me think that she didn't believe that I cared for her as much as she cared for me back then.

"There's something I've never told you before."

She gazed over her shoulder. "Tell me."

"You keep saying that I rejected you back then, and I just want to come clean. Lay it all on the table. I don't like the idea of you thinking that because it's not true."

"It's okay, Ledger. I know you just aren't that guy. I get it."

"I did come for you, Ladybug. I drove several hours up the coast to talk to you your freshman year of college after my football season ended. I hated that we were distant. I fucking hated it. And I wanted to fix it."

"You came to see me at school? When?"

"I was waiting in the lobby of your dorm, and you came walking in with that rich dude you ended up dating, Ryan, and you didn't see me. He couldn't keep his fucking hands off you. I left and drove back to school, deciding I needed to leave it alone. I thought it was for the better. And then you dated him for what? Two years? So I just let it go."

She rolled over again to look at me, her chin resting on my chest and so much empathy in her pretty gaze. "Why didn't you just call me and tell me you were there?"

"Because"—I looked away—"you seemed happy. And Jilly gushed about what a good guy he was, so I figured it was for the better. I only ever wanted the best for you. I just knew that it wasn't me. But I don't want to leave here when this thing between us ends, with you not knowing just how much you meant to me. How much you mean to me now."

"Ledger Dane," she said, her lips turning up in the corners. "You're just full of surprises, aren't you?"

"Only with you." I shrugged. "Let's not make it a big deal. I felt like an idiot for driving there to talk to you, anyway. But I just wanted to make it clear that I struggled with the way things ended between us, too."

"Thank you for telling me. That means a lot." Her voice cracked a little bit, and my shoulders tensed. I didn't want to complicate things for her, and I probably fucked up by coming clean.

My stomach rumbled against her chest, and she laughed. It was late. The sun was threatening to come up soon, and I was hungry.

Hungry for food and hungry for her.

She giggled and squeezed my hand. "It's almost morning. Maybe we should make some breakfast and then go back to bed for a little bit?"

"Sounds good to me. Or I could bury my head between your legs again and call that breakfast."

She jumped up and reached for a towel as she climbed out of the tub. She wrapped herself up and held out a towel for me, raising a brow and smiling. "Real food first, and then we'll see how you feel."

I pulled the drain and stepped out of the tub, drying off before wrapping the towel around my waist. "Deal."

I walked into the bedroom and slipped on my briefs, and she picked up my T-shirt and smiled. "I'm wearing this. It's soft, and it smells like you."

I chuckled, and she went to her drawer and pulled out a pair of panties, but I took them from her fingers and tossed them back in the drawer.

"No panties. I like the idea of you in my shirt with nothing underneath."

She fanned her face. "Okay, then."

We made our way into her kitchen, and she opened the refrigerator and reached for the eggs. I came up behind her and slipped my hands beneath my tee. I slid them up her hips and across her flat stomach, before cupping her tits and kissing her neck.

"Oh my gosh." She whipped around to face me. "I can't make eggs with your hands all over me."

Her head fell back in laughter, and I kissed her neck. "Fine. Put me to work."

She just smiled at me and pointed at the barstool beside

her island. "You sit, and I'll cook."

I dropped my ass on the stool and glanced over at a bulletin board bedside the cabinets. There were a few envelopes pinned there, and I studied them. "What's in the envelopes?"

She turned to look over her shoulder and shook her head. "Those have money in them.

Special things I'm saving for. I take a little out of each paycheck and tuck it inside each envelope. I know it should be in the bank, but I like visualizing. And seeing them motivates me." She placed a few pieces of bacon on a pan and slipped it into the oven.

I got that. I was a visual guy. I made my living that way. I pushed to my feet and walked over because I was curious what the writing said.

Canoe.

Beach vacation.

Dilly.

I ran my fingers along the edge of each envelope, and Dilly's had the most cash in it. "Tell me what these are."

She whisked her egg mixture before pouring it into a skillet. "Well, Dilly graduated from law school not too long ago, and she's studying for the bar right now. I want to get her something really special when she passes, which she will."

"What do you want to get her?"

"We were shopping for Christmas gifts last year, and I found her staring at these pearl earrings. Our mom always wore pearls, and she was buried in her favorite pair. I think they remind Dilly of her. She tried them on and looked in the mirror and told me she'd be wearing them for her first interview someday, but then she gave them back and said today wasn't that day. I want to get them for her. So I've been tucking money away out of each check since."

Charlotte Thomas was the best person I knew. Hell, I loved my mom, Nan, and Jilly—but I didn't know anyone who was as giving as her. She'd always been that way. Making my sister special banners on her birthday and coming over early to our house to decorate year after year. She always went above and beyond for others, which was one of the things I loved about her.

"How much are they?" I asked because I was curious.

She shrugged. "They probably won't seem expensive to you, but I live on a fixed income, so I have to plan for extras, you know?"

"I get that. Hell, I respect the shit out of it. Are you close to having enough?"

"Yeah. They're two hundred and fifty dollars, and I've got a hundred and seventy-five saved up. But I can also take from the other envelopes any time, and I'd have enough. So I'll see how close I get and then I can take the difference out of the others when she has her first interview scheduled. What do they call that? Robbing Peter to pay Paul?" She chuckled. "But it's all mine, so I'm not robbing anyone."

"And what about you? Do you want a pair of pearl earrings?"

"Nope. I'm saving for the other two things."

"A beach vacation and a canoe?" I asked, my fingers running along one of the canoe envelopes that was hanging there.

"Right. Those are long-term goals. I want my own canoe because it's something I like to do as often as possible.

Vivi left one here for me, but it has a hole in it and can't be repaired." She plated the eggs and leaned down to look in the oven before pulling out the bacon. "It's not a big deal. Vivi and Everly both have canoes, and I go over to their houses and can use them whenever I want. I usually go every Sunday and take a picnic, then spend my day alone on the lake with a book before we all head to my dad's for Sunday dinner."

"You guys still do Sunday dinners, huh?" I asked because I'd gone to a few over the years.

"Always. You never miss them if you're home."

"Are you reading Ashlan's books while you're out on the water?" I teased because her baby sister was a romance author.

"I beta read for Ash, so I get to read everything she writes long before they come out. She's so talented, and I love her books. So yeah, I've taken her books out on the water often. But I'd like to be able to do it from my own dock, you know? It's the little things sometimes that we appreciate the most."

I nodded as she set the two plates on the kitchen island.

"Well, at the moment, it's your pussy that I appreciate most."

Her mouth gaped open. "You have a one-track mind."

"Not normally. I mean, sure, I enjoy sex as much as the next guy. But sex with you—it's different."

She sat down on the stool beside me, and I forked a bite of scrambled eggs and groaned.

"How is it different?"

"I don't know. Maybe it's our history or the fact that we're good friends and have a connection. But it's damn good, Ladybug."

"Dilly claims she has a magic vagina, and we *are* twins."
She shrugged, and I barked out a laugh.

"I think everything about you is pure magic."

She took a bite of her bacon and studied me. "Don't go getting all sappy now, Dane. I'm yours for a week. You don't have to sweet talk me. For the first time in my life, I think it's fair to say that I'm a sure thing."

I laughed, but the truth was—this wasn't a game for me. I wasn't saying it to gain anything. It was the way I felt.

"All right. So I understand the Dilly envelope and the canoe envelope. What's the beach vacation about?"

"Well, I love the water, which is why I live on the lake, obviously. And I went to Hawk and Ever's wedding in the Bahamas, which was amazing. But I want to go on a beach vacation where there is nothing to do but drink piña coladas and relax. No agenda. No kids fighting in class. No responsibilities or bills. No wedding. No birthday. Just a vacation to do whatever I feel like."

I nodded. I understood that. I couldn't remember the last time I actually took a vacation that wasn't for work. "Who are you taking on this dream vacation?"

"I haven't decided." She shook her head like the whole thing was ridiculous. "I see the beach, and I can picture myself relaxed. But I don't know who I'd ask to go with me who would be on the same page as me. Maybe I'll go alone and meet my future husband there."

I rolled my eyes. She sure was talking about this fictional dude a lot.

"You're not talking about the ball scratcher, Tobias, are you?"

"No," she groaned. "I will be making it very clear to him that there is nothing between us."

Something about the way she said it had red flags going up. "Why? Is he bothering you?"

"No. He's drunk texted a few times. I never even gave him my phone number, so he obviously got it out of the school directory. I'm not down with that or with him."

"Do you want me to get involved?" I asked, hoping she would say yes because the thought of him drunk texting her pissed me off.

"No. I can handle myself. But thank you for the offer. I'm not worried about him. I just need to make it clear."

"So, Toby-ass won't be going on the dream beach vacation. Why are you looking so hard for a husband, anyway? You're young."

"It's not that I'm looking to get married right now. But I see Jilly and Garrett and obviously Vivi and Niko, Hawk and Ever, and now Ash and Jace—and I envy that kind of love, you know? Someone who would walk through fire for you."

I'd walk through fire for Charlie without hesitation.

"You can have people in your life that love you, who will do anything for you—but you don't have to be married for that." Why did I sound so defensive?

"I know. It's not like I'm desperate to get engaged or anything, but I'd like to meet the person who could be the one, you know? I've always known I wanted to be a mom someday. I want to be married. I love what my parents had. What my sisters have. It's probably very old-school thinking, and I should just be happy to have a good job and a cute house and be able to support myself. It's not that I need a man to be happy. Not at all. But I want a partner. Someone to do life with, you know?"

"Well, you need a man to give you all the orgasms, too." I raised a brow, and for whatever reason, I sounded like a pouty fucking baby.

I didn't want to talk about the man who would give Charlotte Thomas the life she wanted. I wanted to talk about what I could give her right now.

"This is where you come in," she said, turning on her stool to face me. My hands settled on her thighs, and she shivered as I moved them further up her legs. She closed her eyes, and her head fell back as I moved closer to where I knew she wanted me. "You can teach me all the things I need to know so I can let my future boyfriend know what I like," she whispered.

What the fuck?

No fucking way some douchedick was going to use my moves to please this girl. Over my dead body. I'd just have to mix it up so she wouldn't remember what I did—she'd only remember the way I made her feel.

I'd pull out all the fucking stops.

Worship her body until she cried out my name—and only my name.

Even when this came to an end, she would remember this time.

Me and her.

Just like I would.

Chapter 15

Charlotte

When I arrived at school Monday morning, I swear I was still floating on a cloud. Ledger and I had spent most of the weekend in bed. I'd never done anything like that before. Sex had always been a bit of a chore. It had been fairly quick with my past partners, and then we'd go to sleep.

Sex with Ledger was nothing like that. We barely slept, and guess what? I didn't even care. We were both insatiable. And I realized that I needed this. I needed to know how good it could be, and who better to show me what I'd been missing than the boy I'd loved my entire life?

Yes, I still felt some guilt about Jilly, but she was so caught up in the wedding right now that I certainly wasn't going to talk to her about it. And after the wedding, Ledger would be gone, and we'd all go back to normal. There was no need to complicate things by telling her.

What was I going to say?

Your brother is a fabulous lover, and he's giving me all the orgasms for one week, and then he'll go back home, and I'll try to move on.

Jilly had been with Garrett for years. She'd found her person. She didn't know what it was like out there, and this was something I was just giving to myself. A little piece of heaven that made no sense, but it was just for me.

I had Sunday night dinner at my dad's house last night, and Ledger had insisted on coming with me. And even that, just being at dinner with everyone and having him by my side, was nice. I explained that we'd been taking care of some wedding stuff for Jilly, and he'd just tagged along, and no one questioned it. It had been the best weekend I'd had in as long as I could remember.

But now I was back to reality.

I passed Tom, our maintenance guy, in the hall and waved at him.

"Good morning, Miss Thomas. Just a few more days now."

"Yep. We're almost done." I pulled the door open to the gym and walked into the P.E. office. Tobias glanced up, and he looked like a man who'd been up late last night after a whole lot of booze. He had dark circles under his eyes and looked like he hadn't slept as he sat behind his desk. He texted me multiple times again last night, and I didn't show Ledger this morning when I saw the messages because he'd be dying to come down here and make a scene. That was not happening.

"Hello, beautiful," he said, his voice sounding hoarse.

Seriously? That was what he was going to lead with, when

I hadn't even responded to a single message he'd sent.

"No," I said, holding my hand up. "None of that. Listen, Tobias, texting me inappropriate messages in the middle of the night is highly unprofessional. I never gave you my number, and I'd appreciate it if you'd lose it as of today."

"Awww... come on, babe. I was just being honest."

I leaned forward, placing both hands on his desk. "I need you to hear me, or I will report you to Principal Peters. Don't call me babe. Don't text me again. We can be co-workers and remain friendly, but I want nothing more than a friendship with you. Are we clear?"

He smiled like this was a silly game before responding with one word. "Crystal."

"Great. Please remove my number from your phone." And I turned on my heels and walked out the door. It felt damn good to speak my mind. To put him in his place.

How pathetic was that?

But something was shifting in me. Maybe it was all the good loving with Ledger. I was done being walked on. I wasn't even nervous to march in there and tell him to bug off.

I got to my classroom and settled at the reading table and got to work.

Kell strolled into the classroom as I cut sand buckets out of construction paper for today's centers.

"You're here early," she said.

"Yeah. I came to tell Tobias not to text me anymore."

"Tobias? You gave him your number? I thought you weren't feeling it with him? I was hoping you were talking about Hotty-Mc-Dane. Now that guy is who you want texting you."

"I didn't give Tobias my number. And I most definitely am not into him." I rolled my eyes.

"Good. I don't get good vibes from that guy. Have you noticed he's always adjusting his balls?"

We both fell back in hysterical laughter, and I nodded. "I hadn't noticed it before, but now that everyone has pointed it out, I can't unsee it."

"What's on your mind, girl? I know you. That brain of yours is working overtime."

I set the scissors down and turned to face her. "Have you ever had a fling?"

Her head fell back in laughter. Her blonde bob bounced on her shoulders, and she smiled at me. "Yes. Ray and I actually had a fling and fell in love. I know that's not the norm, but let me just say," she leaned in and whispered, "the sex was hot. The banter was fabulous. And we never outgrew the fling. Well, until those two cockblockers entered the world. But you know, we still find time."

I laughed and shook my head at the reference to her two children whom she was crazy about. "Wow. I never knew that. I love that you two ended up together, though. You're one of my favorite couples."

"I guess we are pretty damn cute. So tell me about this fling you're considering."

I chewed on my thumbnail. I needed to talk to someone, and I couldn't talk to Jilly. And telling Dylan any of this right now was risky. She'd make it obvious. I'd have to fill her in later. "I kind of already crossed the line. I've never done anything so irresponsible before. And this person doesn't live here. He's not looking for anything. He's not a relationship guy. We've agreed to just have fun for the week he's here."

She reached for my hand and smiled. "Sometimes flings are just good because you don't have to overthink anything. If it's who I think it is—just enjoy it. You deserve this. Be frivolous for once in your life, Charlie."

Was I that boring that everyone seemed to think I should let loose? But then I thought of Jilly. "What if doing this would upset someone that you love?"

Her face turned serious. "Is he married?"

"Oh my gosh, no. Um, but his sister is my best friend. She wouldn't be happy about it."

She smiled then, as if just remembering that Ledger was Jilly's brother. "Honey, you do everything for everyone. You've spent months making favors for her wedding. You threw a bridal shower, and a bachelorette party. You're an amazing friend. But sometimes, you've got to do something for yourself. And it's no one's business. You're two consenting adults. As long as you go in knowing what it is, no one will get hurt, and no one needs to know about it. This is your business and no one else's."

"I've just never really been a casual girl. But it's just so—" I couldn't find the words, and I could feel my face flush at the thought of what we did last night.

"I get that. But look at you." She chuckled. "Has it ever been this good?"

I shook my head. "Um, no. Not even close."

"Give yourself this. Experience something different. And then you'll know what to look for in the future."

I had already crossed the line, hadn't I? I just needed to make sure I kept the lines clear, moving forward. This would stay between me and Ledger. It was just two friends having sex. Nothing more.

I'd already given him my heart years ago, and he rejected it.

And I was still standing.

I was just fine.

I'd dated plenty since.

I could handle this.

The bell rang, and I went right into teacher mode. And the day moved by in a blur.

· · ·

Before leaving work, I had a text from Jilly. My stomach dropped every time she messaged me, which was probably the guilt I felt about keeping this secret from her.

> **Jilly:** Hey, girl. Guess what? Garrett is taking me out of town for a few days before the wedding because he thinks I need a break. We just got on the road. And my dad called, and he and Brenda are going to join us. It's been so long since I've spent any time with him. I'm hoping this is the start of something new. Keep an eye on my brother for me. He's been MIA a lot, and I think this tension with my dad is getting to him. Nan said he's just staying with her to stay out of my hair. But I always worry about him, even if he is a stubborn ass.

I let out a long breath as I read her words. I kept asking him where he'd tell her he was because he'd stayed at my house all weekend. But why would Nan say he was with her? Did she know where he was?

Me: Of course, I will. Don't worry about a thing. And if you need me to do anything for the wedding this week, just let me know. Tomorrow is my last full day of work, and then it's all half days until I am officially on summer break and walking down the aisle to celebrate you guys. I'm happy you're taking this break before the big day.

Jilly: I will let you know, but I think everything is covered. Thanks for being the best friend a girl could ask for and for helping me so much with this wedding. I love you forever, Charlie.

Me: I love you forever.

I tried to push away the guilt I was feeling as I walked out of school and found Ledger sitting in his car. I walked over to him, and he jumped out of the driver's side and opened the passenger door.

"What are you doing here?"

"Hey. Hop in. I'm taking you somewhere."

"My car is here," I said with confusion.

"We'll come back for it."

I climbed in his car, and he shut the door before jogging around to the driver's seat.

"What are you up to? Is this about sex? You can't wait another minute for me to get to my house?" I laughed, and he shrugged.

"Well, obviously, I'm down for that. But this is something special for you."

I rubbed my hands together as we pulled down the street in front of his house. He glanced over at me. "Jilly and Garrett just left. Relax."

"Oh, yeah, she texted me. But what are we doing here?"

"Nan wants to see you. And she made your favorite chicken salad sandwich, so we're just picking up food."

"Picking up food?"

"I can't just have sex with you, Ladybug. The least I could do is feed you now and then." He barked out a laugh and hopped out of the car. He opened my door, and I followed him inside.

"There's my girl. Ledger told me you've been helping him with his speech for the wedding, and you've been working so hard every night on this," Nan said, and I could feel my cheeks heat.

"Yep. She's put in long hours helping me," Ledger said from behind his grandmother and winked at me.

"Well, that's why I made up a little picnic so you could at least eat when you're working tonight," she said, and she was looking at me strangely. "You look pretty relaxed, my girl. Something's different about you."

I sucked in a breath. Oh my gosh. She knew.

"I've been walking a lot, getting a lot of sunshine. That must be it."

"Yeah. You have that sunny glow," Ledger said with a smirk.

"You do, too, buddy. You must be walking right beside her." Nan waggled her brows, and I wanted to crawl in a hole. "Don't be looking all nervous, sweet girl. I spent a lot of years, er, walking, too. There's no shame in getting your glow on."

Oh.

My.

God.

Ledger's head fell back in a fit of laughter, and he reached for the picnic basket and kissed her cheek. "Love you, Nan. Thanks for this."

"Of course. I love you both. Maybe you two could go for a little walk tonight?" She winked, and my mouth fell open.

"There's nothing little about my walk!" Ledger shouted, and I jumped up and tried to cover his mouth with my hand as we walked toward his car, and he laughed.

He opened my door, and I climbed into the passenger seat, ready to combust as I waited for him to settle beside me.

"You told her?"

"What? No. She knows I've been gone a lot and that I haven't been spending the night at her place or at Mom's, which must be why she covered for me with Jilly, so I'm guessing she has her suspicions. But I don't give a shit. I'm a grown-ass man. I don't owe anyone an explanation."

"So if your sister found out a few days before she was getting married, you wouldn't feel slightly bad that we've been lying to her?" I crossed my arms over my chest and faced him as he pulled out of the driveway.

"Honestly? No. That's all you. I never understood her reasoning about staying away from her friends. I know the whole Lucy Blocker thing was dramatic, but that was on her. I never lied to anyone. I love my sister, and I'd walk through fire for her, but I don't answer to her."

"Yet, you've kept it a secret since you've been here," I reminded him.

He pulled into my driveway. "I've kept it a secret because you asked me to. You care what other people think a hell of a lot more than I do."

"I don't want to upset her. She's my best friend," I said, unable to hide the irritation in my voice.

"I think it's more than that." He turned off the car and faced me.

"Oh, I can't wait to hear this. What else could it be?"

"By not telling anyone, it means you can pretend it never happened. It's safer." He shrugged before jumping out of the car and opening my door.

"That's ridiculous. If I wanted to play it safe, I wouldn't even be doing this," I hissed as I climbed out of the car, and he pressed me up against the passenger door. One hand landed on each side of my shoulders as he caged me in.

"And what is it we're doing, Ladybug?"

"We're having sex. Nothing more."

He nodded. "So, I am your dirty little secret."

"And I'm *yours*," I whispered, as my breaths started coming faster.

"You're not. I don't keep secrets. I date out in the open. I don't lie about who I am or what I'm doing. This is a first for me. Lying because you asked me to."

I shrugged. "It's a first for me, too. I don't normally have a lover that I have to keep hidden."

He barked out a laugh. "Oh, I'm your lover, am I?"

"Yep. And a pretty damn good one."

He leaned down and kissed me quickly before pulling back and reaching into the back seat for the picnic basket. "Come on. I've got something for you."

We walked in the house, and he took my hand and led me straight through the back sliding glass door that looked out at Honey Mountain Lake. When we stepped outside, he kept the picnic basket in one hand and nodded toward the little dock on my property. There sat a shiny red canoe tied to my dock.

"Where did that come from?" I asked as I hurried down the little grassy area between my back porch and the turquoise water.

"Jace took me over to his brother Travis's shop today."

"Honey Mountain Rentals?" I asked as I bent down to admire the gorgeous boat.

"Yep. He said he'd be able to help me order a good one, but when we got there, he had a brand-new shipment in. When I saw the red one, I knew you had to have it. He let me buy it off him."

"Why would you do that?" I asked, pushing to my feet, my eyes welling with emotion as I shook my head in disbelief.

"Because I can. Because you deserve it. Because you're an amazing friend to my sister, to me, hell, to everyone you know. And I wanted to do something nice for you."

I couldn't speak at first. No one had ever done anything this generous for me, and I certainly didn't expect it to come from a guy I wasn't even dating. When I looked at the canoe and then back to him, I saw something I'd never seen before on Ledger's face. He looked... nervous.

Vulnerable.

I moved closer to him, wanting to tell him how much this meant to me, but also nervous about making it more than it was. I tended to lean that way, especially when it came to Ledger.

"Is this a thank you gift because I'm such an impressive lover?" I teased, trying to hold back my laughter.

He chuckled. "Well, I'm not paying you for sex, if that's

what you're asking. I guess it's a thank you for being such an impressive human being."

A lump formed in my throat at his words.

"I feel the same about you," I whispered and pushed up on my tiptoes and kissed his cheek. "Come on, my dirty little secret. Let's get out on the water and eat those sandwiches. I'm starving."

He nodded and moved toward the canoe and set the picnic basket inside. I still couldn't believe he'd done something so generous for me. He stepped into the canoe and held out his hand.

"So now, you can put all the money from your envelope into your beach vacation envelope. You deserve something just for you."

I stared at him.

Maybe that was why I was protecting this secret so much.

Because what I had with Ledger was just for me.

No one was getting in my head and asking what this was or where it would go. No one was warning me to be careful because I would probably grow too attached and get hurt when it all came to an end.

What I shared with Ledger was so much more than a dirty little secret.

It was the greatest gift I'd ever received because he made me feel wanted and needed.

He made me feel beautiful and sexy.

He made me feel like the only girl in the room.

"Thank you for making me believe that's true." I shrugged, and he just studied me as he reached for the oars, and we moved out toward the center of the lake.

We floated around in a little cove that was my favorite place to read. Big trees surrounded us, providing just enough shade. The birds were singing, the sun was setting, and Ledger and I talked for hours while we ate and laughed and enjoyed the moment. No kissing. No sex. Just two people who enjoyed one another's company outside of the bedroom, too.

I knew this would be a day that I would never forget.

And I did everything I could to memorize every last detail.

The sounds, the smells, the words that were spoken.

Because I never wanted it to end.

Chapter 16

Ledger

"So we've got bigger things to focus on. You need to drop this ridiculous school project," Harold said, and I glanced out at the lake. Charlotte had gone to work early this morning, and I'd stayed to enjoy my coffee after she left. I was heading over to take Nan to her doctor's appointment in a little while, but I liked it here.

More than I should.

I knew things were getting complicated because I'd spent every single day with Charlie, and I only wanted more. That was an absolute first for me, because usually, I was ready to bail much sooner than this. Sure, I'd dated women for a few weeks, sometimes months, but we didn't spend every waking second together. Hell, spending the night with a woman usually had me itching to get home and get some space.

But that was not the case now, and it scared the shit out of me because I was leaving. I lived in the city, and she lived here.

I wasn't a relationship guy, and that was all she knew.

She wanted things I could never give her.

A husband. A family. A life.

Thoughts of my father and how fucking badly he'd messed up my view on family flooded my thoughts. How easy it was to manipulate me as a kid. The guilt and shame I'd felt about lying to my mother for years. I can still remember the day I came clean to her. The day I finally told my father what an asshole he was. The day I broke my mother's heart and told her what I'd seen. The fight that followed. My father telling me it was all my fault when he left. Jilly crying and running off to hide in her room. The devastation. And to now learn that he never even wanted to get married, and I was the reason they'd even been together. I shook my head at the memories. I never wanted to be in a position to blow up someone's entire world like I watched him do.

No. It was too much responsibility.

Holding someone's happiness in your hands.

Fuck.

I couldn't go there.

Not even for her.

Because if I let her down, I'd never forgive myself.

"You said you'd consider it if I agree to the new museum project. You know that will be a shit ton of work, and the hours will be insane. But I'll do it, if you take on this small project that I'm asking you to do, Harold. You've got to give me some wins now and then." I shook my head and let out a long breath because I was tired of this song and dance with him.

"I'm considering you for a partner; is that not enough of

a win for you?" he hissed. This was what he always did when I pushed back. He had a little tantrum and hoped it would be enough to sway me. In the beginning, I always gave him what he wanted. But I knew my worth now. I knew he needed me, almost as much as I needed him, but he didn't want to do the work anymore, and that was where I came in. I was willing to do whatever it took.

"Of course, it's a win. But that would also mean that I'd have a say in what we would take on. I don't even know why you're fighting me on this. I'm the one who will do all the work. I just need you to okay it."

"Well, I agreed to let you do your father's project, didn't I? How far are you going to push me on this?"

"Oh, for fuck's sake, Harold. That was a formality. I will do that project as a side job outside of work hours, and you know it. I just needed a doc sent over so he'd quit fucking blackmailing me. You won't have to lift a finger for that project. The school is different. It's a passion project."

"Let's discuss all of this when you get back from the weekend and we take that trip on the yacht that you keep trying to get out of."

I sat down and stared out at the canoe and thought about my night with Charlie out on the water. How simple it was. How easy it was. The laughter. The way the conversation just flowed. The way I could spend hours with her and still want to know more.

About her heart.

About her mind.

About her body.

I cleared my throat. "It would be extremely awkward to

go on a yacht with you and Maureen when Jessica and I aren't dating. It's not like it's a big group, and I don't want to be put in that position. I don't want to lead anyone on. I'm not a complete dick all the time."

He chuckled. "Did you know that Maureen's father was my boss back in the day? He set me up with her. I wouldn't have this booming business if it weren't for him."

What the fuck did that mean?

Was he jumping on the blackmail bandwagon now, too?

I knew that Maureen's father was a very well-known architect back in the day, and Harold had taken over the firm and made it even more successful over the years. But I sure as fuck didn't know that he'd set them up.

"I knew you worked for him. I assumed you went to work there after you and Maureen were married." I ran a hand down my face because I didn't like the direction of the conversation.

"Wrong. I worked for him. He set me up with his daughter, who I truly had no interest in at first. But I was a smart man, Ledger. I didn't have a pot to piss in without Gavin's support. He was my mentor, and he became my father-in-law. It was a win-win."

"Good for you. I'm not much in the market for arranged marriages. The practice is a bit barbaric for me. I'm looking for a partnership with you, Harold, because I've worked my ass off over the last five years. I am not looking for an insta-family, and I'd appreciate it if you'd stop pushing."

"Listen to me. If you're over there fucking some girl and that makes you feel guilty about my girl—I promise you, there will be no questions asked when you return."

I pushed to my feet because I felt like this was some

kind of joke. Plus, the way he was offering up his daughter, knowing I wasn't interested, was beginning to sicken me. This was something my father would do. What the fuck was wrong with these men?

"I'm done discussing my personal life. Think about the school project. The superintendent is breathing down my ass, and I'd like to give him an answer before I leave."

"Then I guess we both have something to think about, don't we?" He chuckled. "Take a look at the museum documents I sent over. It has the timeline and all the information about the building that you need. Just let me know when you think you could get started and how long you think it would take. It's a great résumé builder for you, Ledger."

If I had a fucking penny for every time he used that form of manipulation on me… A few years ago, that kind of shit worked. But my résumé was strong all on its own now. My stamp was on several of those iconic buildings that he took credit for, and people knew it. I had offers all the time from companies we competed with, but I prided myself on being a loyal guy. If I ever jumped ship on Harold, it would be to start my own company. That had always been the goal. But somewhere along the way, I'd gotten comfortable working under the famous Harold Cartwright and the money that came along with that.

"I'll get back to you. Talk soon." I ended the call because I wasn't in the mood to go round and round with him anymore.

My phone vibrated, and I glanced down to see a message from Charlotte.

Ladybug: I wish I were floating on the water right now instead of having my breath sniffed by Darwin.

I barked out a laugh because I fucking loved hearing her talk about the kids.

Me: I wish my head was buried between your legs while we were floating on the water.

Ladybug: OMG! Stop. I'm at school.

Me: Can't help myself. How's your day?

Ladybug: Busy for a half day. I can't believe tomorrow is my last day with the kids.

I knew what she was saying. We'd been talking about it a lot. Her last day with the kids meant our time was coming to an end. I never thought I'd be dreading leaving Honey Mountain. But I was.

Me: Darwin must be crushed, huh?

Ladybug: He doesn't seem too happy about it.

Me: How do you feel about it?

Ladybug: I hate goodbyes, Ledger. I always have.

My fucking chest squeezed, and I moved back inside the house and grabbed my keys.

Me: Goodbye doesn't mean forever, Ladybug.

Ladybug: Are you seriously quoting that "Goodbye Girl" song by David Gates?

Me: What can I say? It's Nan's favorite song. She played it on repeat after she lost Papa.

I thought about the time Charlie had broken down to me

about her mother passing. How she told me she hated change and hated saying goodbye to people because sometimes, they didn't come back. And fuck if I didn't feel like a dick for quoting that song.

> **Ladybug:** It's a good song. I get why she loves it. Okay, the kids are back, and Darwin wants to know what I had for a morning snack.

> **Me:** I'm glad he can't smell my breath because we both know what I had for a morning snack in the shower before you left for work. I can still taste you.

> **Ladybug:** Are you trying to kill me? <panting face emoji> I'll see you later.

> **Me:** You most definitely will.

I left to pick up Nan, and I was still chuckling about my conversation with Charlie. How much fun I had making her blush. Telling her how much I loved her body.

Nan was waiting outside for me, and I opened the passenger door and helped her into the car. "Good morning, my boy."

"Good morning to you," I said.

When I got in the driver's seat and pulled out of the driveway, she started with the questions. Nan should have worked for the CIA because the woman had an insatiable curiosity when it came to mine and Jilly's private lives. We always teased her about it. Maybe it was the therapist in her, or maybe she was just nosy as hell.

"Your mom said you're meeting her at the hospital to have lunch with her today?" she asked.

"I am."

"I only ask because she seems to think you're sleeping at my place every night, too?"

Here we go.

"I've seen her every day since I've been here. Where I sleep does not affect anyone because Mom goes to bed early, anyway." I shrugged as I pulled into the parking lot where her cardiologist's office was.

"I just find it interesting that you're gone every night. My, oh my, you must be working very hard on the best man's speech." She chuckled, and I pulled out my keys and turned to face her. "Or you're going for lots of walks, maybe?"

"Nan. This isn't anyone's concern." I raised a brow.

"If you're sleeping with that sweet girl, you best not hurt her. Because Jilly won't be the only one who has a problem with it. She's not the kind of girl you mess around with, Ledger." Her tone turned serious, and I suddenly felt defensive.

"You're the one who always says that you want me with her," I said, completely outraged by her anger. "Hell, you joked about it the other day."

I knew she'd like me to be the kind of guy to settle down, and Charlotte Thomas would definitely be her pick. I swear, she loved Charlie as if she were her own grandchild.

"As long as you aren't leading that sweet girl on."

"We're adults, Nan. You don't need to worry."

She pushed to get out of the car, catching me off guard, so I jumped out and came around to help her. "This isn't even about Charlie. You know, you always worry so much about being like your dad. And I've always told you that you're nothing like him. But the truth is... you may be just as stupid as him in some ways. Blind to what's right in front of your face."

"What the hell is going on with you?" I hissed. "Did you seriously just compare me to that asshole? And call me stupid at the same time?"

She was marching beside me, all fired up and angry, and I had no idea why. She stepped onto the elevator and clutched her purse like I was going to steal it. "Ledger, you're a good man. Stop running from all the good. Will you do that for me? You're just a guy who has a shitty father. That doesn't make you a shitty man."

I let out a long breath. I thought everyone was getting crazy the closer we got to the wedding. Aside from my sister, who was on some bizarre last-minute vacation with our deadbeat father days before her wedding.

"Just a stupid one?" I tried to tease, but she wasn't having it.

"I call it how I see it."

"Fine. I'm a stupid jackass, I guess. I think everyone has wedding fever. I know I'm a good man, Nan. I know I have a shitty father. I also know that not everyone needs to have a family. Not everyone is meant to be a father. There's no shame in that."

"There is if you're only saying those things because you're afraid of failing. I did not help raise a coward, Ledger." The elevator doors opened, and she stormed off ahead of me.

A coward?

Where the fuck did that come from?

She was all over the place.

Nan and I rarely disagreed. I'd always been her best guy, or so she said.

Disappointing her was not a high point of my day.

But for whatever reason, she was disappointed in me, and I didn't like it.

She came to a stop right before she walked into the doctor's office. "I know you've been through a lot with your dad. You've stepped up for your family, and I respect that. And I know that losing Colt was hard on you. And you're allowed to be sad and angry and grieve—all of that. But the choices that you make for yourself, those are on you. There is no one to blame but yourself."

"I'm aware, Nan. I don't know what this is about." I followed her through the door, and she told me to take a seat.

She didn't let me come back with her for her appointment, and she was quiet on the drive home. When I pulled into the driveway, she turned to me. "Jilly is coming home tomorrow. She's been awfully quiet since she left, and I just hope like hell that your father doesn't ruin this day for her."

Nan had never been so serious before. I didn't like it.

"I won't let him ruin anything for her."

"I know you won't." She reached for my hand. "But someday, you're going to realize that you were so busy trying to make everyone else's life great that you forgot to live your own."

"Where is this coming from?" I didn't hide my surprise at what she'd said today. "Nan, I have a kickass apartment. A job that most guys my age would only dream of. I have no shortage of women that I date. Why do you think I'm unhappy?"

"Because since you've been home, I've seen a difference in you. A light in your eyes that hasn't been there since you were a kid." She put her hands up to stop me from arguing, because I was a happy fucking guy. "I'm not talking about the show you put on for everyone else, Ledger. I know you're the most charming guy in the room. But I want you to be the most fulfilled guy in the room."

I shook my head because I didn't know what the fuck she was even talking about. She pushed out of the car, and once again, I hurried around to help her.

"Let me walk you inside," I huffed, because she was being stubborn and ornery.

"Go meet your mother for lunch. I can see myself inside." And she walked away, leaving me standing there completely dumbfounded.

When I got in the car, the first person I thought of was Charlie, so I texted her.

Me: Do you think Nan could be senile? She's acting crazier than usual today.

Ladybug: I saw her yesterday, and she seemed fine. What did she do?

Me: She's suddenly concerned that I'm not happy, and she seems deeply concerned that I don't want to have fucking kids someday.

Ladybug: You seemed happy this morning. <winky face emoji>

Me: Yes. When I was on my knees for you, I was very fucking happy.

Ladybug: You did appear to be. So she thinks you aren't happy since you've been home?

Me: No. She thinks I'm happy at home, but not happy with my real life back in the city. What the fuck is that about? I'm very fucking happy. She called me charming and unfulfilled. Maybe she's had one too many weed brownies. I think she eats those with her Golden Girls book club.

Ladybug: I thought weed was supposed to make you happy not grumpy.

Me: Don't be practical, Ladybug. Am I charming and unfulfilled?

Ladybug: I don't think you're that charming. <laughing face emoji>

Ladybug: I'm kidding. Just wanted to mess with you. I think you're charming, and you seem fulfilled to me. At least since I've been around you again after all these years. Maybe she just wants you to give her great-grandbabies.

Me: That's a stupid reason to have kids.

Ladybug: That was not a charming response.

Me: Sorry. I don't like Nan being mad at me.

Ladybug: She'll come around. She loves you so much. Should we bring her dinner tonight?

Me: You want to go eat with my grandmother instead of eating takeout naked in your bed?

Ladybug: Hmmmm... I say we eat with her so you

feel better about it, and then we can get naked in my bed after.

Me: I'm both charmed and fulfilled by this plan.

Ladybug: See? You're already making strides. Go spend some time with your mom. See you later.

I almost wrote I love you.

I *wanted* to write I love you.

I never told a woman that I loved them outside of my mother, sister, and grandmother.

I never let anyone get close enough.

I needed to pull back. I was getting in too deep.

I didn't respond. Instead, I drove straight to the cemetery and spent the next forty minutes sitting on the grass beside Colt's grave.

"I fucking miss you, buddy," I said, picking at the grass.

I thought about all the fun we had together growing up.

Our time at the lake, the pranks we used to pull at school. I think a part of me died when Colt did. Maybe Nan was right. Maybe I hadn't been fully living. Hell, I didn't know anymore because I'd been living this way for so long. I let out a long breath and glanced down at my phone to check the time.

I tapped his gravestone twice before walking back to my car.

Colt and I used to say that we were going to open an architect firm in Honey Mountain together. He said I'd draw the pictures—and of course, he made light of it, which still made me laugh to this day—and he'd run the business side of it. That was back in the day when I thought this was the only place I'd ever live after college.

But everything had changed since then.

I drove to the hospital and found my mother waiting outside in the courtyard at a little bistro table with two sandwiches, chips, and drinks.

"I would have bought lunch," I said as she pushed to her feet, and I wrapped her in a hug.

"Well, seeing as my son paid off my house, I can afford to buy him lunch."

"You paid off your house, Mama. You worked your ass off to make those payments," I said, kissing her cheek and moving to the chair across from her as we both sat.

"How was Nan?" she asked before taking a bite of her ham sandwich.

"She was grumpy, actually. She's pissed at me for something."

"Are you keeping her up late? I don't know why you're sleeping on the couch at her place when you have a room at mine."

Maybe Nan was pissed that she felt like she needed to lie for me. Not knowing where I was spending my nights. She didn't need to. I never asked her to.

"I haven't been sleeping at Nan's. I've been hanging out with a friend, but I didn't want Jilly up in my business, so I'd rather not make it a thing."

She studied me. "Oh. Okay. I wonder why Nan lied?"

Because she thought she was protecting me.

"It's not a big deal. Apparently, she's pissed that I don't want to get married and have kids someday. She can't just be happy that Jilly and Garrett are going to give her all those things. She called me *unfulfilled*." I raised a brow and shook my head. I wasn't sure why I was so offended by the word.

"Are you?"

"No. I'm very fulfilled. Look at my fucking life," I grumped, and she gave me a displeased look. My mother wasn't big on f-bombs either.

"I'm looking, Ledger. I see a very successful man who works really hard to provide for his family. But we're all okay. You don't need to kill yourself for us." She studied me, and I reached for my iced tea and took a sip. "It is not your fault that your father left me."

What the hell was going on today? Why was everyone bringing this shit up all of a sudden?

"I don't do things for you, Nan, and Jilly because I feel like what Dad did is my fault. I do it because I love you." Obviously, I felt like shit, learning that the man had only married my mother because she was pregnant with me. But I wouldn't mention that. She didn't need to carry that.

"And we love you, too, but we worry about you just like you worry about us." She reached for my hand and smiled. "You need to know something, Ledger."

"What? You're pissed I don't want to get married and have kids, too?"

She chuckled. "No. But I need to tell you something. I knew about your father's affairs long before he actually admitted it. Long before you told me. I didn't know that you knew or that he asked you to lie for him until that day you let it all out, but that is not the reason that we got divorced. I knew he was messing around on me. I just didn't want to give up on my marriage. But he had an affair before you were even born. Hell, he only agreed to marry me because I got pregnant with you." She paused, and my mouth gaped open. She'd known this whole time?

"Why would you marry him if you knew what an asshole he was?"

She shrugged. "I loved him. I just kept thinking he would change over time. I was young and naïve, and I thought I could change him. But I want you to know this, because I think sometimes you have this ridiculous fear that you might be like him. But you aren't, Ledger. Your father would never care for his mom, sister, or grandmother the way that you always have. You are such a good man, and not because you're successful at your job, but because you have the biggest heart—even if you try to hide it from everyone. And I don't want you to punish yourself for his crimes, because that would be an absolute shame. We've all paid enough, haven't we?"

Her words struck a nerve.

Obviously, I worried that I could be as shallow and selfish as him if I were put in that position.

I always been okay with the idea of dating and having fun and keeping things light. I didn't like complications.

And I didn't know why everyone suddenly had a problem with that.

Since when was being a successful bachelor such a bad thing?

Maybe it was because Jilly was getting married.

Maybe it was because I was getting older.

But it did surprise me to learn that she'd known about the affairs before I had. Known that he only married her because she'd been pregnant with me. It took a little weight off my shoulders that I hadn't said anything sooner. That I wasn't responsible for her staying in a terrible marriage longer than she should have. That it had been her decision, not my doing.

"I'm not punishing myself. I promise. I'm happy... I am." I paused to look at her. "I went to see Colt today. It's the first time I've been to his grave since the day we said goodbye to him."

She reached for my hand. "I'm glad you went to see him. I know losing people we love is not fair, Ledger, but you have to remember that you're still here. And Colt would want you to be out there, living your life to the fullest. You know he'd be the first one to call your father out for wanting to come to the wedding when he hasn't been around in years." She chuckled.

"You're right about that. He would." I nodded.

Colt used to tease me about the way I looked at Charlotte when Jilly wasn't around. He always said he'd bet all the money he had in his wallet that I'd end up with her.

Of course, the dude never had any money in his wallet because he always spent it the minute he got it.

But he did know me well.

Maybe better than I knew myself.

Chapter 17

Charlotte

We stopped by and spent some time with Ledger's mom. I've always been close to Kalie Dane, as Jilly and I had been inseparable since we were kids.

"Are you sure you don't want to join us for dinner? We ordered enough pasta and pizza for a small country." Ledger chuckled. He seemed a little distracted tonight. I had to stay late at school, but I'd come straight here afterward because he seemed like he needed the support.

For whatever reason, he didn't like being called unfulfilled. His grandmother had struck a nerve.

"Well, you know I love spending time with you two, but..." She chewed on her thumbnail and looked away for a minute before turning back to face us. "I actually have a date tonight."

I couldn't help but smile because Kalie deserved to have

some fun. She'd always worked hard, and she'd been such an amazing mother to Jilly and Ledger.

"A date? With who?" Ledger stood there, dumbfounded, before narrowing his gaze at her and crossing his arms over his chest.

I shot him a look. The last thing she needed was to feel bad about this.

"I think it's great. You deserve to have some fun," I said.

"Thank you." She paused and raised her brow at her son before turning back to face me. "I think I do, too."

"I didn't mean it like that. I just want to make sure you're safe. Who's taking you out?" Ledger's tone was much softer now.

"Dr. Bickler. He's been asking me for a while, and I kept putting him off because of the wedding. But Jilly isn't coming home until tomorrow, and there's nothing I have to do tonight, so I said yes."

"Steven Bickler? I like that guy. I think that's great, Mama." Ledger wrapped his arms around his mother and kissed the top of her head.

"Thank you." She chuckled. "All right, that's enough about my dating life. Go fix things with Nan. I'm glad you've got Charlie to help you. Nan's always had a soft spot for you." She winked at me.

"Yeah. Yeah. Yeah. I know. Everyone loves Charlie because she's so sweet. And what am I? Fucking unfulfilled," he whined, and I rolled my eyes.

"You keep dropping those f-bombs in this house and I'll show you unfulfilled," Kalie said, trying to hide her smile, which made me laugh.

"Sorry, Mama. Have fun tonight."

"All right. I'm going to go change. He'll be here soon, and I'd rather not have you lurking around and intimidating him with that scowl." She kissed her son's cheek and wrapped her arms around me, hugging me tight before whispering close to my ear. "Thanks for being there for both of my kids."

I nodded, and she headed for her bedroom.

Ledger glanced down at his phone. "Food's here. Let's go try to schmooze the dirty bird, shall we?"

I chuckled and followed him out the door. The delivery guy was walking up the driveway, and Ledger took the bags from him, and we both thanked him before walking toward Nan's house and pushing the door open.

"Ah… my sweet girl is here. I'm so happy."

"I thought I was your favorite guy?" Ledger teased as he set the food on the kitchen table.

"You are. But you're also the *only* guy in my life, so don't get big-headed about it. The competition is weak."

My head fell back in laughter because Nan was probably the one person who could put Ledger in his place. He loved her fiercely, but she was a no-nonsense woman.

He started unpacking the bags, and I moved to the cabinet to grab three plates and some silverware.

"Why'd you bring so much food? Jilly and Garrett said they aren't coming back until tomorrow, and your mama has a date with Dr. McHottie."

"I feel good about this," I said as I sat in the seat beside Nan, and Ledger took the chair on the other side of me. "He's super nice, really good-looking, smart, and charming."

"But is he fulfilled?" Ledger asked as he scooped an

abnormally large amount of spaghetti on his plate.

I passed Nan the salad, trying hard not to laugh at his comment, and then handed her the lasagna next.

"He looks fulfilled to me." Nan forked some lettuce and popped it into her mouth.

"How can you tell?"

"I have a sick sense." She tapped her temple with her pink fingernail.

"It's *sixth* sense." Ledger raised a brow. "A sick sense would just mean you're mentally disturbed."

She chuckled, which made him smile, and I knew they were getting back on track. "I really struck a nerve with that unfulfilled comment, didn't I?"

"I think you did." I shrugged as I reached for a piece of pizza.

"I can hear you. And yes, you did. Because I'm very fulfilled," Ledger said over a mouthful of noodles.

"Well, I'll give you this, handsome... you do seem very happy lately. So, whatever you're doing, keep doing it. Must be all the walks." She smirked, and I could feel my cheeks heat.

But the fact that she was back to joking with him would make him happy.

"It's definitely all the walks. Especially when I take little breaks and get down on my knees to stretch," he said, and I started coughing because the conversation had me on edge.

Nan just started laughing as Ledger pushed to his feet and rubbed my back until I caught my breath and took a sip of water.

"Are you excited for the wedding?" I asked, desperate to change the subject.

"Yes. I feel like we've been talking about this wedding for so long, I'm excited to see it all done. And, I'm an old lady... apparently, this will be the only wedding I get to attend of my grandchildren. So, it's sort of a big deal."

Ledger set his glass down and shook his head with disbelief. "I don't know where this new concern about me getting married is coming from. You never cared before when I said I didn't want to get married. Why now?"

"I never believed you before. You know, I thought you were one of those wannabe playboys who was just selling his wild oats. I didn't know you actually believed it."

"It's *sowing* my wild oats. If I were selling them, that would make me a whore. I'm not a whore, Nan."

It was impossible not to laugh at how worked up he was over all of this.

"Who are you trying to convince, my boy? Me or you?"

"This is ridiculous. I'm done talking about this. And you sure as shit didn't seem to mind whoring me out to the ladies the other day at the Blue Hair Club." He raised a brow.

This was by far the most entertaining conversation I'd ever witnessed.

"Hey, I said they could look but not touch." She dabbed at her mouth with her linen napkin. She was dainty and sure did look like the perfect grandmother, but she could cuss like a sailor and dirty talk like Dylan.

"Oh, yeah? Well, I don't think Miranda Highwater got the memo. She ran those claws down my chest, and I considered going to the hospital for stitches because she nearly ripped me wide open."

Nan's head fell back just as a loud laugh escaped my lips.

They were going to be just fine.

We chatted for a little while longer until Nan announced that she had a bowel movement on the horizon and hurried us out the door. She made some smartass remark about Ledger dropping me off at home and heading over to his "special friend's" house, and she used her fingers to make air quotes and rolled her eyes. I had a hunch Nan knew something was going on, and that was why she was giving him such a hard time. That was why it was best we keep it to ourselves. Everyone would worry that I'd get hurt. It was almost annoying that no one worried that Ledger would get hurt. Obviously, Nan knew my feelings ran deep. But I still couldn't get myself to stop things from going any further. I was too far gone at this point.

Nan had insisted we take all the leftovers because she said she'd never be able to eat that much. Ledger and I hopped in the car and decided to drop the food off at the firehouse on our way to my house. He followed me up the stairs of the place I'd spent so much time throughout my life. My dad was the fire captain here, and it was his second home.

"Hey, Charlie, I wasn't expecting you." My father pushed to his feet and wrapped his arms around me. "What are you doing here, sweetheart?"

"We just ate with Nan, and Ledger ordered a ridiculous amount of food, so we thought we'd drop it off."

My father extended his hand to Ledger. "Good to see you, son. You ready for this wedding?"

Ledger set the bags on the table and nodded at my father. "Yeah. I think they're ready. We've got the rehearsal dinner tomorrow night and then the big day Saturday."

"I'm looking forward to seeing Jilly walk down that aisle.

And you have your last day of school tomorrow, so you'll be all done just in time." My father winked at me.

"Yeah. One more day. I can't believe it. Why is it so quiet around here?" I asked as my father pulled out some of the food and started piling it on a plate.

"They just went out on a medical call. I'm done for the night. I was just about to make dinner and head home, but I think I'll eat this and let those bastards fend for themselves."

Ledger sat down and chatted with my father while he ate. They've always gotten along well, and I thought Ledger respected the kind of father my dad was. The kind of man who always showed up. He always put his daughters first, and everyone in Honey Mountain knew it.

My dad asked endless questions about the projects he was working on, and Ledger was showing him some photos on his phone.

Dad cleaned up the dishes and put the leftovers in the fridge, and we all walked out together.

"Do you need a ride home?" my father asked when he noticed that we were both in my car.

"I'll drop him off. It's no problem," I said when Ledger's shoulders stiffened beside me.

"All right. Love you, sweetheart. Have a good last day of school tomorrow. I'll see you at the wedding on Saturday."

I kissed his cheek. "Love you, Daddy."

Ledger gave my dad one of those one-armed bro hugs, and we climbed into my car.

"Jesus. I feel like a dick," he whispered.

"Why?" I laughed as I pulled out of the parking lot and headed toward my house.

"Because I like your dad. He'd probably be fucking pissed if he knew what I was doing with his daughter."

"Well, Nan said you are a whore, so there is that." I pulled into my driveway and turned to look at him as I tried to hide my smile.

"You were probably right in keeping me your dirty little secret." He shrugged.

"Stop being a baby. Come on. Let's get inside. Maybe we should take a bath and relax a little."

He followed me up to the door, and when we pushed inside, he just pulled me into his arms and hugged me. He just held me there in the dark for the longest time.

I ran my hands up his back and buried my face in his neck.

After several minutes, he pulled back. "Let's take that bath, Ladybug."

I tied my hair on top of my head while he ran the water. I lit a candle and set it on the vanity and padded to the kitchen to get us each a glass of wine. When I came back into the bathroom, he was already in the tub. His two big arms were draped over the side of the clawfoot tub, and his dark hair was wet.

I handed him our two glasses of wine while I undressed, and then I turned out the lights, leaving just the flame from the candle to light the small space, and I slipped in, settling between his thighs. He handed me the glass, and I leaned back against him and took a sip.

"Seems like you're getting used to the whole bath thing, huh?" I said.

"Yeah. It seems like I'm getting used to lots of things that are new for me." His voice was gruff, not a tone of tease.

I just sipped my chardonnay and stayed quiet as I processed his words.

"Tell me about the future you see for yourself, Ladybug. I want to know."

"What? Why?"

"Because I care about you. And I want you to have the best. So, humor me. I'm interested in this big, full future you have planned out for yourself."

"Well, I've always liked the idea of marriage. You know, finding someone to share my life with." I let out a long breath and took another sip of wine. "And I've always wanted a big family. Growing up with my sisters was the best. I had built-in besties, and then I met Jilly, who is more like a sister to me than a friend."

"How many kids do you want to have?" he asked, and he sounded genuinely interested.

"I'd like to have three or four. I mean, it all depends on who I marry and if he wants as many as I do. I'm not opposed to compromise." I chuckled. "And this is all pending how long it takes me to find that person."

"You're young," he said, his free hand stroking my arm as he kissed the top of my head. "You've got plenty of time."

"Yeah. I'm not in a rush. I mean, look at me. I'm just experiencing my first fling at twenty-five years old, so I'm full of surprises." I tipped my head back to look at him, but he wasn't smiling. He looked so serious.

"I hope I haven't hurt you in any way. Fuck, Charlie, I'd never forgive myself if you regretted this."

I leaned over the tub and set my glass down on the floor before flipping over so I could face him. "Hey. I don't regret anything. This has been the best two weeks of my life, if I'm being honest." I could feel my eyes welling with emotion. Because it was true. The one person that truly *got me*—the one person who made me feel completely alive—was the one person I couldn't have. "I wouldn't trade this for anything. You haven't lied to me, Ledger. You were very upfront with me. I know who you are. I know that we want different things. And that's okay. Sure, it's going to be a little hard when you leave, because…" I looked away for a minute and tried to compose myself.

He swiped the pad of his thumb over my cheek to catch the single tear rolling down. I shook my head, needing to get it all out. "It's going to hurt because it has been amazing. Because we rekindled a friendship that I truly missed. You're such a big part of my heart, Ledger. So, saying goodbye to you is going to hurt, but we'll both be okay."

He froze at my words and stroked the hair that had broken free from my bun away from my face. "You've always been a big part of my heart, too, Ladybug. Hell, you're the best person I know. And I wish I were that guy, you know? The one you deserve. But what if we didn't make this so final? What if we just saw each other every few months? You could come to the city and stay for a weekend, and I could come visit you every once in a while?"

I studied his dark eyes, which were almost black right now. So tortured and pained. He was offering me the best he could, but it wasn't enough. And we both knew it.

"I'm not looking for random weekends, Ledger. I want a boyfriend. I want to be with someone who wants to be with me all the time. Not in between dates with his boss's daughter."

"I'm not seeing her anymore. You know that."

"But you're not offering me forever. I don't hear you saying that you won't date anyone else. That it's just you and me. And that's a deal breaker for me. I want monogamy. I want a man who can't live without me. Not someone who just wants to sleep with me every other month for two days."

He closed his eyes and leaned his head back against the tub. I let my cheek rest on his chest, and we sat there in silence.

"It's never just been about the sex, Charlie, and you know it. But I'm not wired that way. And if I fucked it up with you, if I hurt you—I'd never forgive myself."

Things were already too complicated. This was so much more than a fling. So much more than we originally planned.

And I'd be okay.

But I couldn't drag this out for years, hoping and waiting that he'd change his mind someday.

I wouldn't do that, not even for Ledger.

"Let's just enjoy these last few days and not complicate things. I'll be all right after you go. I'm a little tougher than you think."

"You're the strongest person I know."

Ledger got out of the tub and helped me out before wrapping me in a towel and carrying me to the bedroom. He dried me off and then dried himself. He pulled on his boxer briefs, and I slept in his T-shirt that had become my favorite.

We didn't kiss or have sex.

He just pulled me into his arms and wrapped me up.

We didn't joke or even talk.

I just slept with his arms wrapped around me, breathing him in.

• • •

The next morning was an absolute shitstorm. I overslept and was woken up by Dylan banging on my door. I hurried to open it to find her there with a coffee and a donut, which had been something she started last year on the last day of school. She'd gone by Honey Bee's early just for me.

"Hey, I was on my way to work, and I figured you'd just be heading out." She looked me up and down, her eyes focused on the oversized shirt I was wearing.

I took a sip of coffee and reached for the phone in her hand. "Oh my gosh. I've got ten minutes until I have to leave for work. I love you. Thank you for this, but I need to get dressed quickly."

But, of course, my sister didn't take the hint. This was Dylan Thomas, after all. Awkward situations were her specialty.

"I have five minutes. Let me help you." She took a bite of the donut that I had just pulled out of the bag. "Damn. Yours is better than mine. Typical," she said, pushing past me and heading for my bedroom. I took a bite of my donut and closed my eyes, preparing for what was about to happen.

"Hey, Dilly," Ledger purred as he climbed out of my bed, wearing nothing but boxer briefs as he pulled his jeans on.

"Hey yourself, Ledger Dane. Looks like someone had a slumber party, huh?" she asked, and I groaned as I handed him the donut and the coffee.

"He just needed a place to crash. We were up late working on the wedding."

"Do not insult me, Charlie. I can sniff out sexual tension a mile away. Hell, I walked into Honey Bee's this morning, and there was a girl I'd never seen before standing at the counter, and she kept making eyes at this dude who must have been from out of town, and I swear they are probably doing it right now in his car. I mean, there was some serious heat coming off them." She fanned her face and then looked between us. "But you two could start a forest fire."

She marched into my closet and handed me the white and pink maxi dress that I'd just gotten last weekend. I nodded and hurried into the bathroom and closed the door.

"So," Dylan said, and I tried to listen while frantically changing my clothes. I pulled my hair into a high bun, which was going to raise all sorts of questions for Darwin, because he always got flustered when I wore my hair up for some strange reason. I quickly rubbed on some moisturizer and fumbled through my makeup while trying to hear what they were saying on the other side of the door. "A sleepover, huh? When are you going back?"

"I'm leaving Sunday," Ledger said.

"Ah, so this is almost done, huh?" my sister pressed.

He didn't answer because he didn't want to betray my trust. But then he surprised me when I opened the door and hurried out into the room. His eyes locked with mine, and he turned back to Dylan. "I don't know that it's ever been done."

My stomach dipped at his words, but I pretended I didn't hear him. I reached for the donut and took another bite, noting that he was now dressed.

Dylan leaned over and kissed my cheek. "You're full of surprises, Charlie. I'll call you later."

"Thanks for the donut and the coffee. I love you. We've

got the rehearsal dinner tonight, but I'll call you after."

She hugged Ledger goodbye and made her way out the door to her car and winked at me. "I hope Darwin likes the smell of sugary donuts. Love you."

Ledger grabbed his car keys, and his gaze locked with mine. "You're going to be late. I'll drop you off and pick you up."

I hurried outside and slipped into the car, then he came around the driver's side and got behind the wheel. We were quiet on the drive to school.

"I'm sorry if that's going to cause you trouble with Dilly," he said before clearing his throat.

"It's okay." I turned to face him when we pulled in front of the school. "She already knew something was going on. Our time is up anyway, Ledger. Your sister is back today. She's spending the night with me at my place after the rehearsal dinner. And then tomorrow's the wedding. You leave Sunday, right?"

He ran a hand over the scruff that peppered his jaw. "Yep. Can I spend tomorrow night with you after the wedding? Jilly and Garrett will be staying at the hotel."

"Let's play it by ear, okay? I'll see you after school." I stepped out of the car, needing air and space and a minute to pull myself together.

He rolled the window down. "I'll see you in a few hours, Ladybug."

I just nodded and held up my hand before walking away.

Because that was exactly what he'd be doing in two days.

Chapter 18

Ledger

Fuck me. She was pulling away, and I couldn't blame her.

That talk we had last night had left my mind spinning.

I didn't know what was wrong with me. Why commitment scared the shit out of me. I dialed Nan. She'd always been my go-to when I needed an ear.

"Hey there. I'm in a much better mood today, if that's what you're calling about." She chuckled.

"Remember back in the day, after Dad left, you'd put on your therapist hat and talked me through things?" I pulled over near the park and let out a long breath.

"Of course. My therapist hat is my favorite next to my dirty bird hat. Tell me what's going on."

"You still believe in patient confidentiality, right?" I asked.

"Ledger, you know that you can trust me always. Unless I'm worried about you hurting yourself, I will take your dirty secrets to my grave. I will love you in spite of your bad choices."

"Jesus. I didn't kill anyone, Nan. I'm just struggling with a few things. Coming home has been—I don't know. There's just a lot running through my head."

"Start at the beginning."

I told Nan about the deal with my father. How he basically blackmailed me to agree to walk Jilly down the aisle. She didn't say a word; she just listened.

"Well, they always say that when people show you who they are, you should just believe them. He continues to be the same man he's always been. But you, my boy. You continue to be better than you think you are. That was very big of you to agree to his terms, because I know it must have killed you to give him what he wanted. But love has a way of making us do crazy things, right?"

"I guess it does. I just hope he doesn't disappoint her, you know? I mean, how in the hell are they on a vacation together?"

"It's all out of your control, Ledger. These are decisions that your sister is making for herself. You agreeing to design his home so that he'll give her what she wants is the decision that you made. I don't know that I would have done it, but I respect that you would. That you'd go to that length to protect her from knowing who he really is."

"Thank you."

"So, what else is running through that thick skull of yours? Is this about Harold pressuring you to get back together with Jessica? Is she still reaching out?" I'd filled Nan in on that situation a few days ago.

"Yeah, that shit is still going on, too, but I don't really care about that. This is about Charlie."

There was a long pause, and then she spoke. "About all the time you've been spending with her?"

I cleared my throat. I wasn't going to tell her all the details, but I could still open up enough to get her advice. "Yep. We've been spending almost every day together since I've gotten home. I mean, obviously, we have wedding stuff to do, but it's more than that."

"You don't say?" I could tell she was smiling just by the tone of her voice.

"Don't get all smug. Pretend I'm a normal client, please."

"All right. Well, I'd say it's noticeable to me because you've always liked your space so much. Always had so many boundaries when it came to your dating life. I think you had that two-day-a-week rule with Jessica, didn't you?" She laughed, and I rolled my eyes.

"What can I say? I like my space. But not with Charlie. I think she's the one trying to put up some boundaries now because she knows I'm leaving, and I don't know... I don't like it. I asked if we could still, um..." I cleared my throat again because I didn't want to share too much. "See one another occasionally. You know, maybe get together every few months."

"What did she say?"

"She shut me down. You know Charlie. She wants the whole package. The husband and the kids... that whole sappy future that works out for less than half of those who try it."

"Such a cynic." She let out a long sigh. "Well, you told her what you were willing to give, and that wasn't enough for her. Sounds fair."

"So, what? It just ends? We just go back to our lives?"

"Isn't that what you want?" she asked.

"Yes, of course. I just didn't expect to like being with her so much, I guess." It wasn't just the sex, either, though I wasn't about to tell Nan that. Not even close. I was taking goddamn bubble baths, for God's sake. I was not a bubble bath type of guy. But I didn't even mind it. Charlotte just kind of got me. She called me out on my shit. She supported me when I needed it.

"That's not a bad thing, Ledger. You know it's okay to change the rules, right? Just because you thought you wanted your life to be a certain way doesn't mean that can't change."

I let out a long breath. "I'm just getting in my head. It would never work. I'd fuck it up. I'll go back to my life, and get back into my routine, and she'll do the same."

"It may not be as easy to do as you think," she said, and there was no tease in her voice now.

"It'll be fine, Nan. Thank you for talking to me."

"You're my special guy. I'll always be here for you, my boy."

"All right. I love you. I'll see you tonight at the rehearsal."

I ended the call and drove to my mother's house. Jilly was due home later today, and I was curious to see how things went with my father. The house was quiet when I got there, and I took a quick shower and changed my clothes. I texted Mom to find out how her date went, and she sent back several heart eye emojis, which I was guessing meant it went well. She said she'd meet me at the house at five tonight, and she and Nan would drive over with me to the Honey Mountain Country Club for the rehearsal.

I'd just gone to the kitchen to make some toast when the door flew open. My sister's face was puffy and red. Garrett stood behind her, making a face at me that let me know things weren't good.

"Ledger Dane, is there something you want to tell me?"

"I don't know. Why don't you tell me what's going on?" I asked as I moved closer and placed a hand on her shoulder. My heart raced because if she'd found out about Charlotte and me and was this upset, then we'd royally fucked up.

"Dad's the devil, isn't he?" she asked; her bottom lip started to quiver.

"I think that's a fair assessment. What happened?"

"Brenda told me that you were designing their house for them. And I knew you'd never do that by choice because you despise the man. And then I remember him making me call you to ask you to call him—the whole bullshit excuse about Brenda's mom being sick. Guess what, Ledger?"

"What, Jilly Bean?"

"Brenda's mom isn't even alive!" she shouted and stormed through the kitchen before pulling out a chair and sitting down, burying her face in her hands.

I glanced at Garrett, and he shrugged before moving to sit beside my sister. "Jilly asked her if her mom was even sick when she started to put things together, and Brenda seemed genuinely out of the loop. She said her mom had passed a few years ago."

"Fuck." I pulled out a chair on the other side of my sister and turned to face her. "I'm sorry that he's such a dick. I truly am. I don't want this to spoil your special day."

Tears dripped from her eyes, and she blinked a few times

and looked at me. "Stop apologizing for him, Ledger. I should be apologizing to you."

"For what?" I asked, shaking my head.

"You've been more than a brother to me. You've been an amazing father to me all these years. You were there at my graduation from both high school and college. You've helped me so much financially, emotionally, and in every other freaking way that a father should. And I was too goddamn blind to see it. Thank you for being such a good man. It's the reason that I found myself a good man." She smiled and then winked at Garrett before turning back to me. "Will you walk me down the aisle tomorrow, Ledger?"

"Of course, I will. I'll walk you wherever you need me to, as many times as you need me to." I pulled her in my arms and hugged her.

"Just down the aisle the one time should be enough. No need to do it more than once," Garrett said, and we all started laughing.

She pulled back and swiped at her face. "How are you going to get out of doing that house now?"

"Don't worry about the house, Beans. It'll all be fine. No more crying. You're getting married tomorrow. Let's start acting like it."

She pushed to her feet. "Okay. No more tears. That is the last time I cry over that man. I've got a rehearsal to get ready for."

Jilly left to go take a shower, and Garrett and I put on a pot of coffee and sat at the table.

"How bad was it?" I asked, keeping my voice low.

"It was pretty ugly. He ended up admitting that he made

that deal with you. Jilly told him she didn't want him at the wedding, and he said he was fine with it because he had a contract from you, so if she didn't want him there, it was no skin off his back."

"He's such a fucking asshole, right?"

"Yeah. He really is." Garrett sipped his coffee. "You know that everything your sister said about you is true, right? You're the reason that she and your mom are actually okay. You've been the man of the house longer than you even know. You stepped up, Ledger. And you were a fucking teenager when all this shit went down. And even after you lost your best friend, you continued to show up for them. It's honorable." His blue eyes were wet with emotion.

His words hit me hard because I wanted to be that for them. I wanted to take away some of the hurt and make them feel safe and not completely abandoned.

"Thank you, brother. That means a lot to me."

Garrett cranked his neck to look down the hall and lowered his voice. "What's really going on with you and Charlie?"

I didn't know how to answer him, because I honestly didn't know what was going on with us. A hell of a lot more than I expected, that much I knew.

"It's complicated."

He nodded. "Don't run, Ledger. She's one of the good ones. Hell, she's amazing. Why does it have to be complicated? You know Jilly won't care as long as you don't hurt her, right?"

I scrubbed a hand down my face. "We want different things. We don't live in the same fucking place, for starters. She wants the fairy tale, man. I am not that guy."

"Says who?" He raised a brow. "You've always been so

vocal about not wanting anything serious, but look at you. You're a family guy, dude, whether you want to admit it or not. Look how you've stepped up for your sister, your mother, and your grandmother. You might not want to believe it, but you actually are the guy on the white horse. You've just been hiding your horse when it comes to yourself."

My mouth gaped open. "Are you drunk?"

He barked out a laugh. "Not even a little. I've had two waters and a coffee this morning. Nice try. Just calling it as I see it."

I heard the bathroom door open, and Jilly called out for Garrett.

"Thanks for the talk, brother. I'll see you tonight. One more day and you get to marry the love of your life."

"I'm so ready." He clapped me on the shoulder and left the kitchen.

I spent a few hours working on the specs for the project Harold had just sent over. I had lunch with Nan, and she didn't bring up our conversation from this morning because she respected the doctor-patient relationship. Instead, we talked about the wedding and what a piece of garbage my father was for doing what he did to Jilly.

I got a text from Charlie saying she'd be off in a few minutes, and I headed over to the school. I filled her in on what happened with Jilly and my father, and she was quiet as she listened.

"I'm glad you're walking her down the aisle. That's the way it should be. You've been more of a father to Jilly than he ever was," she said, and I pulled into her driveway.

That seemed to be a common thread today.

My father had sent several texts, letting me know that he'd been uninvited to the wedding but that he expected me to hold up my end of the deal.

I'd yet to respond to him, nor did I plan to deal with his bullshit until after the wedding.

"Do you want me to drive you tonight?"

"I don't think that's a good idea." She shrugged. "We've kept this thing a secret all this time, so why risk blowing it right before it's about to end, anyway?"

I nodded. But I wasn't ready for it to end.

"I thought we said if we were both without dates, we'd attend the wedding together?" I asked, reaching for her hand.

She sucked in a breath. "We'll be there together, no matter what. We're the only two people in the wedding party. So, consider it a date, just due to the fact that you're kind of stuck with me as you have to walk me down the aisle."

She tried to make light of it, but there was something in her tone. She was pulling away. Protecting herself. Preparing for what we both knew was coming.

"I've never been stuck with you, Ladybug." My thumb stroked the inside of her palm. "I know you're with Jilly tonight, but please let me stay with you tomorrow night."

Fuck. I sounded like a desperate, pussy-whipped asshole, but I didn't even care. I wanted every last second with her. She'd already shut me down for trying to keep it going after our arrangement came to an end, but at least I could fight for tomorrow.

"Sure." She smiled and leaned forward, kissing my cheek before hopping out of the car. "Thanks for picking me up."

"Of course!" I shouted as she walked up her driveway

toward her door. She waved, but she didn't look back, and my chest squeezed.

I'd let things go too far, and now I was fucked.

Charlotte Thomas was preparing for me to leave.

And I was the one who wasn't prepared.

• • •

"So, Ledger, I think that worked," Caroline, the wedding planner, said after making me practice the ridiculous routine twice. "Just like you did here, you're going to walk Charlie down the aisle and then go back to get Jilly."

It wasn't all that complicated. It was two trips down the aisle.

My sister seemed completely over what happened with our father, and she was busy bossing everyone around. My eyes scanned the space and found Charlie talking to Garrett's cousin, Robby, and my blood boiled.

"Yeah, I got it," I said, but my gaze never left Charlotte and Robby. He was laughing and standing way too close, and my hands fisted at my sides.

"Okay, guys. We're good to go. Let's go eat." My sister waved her hand above her head for everyone to leave the outdoor area where they'd be saying their vows tomorrow and head inside for dinner.

Nan reached for my elbow, and my mom found the other side, and I led them both into the clubhouse. We had a few aunts, uncles, and cousins fly in for the big day, and they were all joining us for dinner tonight. Garrett's family invited out-of-town family members to join us tonight, as well, so we had around twenty-five people eating together.

When we made our way to the long table that they had set up in a private room off the dining area, I glanced over to see where Charlotte was. That butt-kissing cousin of Garrett's was staying close to her, and it was pissing me off.

Who the fuck was this guy?

I raised an eyebrow at her when her gaze locked with mine, and I pulled out a chair for her. "I'd like to sit next to you so we can discuss some things about our toasts tomorrow."

She smiled, but the douchedick made a face. "It looks like it's open seating, so I'll sit right here so we can continue our conversation. I want to hear more about these cutie patootie kindergarteners of yours."

Cutie patootie?

Are you fucking kidding me with this shit? This guy was pulling out all the stops.

She just smiled and took the seat beside me, while that ass-kissing motherfucker sat in the open seat beside her.

Nan was on the other side of me, and Jilly and Garrett were sitting across from us with my mother. Everyone else settled into the empty seats.

Our glasses were filled with wine, and there was a set menu just like there'd be tomorrow, and we quickly chose our entrées. Nan was talking my ear off about some big news down at her ladies' club. Apparently, they'd hired a new water aerobics instructor named Bull, who was in his late fifties, and all the girls were enjoying the view.

Did I want to hear about this? Hell no. But it was Nan, and I'd do my best to act like I gave a damn.

Mind you, the dude sitting on the other side of Charlotte hadn't come up for air. He was talking nonstop and asking endless questions. I looked up to see Garrett watching me with a mischievous smirk on his face as he sipped his wine.

He was enjoying this. The fucker.

I was his best man, for God's sake.

He shrugged and set his glass down, sending me a message without actually speaking.

Shit or get off the pot, dumbass.

Not everyone wanted to get off the pot. But that didn't mean I wanted her to be sitting here talking to this needy bastard.

Our salads were set down in front of us, and thankfully, Aunt Shirley was interested in Nan's story about Bull and his pelvic thrusting exercises that he'd introduced to them this morning.

"I hate to interrupt this riveting conversation," I said, placing an arm on Charlotte's shoulder. "But I need to discuss our timeline for tomorrow. Can you give us a minute, Robby?" I shot him a death glare, and he wiped his mouth with his napkin and nodded.

Thankfully, he turned his attention to Garrett and started firing off multiple questions about the wedding venue.

"What is your problem?" She kept her voice low and didn't hide her anger.

"My problem is that he's hanging all over you."

"So, what, Ledger? What do you care?"

What the fuck? She wasn't even feeling bad about it?

"He doesn't even live here," I hissed, glancing over to make sure no one was listening. Thankfully, my sister was deep in conversation with my cousin Janey, and the loud chatter around us made it easy to speak.

"Neither do you, remember?"

Well, that shut me up, at least for a minute. "Touché. But I'm here now."

She rolled her eyes. "You're being ridiculous."

I hated how distant she was being. I craved her warmth. I wanted those eyes on me. My hand found her thigh under the table, and it slipped beneath the hem of her dress. She sucked in a breath, and her cheeks pinked just a little. No one else would notice, but I noticed everything about Charlotte Thomas.

The way her dimples popped when she smiled. The way her eyes turned from brown to green, depending on the lighting. The way her breaths came faster when we were together. The way her nipples pebbled beneath her dress every time I touched her.

My hand climbed up, and I studied her.

She didn't stop me.

"Ledger," she whispered, and I didn't miss the desire in her voice. The need that I felt when I was near her. She felt it, too.

"Do you not like your salad?" Robby asked, bringing his attention back to her, and it took all my strength not to throw my fork at his face.

"Oh, yes. I was just talking about my speech," Charlie said, her voice gruff as she reached for her fork, and my fingers found her damp panties between her legs. I stroked her a few times, wishing like hell that I could carry her away right now. That it could just be her and me.

Her legs parted a little bit more, allowing me access as the fucker on the other side of her started the conversation back up.

"Did you always want to be a teacher?" he asked, and I slipped my finger beneath her panties, and she dropped her fork on the plate and quickly reached for it again.

"Yes. Yes. Yes, I did," she said. Her words were a little breathy, but he didn't seem to notice.

"You see, that's the same way I feel about being an accountant." He took a bite of salad and then continued. "I love numbers. I'm a numbers guy."

She nodded as I slipped a finger inside her, and she startled but kept her composure. I glanced around, and everyone was talking at the same time. The wine was flowing, the conversation animated, and all I wanted was to make the girl beside me come apart beneath my touch. I cleared my throat and moved my chair a little closer as I slipped another finger inside. Her hands looked like they were resting on the edge of the table, but upon closer look, she was gripping the white cloth covering the wood table, pretending to be completely entranced by the dude beside her.

I moved in and out. Slowly at first and then quickly. Feeling her clench around my fingers had my dick so hard I knew I'd have to sit here for a while after I made her finish before I'd be able to stand up. Her knuckles were white, and her chest was rising a little faster now, but numbnuts next to her didn't miss a beat.

"I won every math competition known to man when I was in high school."

"Mmmhmmm," Charlie said, tucking her lips into her teeth and trying to stay composed as I moved faster. "That's very exciting, Robby."

A slight moan left her mouth, and her head fell back against the chair.

"Are you okay?" he asked with concern.

Yeah, welcome to the ballgame, douchedick.

"Yes," she whispered as she clenched against my fingers and rode out every last bit of pleasure, all while keeping herself completely composed. It was the hottest thing I'd ever fucking seen in my life. "Sorry. I have a little charley horse in my foot. I just need a minute."

I smiled. She was so fucking sexy. I slipped my hand out from between her legs and moved it back to my lap.

"Do you want me to *rub it* for you?" I purred.

She glanced over at me, her eyes sated, and the corners of her lips turned up.

"I'm okay. Thanks, though."

"Anytime, Ladybug."

Chapter 19

Charlotte

Oh.

My.

God.

My entrée got set in front of me, and I could barely pull myself together enough to reach for my fork. My body was still tingling.

I just had an orgasm at Jilly's rehearsal dinner.

From her playboy brother.

This had to be an all-time maid of honor low.

But I didn't even care because I was so relaxed.

And the guy on the other side of me was still talking about his 401K, and I was trying to feign interest.

But the guy on the other side of me—Mr. Orgasm himself—pushed his chair back and leaned down close to my ear. "I'll be right back. I'm going to go wash my hands, even though I'd prefer to never wash them again."

He winked and walked off.

"So, I'm hoping you're taking a good percentage of your paycheck out each month to put toward your future. If you want any financial advice, I'm your man." Robby cut into his steak and remained quiet for less than fifteen seconds before turning to me. "Hey, why don't we set up a Zoom call next week and work on your financial portfolio?"

I nodded. "Sure. We can do that."

I leaned back in my chair to glance down the hall to look for Ledger. When he came strolling into view, my breath caught in my throat. Tall. Lean. Broad shoulders and a big ole grin spread across his handsome face as his dark gaze locked with mine.

I turned back to face Robby when he asked me about the equity in my home.

"Um, well, homes have been going up in Honey Mountain, so I've definitely got some equity."

"Ah, I see we're still having a riveting conversation," Ledger said under his breath, and I chuckled. Garrett jumped in and started asking Robby questions about selling the condo because he and Jilly were looking for a new house, and I was grateful for the reprieve.

"You were gone to the bathroom for a while. Everything okay?" I quirked a brow.

"Ah, are you keeping tabs on me?"

I reached for my glass of wine. "No. I just noticed you were gone longer than usual."

"Well, let's just say that I had a little situation that I had to take care of. I certainly don't want to be sitting next to Nan with a raging boner."

I coughed as the chardonnay went down the wrong tube, but I quickly pulled myself together. "Glad you got that under control. And thanks for being so helpful earlier."

He barked out a laugh. "Happy to give you a hand. Literally and figuratively."

"Is this dirty talk going on over here?" Nan whisper-shouted as she leaned in with her cheek resting on Ledger's chest. "I thought I heard someone say boner?"

"Well, if there was, you certainly managed to be a major buzzkill, you dirty bird," Ledger said.

"We're just talking about Ledger's stomach issues." I set my wine glass down and tried to hide my smile. "Apparently, he's all backed up, and he's very uncomfortable."

"Ah, yes. I definitely need a release."

Now it was my turn to laugh. "I'll bet you do."

Nan turned away when Garrett's mom asked her about her garden, but she winked at us before she did.

"Maybe you could help me out, seeing as I was so helpful to you."

"I would, but I promised to talk about my retirement plan with my financial planner over here," I teased.

He leaned close to my ear, his lips grazing the sensitive skin there and sending chills down my back. "Do you like him, Ladybug?"

I shrugged because just having Ledger this close again had my mouth going dry.

"Because I like you," he whispered.

I chuckled, and when I looked up, I locked eyes with Jilly, but she turned away quickly. It was a reminder that we weren't alone. Ledger must have caught the move because he straightened, as well, and started eating.

I spent the next hour listening to Robby explain the benefits of investing in the stock market young and considering a college fund for the children that I didn't even have. My eyes were heavy and tired. I think it was the combo of the wine, the mid-dinner orgasm, and the lengthy, one-sided financial discussion from Robby.

Did Garrett really think that this would be a good setup? I mean, I'd barely gotten a word in edgewise, not that I'd even tried. I was doing my best to listen, all while keeping my eye on Ledger Dane. We'd all moved to the bar area for an after-dinner drink, and a cocktail waitress had taken in interest in him while I'd been cornered by Garrett's cousin once again.

"I'm so sorry to interrupt, Robby. But I need to take care of something real quick. Please excuse me." I hurried over to where Nan sat talking to Garrett's parents, and I whispered in her ear, "Do you still keep those antacids in your purse?"

She smiled at me and unzipped her handbag. "Of course, I do, my girl. You never want to get caught somewhere with a gas bubble in your belly."

Garrett's father, Doug, barked out a laugh as she handed me a couple antacids, and when I saw the bottle of anti-diarrhea medicine, I helped myself to two of those.

I kissed her cheek. "You're the best."

"No argument there," she said as she turned her attention back to the sweet couple.

I walked by Jilly and Garrett, who were deep in conversation with his uncle and his aunt, and she leaned over and whispered in my ear, "Have you had enough investment talk?"

I raised a brow. "You know me so well."

"Shall I come save you in a few minutes, and we can head home and do face masks?"

"Yes, please. I just have to give this to your brother, and then I promised Robby I'd be back over. So please don't wait too long," I said, looking around to make sure no one else could hear me.

I sauntered over to Ledger, whose eyes were fixed on me the entire time I closed the distance between us. The girl beside him seemed unaware as she continued talking. I'd caught him looking at me nonstop over the last forty minutes since we'd moved to the bar.

"Hey," I said. "I'm so sorry to interrupt."

"Never apologize for that, Ladybug."

The woman beside him was glaring at me, so she clearly didn't feel the same about my intrusion.

"I just knew how bad that diarrhea was, and I was worried about you. Take two of these, and hopefully, you won't have a bad case of the shits in an hour." I held out the pills, and instead of looking annoyed like I expected him to, a wide grin spread across his handsome face. Like he loved every minute of this.

"You are always thinking of me, aren't you?"

"I wouldn't say that. I just had to sit next to you at the table, and let's just say you didn't hide your discomfort very well." I waved my hand over my nose, and the woman chuckled and said she'd leave us be and walked away.

"I don't think you minded sitting next to me at that table. I can't put my *finger* on it, but I think I helped make this night very... pleasurable for you."

My head fell back in laughter, and I wanted to kiss him so badly it was almost painful. "I'm sorry I can't pay back the favor tonight."

"You want to, though, don't you?" he said, and I squeezed my thighs together because I couldn't stop myself from reacting to him.

"I do." I moved even closer.

"There you are. I was worried about you." Robby moved to stand between us.

"Oh, I'm sorry," I said, stepping back and putting some distance between Ledger and me. I'd sort of lost my head a little with him tonight. We hadn't been in a crowd together since we'd started whatever it was that we'd started. So, I wasn't used to not being able to touch or kiss him when I wanted to. But this was a good wake-up call because after tomorrow, I wouldn't be doing any of that. "Ledger had a stomachache, so I went to find him some medicine."

"That's very thoughtful. And very practical. Instead of buying your own on the way home, Ledger, she just saved you some hard-earned money."

"She's very thoughtful that way." Ledger smiled just as Jilly walked over and put a hand on my shoulder.

"Garrett's ready to drop us off at your house if you're ready?"

"Yes, of course."

Jilly's eyes locked with her brother's, even though she was speaking to Garrett's cousin. "Sorry to steal her away, Robby."

"Not a problem. I will be at your beck and call tomorrow at the wedding," Robby said, as he used his hand to do some sort of royal gesture, where he half-bowed and tucked his head down before waving me along. He really was a sweet guy, but it was never going to work for me. Not when Ledger was in the room. And in my mind.

And technically, in my pants.

"She'll be very busy tomorrow. She's the maid of honor," Ledger hissed, and I could feel my cheeks pink.

"Her duties are over fairly early." Jilly slipped her hand beneath my elbow. "Good night, gentlemen."

We made our way through the bar, saying a quick goodbye to everyone before stepping outside while we waited for Garrett to pull up in his car.

"Did you really think that setup was going to work?"

"Are you kidding? No. He's such a nice guy, though. But it's going to take a very patient person to put up with that finance talk. The last time we visited, I fell asleep at the kitchen table. But Garrett thinks he's so brilliant, and he loves you, so he means well."

I laughed. "Then let's not break his heart. Robby doesn't live here, so we can just chalk it up to a distance issue."

"You're such a good friend." She kissed my cheek as Garrett pulled up, and we climbed in his car.

He didn't ask anything about Robby on the drive home, which surprised me. In fact, he hadn't mentioned his cousin in over a week. Maybe he'd forgotten about it.

I mean, the man was getting married tomorrow.

When we arrived at my house, I left them outside to say their goodbyes, and I made my way inside and started a pot of tea for Jilly and me.

She came in and closed the door behind her. We drank

our tea and talked about all the characters that had been at the rehearsal dinner.

"I think Garrett's grandfather was flirting with Nan."

I gasped. "Really? How did she react?"

"Like a cat in heat. She was pouring on all the charms and flirting like a fool."

I chuckled. "I love her so much."

"Me, too." She yawned.

"Come on. Let's get our face masks on and clean up for bed. Big day tomorrow."

We washed our faces and put on a face mask while we both tied our hair up in a bun. We took a selfie and sent it to Dylan, because we knew she'd love it, and then we rinsed our faces and climbed into bed because it was late.

"Thanks for letting me sleep over the night before my wedding," Jilly said, as she lay beside me beneath the covers. The room was dark, and I could hear the crickets singing outside through the window.

"Of course. Big day tomorrow."

"Yeah. I was just thinking about how many times we had sleepovers growing up and would lie in bed talking about our wedding days."

I chuckled. It was true. Jilly and I had sleepovers every single weekend from fifth grade on, trading off from my house to hers.

"And now, you're getting the wedding of your dreams."

"I am. No thanks to my father, but luckily, I have the best brother in the world," she said.

My stomach flipped at the mention of him. What he'd done to me with all those people sitting around us, completely unaware of what was going on beneath the table. I squeezed my eyes closed at the memory because he knew my body like no other.

"He's the best," I whispered.

"How about you, Charlie? Do you still think about your wedding day?" she asked.

"Not really. I mean, I'm not dating anyone, so I haven't really thought about it in a long time."

I was lying because I'd been daydreaming about Ledger lately, and I knew that it was wrong. I knew that this was temporary, but I couldn't help myself from wanting it to be more. I was trying really hard to pull away and prepare myself for what was coming—but it wasn't easy. I knew it was going to hurt like hell.

She remained quiet, and I thought she'd fallen asleep.

"You know you can tell me anything, right?" she asked, and her voice cracked a little bit, which startled me.

"What? Of course, I do."

"I love you forever, Charlie. There's nothing that would change that." My heart raced, and guilt flooded every inch of my body because I'd kept this huge secret from my best friend. I'd never kept anything from her before, aside from the crush I'd had on Ledger.

Did she know?

"I know you do. And you know I love you forever, too, right? Where is this coming from?"

I swear I held my breath as I waited for her to respond. Waited for her to call me out. At this point, it wasn't even about what was going on with Ledger and me that I was worried about—it was the fact that it was her wedding day tomorrow, and this was not the time to talk about that.

To talk about me and my heart.

"It's not about anything in particular," she said, and my shoulders relaxed. "I know I've been so crazed over this wedding, and so many things are changing. I just wanted to say it. You're the best friend a girl could ever ask for."

"So are you," I whispered. "I love you. Now get some sleep. You're getting married tomorrow."

"Love you more," she said.

And I rolled over and squeezed my eyes closed, praying for sleep because I realized that I'd had Ledger in my bed every night for the last week. And I didn't like sleeping without him.

And I knew that was a recipe for disaster.

• • •

Nan, Kalie, and I sat on the couch, watching Jilly slip into her wedding dress. Honey Mountain Country Club was a popular wedding venue in town, and it had a suite that we used to get ready. There was an entire wall of mirrors, and Jilly twirled around. She looked stunning. The lacy, strapless gown hugged her curves, and the tiny pearl beads covered the bodice. A long tulle train puddled behind her. Her brown hair was braided along the side of her head and twisted into a gorgeous chignon at the nape of her neck.

"Jilly." I hurried to my feet after she turned to face us. "You look gorgeous."

I'd seen her in her dress at her fittings, but seeing her all done up on her special day—it was almost overwhelming.

"My sweet girl." Kalie had her phone out and was snapping pictures of her daughter. "You are a vision."

"Well, Garrett is going to want to get you out of that dress as soon as possible. Oh, boy," Nan muttered. "You are all woman."

"Mother!" Kalie's eyes doubled in size before her head tipped back in a fit of laughter. "Let's try to behave until after the wedding, okay?"

"What fun is that?" Nan whispered in my ear, and I chuckled.

Kalie was adjusting the pearl buttons on the back of Jilly's dress, and Nan pulled me aside. "How are you doing?"

"I'm great. It's a special day, and I couldn't be happier for Jilly and Garrett."

"Me, too." She nodded. "Your day is coming, too, my girl. I promise."

I laughed because I had no idea what she was talking about, and I was still a little uncomfortable with the idea of her knowing what was going on with Ledger and me. He wasn't certain she knew, but she was acting awfully weird around me. "Thanks, Nan. I love you."

She smiled. "I love you, too. Did you see the way Garrett's grandfather, Benjamin, looked at me last night? That man is hotter than the devil's behind."

I chuckled. "Well, he'd be lucky to date you, Nan."

There was a knock at the door, and Caroline peeked her head inside. "It's time, ladies. Ledger is here, and Garrett's dad is going to walk Nan and Kalie to their seats while Charlie gets Jilly's train ready outside the doors."

We all nodded in agreement. Kalie whispered something to Jilly, which caused a massive lump to form in my throat. Thoughts of my sweet mama were always there, but seeing them together on Jilly's wedding day had me thinking of her even more than usual. I glanced up to see Ledger watching me.

And we stepped out into the foyer, where a massive floral arrangement sat on a round marble table. Enormous glass doors led outside to the ceremony.

It was time to get my best friend married.

Kalie took my purse for me, and Garrett's father stepped inside and stood between them. They each wrapped their hands around his arm, and he led them outside. Caroline positioned Jilly right in front of the doors as I bent down in my strapless champagne satin gown so I could straighten her train and adjust it just right.

I pushed to stand and looked at Jilly; the tears welling in my eyes made it hard to see. I fanned my face and tried desperately to push the lump away.

"Don't you dare cry, Charlotte Thomas." She laughed, but she sounded weepy, too.

"I won't. I'll see you at the end of the aisle."

"I'll be right there." She winked, and I hooked my hand through Ledger's elbow, and he smiled down at me.

"You ready, Ladybug?"

"Yep. Let's do this."

Caroline opened the door and reminded Ledger to hurry back for his sister.

When the doors closed behind us, and the orchestra music filtered down below on the large grassy area beside the lake, he leaned down close to my ear.

"You're beautiful. You took my fucking breath away."

You always take my breath away.

I smiled and shook my head. "You clean up nicely, too."

We made our way down the aisle, the turquoise water sparkling in the distance. The property sat right on the lake, and the sun was shining down on us. The most beautiful pink and white florals lined each row of chairs. I smiled at my dad and my sisters and my brothers-in-law as I walked by. Everyone in town was here, and I just took it all in. Someone waved frantically, and I nearly burst out laughing when I realized it was Robby. I swear I heard Ledger growl under his breath, and it took all I had to keep my face straight.

Ledger walked me to the front, where Garrett stood, and then kissed my cheek, which I didn't believe was part of the plan, but I wasn't complaining. I glanced out at the audience and saw Dylan mouth the words, *he's so hot*, in dramatic fashion. I turned my attention to Garrett, who looked like a kid at a candy store who was tired of waiting.

For just a minute, I wondered what it would be like to have a man waiting for me at the end of the aisle.

And there was only one man that popped into my head.

The one who swore to hell and high water that he'd never get married.

Chapter 20

Ledger

I made my way back through the doors, where my sister stood with a big smile on her face.

"Are you ready?"

She nodded and then reached for my hand. "Thanks for walking me down the aisle. I hope someday I will get to watch you do the same thing."

I raised a brow. "Don't hold your breath, Jilly Bean."

She held her hand up to Caroline as she walked toward us and asked if we could have a minute before turning back to face me.

"Where is that coming from, Ledger? I mean, why are you so adamant about remaining single?"

I scratched the back of my neck. "You really want to do this right now? I'm about to walk you down the aisle."

"I really do. There's no way you can weasel out of it

because you kind of have to stay right here." She chuckled.

"I guess just the way our family blew up left me wanting something different, you know? I don't ever want to hurt anyone the way Dad hurt Mom and hurt you." I shrugged. My stance weakened with each day because I didn't even know how I felt anymore.

"And hurt you."

"Sure. But I survived."

"We all did, Ledger. But I think because of the way everything went down, you're actually protecting yourself from ever getting hurt like that again. And I never took you for a coward."

What the fuck was this? If I had a nickel for every family member who had called me a coward this week—well, I guess I'd have a dime.

But still. I didn't appreciate it.

"I'm going to let you get away with that comment because it's your wedding day." I cleared my throat and shot her a warning look. "But I'm not a fucking coward."

"So why are you hiding what's going on between you and Charlie from me?"

I ran a hand through my hair.

"Because it's not your business. We didn't want to upset you. It's... temporary."

"It's Charlotte fucking Thomas, Ledger. She's my best friend. You're my brother. Of course, it's my business," she whisper-hissed. "You don't think I saw your shoes at her house that morning I stopped by? Your phone was on her nightstand, for God's sake. But for the record, nothing would make me happier than you two being together. I don't know why you would hide that from me."

"It just sort of happened." I shrugged. "And it's been pretty damn good, so I didn't want to add any drama. It was just something we did for us."

"If you hurt her, we're going to have a problem. You know that, right?"

"No one is going to get hurt. We talked it out, and we had a plan going in."

She studied me for a minute. "I'm not sure she's the one I need to worry about."

"What the hell does that mean?"

"It means you've seemed happier these last two weeks than I've seen you in a long time. It might not be so easy to walk away from Charlie. She's one of a kind, which is why she's my best friend." She tapped her finger against her mouth. "Mom and I had a heart-to-heart two nights ago. You know that Dad cheated on her throughout their marriage, right? You and I were just in the dark. I mean, they only got married because she was pregnant. The odds were against them from the beginning."

I raised a brow, surprised by her words. "You know about that?"

"Yeah. She told me the other night, and it all sort of made sense to me. They never had a strong foundation. She gave it her best shot, but he was never going to change. I know that now. But I'm sure as hell happy they got married because of *you*, or there would be no *me*." She chuckled, and I couldn't help but smile.

"It's pretty fucked-up, Beans."

"It is what it is, Ledger. We have a rock star mother. Things could be worse. But that doesn't stop me from wanting to be happy. We aren't doomed because our dad is a jackass." She shrugged. "It takes strength to put yourself out there. Loving someone is scary, but it's also wonderful. It's cowardly to run from it just because you're afraid you might mess things up—or worst of all... they might hurt you. You have to keep moving forward."

"Okay, Dr. Know-It-All. Can we please walk you down the aisle now? Caroline looks like she is about to have a coronary."

"Yep. Glad we cleared the air."

"Hey, can I ask you a favor?"

"Of course." She patted her hair into place and smiled.

"Don't tell Charlie that you know. I'll tell her later. She doesn't want everyone judging her or reading into this and hounding her about it."

Her gaze narrowed. "Wow. You're so protective. I'm loving this. I won't say a word."

"Love you, Beans. Let's go get you married."

"We're ready." My sister looked over her shoulder and called out to her wedding planner.

"Thank goodness. You had me sweating over there. Let's do this." Caroline said something into her earpiece and then pulled the double doors open that led outside.

The wedding song played, and Jilly put her arm through my elbow and leaned close to me. "Let's do this."

Everyone moved to their feet as we made our way outside.

I glanced around at all the people who were here to support my sister. People who I'd grown up with. People who I'd forgotten meant the world to me when I left Honey

Mountain, desperate to leave this town behind me because of all the shitty memories with my father. Colt's parents were here. All the ladies from my grandmother's club and family and friends had all come out in full force. The only one missing was my father.

Everyone else was here to support her, and he wasn't.

And it didn't even fucking matter. His presence wouldn't be missed.

My eyes locked with Charlotte's, watching me walk my sister down the aisle.

The sun was just getting ready to set, and pops of copper and gold shone in her hazel gaze.

My stomach dipped.

Visions of Charlotte Thomas walking toward me down the aisle flooded my thoughts.

What the actual fuck was that about?

I wasn't a guy who daydreamed about his wedding day. Not even once had that happened.

At least not before today.

I was probably getting caught up in the nostalgia of this being such a big day for my sister.

I handed her off to Garrett and shook his hand before I moved to stand beside him as he and my sister recited their vows.

Charlie's eyes were wet with emotion as she watched Garrett dip Jilly back and kiss her like he wasn't standing in front of a couple hundred close family and friends. Father Davis did not look pleased, and I cleared my throat, because they either needed to get a room or pump the brakes on this over-the-top kiss.

Garrett pulled back, glanced over at me, and winked. I rolled my eyes, and the crowd erupted in laughter.

"I'd like to introduce Mr. and Mrs. Garrett Jones," Father Davis announced.

Everyone pushed to their feet once again, clapping and whistling, and I reached for Charlie's hand before following them down the aisle.

We were ushered out to the grassy area for photos before the DJ introduced Charlotte and me and then my sister and Garrett into the tented reception. There were large crystal chandeliers hanging above, and round tables with white linens surrounded a dance floor, which sat in the middle of the space.

The party went from tame to wild over the next few hours. Charlotte and I both said our speeches, and she kept her distance from me for the rest of the evening, but her eyes locked with mine every time I looked over. She left me no choice but to text her.

Me: Are you avoiding me?

Ladybug: Probably. It is Jilly's wedding day.

Me: She knows about us.

Ladybug: What? How do you know?

Me: She confronted me right before we walked down the aisle.

Ladybug: What does she know?

Me: That something's going on. She wasn't upset at all, as long as I promised not to hurt you. I'm not hurting you, am I, Ladybug?

Ladybug: No. You've been very upfront. We have an agreement, and we've stuck to it. Tomorrow, we say goodbye, and this comes to an end. Next time you're home, we'll just go back to being friends. Easy breezy, Dane.

I didn't like how casual she was being. Like maybe we'd speak again someday, and maybe we wouldn't. That shit didn't sit well with me.

Me: Your cousin, Hugh, texted me this morning and invited me to the grand opening of his restaurant in Cottonwood Cove. Maybe you'll want to come check it out?

Charlotte's cousins all lived in a small town outside of the city on the coast. I'd met them several times when we were growing up, and Hugh and I had hit it off and became good buddies. He'd come to me for some help on his restaurant design, and I'd been happy to be part of it. I also wanted to find a reason to see her again.

Ladybug: I spoke to him a few days ago, and he sent me photos. It looks great. He said you helped with the design. I may come visit in a few months. Why are we texting when we're in the same room?

Because I can't get enough of you.

Me: Because I'm your dirty little secret, and if I come sit by you, my mouth will be on yours within seconds, and I know that will complicate things.

Ladybug: Good point. Let's save it for when we're alone.

Me: How long until we can get out of here?

Ladybug: After they cut the cake.

"What are you up to?" Nan asked after she returned from the dance floor.

"Nothing. Are you ready for cake?"

"Ohhh... I did work up an appetite on the dance floor with Benjamin. I think that man was getting a little frisky."

"Don't you worry. I've got you." I ignored her comment about Garrett's grandfather because I did not want details on what getting frisky entailed at their age. But I was determined to get this party moving forward.

I had no shame in my game. It was my last night with Charlie, and it was getting late. I knew I'd be fine once I got back to the city and back into my routine. She'd be fine, too. But I wanted this last night with her. I missed her last night, which had shocked the shit out of me.

"Hey," I said as I walked over to Jilly and Garrett when they stepped off the dance floor.

"Are you having fun?" my sister asked.

"Yep. Great wedding. Everyone is having a good time, but I think Nan is getting anxious for cake. You should get things moving so the older people can cut out."

She nodded and glanced down at her phone. "Oh, yes. It's so late. Let me tell Caroline it's time."

Jilly hurried off, and Garrett raised a brow at me and pursed his lips.

"Are you seriously playing the elderly card?"

"It's late," I said dryly. "These grandparents need to get their rest."

"Oh, really? It's not because you and the maid of honor

have been making googly eyes at one another all night while you stay on separate sides of the room, even though your sister already knows what you're up to?"

"Are you really in a position to talk? I mean, you practically stripped my baby sister naked in front of family and friends after you said your vows. Poor Father Davis was traumatized. It was bordering on pornography."

"Okay, horndog. We'll cut the cake so you can get your girl home." He barked out a laugh before walking away to join his wife.

My girl.

The words did not make me cringe. Just the opposite, actually. My chest squeezed. And that was not a common reaction for me. It was definitely time to get the hell out of Honey Mountain.

But I didn't argue with him, because right now, I wanted them to cut the cake so we could sneak out of here.

The DJ asked everyone to gather in the center of the room so the cake cutting could commence. Charlie walked over to stand beside me.

"Well, you didn't waste any time, did you?" she purred as she stared straight ahead at my sister and Garrett as they cut into the seven-tier cake.

Garrett gently held the slice of cake up for her to take a bite, and I rolled my eyes. The dude was so pussy-whipped it was almost embarrassing to watch.

"What can I say? I have a taste for something sweet."

"So, should we get a piece of cake and then sneak out?" she asked.

"I'm not talking about wedding cake, Ladybug. I'm talking

about burying my head between your legs and eating your—"

"There you are, stranger. You promised me a dance. How about we go take a twirl around the dance floor while they're passing out the cake?" I was cut off by the bane of my existence, Robby.

This dude gave cockblock a new name. He was relentless.

"Oh, um, I probably need to help pass out the cake," Charlie said, and her excuse sounded lame at best.

"Nonsense. You've done enough, according to my calculations, which you know are spot on. You deserve a dance."

And you deserve to get punched in the dick, Robby.

"Okay. Sure." She glanced up at me and winced before following him onto the dance floor.

"Kudos for getting that cake cutting started—but I think someone else has his eyes on your girl," Nan said as she sidled up beside me.

What was it with everyone calling her my girl?

"I have no idea what you're talking about, per usual." I crossed my arms over my chest because I was irritated.

A server brought a slice of cake over to Nan and me, and I pouted as I took a bite.

Not what I had in mind for dessert.

"Ah… and now you're grumpy. That's stage one of a bad case of blue balls."

I took my time chewing the vanilla and coconut cake before shooting her a look. "Aren't you supposed to be home knitting and reminiscing about my childhood? Why must you always take it there?"

"I've always had a one-track mind, and I have a hunch it

runs in the family." She winked as she led me over to the table a few feet away and popped a bite of cake into her mouth once she took a seat.

I watched as king cockblocker spun Charlotte around on the dance floor, and her head fell back in laughter. The chair beside me pulled out, and Dylan sat down.

"Well, don't you look like a sad sack sitting over here watching her on the dance floor with the mathematician," she said.

"What are you talking about?"

"Please. You look like you're about to tear his head off. The cat's out of the bag, if you know what I'm saying?" She waggled her brows.

"I think you two have both lost your minds," I said, looking from Nan to Dilly.

"Did you say the *pussy* cat is out of the bag?" Nan asked Dylan, and she cackled as the words left her mouth.

"You're my kind of girl, Nan." Dylan fist-bumped my grandmother, who was behaving like a raging hormonal teenage boy.

"I think she's trying to tell you to shit or get off the pot," Nan said over her laughter.

"Yes." Dylan clapped her hands together and glanced down at her phone. "It's nearly twelve-oh-*cock.*"

"I'm begging you both to stop talking."

"Don't be ri-*dick*-ulous," Nan said over her hysterical laughter. Tears were streaming down both of their faces because they thought this was the funniest thing in the world.

"It's very un-be-*come*-ing," Dylan piped in, and I rolled my eyes.

I took one last bite of cake and pushed to my feet because I was done with their shit at the moment. I stormed out to the dance floor and leaned in so I could whisper in Charlotte's ear.

"Please leave with me now."

Her gaze searched mine with concern, and she nodded.

"I'm sorry, Robby. I'm needed for wedding duties."

"Not a problem. I'll round up your phone number from Garrett and give you a call when I get back home so we can continue our talk about your future."

"Thank you," she said with a chuckle before I placed my hand on the small of her back and led her off the dance floor.

We made our way over to my sister. "I love you. We're leaving. I have a headache."

Jilly barked out a laugh and then narrowed her gaze at me. "Oh... you *both* have a headache?"

"We do. Nan and Dilly just dirty talked their asses off to me, and I'm done. I'm tapping out. The wedding was amazing, and we're both exhausted from our duties."

Charlotte fell forward, laughing. "Real smooth, Ledger. I love you forever, Jilly."

"I love you forever. Get my girl home safely, okay, brother dearest?"

"Yes," Garrett said as he sipped his champagne. "That's awfully kind of you to take the maid of honor home, seeing as you have that awful headache."

I used my middle finger to scratch at my cheek, and his laughter bellowed around us. I took Charlotte's hand, and I didn't give a fuck who saw us, and I led her right out the door. I had a couple cars on standby out front so no one would have to drive home, and I walked toward the front car and gave him her address as I opened the back door for her.

I settled beside her, and the driver pulled out of the parking lot and headed for her house. My mouth was on hers before we even made it to the road.

I kissed her like my life depended on it because that was how it felt.

It had been torture being that close to her all night without touching her.

She kissed me back with the same need, and I almost unbuckled her and pulled her onto my lap, but we were already in her driveway. I handed him twenty bucks and hurried her out of the car, then we made our way inside.

It was our last night together, and I had every intention of spending every last minute with her.

Worshipping every inch of her beautiful body.

Making her cry out my name over and over.

Chapter 21

Charlotte

I dropped my purse on the counter and walked to the back wall of windows with Ledger right behind me. "I've never seen so many stars out before, have you?"

His head rested on my shoulder as we both gazed out at the dark water.

"No. It's fucking beautiful, though."

I turned around in his arms. "You want to take the canoe out?"

"Now?" he asked, but the corners of his lips turned up.

"Yeah." I smiled up at him and kicked up one foot at a time toward my butt and pulled off my heels. "Let's go sit under the stars."

He stepped back and slipped his tuxedo coat off, tossing it onto the couch and rolling up the sleeves of his dress shirt. He tugged off the tie and dropped it onto the couch, as well.

The move was so sexy that I squeezed my thighs together and sucked in a breath as I watched him unbutton two buttons of his dress shirt before kicking off his shoes and bending down to tug his socks off.

He moved toward me, almost predatory. Eyes hooded as they scanned my body.

"Whatever you want, Ladybug."

"I want you in a canoe under the stars," I said, my voice gruff.

He scooped me up and held me like a baby as he turned the outside light on and pulled the back door open and carried me outside to the dock. He set me down and held out a hand as he helped me climb in. He carefully untied the boat and easily stepped in before reaching for the oars.

Ledger paddled us out to deeper water, his muscles straining against his white dress shirt under the moonlight and the glow from the stars.

"I think that's the Big Dipper," I said, pointing up at the black starlit sky as the stars reflected on the water.

"Do you now? I thought this was the Big Dipper." His gaze moved down to his bulging erection, and he waggled his brows.

I chuckled. "Trust me. That is most definitely the most impressive dipper out here tonight."

He just smiled as his eyes scanned me. "You're so fucking pretty, Charlie. I swear I couldn't take my eyes off you tonight."

I sucked in a breath, and my teeth found my bottom lip as I reached for the back of my head, removing the pins from the chignon at the nape of my neck and allowing my hair to fall free.

"So don't."

His tongue swiped out to wet his lips as he pulled the oars into the boat and set them down.

"I don't plan to."

"It's our last night." I moved closer, holding up the hem of my dress and carefully sitting on the bench right in front of him. My legs slipped between his as the satin fabric puddled around me. "So let's stay up all night and enjoy it."

"I plan on it." He winked, and my stomach dipped. I was in too deep, and I knew it, but this was our last night, and I wasn't going to pull back now.

"Are you looking forward to going back to the city? To your regular life?" I asked, as his hands found mine and he intertwined our fingers.

"I'm looking forward to going back and seeing if Harold stays true to his word and makes me a partner. I want to talk to him in person about the middle school project and see if I can get him to bend a little bit. But I'm not as anxious to get back to the city as I thought I'd be."

I nodded. "Why is that?"

"I've had a good time being home, and that's all due to you, Ladybug."

"Yeah? It's been fun, huh?"

He tugged me forward onto his lap and the boat rocked a little, and nervous laughter escaped.

"I got you." His mouth found mine as one knee settled on the bench on each side of him so I was straddling him.

"I know you do," I whispered against his mouth.

He tipped my head back so he could take the kiss deeper, but his fingers traced a path across the cylinder of my neck as they spread out just below my jaw. His thumb stroked the edge of my ear as his tongue explored my mouth. My hips ground against him, his erection swelling beneath me, and every once in a while, the boat rocked excessively, and we slowed our movements down.

When the boat nearly flipped us, he chuckled against my lips, and his fingers tangled in my hair as he tipped my head back. His lips moved down my throat.

"Are you eager tonight, Ladybug?"

"Yes," I panted as I continued grinding up against him.

"Are you willing to take the risk that we could end up in the water?" he teased as he continued kissing his way down to my collarbone.

"I'm fine with it." My voice was barely recognizable and laced with desire. "I love to swim."

A light wind swirled around us, and I shivered at the feel of his lips on my skin and the whisper of a breeze.

His hand found the zipper on the back of my dress, and he guided it down slowly. He pulled back, allowing the satin fabric to puddle at my waist, exposing my breasts as I wore nothing beneath.

"I want to memorize every inch of you. You're a work of fucking art." His thumbs gently traced over my nipples, and I gasped.

"Please tell me you have a condom," I said, my fingertips tracing the scruff on his jaw as I searched his gaze.

He wanted me as badly as I wanted him.

"Shit. They're in my wallet, which is at your house." He let out a long breath.

"I've never been with anyone without a condom, and I'm

on the pill."

His gaze was so tender it nearly stole my breath. "I've never been with anyone without a condom either, and I've been tested recently. Are you sure?"

"Yes. I need you right now, Ledger. Right here. Under the stars."

"Just you and me, Ladybug." He carefully lifted me, pulling my dress up to my waist and then reaching for the top of my thong. The boat started to rock, and I grabbed his shoulders.

"Tear them off," I said, and he didn't hesitate. He quickly tugged at the band and the fabric came apart easily, and he dropped it at my feet.

I reached for the button on his pants, and he lifted up just enough for me to unbutton and pull the zipper down. I found the edge of his boxer briefs and tugged them both down just enough to allow his cock to spring free.

The urgency that I felt was unexplainable. The need I had for this man was overwhelming.

I didn't want to think about tomorrow or next week—or the fact that everything would come to an end after the sun came up.

I just wanted to be in the moment.

I'd wanted this boy my entire life... and now, the man version was all mine. At least for tonight.

"Fuck, Charlie. I want you so bad." His fingers dug into my hips as he positioned me over him.

The tip of his erection teased my entrance. "Are you sure about this?"

"Yes. I want you right now." I slowly slid down his shaft,

feeling every nerve come alive in my body. The sensation was too much, but not enough at the same time.

I wanted more.

I wanted everything he was willing to give.

"Holy fuck," he hissed as he filled me—inch by glorious inch. His eyes hooded, his breaths coming hard and fast, and he groaned as my head fell back, and I adjusted to his size. "This feels so fucking good."

"It always does with you." The reality that it had never felt like this with anyone else loomed like a dark cloud above me, but I refused to acknowledge its presence.

I started to move, and we both slowed down when the boat tipped from side to side, and water slipped in. He placed both hands on my hips and spread his legs farther apart, which made the canoe feel more balanced.

"I've got you," he whispered just before his mouth came over my breast, and he tugged at my nipple, which caused my entire body to jolt. But Ledger was right—he had me. He moved my hips up and down as he took turns kissing one breast and then the other.

My head fell back again, and my hair tickled my lower back as I continued to ride him. We found our rhythm, and we continued to move for what felt like forever.

The stars danced above, and the light breeze cooled my heated skin. But the man beneath me knew just what I needed. He moved faster, and my entire body started to shake. I didn't care if the boat tipped over. It would be worth it because I couldn't slow things down now even if I tried. Nothing had ever felt so good, and I never wanted it to end.

Without saying a word, Ledger's hand came between us,

knowing just where to touch me. The bundle of nerves that was so exposed at the moment, just the graze of his thumb had my hands fisting in his hair.

"Ledger," I cried.

"Come for me, baby."

And that was all it took.

I rocked against him one last time as I went right over the edge. The boat was rocking, my body was shaking, and bright light exploded behind my eyes, just like the stars that were out tonight. Pleasure coursed through my veins, and he pumped into me one more time before he followed me into the abyss.

He shouted my name and continued moving my hips up and down as we both rode out every last bit of pleasure.

The boat slowed, and he wrapped his arms around me, burying his face in my neck.

"I fucking love—" He paused, and our breaths filled the air around us. My heart raced as I waited for him to finish what he was saying. "This."

My chest squeezed because that wasn't exactly what I was hoping he'd say, but it was the best he could give me, and I accepted that.

But I was done being afraid. I knew this would never be what I needed it to be, but it wasn't going to be because I was afraid to say how I felt this time around. And it would give me the courage to keep searching for it.

Searching for someone to love me the way that I loved this man.

I put a hand on each side of his face, and I smiled. "I love you, Ledger Dane. I think I have my entire life." A tear ran down my cheek, and the panic in his eyes made my chest heave. "I'm not saying it for you to say it back to me. I know who you are. I just love you in spite of it."

"Fuck. Charlie. Please don't say that." His hand moved to my face, his thumb tracing across my bottom lip.

"I'm not afraid to say how I feel anymore. And it's okay, you've been honest about what you have to offer. I knew this was going to come to an end, and I wanted to do it, anyway." A lump formed in my throat as another tear escaped and made its way down my cheek.

"You deserve a lot better than me." He studied my gaze with an intensity I'd never seen from him.

"Well, I actually agree." I smiled because I was at peace with this. It felt good to tell him how I felt. I knew it was going to hurt like hell tomorrow, but I wanted to leave it all out here tonight. "I mean, you showed me how it should be. How good this should feel. But you've also helped me to see what I need and what I want."

"And what is that?" He almost looked like he was bracing himself for what I was going to say next. As if he knew the answer before I said it.

"That I want to have everything. This," I said, motioning between us. "The fireworks and the connection. But I want it with a man who loves me the way that I love him."

"You know that I love you, Charlie. As much as I'm capable of." He shook his head as if this was torture.

"That's a copout, Ledger. Because you're capable of love. Look at how you are with Jilly and your mom and Nan. You're one of the most loving people that I know. And the way you've been with me these last two weeks has been... amazing. But I want a man who isn't afraid to fight for me. Who values me more than his own fears. And you've made it clear that you aren't that man."

I swear I saw his eyes well at my words, but he quickly pushed it away, his face losing all traces of emotion as he nodded.

"You deserve the best. I couldn't agree more."

"Thank you for showing me what it feels like. Showing me what I want. And giving me the confidence to say it."

"There isn't anything I wouldn't do for you," he said so earnestly that I almost believed him.

But that wasn't true.

He wouldn't give me the one thing that I wanted.

Which was him. All of him.

"Thank you. And hey, we didn't fall in the water."

"Well, we definitely rocked the boat, Ladybug." He chuckled, but he looked lost in his thoughts.

I pushed up slowly, and he helped me to settle on the bench in front of him. And then he did the most intimate thing yet— and we'd been more intimate than I'd ever been with anyone in my life. This man knew my body. Knew what I wanted. What I needed.

But he tugged off his dress shirt and dipped it in the water, and then moved to kneel between my legs, and he gently cleaned me up. I closed my eyes as the cool water hit my core, and I leaned back, allowing him access. I never in a million years thought I'd be comfortable doing this with a man.

But here we were.

Ledger leaned forward and pulled my dress up, reaching behind me to zip it in the back.

And then he tugged his pants up and buttoned and zipped

them, leaving his shirt in a ball beside him. I kneeled enough to pull the skirt of my dress down and reached for my torn panties.

"Sorry about that. I will replace those for you."

I shook my head. "Don't be silly. I'm the one who said to tear them off. And honestly, it was pretty hot."

He chuckled. "You're pretty hot, Charlotte Thomas."

He reached for the oars and started paddling us back toward my house.

"So what happens now? We've had mind-blowing sex, and you leave tomorrow. Should we call it done right now?"

"Not a fucking chance," he said. "We made a deal that we had until tomorrow. So, I'm not going anywhere until tomorrow afternoon."

"I figured you were out of tricks. I mean, sex in a canoe, without falling in the water—all with a sky full of stars above us. I don't know how you can top that."

He smirked and continued to plunge the oars into the water as I watched all the muscles in his bare chest and arms flex each time he pulled. "You ain't seen nothing yet."

I leaned back and closed my eyes for a minute to take it all in. I bared my soul to this man, and I didn't have a single regret.

It felt good to find my voice.

And now that I had, I wouldn't settle for anything less than what I wanted.

Even if it meant I couldn't have it with the man I loved.

Chapter 22

Ledger

I stared at Charlotte as she slept. Her hair was splayed out in dark waves around her. Her long lashes rested on her cheeks, and her plump lips taunted me to take one last taste. It was difficult for me to be in her presence without touching her. And she made it clear that we couldn't keep this arrangement going in the future. She knew what she wanted.

The impossible dream.

So this was it. We stayed up until the sun came up. We come home and made pancakes and then had sex again. And then we soaked in a bath together. And fuck me if I didn't enjoy a nice hot bath after sex now.

Who fucking knew that was possible?

And then we dozed off, or she had. And I've just been lying here, watching her sleep like some fucking crazy stalker. Because leaving her was much harder than I ever imagined.

She told me she loved me. I almost said it first.

It wasn't that I didn't feel it.

It was that I didn't believe I could do it justice.

The idea terrified me.

There was too much room to fuck up.

To let her down. To lose her. To hurt her.

Fuck no.

I knew all too well how easy it was for the train to derail.

A part of me wanted to sneak out like a coward. Wasn't that what Nan and Jilly had called me, anyway?

I hated goodbyes.

But I wouldn't do that to her.

I couldn't.

I stroked her hair away from her face, and she smiled. In her fucking sleep, the girl smiled because I touched her.

She was a goddamn angel.

She moved closer, resting her head in the crook of my neck. I wrapped my arms around her and breathed her in.

My body relaxed against hers.

Her soft breaths lulled me until my eyes closed.

And sleep finally took me. Giving me a break from the torture of my own thoughts.

The mattress shifted, and my eyes sprung open in a panic at the loss of her warmth against me.

"Sorry, I didn't mean to wake you. It's already noon."

"Oh, shit. I need to go say goodbye to my mom and Nan and then get on the road." I scrubbed a hand down my face.

Jilly and Garrett flew out to Mexico this morning for their honeymoon, so at least that was one less goodbye that I'd need to say.

I never understood the reasoning behind goodbyes.

It always felt so permanent. If you were just leaving for now and not forever—why say anything?

Just know that you would see one another again soon.

Why go through all the formalities and sadness when it wasn't forever?

"All right. Let me get you a cup of coffee and a bagel to go."

Ouch. Someone sure wasn't nearly as anxious as me about saying goodbye. She seemed perfectly at peace with things, which surprised me after she bared her soul to me last night.

"Thank you." I pushed out of bed and went to her bathroom to splash water on my face and brush my teeth.

I came out and found my pants on the floor and pulled them up. The dress shirt I wore to the wedding was in a ball on the floor after I'd soaked it and cleaned her up. So I tucked it under my arm and pulled my jacket on with nothing beneath it. I saw my T-shirt hanging over a chair in her bedroom. It was the one she slept in every night, and I'd be damned if I took it. I liked the idea of her sleeping in my shirt.

Would she still wear it when she moved on and started dating someone else? The thought had me stopping dead in my tracks. Nausea pooled in my throat, and I took a few minutes to breathe through it.

What the fuck was that about?

I walked out to the little living space, which was a small kitchen, dining room, and family room all in one. She was just pouring the coffee into a to-go cup, and she handed me a bagel wrapped in some sort of white paper that I'd seen Vivi use at her bakery.

"All right. You need to get some coffee and some food in you before you get on the road." She smiled, but there was a sadness in her eyes that she was trying to mask.

I was glad I wasn't the only one who felt like the world was ending. Another example of what a selfish prick I was.

"Thank you." This girl knew exactly what I needed. She always had, hadn't she?

"Of course. And listen, I know we said a lot last night, and it's important to me that you know I'm going to be fine. This was a good thing, Ledger. I'll move on in no time, okay? So please don't worry about me."

What the fuck was her deal with telling me how quickly she'd be moving on? This wasn't the first time she mentioned it. Like I should get some sort of medal for showing her how good sex could be, and she'd be hurrying off to find someone who could deliver the goods and give her the future that she wanted?

Fuck that.

I didn't want to hear about it.

I sure as shit wouldn't find what I had with Charlotte with anyone else.

I just understood that I wouldn't ever have that long-term.

But she was going to go find it, and apparently, she was putting that plan into action right away.

And I wanted to punch a fucking hole through the wall.

I know. I know. Nothing about my way of thinking was right.

I nodded. "You don't have to be in such a rush."

She smiled. "Well, now that I know what I want, I'm ready to find it. So please, don't leave here feeling bad or feeling sorry for me. I agreed to this. I knew this day was coming, and I actually feel fine about it. I'm good." She shrugged, and though her smile looked a little forced, she was obviously okay with it because she was rushing me out the door.

I reached for the coffee and bagel. "Okay. Good to know."

And now I felt like a dickhead because I had a lump in my throat and was anything but okay.

"Tell Nan I'll come by later this week to help her plant those new flowers she wants to get in her garden." She patted me on the shoulder like I was a fucking buddy of hers. Not like I was the man who'd literally just rocked her world out on the water under the stars last night.

I mean, how many people could have mind-blowing sex in a canoe on the water and not tip over? My fucking legs were throbbing today from the workout I'd gotten from trying to keep our balance.

And I was getting a pat on the shoulder?

A motherfucking attaboy?

I deserved this. I was the prick who couldn't commit, so I had to take the shit that came along with that. Usually, it was me trying to end things amicably. Hurry my ass out the door. Mind you, Jessica was still relentlessly messaging me that we needed to speak when I came back to the city. I hadn't responded. I'd made myself clear, and I wasn't going to complicate things.

But this, this was new.

"I will let her know."

She moved forward as if she were trying to get me to step backward toward the door.

"Are you in a hurry, Ladybug?" I asked, raising a brow.

"You expecting someone?"

"No. Of course not. I just know you have to get over to your mom's and Nan's, and then you have a long drive since you have to work tomorrow. I'm sure Harold is going to push for you to go on that trip with him and his wife and Jessica. And I just want you to know that I'm fine with whatever happens there."

What? Where did that come from?

"Whatever happens there?"

"Yeah. I mean, you were dating your boss's daughter, Ledger. She wants you back, so it won't be too surprising if that happens. That's all."

"It was never serious. I told you that. I don't do serious," I said, and I squeezed the bagel so hard in my hand I was certain I'd smashed it.

"I'm aware. But maybe you'll bend the rules for her. I mean, there's a lot at stake. I know how much your job means to you. You make the big bucks, right?"

If I were ever going to bend the rules, it would be for Charlotte Thomas. And she knows that, doesn't she? Was she trying to start a fight with me?

If she was, she wasn't very good at it. I was totally fucking confused.

"Hey," I said, reaching out with my free hand and tipping her chin up, forcing her to meet my gaze. "I'm not getting back together with Jessica. Hell, we weren't really a couple, anyway. It was nothing like—" I stopped myself from saying more.

It was nothing like what Charlotte and I shared.

Not even close.

But this was already complicated.

"Listen, we don't need to go over it again. This was the deal. Today is the day. There's really nothing more to say. So..." She raised a brow, chin high, shoulders squared. Her hazel gaze was lacking the normal warmth.

Her guard was up.

I should be happy. This was what I wanted. What I asked for.

She wasn't sad. She wasn't torn up.

"Right. Well, if you decide to come to town for Hugh's restaurant opening, let me know." Was my voice trembling?

"Okay. Maybe."

"And I'll be back soon. I mean, Nan's getting older."

"Sure. Maybe we'll run into one another. Take care, Ledger." She reached around me for the door handle.

Wow.

She was much better at goodbyes than I was.

It was like we'd switched roles. I was the one trying to drag this out.

"I had a great time these last two weeks," I said. "It meant something to me."

"Ledger," she said, and there was a warning in her voice. "Please."

I nodded. Why couldn't we still talk now and then? Or even text once a day? I wasn't opposed to that.

"Yeah, yeah. I get it." I leaned down and kissed her cheek. I wanted to kiss her goodbye, but I thought she might punch me in the face if I did. She seemed a little hostile at the moment.

I wasn't one step over the threshold when the door shut abruptly. My nose even got thumped because I had barely cleared the doorway.

She was done with me.

I wouldn't be surprised if she was already on a dating app, finding Mr. Right.

I'd given her the road map because I'd been a perfect *Mr. Right Now*. But that wasn't enough. I'd fucking cleared the way for some other lucky bastard to end up with the girl of my dreams because I was too fucked up to claim her myself.

When I pulled up at my mom's house, I stepped inside, and she and Nan were sipping coffee at the table in the kitchen.

Nan burst out in laughter. "Oh, my. The girls would get a real kick out of this. You look like you just came from *Thunder from Down Under*."

I glanced down and rolled my eyes when I remembered that I'd left without a shirt. I was wearing tuxedo pants and a jacket, with nothing else. And I'd all but been pushed out the door like she couldn't get rid of me quick enough.

"Thanks." There was no humor in my voice. "I'm going to take a quick shower, and I need to get on the road."

"Oh, someone's in a mood. I'm guessing saying goodbye wasn't as simple as we expected."

There was nothing simple about saying goodbye to Charlotte Thomas.

The only thing that had been simple was making her mine over the last week.

"Nan, I am in no mood," I said before turning and heading up the stairs to the bathroom. I took a quick shower and found my laundry all washed and folded on my bed. I packed up my suitcase and went back downstairs.

"Thank you for doing my laundry, Mama." I kissed her cheek.

"Thank you for giving your sister her dream wedding and for helping me with the house."

"You're a good boy, which is why you're my favorite guy," Nan said as she pushed to her feet and hugged me.

"Thank you. I love you both. But I need to get going." I leaned down and kissed my grandmother's cheek and then pulled my mother in for a hug. I needed to get out of here. Get on the road. Put some distance between me and this town.

Me and this girl.

I was tempted to call Charlie from the road, but after that awkward-as-fuck goodbye, I knew it wasn't what she wanted.

If I wasn't all in—I needed to be all out.

Those were her rules, not mine.

But I needed to respect them.

I made good time getting home and already missed the mountains and the lake in Honey Mountain. I loved San Francisco, the buzz of the city, but it wasn't peaceful. Cars were honking, and the traffic was a bitch, and I'd only just returned. I pulled into my underground parking spot and made my way up to my condo on the top floor. I'd been proud as hell when I bought this penthouse in the iconic downtown building. But as I pushed the door open, I glanced around, and it felt a little sterile.

I dropped my keys on the foyer table and made my way inside and over to my favorite feature, floor-to-ceiling windows on the entire back wall with city views. People moved in both directions down below at a rapid pace, and I thought about Charlie's view of the lake. The warmth in her home and the way it always smelled like peaches. I liked being at her place, even if it wasn't much bigger than a shoe box.

I called to have groceries delivered and spent the next few hours answering emails and getting caught up on work. I sent Jessica a text that I would not be going with her family on the yacht next week, and once again made it very clear that I was happy with our decision to remain friends and nothing more.

I checked my phone a couple dozen times to see if there were any messages from Charlie. I'd grown accustomed to texting and talking to her all day, and even though I was in one of the most lively cities in the world, it was a little quiet tonight.

Too quiet.

I was thankful when it was time to go to bed, but I had a restless night's sleep, as I'd grown used to the warmth of her body beside me when I slept.

These were habits that I'd fallen into quickly with Charlotte, and I was certain I could fall out of them just as fast. I made my way to my usual coffee haunt downstairs in the building I worked in before heading up to my office. I was the first one to arrive, which wasn't unusual, and I settled behind my desk and took a sip of coffee, cursing when the hot lava nearly blistered my tongue.

"I see we're in a good mood today," Harold said as he stood in my doorway.

"Yes, of course." I pushed to my feet and extended my hand. "I just forgot how fucking hot they make their coffee downstairs."

"The best in the city. It's got to feel good to be back, son."

He called me that often, and I couldn't tell if it was a term of endearment or if he was being condescending. I never could put my finger on Harold Cartwright's motives if I were being honest—but I'd never much cared to dissect them, either. We were both benefiting from our relationship, so I hadn't read a whole lot into it.

Before now.

"Yes. Definitely. So, are we still set for our nine a.m. meeting?" I asked, because today was the day that we were supposed to discuss the dynamics of me coming on as a partner with his chief legal, Stew Harrison. This opportunity had been dangled over my head for a long time, and Harold finally seemed ready to come up with an agreement.

"We are all set. Stew will just go over the terms, and we can sign today if you're ready." He cleared his throat. "And I need an answer on that museum job this week. You'll be traveling a lot if you take it on, and I'd very much like you to do so, which is why I'm agreeing to make you a partner. Maureen and I plan on going to our vacation home in the South of France, and I want you to keep things going here while I'm gone."

This was what I wanted.

What I worked so hard for.

"I do have some concerns about the museum project, so I placed a call to John Levins to discuss things in a bit more detail, as the email and contract were both very vague."

"There's no need to do that. What is important is that this museum is going to give us another leg up on projects in this city. Make this firm, which you are being offered a partnership in, even more iconic. More lucrative. And your name will go on this building as a lead architect along with mine. Don't look a gift horse in the mouth, Ledger."

I nodded. But the email from John didn't sit right with me.

My name was nowhere on it, yet I was the lead? I'd still keep my meeting with him just to clear things up, at the very least. We'd met several times over the years, and he was a good guy. We'd become friends, and we both worked for difficult men, so we had a mutual respect for one another.

"I told you that my father didn't end up attending the wedding. Is there a loophole that Stew could find to get me out of the agreement?" I rubbed my temples because the mention of my father had me on edge.

"No. I mean, your name isn't technically caught up in it. It was a vague agreement sent over by the firm to do the house drawing pro bono. So, I think you're stuck, unless you can find someone else here at the firm to do it, which I can't think of anyone else that would do anything pro bono, not even for their own family members." He laughed, and I nodded.

Cartwright Designs was not a pro bono type of firm. I knew that. It still didn't stop me from trying every now and then.

"All right. I guess I have no choice. I'll do it outside of work hours, obviously. But I do want to continue discussing the middle school project. They aren't asking for pro bono work. They're asking for a fair price. They have a budget, and they'd like us to work within it. I think it would be positive press for us. You know, showing that we give back. Honey Mountain is a small community. Good people. I think it's the right thing to do."

"How about this? You join us on the yacht, and I'll think about it." He turned for the door because he was done. He had a way of dismissing me, and I didn't care for it.

"Harold, I am not joining your family on that trip. I've said it multiple times to both you and Jessica. We are not dating. I told you from the beginning that I didn't want things to get messy or interfere with work, but you pushed. You pushed hard. And she is a lovely lady, but I am not looking for the same things that she is. It ended amicably, and I'd appreciate it if you'd respect that." It wasn't because we didn't want the same things. It was because we had nothing in common, but I didn't want to be disrespectful.

His neck turned red, which was his tell that he was pissed. "We'll talk about it later. Keep in mind you're saying no to the man who is agreeing to make you a partner."

"Because I'm damn good at my job and I've put in the work. Not because I'm dating your daughter. Jesus, Harold, this is so fucked-up."

"This is business, Ledger. You want to play with the big boys? You want to make the big bucks and be a baller? You best get on board with what it takes to do that." He turned and walked out of my office, and I stood there with my jaw hanging open.

What the fuck?

Had he always been this out of tune and I'd just dealt with it?

Well, I wasn't dealing with it anymore.

Chapter 23

Charlotte

I set my water on the counter and glanced at the vase filled with beautiful pink peonies. Ledger had sent them a few hours after he left, and the card had simply read:

I'll miss you, Ladybug. xx, Ledger

I slipped on my sunglasses and made my way through the backyard as I climbed into the canoe and sat on the bench, closing my eyes.

I wasn't ready to paddle out to where he'd rocked my world just yet. I'd just sit here and meditate.

I leaned back and let the sun warm my skin.

I knew when I woke up this morning that I needed to just get up and out of bed. Pull up my big girl panties and own up to what it was—a damn fling, one that I'd signed up for. Yet it felt like my heart had shattered into a million pieces when we'd said goodbye. I hurried him out the door because

I knew I was going to fall apart, and I certainly didn't want to do it in front of him. I didn't want him to feel sorry for me; it was embarrassing enough that I'd grown attached all while knowing this was going to come to an end. I needed to wallow in this on my own.

Today had been my first day out on the water since he'd left. He'd gifted me that beautiful boat, and now it was tainted because the last time I'd been out there, it had been... everything.

Intimate. Sexy. Mind-blowing. Erotic. Romantic.

"Hey, what are you doing out here?" Jilly's voice startled me, and I sat up.

"What are you doing here? You're back from your honeymoon? I thought you didn't get back until tonight?"

She walked across the grass and onto the dock before climbing right into the boat and sitting on the bench across from me. "Yeah. We got back this morning, and I wanted to come see you."

"How was it?" I asked, trying very hard to act excited. I'd been moping for days, and Jilly was the last person I wanted to know.

"It was great. We had so much fun, but I missed you. That was the longest you and I have ever gone without speaking." She shrugged.

"We texted every day." I chuckled. "I wasn't going to call you on your honeymoon."

"Take off your glasses," she said just as she slipped hers up onto the top of her head.

"What? Why? It's so bright out here." I shook my head because she was being ridiculous, and I did not want her to see my puffy eyes.

She leaned forward and plucked them right off my face, and studied me. "What's going on, Charlie? I tried calling you multiple times, and you didn't pick up. You just sent those overly bubbly texts back to me. Come on. This is me. I know you. And those dark circles under your eyes are telling a story of their own."

"I'm fine. I swear I am. Tell me about your honeymoon." I tugged the glasses back from her and slipped them back on my face.

"It was sunshine, lots of food, and good sex. There's really nothing more to report." She smiled, but I knew my best friend well, and she was not going to let this drop. "Did he hurt you?"

"No. Of course not. I'm sorry you even had to find out about it."

"Please, girl. I caught it early on. But you didn't tell me, which surprised me. We've never kept secrets."

I'd kept one from her for years. The fact that I had a massive crush on her brother.

"I never told you that I had a crush on him when we were younger, either."

"I knew you did, but I just didn't think it was all that serious. But what happened while he was home this time—it seemed like it was a whole lot more than a crush."

I shook my head, trying desperately to push away the lump in my throat. "It wasn't."

She pulled the glasses off my face again and held them up with a firm look in her eyes. "Stop hiding from me."

The tears started to fall, and I couldn't stop them. "Jilly, it's fine. I'm fine. I knew what I was getting into. I'm the one who agreed to it."

She reached for my hand. "So, that doesn't mean it doesn't hurt. You can talk to me, Charlie. You're my best friend. Let me be there for you. You are always there for me. Hell, you're always there for everyone. Let me help you. Stop being stubborn."

I shook my head and swiped at my tears, reaching for my glasses again because I didn't want to do this. "He's your brother. I'm fine. Please give me my glasses."

She held them over her head, and I dove toward her.

"Tell me what happened."

"Nothing happened!" I shouted. I didn't know why I was getting so worked up. I just wanted to float in a boat alone today. Why couldn't she just let me be?

She chucked my sunglasses in the water, and my mouth gaped open. "I can't believe you just did that."

"And I can't believe you won't talk to me."

I reached for her sunglasses and tugged them off her head and threw them as far as I could into the water. "I don't want to talk to you about this. Why can't you understand that?"

I turned to climb out of the boat, but she reached for my hand. "I can't believe you threw my glasses in the water."

"Let me go, Jilly," I said, before losing my balance and stumbling back. She reached for me, her hand grasping mine, as we both tumbled right over the side of the canoe and into the cold lake water.

"Oh my gosh," she said over her laughter as we both gasped for air. "It's freaking cold in here."

My feet barely touched the bottom of the lake, and I swam

over to grab my sunglasses and put them on my face, even though I could see nothing through them at this point.

"What is your obsession with wearing those damn glasses?" she shouted and lunged toward me.

And that was all it took. I lost it. I pulled the sunglasses off my face and chucked them.

"I'm not obsessed with the glasses. I just wanted to be alone. I don't want to be sad in front of you, okay?" I was still shouting, but it was mixed in with my sobs, and she wrapped her arms around me and let me cry.

"It's okay to be sad in front of me. How many times have I cried to you? How many times have you just sat there with me and let me be sad? Why can't I do that for you?"

"Because," I croaked. "He's your brother. And you just got married."

"Charlie, none of that matters. First off, he's my brother, and I love him no matter what you tell me. But I'm also aware that he can be a big, stubborn ass. Second, I plan on being married for a long ass time—forever, hopefully." She bellowed out in laughter. "So, stop handling things by yourself and let me in."

I sobbed and cried and did everything I didn't want to do, standing neck-deep in the lake with my best friend. She didn't care that she was in a floral maxi dress or that I was having a complete meltdown of epic proportions.

"I agreed to all of it, Jilly. I just didn't know it would hurt so much when it ended." I let out a long breath and tried to calm myself down.

I'd never experienced heartache like this. I experienced severe grief after my mother passed away when I was just thirteen years old. I ached, and I hurt, and I cried night after night.

I was familiar with grief.

With losing someone that you loved because life was unfair and took them away. It wasn't their choice.

But heartache was something different altogether. It was loving someone who didn't love you back. At least not the way you needed them to. I'd never love another boy or a man the way that I loved Ledger Dane.

"I get it," she said. "But you have a connection, you always have. I can tell you this much about Ledger—he loves you in his own way. He has had you up on a pedestal since we were kids. I think he wanted this to happen as much as you did, and I highly doubt that he just walked away and isn't feeling the aftermath, too."

I reached for her hand, and we walked over to the dock and jumped up to sit on the edge. "The part that stings so much is that it's his choice that we aren't together. He doesn't want me the way that I want him. It's just not his thing. He was completely upfront about it. But that doesn't mean that it doesn't hurt. But you know I'll get over this, right? So please don't worry."

"What is so bad about worrying about you, Charlie? It's okay to let people be there for you. Have you been dealing with this all on your own?"

"Well, of course, Dylan showed up an hour after he left with a few tubs of ice cream and a bottle of tequila. She knew something had been going on with him, but not how deep things had gone.

So I broke down to her, ate way too much ice cream, and

my head still hurts from the tequila shots." I chuckled, which sounded more like a laughing sob.

It had been almost a week now, and I was trying to pull myself out of my slump. I had Sunday dinner tonight at my father's house, and we never missed that, no matter what was going on in our lives. I turned down invitations from my sisters this week to go to lunch and spend the day at the lake. I said I was sick and allowed myself some time to just be sad.

There was this small part of me that always thought I'd end up with Ledger. Hell, I've loved him for as long as I could remember.

"Of course, you can't hide from Dilly. And she always knows exactly what you need, doesn't she?" She squeezed my hand.

"She does."

"I just wish my brother would stop being so afraid. I think all that went down with our father abandoning us, and the guilt Ledger carried about lying to Mom, he's just become so guarded." She shook her head, and a tear rolled down her cheek. "He deserves to be happy, too. I don't know why he can't see it."

"I don't know either. But spending two weeks with him was better than I imagined—and I want you to know... I'd do it all again just to have that time with him, even knowing how much it would hurt when it came to an end."

But the reality had hit me hard.

It was over.

"I know he feels the same way, Charlie. He's just a scared, stubborn ass. How did it end? Did he ask to see you again?"

"He actually did. He said he'd like to see each other a

couple of times a year. Every few months. Keep things casual. But I know myself, Jilly. I'm not that girl. Even this fling was very out of character for me, and it only worked because it was Ledger. I want a partner. A man who loves me and wants to be with me all the time."

"What is he even thinking? Well, that tells me that he didn't want it to end. But Ledger is so freaking terrified of following in our father's footsteps, which is comical, really."

"Why?"

"Because my dad never stopped and worried about hurting anyone. He just continues to do what he wants. Ledger takes care of the people he loves." Jilly chuckled. "He's just not looking at the whole picture. He's just a dumb boy."

I wrapped an arm around her and leaned my head on her shoulder. "He'll be fine. We'll all be fine."

"But will our sunglasses ever recover?" she asked, and we both burst out in a fit of laughter.

We sat on the dock, talking for hours, and I actually felt better than I had in days. We managed to dry off while sitting out in the sun. Jilly left to go meet Garrett for dinner, and I took a quick shower to get ready for Sunday dinner at my dad's.

It was the first day in a week that I wore makeup and actually put on a sundress and rejoined the living.

It was time to move on.

When I pushed the door open of the home I grew up in, I was surrounded by the smell of garlic and basil. Dad was making his famous spaghetti.

Vivian was the first one I saw when she came around the corner holding my niece, little Bee's hand, as she waddled along, putting one leg in front of the next. She had dark hair and the most beautiful eyes—a mix of both Niko's and Vivi's, which made them a dark gray. Her hair was in two tiny buns on each side of her head, and she wore this little white eyelet sundress, smiling the minute she saw me. I bent down and held my arms out for her. Vivian let go of her hand, and she took two steps and fell into my arms. I wrapped her up and breathed in all that sweetness.

She always smelled like honey and baby powder.

This was exactly what I needed. I pushed to stand and held her in my arms.

"Hey, are you okay?" Vivian asked as she put a hand on my shoulder.

"Yes, of course. I just needed my baby Bee fix." My niece's head fell back in a fit of giggles, and I spun her around.

"Okay, good. I know you weren't feeling good, so I was getting a little worried." She had that big sister look on her face, and I immediately knew that Dylan had filled them all in on what happened. I couldn't be upset. It was how we worked in the Thomas family. We were all in it together. If you didn't want to talk about something, that was fine—but everyone was on call and aware of what was going on.

"I'm fine, I promise. Just getting used to being on summer break, and it's nice to sleep in."

"Darwin and his mom came into the bakery yesterday, and she said he misses you so much. She said you are the best teacher he's ever had." My sister looked so proud as she said it. Like I'd found the cure for cancer or something fabulous like that.

"Well, he just finished kindergarten, so I'm kind of all

they know." I chuckled. It felt good to laugh.

"Vivi and Charlie, we need you!" Everly shouted from the kitchen. "We're having a little disagreement, and we need your input."

I set Bee down on the floor, and Vivian and I each held one of her hands and led her toward the kitchen.

Dylan, Ashlan, and Everly were standing at the oversized kitchen island, each with a glass of wine. Vivian picked up the glass she must have left on the counter earlier.

Ashlan poured me a glass of chardonnay and handed it to me before kissing my cheek.

Yep. They definitely all knew I was going through something.

"What's the disagreement?" Vivian asked as Bee padded over to the table to stand beside Paisley and Hadley as they all three looked at my nephew, Jackson, who was sleeping in his car seat.

Dylan flicked her thumb at Everly and laughed. "Bossy, over here, thinks that I was the reason that we got busted for ding-dong-ditching back in the day. Listen, I'd own it if it were true. But I don't get caught. I'm too sly."

Everly bit off the tip of a carrot stick and rolled her eyes. "You were the one that insisted we do just one more house. And then you went and chose a house that had that crazy, yappy dog—what was his name? Hotdog?"

"His name was Hot Tamale," Ashlan said over her laughter. "He's still alive. I saw him when I took Buddy to the vet last week. That poor dog has no bark left. He sounded like he had a bad case of the croup."

"How is he still alive? He was ten years old back in the day when we got caught. I remember Mr. Peterson kept shouting that we were going to be responsible for giving his ten-year-old dog a heart attack by ringing the bell," Vivian said as she took a sip of wine.

"He was so freaking dramatic to call the police on a bunch of kids who were just having fun." Dylan shook her head and didn't hide her irritation. "But I am not the one who got us caught. I made it onto the front porch and to his doorbell like a freaking gazelle. I could seriously help Matt Damon in *Bourne Identity*… I'm that stealthy."

"So we just got caught because he was waiting at the door for you?" Everly asked, raising a brow and trying to hide her smile.

"Hey." Dylan held up a piece of celery and pointed it at her. "I'm the one who suffered. I got tackled by that crazy son of theirs. What was his name? Dick? And he was like a man-child, right?"

Ashlan motioned to her that the girls were standing behind her and made a face. "His name was Drake. He was not a man-child. The guy was, like, twenty-five when he tackled you."

"Well, why was he always wearing those baby onesies, then?"

I barked out a laugh now because I couldn't hold it in even if I wanted to. "He was a mechanic, and he wore those jumpers for work, you fool."

"Well, let me tell you, he was not a little dude. He freaking pummeled my ass—I mean my *booty*." Dylan glanced at the kids and raised a brow to make it clear that she was being respectful.

"I'm still sad I missed that." Yes, I had stayed home with my parents because ding-dong-ditching scared me. I was a born rule follower. Always had been.

Up until the time I decided to have a week's worth of hot sex with my best friend's brother and then accidentally fall deeper in love with him than I already was.

This is why some people should not step out of their comfort zones.

"Oh, yes, little miss angel face was home with Ash and Mom and Dad, watching holiday movies." Dylan shook her head in disgust.

"I stand by that decision," I said.

"Well, I was, like, seven when this went down. Didn't Dad say you guys had police records?" Ashlan fell forward because she couldn't stop laughing.

"I was so terrified that I wouldn't get into college. Dad said we had records, and it scared me so bad. I remember crying for days to Mom that I hoped I could turn my life around." Vivi sighed.

"And Dad was furious with me for being the oldest and joining in, even though it was all Dilly's idea. Hawk kept telling me that Dad was just messing with us and we didn't have police records, but I believed it for a few days. At least during the time that we were grounded."

"I was not concerned about the police record because I was still trying to figure out why no one was upset that a grown man tackled me. I was, like, nine years old. That guy was a nut job. We didn't come to storm the castle. It was freaking ding-dong-ditch."

I smiled and shook my head. "Ash and I kept sneaking

you guys cookies in your rooms while you were grounded," I said. "And for the record, Drake Peterson works at Honey Mountain Auto and still rocks the jumpsuits."

"So why do you blame me? I think there was a snitch. That man knew I was coming to his door, and Dick came out of nowhere and took me down. And let me tell you, ladies... I have spider-like reflexes. So I don't go down without a fight. I didn't see that fucker coming."

The kitchen erupted in laughter, and Paisley's eyes grew wide as she stared at my sister. "Aunt Dilly, you should go to timeout for that one."

"Sorry, my love. I'll take a timeout right here in the kitchen." Dylan took a sip of wine just as our dad stepped into the kitchen. Niko, Jace, and Hawk were all out on the porch chatting with the guys from the firehouse who had come for dinner.

"Dad, we have a question," Vivian said.

"Ask away." He moved to the refrigerator and grabbed a beer.

"How did the Petersons know we were coming that night when we got into all that trouble for ding-dong-ditching?" Everly raised a brow.

"Ah... the night you all almost went to the big house." He smirked and ran a hand over the scruff on his jaw. "Didn't I ever tell you what happened?"

"Um, nooooo. I have been blamed for years," Dylan huffed.

I bumped my shoulder against my father's. "Do you know?"

"Of course, I do."

"Well?" Ash said, throwing her arms out to the sides.

"Charlie came home acting all nervous. So your mother figured it out, and I called all the neighbors to warn them. I told them to scare you if you rang their bell."

"You set me up?" Dylan shouted. "I can't believe you sold us out."

"It was a whole lot of fun watching you squirm. Joey wasn't even on duty that night. We asked him to come over in uniform and scare you. I wasn't about to raise a bunch of criminals. You kept it straight from then on." He took a long pull from his bottle and chuckled.

"I got tackled by a grown man," Dylan said, throwing her hands in the air.

"Yeah, that wasn't part of the plan." He barked out a laugh. "I did go over and have a talk with Drake about that afterward."

"Well, thank you for clearing my name, at least. I was not to blame, and I'd like that on the record." Dylan held her glass up, and we all clinked ours together.

This was exactly what I needed tonight.

Time with my sisters might not mend my broken heart, but it sure was a good distraction.

Chapter 24

Ledger

I hadn't felt right all week. I hadn't slept, and I missed the hell out of Charlotte. I sent her the flowers, and I texted her a couple times just to say hi, but I hadn't heard back. I felt like I was going out of my mind. I dreamed about her in the little time that I actually did sleep, and I thought about her all day.

I felt like something wasn't right at the office ever since my meeting with Harold and Stew. I even hired an outside attorney to take a look at the legal doc for the partnership. Hell, a couple weeks ago, I'd have just been happy to have an offer, but ever since I returned, I was seeing Harold differently than I ever had. Maybe it was the fact that Jessica and I had broken up, and he didn't like that. He had her come to the office for lunch twice this week, which was awkward as fuck because those were the days that I had a scheduled lunch with him. I was cordial to her, but when she came into my office after lunch on Monday and tried to climb me like a spider monkey, I was angry. I made it clear that I wasn't interested and asked her to leave. And the first person I wanted to talk to about it was Charlotte. I'd gotten used to sharing everything that happened in my day with her, and I missed it.

Today, I was having lunch with John Levins, and I hadn't even mentioned it to my boss because he'd been so against it. But I wasn't moving forward on a project of this size without having all the information before I agreed to do it. And Harold liked leaving out the details.

"Ledger," John said as he pushed to his feet from where he sat at a table in the back of the fancy dining room at one of our local lunch spots.

I shook his hand before taking the seat across from him. "Thanks for meeting me. I just wanted to make sure I had all the info before we got started."

"I understand," John said. "I'm always happy to discuss future projects. You know that Scott Bernard really wants you to take on this job."

I nodded, and we paused to place our lunch orders, and I reached for my water and took a sip. "I know that he wants Harold Cartwright's name on the building. I can respect that. But I'd like to be mentioned as the lead designer, as well. I know their friendship goes way back, but if I'm going to be the designer on this, I want to know that he'll work directly with me and not run to my boss behind my back."

He looked over his shoulder and leaned forward before whispering so only I could hear him. "You know that Scott doesn't care for Harold, right?"

"Haven't they been close friends for years?" That was

what Harold had told me.

"No. They are most definitely not friends. Scott is only taking this job because he wants you to design the museum. He saw what you did with the Charter building downtown, and you are the only architect he has in mind for this. But Harold said that the only way you can design for Scott is under his name. I believe his exact words were: *If you want him, you have to go through me. I own him.* Harold is the one insisting that his name gets top billing. Between you and me, Scott would prefer to do this without Harold or his slimy attorney, Stew. Just be careful with that contract, Ledger. They pushed hard to make sure you don't get top billing, even though Scott has included a clause that you and he have the final say in all the designs."

What the fuck?

I shook my head. "Wow. I'm in the middle of negotiating a partnership, but it sure doesn't sound like he's there, does it?"

"He hasn't designed in years. Everyone knows you are his secret weapon. Hell, I was at a party a few months ago, and he joked about you being his boy and how he and his daughter had a plan to make you part of the family. Everyone thought it was funny, but it was creepy as fuck. Just watch your back, okay?"

"Yeah. Thank you. So, we haven't signed anything with Scott yet, correct?"

"Nope. We're waiting on you, because Scott demanded you be on the contract since you're the one he wanted to work with. And let me tell you, Harold didn't like it. He tried to sign without you when you were out of town. I'm sure he's pressuring you to sign it because he's added some small print that is pretty shady. You're barely being acknowledged, Ledger."

I nodded. This wasn't all a complete surprise. I'd been warned many times about Harold. I didn't fully trust the man, but he had put a lot of faith in me as far as designing projects that I wouldn't have been able to work on if I hadn't been at his firm. But it sounded like he was shadier than I thought. I thought he was on the way out of his career and scraping to hold on.

And he was *using me* as a way to do that.

"Do me a favor. Ask Scott not to sign anything just yet. I'm working on something."

Our food was set down on the table, and we both paused and waited for the server to walk away.

"Oh, yeah? What are you up to, Dane?"

"Something I've been thinking about for a couple of weeks." It had been something I'd thought about for years before but had kind of given up on. But after being home for those two weeks, something had shifted in me, and I couldn't shake it.

"Good. Scott will have no problem if you make a move. This job is yours, regardless of who you work for."

"That's all I needed to hear. Thank you for being honest with me."

"Always."

My mind was still spinning after I left lunch with John as I made my way back to the office. Had Harold been playing me this whole time? The wording on the partnership was unclear, which was why I brought in a third party. Stew was not looking out for my best interest. He was Harold's attorney, and I needed to keep that in mind.

When I arrived back at the office, I made my way to Harold's office. Mariana, who'd been his assistant for years, was walking my way.

"Hi, Ledger. Are you looking for Harold?" she asked.

"I am. Is he in?"

"He is. But he's in a meeting with Stew. I just called them because Jessica called, but he asked me not to disturb him. So, it must be serious if he didn't take her call." She shrugged. "You can wait or leave him a note to ask him to come see you when he's done. Otherwise, three hundred things will come up before I get back to my desk, and I don't want to forget to tell him that you need to see him. I'm just going downstairs to grab a coffee and a cookie. Can I get you anything?"

"Nope. I just came from lunch. I'll just leave a note on your desk, and if you can have him stop by before he leaves today, that would be great."

"You got it." She waved, and I headed farther down the hall and turned into his waiting area outside his office.

I moved behind her desk and pulled out a sticky note just as a voice came over her conference phone.

"What if he doesn't sign it?" That was Stew talking. I was about to pick up the receiver and hang it up when Harold spoke.

"Ledger may be talented, but he isn't quite that sharp. He'd do just about anything to make partner. He'll sign it."

I dropped down in Mariana's chair and fumbled to get my phone out and clicked it on record to capture the rest of the conversation. I figured I might need this sooner than I thought. After my conversation at lunch, nothing was sitting right with me. And this conversation that I was overhearing only proved that more.

"What happens a few years down the line when he no longer likes the arrangement? I mean, you aren't giving him anything more than he already has now, aside from telling him he's a partner. He'll have no say in anything, nor will he have a piece of the pie financially." Stew sounded hesitant.

"He'll have a career working under my name. I made him. This is how he can thank me. I mean, you'd think the asshole would be more than willing to go all-in with Jessica. Then this would be a family business. But he's being a stubborn ass about that, and I don't appreciate it."

"Well, it would be a family business that he'd be an employee at. It would never really be his, right?" Stew asked with a laugh.

"Well, if he ends up with my daughter, he'll have ownership at some point." He sounded so smug and cocky.

"I don't think Jessica would be very happy to know that you're marrying her off to keep your business alive." Now, it was Stew's turn to chuckle. Like they were discussing the weather, not my life and his daughter's life.

Obviously, Jessica wasn't in on this plan, which I was grateful for.

"My daughter wants to be taken care of. She wanted me to set them up because she likes him. She doesn't need to know that it would help me, as well. It's just killing two birds with one stone."

"Well, we need him to sign that damn museum contract, or I think Scott will pull out if Ledger doesn't do it." Stew seemed slightly concerned, and he had good reason to be.

"He'll sign. Where the hell is he going without me?" My hands fisted at my sides, and I pushed to my feet. I clicked off my phone, knowing what I needed to do. I probably wouldn't need the recording, but I had it if things got ugly.

I'd heard all I needed to.

I stopped by my office and dropped the contracts into my briefcase, and I made my way back to my condo. My sterile, quiet, expensive condo.

I paced in front of the wall of windows, looking out at the city. But it wasn't the fact that my boss and mentor was a pretentious, scheming prick that was on my mind. I'd always known it, hadn't I?

I just never cared before.

Before her.

Before I looked at everything differently. It wasn't the view at Charlotte's house that I missed. Of course, I liked the lake. But what I missed was the girl.

Her smile.

Her warmth.

Her laughter.

Don't even get me started on her body.

Fuck. I fucked up.

I missed our talks. I looked forward to seeing her first thing in the morning. I looked forward to hearing about her day and sharing mine with her.

My grandmother was right. I was a coward.

I'd been so afraid of doing something to hurt her—but that was exactly what I'd done, anyway. And I'd hurt myself, too.

If I were being honest, I'd always missed Charlie. I'd been dating women that didn't compare to her. Dating women like

Jessica because there was no risk. No connection. No real feelings.

But Charlotte had always been different.

She wasn't just a part of my past.

She was my future.

Why did I fear the future?

I picked up my phone and dialed my sister.

"Hey, how are you?" she asked when she answered.

I let out a long sigh and dropped to sit in the leather chair in the corner. I ran a hand over the top of my head. "I don't know, Jilly Bean. I've been better."

"Well, that's very honest of you. What's going on?"

"I don't know. When I went back to Honey Mountain, I thought it would be a long two weeks, but it was fucking great. And now I'm back, and nothing's really working for me here, and I'm wondering what the fuck I'm doing with my life." I leaned my head back against the chair and let out a long breath.

"It's about time you admitted it. I'm not sure what the fuck you've been doing with your life for quite a while," she said.

"I can always count on you for honesty, can't I?"

"You can. Is it the job or the fact that you're lonely because you don't let yourself go deep with anyone outside of our family?"

"The job will be fine. I know I'm good at what I do, and I've always trusted my gut professionally. So, it's time to jump. No question there. But, that's not where my head is..." I admitted.

"Where's your head?" she asked.

"I'm in love with Charlotte Thomas. It wasn't supposed to happen, although I'm fairly certain I've loved her for a long time. I crossed the line and came up with this ridiculous plan. I thought I could walk away, Jilly. But I'm fucking miserable. I can't sleep. I can't eat. Hell, I'm in the middle of a crazy-ass disaster at work, and I don't even fucking care." Here's the thing. I knew my position at work; I knew how I was treated and what was going on. When it was just me, it was no big deal. I'd work through it. But now there was someone else, even though I tried to deny it. Someone else that I loved and wanted to have it all with, and knowing what I knew now, this job wasn't going to work anymore.

She'd changed that.

Hell, she'd changed everything.

I heard chuckling in the background and was fairly certain Garrett was laughing, too. "Are you with Garrett, and are you two fucking laughing at me?"

"Take it down a notch. We just both predicted this, but we weren't sure that your stubborn ass would ever admit it," Jilly said.

"Hey there, brother-in-law. I hope you don't mind being on speakerphone." Garrett laughed. "I think Robby is going to be very upset if you swoop in and steal his girl."

"She isn't talking to that dude, is she?" I hissed. "No offense, Garrett, but your cousin is not getting in the way of this."

"She isn't talking to him. Don't be ridiculous. Garrett just wanted to make you sweat a little."

"It's more like I wanted to give you a wake-up call to get off your ass. You deserve this, brother. I saw it when you were here. Hell, I think we all did. Time to put your guard down and stop being a big pussy about it," Garrett said.

Wow. Tell me how you really feel.

"And what happens if I fuck it up?"

"Well, she's pretty devastated right now, and so are you, so I can't imagine you could fuck it up more than this," Jilly said.

"She deserves better," I whispered.

"Ledger." Jilly's voice cracked, and a lump formed in my throat. That was the thing with my baby sister, we could be joking one minute and then go deep the next. We'd always been straight with one another. "It is not your fault that Dad left. He's a cheating bastard; it was going to happen. That had nothing to do with you. You're the most loyal man I know. You won't mess this up because you love her. And you always protect the people you love. Trust me—I can vouch for you."

I scrubbed a hand down my face and was surprised that a little moisture was there. Emotion welled, and it wasn't something I was used to dealing with.

But I was feeling all of it right here, right now. Everything was happening at once, and maybe that was how it was meant to be.

"Thank you, Jilly. That means a lot to me."

"It's all true," she said, and her words trembled.

"Ledger, you know I'm not much of a sentimental guy— but she's right. I love Charlie like a little sister, and I have zero concern about you doing anything to hurt her. Well, anything you haven't already done to hurt her by being a scared little pussy."

"What is it with you and calling me a pussy all of a sudden?

Why don't you call Robby and tell him to back the fuck off? She's spoken for. She just doesn't know it yet." I pushed to my feet, pacing around my apartment.

"Yes!" Jilly shouted, and I held the phone away from my ear. "What are you going to do?"

"Whatever it takes." I hurried to my room and started throwing things in a bag. "Don't say anything to her, Jilly. I want to talk to her myself. Hopefully, I haven't fucked things up so badly that she won't hear me out."

"She'll hear you out. She's been pretty down, Ledger."

My chest squeezed. "I've tried reaching out, but she doesn't respond."

"Well, you offered her a permanent hook-up situation with no strings attached. She's not that girl, and you know it. Having this fling—or whatever the hell you two called it—that was big for her. She only did it because it was you. And she wanted it with you so badly that she bent her rules," Jilly said, and I could hear the disappointment in her voice.

"Hey. I'm more than aware that I fucked up, okay? I'm going to fix this. I'll let you know when I get there."

I ended the call and sent Charlotte a text.

Me: Hey. I need to talk to you.

I waited ten minutes while I threw a bunch of clothes in my suitcase, and I grabbed my car keys.

If she wouldn't talk to me on the phone, she'd talk to me in person.

It was time to get my life on track. I'd wasted too much time already.

My phone rang, and I glanced down to see Harold calling. I sent him to voice mail, and I chuckled because that would piss him off. The man liked me at his beck and call. But I was done with that.

Done with a lot of things.

I pulled out of the parking garage, and I had my Bluetooth call Dan Garfer.

"Ledger, glad to hear from you. I was afraid you'd go back home and forget about us," he said through the speaker system.

"Nope. That's not going to happen."

"Have you talked to your boss? Is he still considering it?"

"I need to ask you something, Dan."

"Sure, what is it?"

"Are you hoping to work with *me,* or were you hoping to work with Harold Cartwright?"

"Uh, no offense, but I don't know anything about Harold Cartwright. We'd like to work with you because you're talented. I mean, that architecture magazine did that article on you last year, and I think everyone in Honey Mountain bought it and hung it in their shops. You're from here, and we trust you. And your grandmother makes the best pie in town, so that doesn't hurt. Either."

I laughed. "Good to know, Dan. You can count on me to do it. It'll be just me that you're working with. I won't be doing this through the firm."

"I have no problem with that. I actually prefer it. And you'll be able to work with us on the price, like we discussed earlier?"

"Absolutely. We can make that budget work."

"This is great news, Ledger. When can I announce it?"

"Give me a few days to get my ducks in a row. But I'll be

back in town this week, and I'll personally bring the contract over."

"I can't thank you enough. Looking forward to working with you, Ledger."

"Me, too." I ended the call, and my fingers itched to call Charlotte.

But I'd have to wait and do this in person.

I wanted to tell her that I was leaving my job.

Making changes in every area of my life.

Most importantly, I was coming for her.

And I wasn't going to stop until she heard me out.

Chapter 25

Charlotte

Nan had invited me to come over to her place for dinner, as we'd spent some time in her garden yesterday. She asked numerous times if I was okay, and I insisted that I was. It was embarrassing how not okay I was. My first attempt at a fling was an epic fail. I've had relationships that lasted years, where I felt completely fine when they ended. Yet a two-week fling left me barely functioning.

My sisters and Jilly kept coming over to check on me, and I'd become pretty good at putting on a fake smile and acting like I was okay. And every time Ledger texted me just to say hi, it felt like a punch to the gut. I needed to get over Ledger, and making small talk every day with him was not going to help me do that.

For him, it was probably easy because he wasn't hurting. He wasn't tossing and turning all night because he missed the feel of my body beside his. He didn't ache for my presence or to hear my voice or laughter.

But being with Nan had been the most content I'd felt since he left. Maybe it was the familiarity or the fact that they were so close and had similar senses of humor. Or that she didn't push me to talk about it, even though I was sure she knew something had gone on between us.

I walked up the three steps to her front door and knocked.

"Come in, my girl!" she shouted.

I pulled open the door and was immediately hit with the smell of peaches and honey. The woman was a fabulous cook, and her pies were as good as Vivian's.

"Hi, Nan. The house smells so good," I said as I made my way into the kitchen and kissed her cheek.

"Well, you're looking too skinny lately, and I'm determined to put some meat on those bones." She wore the cutest floral apron, and her hair was curled tightly against her scalp. She was one of my favorite people on the planet because she had a side to her that was this sweet grandmother, and then she had a wild side that always made me laugh. I imagined my sister, Dylan, would be a lot like Nan when she got older.

"I'm eating plenty, trust me." I was fibbing just a little bit as I hadn't had an appetite in days, but I knew it was temporary. This feeling would eventually pass, and I'd move on. What choice did I have? I took the glass of sweet tea that she offered me. "What can I do to help?"

"Nothing, my love. I want you to sit right here and tell me what you did today." Nan sat down in the chair across from me.

"I floated in the canoe for a few hours and read Ashlan's

new book that she just finished. I'm her beta reader."

"Oh. What's a beta reader?"

"I read what she writes early and give her feedback. It works out great for both of us because she appreciates the input, and I love reading, especially her books."

Nan rubbed her hands together, and her eyes sparkled. "I've been meaning to pick one up. I've never been much of a reader, but maybe I should start. Are they sexy?"

I laughed. "They are pretty sexy. This one has this alpha hero, and he's in the military and is the heroine's bodyguard. It's really good."

"Oh, my. You know my husband was in the military, and let me tell you... that man could rock my world with just a look. I can't count how many times he undressed me with his eyes in front of a room full of people."

My mouth fell open. Nan was quite the dirty bird, as Ledger and Jilly called her, but she never talked to me about her own sex life. "Really? I knew you had a great marriage, but I didn't know it was so—steamy."

"Oh, my girl, we took advantage of every moment we had alone," she said, and I took a sip of tea as I listened. "And for the record, the man was very well-endowed. He had some kind of award-winning penis."

I spewed iced tea all over the table and coughed so hard I could barely catch my breath. Nan was on her feet with a towel and patting my back as she laughed hysterically. "Have you never seen a penis, Charlie?"

It took me a minute to catch my breath. "I have. I just didn't expect you to talk about your husband's penis."

She handed me a few paper towels to clean myself up and

sat back down. "Please don't tell me you've never had good sex. That will break my heart."

Thoughts of Ledger flooded my head. In my bed. In the canoe. In the living room. In the kitchen.

I could feel my face heat, and I was certain that I was three shades of red.

"I have... I mean, not often. But..." I certainly couldn't tell her that her grandson had rocked my world in more ways than one.

"Well, look at you. Welcome to the club. It looks like you're a new member from the way you're blushing, like you're still trying to process it all." She took a minute to think and tapped her finger against her lips as if a lightbulb had gone off. She leaned forward and whispered, "Apparently, the apple doesn't fall far from the tree. Glad to hear my boy is a giver."

My eyes doubled in size, and I shook my head. But there was no sense denying it. The woman would never believe me, anyway, and she was right. Ledger clearly had an award-winning penis, too.

"Don't worry about it. Your secret is safe with me. So tell me how you're really doing. Don't sugarcoat it for me the way you do for everyone else. I may be a nosy old lady, but I can keep a secret. I know you're hurting."

"I'm really okay." I bit down on my bottom lip.

"What if we talk without names? Would that help you?"

"What do you mean?"

"Well, did someone I don't know maybe hurt your heart? Some stubborn little turd that can't get his head on straight?" She chuckled.

I smiled and shook my head, but for whatever reason,

talking to Nan felt safe. She had a way of making you feel comfortable. "It wasn't like I didn't know what I was getting into."

"But you can't stop love, my girl. And remember this... just because someone is afraid of it doesn't mean they don't feel it. You know that, right?"

Not really, but I liked the idea of thinking it was true.

"Maybe."

"Let's take my grandson, for example." She held her hands up to stop me from insisting it wasn't him that we were talking about, even though we both knew it was. "He's this strong, charismatic man. He's determined to take care of his family because his own father failed at the job. He's afraid to love because he's been let down so many times by his own father, and then losing Colt the way he did just added to his fear of allowing himself to go deep with people. Sure, he loves me and Jilly and Kalie because he already did. But allowing himself to go there with others now—not happening. But that doesn't mean he doesn't feel it. It just means he's terrified of it. I think my favorite grandson has been terrified of his feelings for you for a long time."

Her words resonated with me. "I'll bet you were the best therapist back in the day, huh?"

"Oh, yes. I had a mile-long waitlist. I'm good at helping people work through their shit. Except for Ledger." She said his name, and her tone turned serious. Her eyes welled with emotion. "I haven't gotten through to him yet. But I'm not giving up on him, and I hope you don't either."

A lump formed in my throat. "You can't make someone love you, Nan."

"Oh, my girl, loving you is not the problem. It's loving himself that he has to come to terms with." She patted my hands, and I let out a long breath. I didn't want to talk about him anymore because hoping for something that wasn't going to happen was not a way for me to move on.

"So, tell me what we're having for dinner."

She smiled, her eyes filled with empathy and understanding. "I made pork chops, mashed potatoes, applesauce, and a green salad with all the fixings from my garden."

"That sounds delicious."

Nan dropped the subject, and we ate and talked and laughed over the next hour. She didn't eat nearly as much as me, as she said her stomach had been a little off all day. But she continued pushing food on my plate, which made me chuckle.

I groaned when I ate the first bite of peach pie. "This is so good."

"I'm just happy to see you eating." She smiled and something crossed her face that I couldn't read. She leaned back in her chair and cleared her throat.

"Are you all right?" I asked as I spooned another bite into my mouth.

"Yes. I think I'm just having a little indigestion. My arm has been bothering me, so we must have worked a little too hard in the garden yesterday." She rubbed her chest, and her smile looked forced.

"What? Is your chest hurting?" I jumped to my feet and hurried to stand next to her.

"I'm all right, my girl. I just need a second."

I rubbed her back, and before I could even process what

was happening, Nan fell forward and gasped. I wrapped my arms around her and tried to stop her from falling out of the chair. But we both went down, and thankfully, my arms shielded her head from hitting the floor.

"Nan, what's happening?" I shouted, patting my hands over her face, but her eyes were glazed over. She wasn't speaking. A layer of sweat covered her forehead.

I ran to get my phone and dialed 911, leaning my ear to her mouth to make sure she was breathing. Her breaths were labored, but she was breathing.

"I'm breathing, Charlie. But you're going to suffocate me if you put that ear any closer," Nan said, and I pulled back and gaped at her. My tears dripped down, landing on her neck. Her voice was weak, and I saw the fear in her eyes.

"Nine-one-one, what's your emergency?"

I rattled off Nan's address and said I thought she was having a heart attack.

"Is she conscious?"

"Yes, she's talking to me a little bit," I croaked. "But she's on the floor, and her breaths are shallow. She's sweaty, too."

"It'll be okay, my girl," Nan whispered.

"Okay, keep her talking. We've got an ambulance on the way."

"Okay," I said, and I pushed the hair back from her face as the tears continued to fall. "You're okay, Nan. They're on their way."

"I'm sorry." The words were barely audible.

"I need to call Kalie and Jilly," I said when she squeezed my hand. I knew Kalie was on a date tonight, so she wasn't at home.

"We've got time." When Nan spoke, her words were labored and spaced out, and I was scared to death I was going to lose her. I couldn't hang up on the 911 operator, so I just sat there, holding her hand and talking to her.

"Tell me what your favorite flower is," I said, because I wanted to keep her talking.

"The peony. It's going to be okay, Charlie." Her voice faded with my name.

"Nan," I cried. "Please keep talking to me."

"Are you there, Charlotte?" the operator asked.

"I'm here."

"Okay, they just pulled in. Can you go to the door and open it for them? Is she still talking?"

"Yes," I sobbed.

Memories of the day I came home from school and saw an ambulance outside of my house came crashing down on me. The day my mother passed away.

I couldn't lose Nan.

I hurried to the door and opened it, just as four men surged past me. They hooked her up to all sorts of machines and asked her questions before getting her onto some sort of bed and lifting it up so they could wheel her out.

"Can I come with her?" I asked, swiping at the tears as I frantically sent a group text to Kalie, Jilly, and Ledger.

Ledger.

He wasn't here. This would kill him.

I just said that she was being taken by ambulance to Honey Mountain Hospital.

"Absolutely," one of the paramedics said with a smile that told me he empathized with my concern. I hurried over to shut off the stove and blow out the candle before chasing them out the door and climbing into the ambulance.

Nan wasn't saying as much anymore, and that had me in full-blown panic mode.

"Nan, keep talking," I said as I took the seat beside her and reached for her hand.

"It's okay, my girl," she whispered, the last words even more light and airy. The paramedic who sat beside me stood and read the numbers on a few machines that were set up around her.

"Let them know we're coming, and she's in distress!" he shouted to someone as we tore down the road toward the hospital.

My heart was racing and breaking at the same time. Suddenly, all that food I ate was threatening to come back up.

A sob escaped, and I desperately tried to push it away. To stay in control. Not to lose it in front of Nan because that would only scare her.

The lump in my throat made it painful to breathe.

When we arrived at the hospital, there was a team of people waiting outside, and I got shoved back against the wall as they hurried her out of the ambulance. Nan was whisked away, and I jumped down and chased after her.

"I'm right here, Nan!" I shouted.

When they got to the double doors, a nurse turned around, and I came to an abrupt stop. "I'm sorry. You have to wait here. We need to see what's going on. I'll let you know as soon as I can."

I nodded and pressed my back against the wall after she walked through the double doors, leaving me standing here alone. I slid down the wall until my butt hit the floor, and I buried my head in my knees and sobbed.

My phone was vibrating like crazy in my pocket, and I knew they were probably worried sick and frantic to know what was happening. When I pulled my phone out of my pocket, I saw Ledger's name light up the screen.

I answered his call, but I couldn't speak.

"Ladybug, what's happening? Is she okay?"

"I don't know," I sobbed, and I didn't even know if he could make out the words that I was saying because they were muffled by my cries.

"I'm on my way, okay? She's going to be all right. She has to be."

I looked up to see Jilly and Garrett sprinting toward me. "Jilly's here."

Jilly bent down in front of me, tears streaming down her face. I dropped my phone, and I didn't know if I even ended the call.

"What happened?" Jilly asked, as she swiped at the tears, and Kalie came running around the corner with Dr. Bickler on her heels.

I tried my best to tell them everything that had happened. But my words were shaky, and it had all happened so fast.

"She was fine one minute, and then she was on the floor," I said, shaking my head in disbelief.

"Let me go see what I can find out," Dr. Bickler said as he squeezed my knee and kissed Kalie on the cheek.

"Thank you," she said as she slid down to sit against the wall beside me and wrapped an arm around me. "Thank you for being there with her, honey."

I nodded, swiping at the moisture that was making it difficult to see. "Of course. I just hope she's okay. She was talking at first, but then she got quiet in the ambulance."

"Hopefully, Steven can find out what's going on," Kalie said, just as I looked up to see Dylan running toward us.

"Is she okay?" she asked, and as strong as she liked to be, she didn't hide the fear in her eyes.

I didn't think there was a person in Honey Mountain who didn't love Nan.

"We don't know. It sounds like she had a heart attack," Jilly said, as she sat on the other side of me and held my hand.

"How did you know we were here?" I asked, shaking my head because my sister always knew when I needed her. All of them did, actually, and I had a hunch the rest wouldn't be far behind.

"Ledger called me," she said, bending down in front of me as her gaze searched mine to make sure I was okay.

"He did?" I gasped.

"Yeah. He said you got Nan to the hospital and that you were very upset, and he was worried. He sounded frantic, honestly."

"I need to go call him back." Jilly moved to her feet and paced over by the row of chairs in the waiting room.

"Why don't we all move over there to sit," Garrett said, as he helped Kalie to her feet and Dylan pulled me up.

Vivian came around the corner, wearing pajamas with her hair in a messy knot on top of her head. "Is she okay?"

"We're waiting to hear," Kalie said as we each took a chair in the waiting room.

Jilly was talking to her brother on the phone with her

hands flailing around.

Ashlan and Everly rushed in and hurried over to me. Everly's face was completely panicked as she squeezed my arms and looked me up and down as if I were injured.

"I'm fine. It's Nan I'm worried about," I said, finally pulling myself together and speaking without sobbing.

"That had to be traumatic for you, though," Everly whispered. "Thank goodness you were there."

Dr. Bickler came around the corner and sat beside Kalie as he filled us in. He didn't know much more than we did, but he said it sure sounded like she had a heart attack. He said that they promised someone would be out to fill us in soon.

I looked up to see my father walking toward me. He was in his Honey Mountain firefighter tee as he stepped in and searched the waiting room until his eyes locked with mine.

There was something about my dad that had always made me feel safe and loved and cared for. Even with all he'd lost when my mom passed, this man had shown up for us every single day.

I pushed to my feet and ran toward him. He wrapped his arms around me, and I broke down in tears all over again.

"You're all right, sweetheart." He patted me on the back, and my cheek rested on his chest. "Any updates on Nan?"

"We're just waiting," I said.

We moved to the chairs, and my father took the seat beside me.

And we all just sat there quietly as we waited.

Chapter 26

Ledger

I had too much time to think in the car as I made my way back to Honey Mountain. Jilly had filled me in on what happened, as Charlie had been hysterical when I spoke to her. And they still didn't know shit. I pulled into the parking lot and ran toward the hospital.

When I stormed into the waiting room, my mother and Jilly were standing with a man in scrubs, who I assumed was the doctor. I made my way over to them, but my gaze locked with Charlie's as I walked past the group in the waiting room.

The sadness in her eyes nearly brought me to my knees.

"This is my brother," Jilly said as she turned around to see me coming. "Dr. Robings is just filling us in."

"Your grandmother suffered a heart attack, and thankfully she wasn't alone, and you got her here in time. This could have turned out very differently, so you saved her life by getting her here." He let out a long breath.

"What does that mean?" I asked, because I knew heart attacks weren't good, but I didn't really know much more than that.

"It means the heart muscle is not getting the oxygen that it needs to function. We're prepping her now for bypass surgery, which will create a new path for the blood to flow around the blocked artery."

Fuck. This wasn't good.

"How long will she be in surgery?" I asked as I glanced at my mother and sister, who both had tear-streaked faces and looked like they were at a loss for words.

"It can take anywhere from three to six hours. You all can go home, and we can call you when she gets out."

"No. We'll be here." I cleared my throat. No fucking way would Nan be waking up alone.

"All right, well, at least go get some coffee. It's going to be a long night. I'll keep you posted."

"Thank you, Dr. Robings," my mother said.

"Oh my god. Nan's having bypass surgery?" Jilly asked over her tears. I wrapped my arms around her and hugged her.

"She's the toughest woman I know. She'll be okay." I wasn't certain, but I damn well wasn't going to say that.

My mother updated everyone in the waiting room and told them they should head home because we were going to be here until morning.

Jack Thomas, Charlie's dad, pushed to his feet and looked over at his daughters. "Let's give them some privacy, and we can come back in the morning."

The Thomas girls pushed out their chairs to stand, and

my gaze locked once again with Charlie's. There was so much that I wanted to say to her, but this was not the time or the place for that conversation.

"Thank you for being there with her," I said, shoving my hands into my pockets to keep from reaching for her.

"Of course. I'm just so sorry," she said as she lunged herself at me, and I wrapped my arms around her.

"The doctor said you saved her life," Jilly croaked from behind her. "He said we are so lucky you were there, and you got her here so quickly."

Charlotte pulled back and swiped at the tears falling down her face and nodded. "Please keep me posted, okay? I'll come back in the morning."

I nodded and watched as she hugged my sister and my mother before following her family out the door.

The next six hours were the worst of my life. I couldn't think straight. I thought about Nan and how big of a role she'd played in my life all these years. She'd been my rock. My sounding board.

I couldn't imagine existing in a world that she wasn't in.

I also thought about how precious life was. How so much of it was out of our control. How I'd spent so many years trying to control everything. Who I let in. Who I trusted. Who needed me and what I could do for them.

And at the end of the day, none of that fucking mattered.

You were lucky to have this time with the people that you loved—and you should be fucking grateful for every day that you had with them.

My mother had insisted that Dr. Bickler head home, and she, Garrett, Jilly, and I took turns going to get coffee and sharing funny stories about Nan.

"You know Nan calls your boyfriend McSexy, or something crazy like that," I said as I pushed to my feet and tossed the empty paper coffee cup in the trash.

"McHottie," Jilly said with a laugh.

My mother blushed. "He is easy on the eyes, isn't he?"

"Yeah, this is a conversation I am happy not to take part in." I rolled my eyes, and Garrett laughed so loud it prompted the rest of us to join in. And then we fell into silence once again. At a loss for words.

"Thank God Charlie was there with her," my mother whispered.

The irony was not lost on me. This girl had been what was missing from my life. It didn't surprise me that she'd be the person to be there when Nan needed her most. That was who Charlie was.

All that sweetness wrapped up into the most beautiful woman I'd ever known.

"I just texted her, and she's still so shaken up. She wanted to come back, but I told her to get some sleep, and we'd see her in the morning."

I nodded. There was so much that I wanted to say to her. I didn't even know where to start.

I hated that she was upset and that I was so shaken up.

I hated the fear in her voice when I'd called her, and she'd sobbed and cried.

I knew it probably brought back memories of the day her mother passed away at their family home.

Charlotte Thomas loved with her whole heart, and I knew she loved my grandmother fiercely.

We all did.

I prayed like hell that she would be okay.

And I made a silent promise that I would never take the people in my life for granted again.

I was going to start living the life that I was meant to live.

Not the safe life I'd been living for the last few years.

• • •

It had been a painfully long night. Nan's surgery had gone well, and she was in recovery. They were going to keep her here for a few days, but the bottom line was—she was going to be okay. They said we could head home and get some rest as she wouldn't be ready to see anyone for a few hours.

My mother and Jilly sobbed, and I just buried my face in my hands and let out a long breath I hadn't even realized I'd been holding.

"You okay, brother?" Garrett asked as he clapped me on the shoulder.

"Yeah. I'm fucking relieved."

"Life is short, man. It sure makes you appreciate things, doesn't it?" he asked.

"It does." I nodded.

"I'm going to go take a shower, and then I'll be back," my mother said.

"Yeah, let's do that." Jilly looked at her husband, and he pushed to his feet. I realized in that moment that if you wasted all your time worrying about who was going to hurt you or who you were going to let down, you'd miss out on the little things. The important things. This man was standing here by my sister's side because he loved her. He was supporting her any way he could.

And that was love.

It was showing up for the good days and the bad days.

I thought about Charlotte. She called 911 and held Nan's hand all the way to the hospital. It hadn't brought back good memories for her—but there she was. Showing up because she loved Nan. Not running away because it was hard.

"You guys go. I'm just going to hang here for now."

"Are you sure?" my mother asked as I pushed to my feet and hugged her one more time.

"Yep. I'll go catch a shower when you get back."

Jilly pushed up on her tiptoes and kissed my cheek. "Thanks, brother. I love you."

"Love you, too."

I spent the next few hours thinking.

Planning.

Dreaming.

Just the way Nan would want me to.

"Ledger Dane?" A nurse called out. I'd let them know I'd be staying here until she woke up.

"Yep." I stood.

"Your grandmother is awake, and she's asking for you."

I smiled. Of course, she was. She knew I'd be here, waiting for her dirty bird ass to wake up.

I followed the nurse down a long hallway. Machines were beeping, and the lighting was dim as we turned right at the end of the hall, and she pushed open the first door.

Nan was propped up, sipping some water, and her lips turned up in the corners when she saw me.

"There's my favorite grandson."

"Your only grandson." I smirked. "How are you doing, Nan?"

I dropped into the chair beside her and reached for her hand.

"I'm doing fine, my boy. Looks like my ticker just needed some new batteries."

I rolled my eyes. "I think it was a little more than that."

Her smile fell. "How's Charlie? I know I scared the bejeezus out of her."

"She's all right. Just worried about you. She'll be back over here to see you in a little bit, I'm sure."

She nodded and shifted in the bed, and I pushed to my feet and reached for her. "Are you hurting?"

"Oh, boy, is this how it's going to be? I'm just sick of laying down, and I want to sit forward."

I rolled my eyes because Nan being the patient was not going to be easy. "Just let me help you, you stubborn woman."

She chuckled. "Well, it takes one to know one. Sit back down, I'm good. Just because I had a heart attack does not mean I'm some fragile flower."

I sighed and dropped back down in the chair. "I know. You're a tough old bird."

"Damn straight. Now, let's talk about you. Are you okay that you're missing work again after just getting back a week ago? I feel bad that you drove all the way back."

I cleared my throat and leaned forward in my chair, clasping my hands together. If I was going to start making changes, it was time to do it now. "I was already in the car, driving back, when I got the call."

Her gaze narrowed. "Really? Are you just trying to make

me feel better?"

"No. I'm not that nice."

She let a loud laugh escape, and I smiled because I loved seeing my grandmother happy. "Good point. What were you coming back for?"

"I'm thinking of making some big changes in my life." I raised a brow.

"What kind of changes are we talking about? Like becoming the new stripper for my bridge club or moving to a new country?"

"I'm thinking of moving back here."

"Will that snobby, rich boss of yours allow that?"

"I sent him my resignation along with the bullshit contract he sent me without a signature this morning when I had all that time to think. My attorney told me it was all fluff. There was never going to be a partnership. The truth is—I don't want to be his sidekick anymore. I'm ready to branch out on my own. Choose the projects that I want to do and do them. Not because they'll make my name famous or people will be impressed, but because I'm passionate about it."

"Interesting. And you can do that back here?" She had the biggest smile on her face, and it made my chest squeeze.

"I can. I'm going to take on that museum project on my own, along with the Honey Mountain Middle School project. I can do both from here. I'm also going to invest in that house-flipping business with Niko, Jace, and Hawk. I'll keep my condo in the city and get a place here—and go back and forth."

"What about your father's house? Do you still have to design it?"

I chuckled. "I may or may not have recorded my boss

planning to screw me over and threatened to go public with the info. So, we made a deal."

"What kind of deal?"

"I go away quietly and don't destroy his reputation, and he honors the contract that the firm agreed to design the house. I get to walk away, free of both of them," I said.

"Wow. You've thought of everything. You're not doing this for me, are you?" she asked, and her eyes studied mine with an intensity I hadn't seen in a long time from Nan. She wasn't normally this serious, but she clearly didn't want me doing this for her.

I'd do anything for this woman, but she wasn't the reason I was coming home.

"I decided this before you had your heart attack. I'm doing this for me," I said.

And for Charlotte.

"Well, it's about damn time. Are you ready to start living, Ledger? Really living? Not just making the big bucks, although I don't mind getting those fancy Christmas and birthday gifts." She waggled her brows. "But I'd sure like to see you happy. Rich in other ways than just money. And I think you've found that here, haven't you?"

"I'm not giving away all my secrets just yet. We all know how chatty you get when you're gossiping."

She rubbed her hands together. "How about after you seal the deal, you haul that booty back here and tell me about it first? I'm getting old, Ledger. If you're ever planning to get hitched, you best get a move on."

I groaned. "And this is why I like to keep some things to myself. I've got to win the girl over first. Let's not put the cart before the horse."

"Well, I hope she makes you grovel."

I kissed the back of her hand. "I'll do whatever it takes."

Her eyes were wet with emotion. "Finally. I'm sure happy that you're moving back here, because you were a real hit with the girls down at the pool. I'm running for president of the club, so if I can work in a once-a-month striptease, that would sure help me out."

"Didn't you just have a heart attack? Do you have no shame, woman?"

"None at all." She chuckled.

"Mom and Jilly will be here soon. Keep this between us so I can tell them later, all right?"

"Your secrets are always safe with me, Ledger."

"I love you, Nan."

"I love you more, my boy."

The door opened, and Charlotte walked in, and my breath caught in my throat.

"Is it okay that I'm here?" she asked; her bottom lip trembled as she looked from me to Nan.

"Of course, it is, my sweet girl. Come on over here." Nan patted her bed, and Charlie hurried over to her.

"I was so worried. I'm so glad you're okay." Her voice wobbled, and tears streamed down her pretty face.

"I'm fine, sweetheart." Nan covered her hands over Charlie's.

"All right, I'm going to leave you two alone." I pushed to my feet. What I needed to say to this girl wasn't going to be said here with an audience. I owed her more than that. She needed to know how I felt and what I was willing to do about it.

She'd always felt like I hadn't fought for her, but starting today, I was going to fight like hell.

"I'm sorry. I don't want to take away from your time with Nan. I'm sure you've got to get back to the city soon."

My gaze locked with hers. "Take your time. I know you were terrified yesterday, and it's important that you see that she's okay. It's important that you know that you saved her life by getting her here so quickly, Ladybug."

"Okay," she whispered. "Thank you."

I leaned over the bed and kissed Nan on the cheek and winked at Charlotte before walking out the door.

I heard Nan's voice. "Oh, swoon. He is something, isn't he?"

I barked out a laugh as I made my way down the hall.

I was preparing for how I was going to win Charlotte back.

Not that she was ever really mine.

But I was ready to change that.

Chapter 27

Charlotte

I came back home and took a nice, long, hot bath after spending a few hours with Nan, Jilly, and Kalie at the hospital. I hadn't slept much last night, and I was exhausted but relieved that she was doing okay. Dilly had spent the night with me because she was convinced that I'd have nightmares like I used to after our mother passed away.

But I knew this was different.

It had been terrifying and scary seeing Nan on the floor like that—but I'd realized something. I was stronger than everyone thought.

Stronger than even I thought.

Because I learned at a young age that I could survive anything.

Seeing Ledger didn't hurt the way I thought it would, because I realized that I wasn't ever going to get over that man. He was the love of my life, and I was lucky to have experienced that. Even if I didn't get to keep him forever, I knew that I'd never love anyone the way that I loved him, and that was okay.

I pulled on a tank top and some jean shorts so I could paddle out to the lake in my boat. I wasn't going to let my canoe stay tied to the dock forever, just because I missed him. I was going to hold on to those memories with everything I had.

I pulled my hair into a ponytail and jumped when someone knocked on the door. I glanced through the peephole and was surprised to see Ledger on the other side. I tugged on the doorknob and met him face-to-face.

"Hey. What are you doing here?"

His eyes scanned my body from my feet up to my eyes. "I wanted to talk to you. Do you have a minute?"

"Yeah. I was just going to take the canoe out."

"How about we talk out there?" he said.

"Okay." My stomach dipped, and my fingers itched to reach out for him. But I stopped myself and led him out the door and down to the dock.

Ledger was wearing a pair of khaki shorts and a white tee. He looked so freaking good, it was hard not to stare. He climbed into the boat after me and untied the canoe before reaching for the paddles.

"I just stopped by to see Nan on my way over here, and she said you stayed for a few hours today."

"Yeah. I'm just so glad she's okay. That was pretty scary. It really puts things in perspective, doesn't it?"

"It does. That's what I wanted to talk to you about."

My stomach dipped at the way he was looking at me. His

shoulders strained against the white cotton fabric, and the veins in his forearms were on full display as he pulled the paddles, and we glided through the turquoise water. The sun was just starting to set, and the sky was a beautiful mix of oranges and pinks and yellows.

"What's on your mind?" I asked as I leaned back and closed my eyes, letting the last of the sun beat down on my face before it tucked behind the clouds.

"You are."

I stayed perfectly still, because I wasn't expecting that, and I didn't want to read into it or try to figure out where he was going.

"What about me?"

"Look at me." His voice was firm and serious.

I opened my eyes and sat forward. "I'm looking, Ledger."

"I love you, Ladybug. I was a coward for not saying it sooner. It certainly isn't because I wasn't feeling it."

I tucked my lips beneath my teeth and tried to compose myself. It had been an emotional rollercoaster this last week. Between him leaving and Nan's heart attack, I couldn't take much more.

"Don't play games with me," I said, my voice betraying me as it shook.

"I'm not. I'm here because you are all that I want, Charlie. I've been fucking miserable. I haven't slept. I haven't eaten. I hate my job." He reached for my chin and forced me to look at him. "My life does not work without you. You are what's been missing. What's always been missing. Only you."

A tear broke free and trailed down my cheek, the salt hitting my lips as I shook my head. "Is this because you thought Nan was going to die, and you're just reacting?"

He pulled me into him, wrapping his arms around me as the boat rocked. "I was on my way here to talk to you before she had her heart attack. I was already coming for you. You weren't taking my calls or responding to my texts, so I got in the goddamn car and started driving. And then Nan had a heart attack, and you saved her, just like you saved me."

"From what?" I croaked as I pulled back, needing to look into those dark eyes of his.

"From my miserable, lonely life. No one ever felt right, because I'd already found the other half of my heart when I was young. I was just too much of a coward to admit it."

"So what does this mean? You want to see me twice a month?" I shrugged as his hand found my cheek.

"It means I want to see you every fucking day for the rest of my life. I want you to be the last person I see before I go to sleep and the first person I see when I wake up. I will fight like hell for you, Charlotte Thomas."

I was at a loss for words as tears streamed down my face, when he did the most unexpected thing of all. He pushed back and got down on his knee and reached into his pocket.

"Nan and I had this deal that if I ever did tie the knot, it would be with her wedding ring. I never took it seriously because I never thought I'd feel this way. But I told her that I was staying in Honey Mountain, and I drove back over to the hospital after you left to tell her that I loved you. And that I would be needing that ring of hers."

My mouth gaped open, and I laughed and cried at the same time, trying to stay put in the boat without flipping out of it.

"Why did you need the ring, Ledger?" I asked. My voice trembled because I couldn't believe what was happening.

"Because when you finally realize that you've found your person, you want to start forever right now. And I know it's fast and unexpected, and I'll wait for however long you need. But I want to marry you, Ladybug. I want to spend my life with you. I don't want to hide it from anyone or anything."

I nodded, trying to speak over the gigantic lump lodged in my throat. "I love you. It's not fast for me, because I've loved you for as long as I can remember."

His thumb swiped at the tears running down my cheek. "I want you to know that I went to the firehouse after I left the hospital, and I asked your father for his blessing. I told him that I've loved you since we were kids, and I'd do whatever it took to be the best husband I could be, if you agreed to be my wife."

I shook my head and smiled. "I can't believe you did all this."

He reached for my hand. "I'm going to ask you officially so there's no question about what this means."

"Okay," I whispered.

"Charlotte Thomas. Will you make me the happiest man in the world and marry me?"

My lip quivered as I was completely overcome with emotion. "Do you even need to ask?"

"I just want to hear you say it," he said, as his thumb stroked my palm.

"Yes. You had me at *Ladybug* all those years ago."

He chuckled and slid the gorgeous antique ring on my finger. "You know if you want a different ring, we can go pick one out. But this one is yours, too. This one represents the greatest love I've known in my life. Everything that I want to share with you."

I glanced down at the ring and shook my head. "It's absolutely perfect."

"You're perfect." He tugged me onto his lap, and the boat rocked back and forth as his mouth found mine.

When we landed in the cold water, I didn't even care. Our mouths were tied together, and his hands came around my hips to hold me against him. When we finally came up for air, my head fell back, and laughter bellowed out of me.

"This is crazy. I can't believe we're getting married. We don't even live in the same city."

His feet found the bottom of the lake, and my legs wrapped around his waist.

"Oh. I quit my job. Did I not mention that?"

"You quit your job?" I gasped and searched his gaze with concern. "Why? You love your job."

"No. I love architecture. I love creating things. And my boss is an enormous dickhead. He wasn't ever going to make me partner, and it's time for me to branch out on my own."

"I like the sound of that. Start chasing those dreams, Ledger Dane."

"I already got the one that matters most. The rest is just icing on the cake."

I pushed his wet hair away from his face and smiled. "Is it weird that we're getting married when we never really dated?"

He barked out a laugh. "I really don't give a fuck. We haven't done anything right, but for whatever reason, it just works for us."

"It does, doesn't it?"

"So, I have an idea. I've got two jobs lined up, but there's no rush to get either started immediately. We're still working on the details."

"Okay," I said.

"You're on summer break, and we can wait for Nan to get out of the hospital, which will give us time to plan…"

"Plan what?"

"That beach vacation you've always wanted to take. Let's do it. You and me."

"You and me. I like the sound of that."

He pulled my head down, and my mouth crashed into his. And it was the most magical moment of my life. I learned that life was full of ups and downs, but as long as you kept moving forward, you would find your way.

And this boy had always been the direction that I wanted to go.

We stood out in the lake, kissing for what felt like forever.

And I never wanted it to end.

• • •

CANCUN, MEXICO

"How's that piña colada?" he asked as I took one more sip of my fruity cocktail. We were both lying on a large daybed on a private beach in Mexico. Ledger didn't do anything small. He planned this entire vacation for us. Once Nan had been released from the hospital, and Ledger had come to an agreement regarding the museum project and with Dan Garfer for the middle school, we caught the next flight out of Honey Mountain.

No one seemed to be surprised that we decided to get married.

Jilly jumped up and down, and Garrett shook his head and laughed because apparently, he'd known this day was going to happen all along. Nan got a little weepy, which surprised us, and Kalie cried. As far as my family goes... my father insisted everyone come and hear the news at Sunday night dinner that weekend. He couldn't stop smiling when I told him how Ledger had proposed, because all my father ever wanted was for his girls to be happy.

Dylan gave me an I-told-you-so look and then made some comment about how she was the last Thomas girl standing. Everly and Vivian both hugged me and offered to do anything they could to help plan the wedding, and Ashlan jumped in my arms and thanked me for all the new book material I'd given her.

"It's heavenly, just like this entire vacation." I had my legs draped over his, and the bed had a sheer white fabric that shielded some of the sunshine from us.

"I wish we could just get married here, but I know your family would be pissed, and Nan would lose her shit."

"Yeah. I don't think that would go over well, but I'm not really feeling the big wedding thing. Jilly was so stressed out, and I don't know, I just have a few things that are important to me."

"What are they? I want you to have everything you want."

"I already do," I said, rolling onto my stomach and pushing up on my elbows.

"So, what are these *things*?"

"I'd like to wear my mom's dress. I claimed it a few years

ago, and no one fought me for it. It's stunning and chic and perfect. We've got Nan's ring and my mother's dress—I'd say we have about all the positive mojo a wedding can have."

He reached for my cheek, the pad of his thumb tracing across my bottom lip. "I'd say we do, too. What else?"

"I've got the groom I've always wished for. I'd like to have our families there surrounding us, a handful of pink peonies, some good food and drinks, and I think we call it a day."

"Oh, yeah? That's all you need?"

"It is."

"So, we'll keep it simple. Only the people we're closest to. If you agree to get that piece of land I found for us, we could do it right there on the property. Bring out a tent and tables and whatever you want."

Ledger had wasted no time. He found a gorgeous piece of land on the lake, and he wanted us to build something together. He said he'd draw whatever my vision was. He just hoped it would be larger than the postage stamp I currently lived in.

"Well, you make a very good case, Mr. Dane."

"Only when it comes to you."

"I think I can get on board with this idea." I gave him a chaste kiss and leaned over to get my journal. I thought about my mom and how I wished she could be here to see how happy I was.

But in a way, I knew she was here with me.

When I wrote the three things that I was thankful for today... I chuckled.

Happily.

Ever.

After.

Wasn't that what everyone wanted? To find what makes them happy and then do it every day after. Whether it be a job, or a passion, or another person who feeds your soul. It's your version of happiness, and that's what I've been chasing for years.

There are times in your life when you feel like nothing is ever going to work out the way you want it to.

And then the man of your dreams shows up at your school and makes your stomach flip.

Maybe you bend the rules to make it work. Maybe you find your new normal.

But either way, you're doing it with the one who makes your heart race.

And Ledger Dane was that for me.

I looked up to find him staring at me, and I set my journal down and smiled. "What are you looking at?"

"My whole world," he said, and tugged me down to him.

He kissed me like *I was* the only girl in the world.

And I kissed him back the same way.

Because I found my forever.

I found my happily ever after.

"I love you, Ladybug," he said when he pulled back to look at me.

"I love you." I tangled my fingers in his hair.

"Forever." He rubbed his nose against mine.

Forever.

Epilogue
Charlotte

We were all over at Everly and Hawk's house, because Jace asked us to be here and not to tell Ashlan that he'd invited us. He was being very secretive, as was Ledger, who had been over here with Hawk and Niko doing something all afternoon. I'd tried to get it out of him, but he said he would be breaking guy code if he told me.

We were all gathered in the kitchen, and Hawk had the lights off.

"This is super odd," Dylan said. "Why are we in the dark? I can barely see the salsa. How am I supposed to eat my chips?"

Hawk barked out a laugh. "Well, I do have some news for you while we're waiting, you smartass."

"Oh, do tell," she said.

"There are some big changes happening with the Lions."

"Are you really retiring after this season?" she asked.

Everly came to stand beside him, and he smiled at her before turning back to my sister. "I really am. We want to have another baby, and I can't be doing that when I'm getting my ass kicked out on the ice, day after day. They want to bring me on as a part-time coach, and I'm thinking about it. But, the big news is that the owner, Duke Wayburn, told me that his chief legal, Roger Strafford, is retiring after this season. I told him about you and that you graduated first in your law school class and how you've been clerking for some big judge." He smirked. "Basically, I told him that my sister-in-law was a complete badass."

Everly beamed and reached for his hand. "He really pushed hard to get you an interview, and the Wayburns are all about family, so he said he's going to give you a call next week."

"Shut the front door. You got me an interview with the San Francisco Lions?"

"Damn straight. I mean, your sister is being humble. She jumped in and told Duke that he'd be a fool not to give you a chance. I believe she called you the *legal mind of the future*."

Dylan fist-pumped the sky. "Damn straight. I am going to bring my A game and knock Duke Wayburn on his ass."

"Well, he won't be the only one you need to impress," Everly said. "You may be interviewing with him and Roger next week, but his son, Wolfgang, is going to be starting with the Lions in a few weeks. Duke is going to be stepping back from his duties after this year, as well, and his son, Wolf, is being groomed to take over the whole operation. He'll be recruiting and finding new players for next season and getting the lay of the land."

"Where is he now?" Dylan asked.

"He's been a Navy SEAL for the last decade, and I've only met him a few times, because he's been traveling so much with the Navy. He's a kickass dude that will take no shit. He'll be good for the team. He'll be back in a few weeks, so whoever replaces Roger will be working closely with Wolf."

"Hmmm... a Navy SEAL slash billionaire? That's an interesting mix." Dylan tapped her finger to her lips.

"He's a really good guy." Hawk reached for a chip and popped it into his mouth.

"Says the guy who likes everyone. I've only met him once. He's confident. He takes his business very seriously, and he can be a little intimidating. I think if you end up working with him, you'll have met your match," Everly said.

Dylan leaned close to me and whispered in my ear, "Do they really think there is a male version of me out there? I wouldn't count on it. The big guy broke the mold after he made me." She put her hands together as if she were praying and nodded with a big smile on her face.

"He sure did."

"And I've got my lucky earrings that I'll be wearing to that interview, so how can I miss?" Dylan lifted her hair and tugged at her earlobe to show me that she was wearing the pearl earrings that I gave her last week when she started sending her résumé out.

I laughed, and Ledger came up behind me and wrapped his arms around my waist.

I turned in his arms and faced him. "Are you going to tell me what's going on?"

"You're about to find out."

"Okay, they're pulling up. Let's all go out on the patio and try our best not to make a sound," Niko said as he reached for Vivian's hand, and she held a sleeping Bee on her hip.

"Does anyone in this family ever do anything simple anymore?" my father asked as he stood beside Ledger and me when we stepped outside.

"Well, we're having a small wedding," Ledger reminded him.

"Please. You bought a plot of land to have your wedding and build a house on. There is nothing simple about that." My father chuckled.

"Here they come," Everly whispered.

"Daddy, it's dark out here!" little Paisley shouted as they came through the back gate, and we all tried not to make a peep.

"Why aren't we going through the house?" Ashlan asked in the distance.

"Daddy, I don't like the dark," little Hadley said.

"Well, then we best do something about that!" Jace shouted, and Hawk hit something in his hand, and the entire backyard lit up with twinkle lights. There were white paper lanterns hanging in the trees. Strings of lights strung from the back porch to the trees down by the water.

A slew of gasps surrounded us, and Ashlan turned to see everyone standing there.

"What's going on?" she asked.

"The girls and I have something to ask you, sunshine." When she turned back, Jace, Paisley, and Hadley were all three down on their knees.

Dylan came to stand by me and squeezed my hand.

"Yes!" Ashlan shouted before he even asked, and everyone laughed.

Jace chuckled and reached for her hand. "Well, that'll give a guy a big head before he actually asks."

More laughter.

"Daddy, ask her," Paisley said.

"Ashlan Thomas, I love you more than I ever knew possible. I want to spend my life with you. Will you marry me?"

Her head was bobbing up and down, and she dove into his arms. "Again... yes."

"Let me put this ring on your finger, baby," Jace said.

"We ask, Wuvie!" Hadley shouted, and Ashlan looked at her and reached for her hand, moving to stand in front of the girls.

"You want to ask me something?" Ashlan was swiping at the tears rolling down her face.

"We do," Paisley said, holding something up in her hand. "Will you be our mama?"

That was it. Every single one of us was in tears now.

"I already am," Ashlan cried and dropped to her knees, and the four of them just sat there hugging.

"Damn. Four down, one to go," my father said as he glanced over at Dylan.

"Don't hold your breath, Daddy-O. I've got big plans for myself, and they don't include being tied down to some guy who can't keep up with me. Not that there's anything wrong with that." She held her hands up defensively and glanced around as we all laughed.

"I can't wait for the day someone knocks you on your ass," Everly said.

"Well, keep waiting. I plan on knocking a whole lot of people on their asses for years to come." Dylan smirked. "But it looks like I'm going to have to start with Wolf Wayburn if I want to lock down this job."

"Good luck with that one," Hawk said with a laugh.

"I don't need luck. I've got my secret weapon." She waggled her brows.

"And what's that?" our father asked.

"The charm of royalty and the killer instincts of a ruthless savage. Buckle up, kids, I'm going after this job, and I will hold nothing back."

"I don't think there's anything that could stop you," I said as I reached for Ledger's hand.

"I guess Wolf Wayburn better be ready for you," Ledger said.

"They rarely are." Dylan waggled her brows.

Ashlan, Jace, and the girls made their way over, and we were all hugging and congratulating them. We spent the next two hours eating and drinking and visiting.

Ledger wrapped his arms around me from behind after I'd just said goodbye to Dylan, who was heading home to start studying up on the Lions. My back rested against his chest, and I waved to her as she walked to the guest house, and I leaned my cheek into the crook of his neck.

"Damn, I can't wait to marry you in a few weeks," he whispered.

"Me either. Life just keeps getting better, doesn't it?"

"Everything is better with you, Ladybug."

"Don't you forget it," I teased.

"Never." He nipped at my ear. "How about we revisit that whole canoe-under-the-stars thing tonight?"

I turned in his arms to face him. "The stars are out. It would be a shame not to."

"Should we go say our goodbyes?" he asked, the pad of his thumb tracing my bottom lip.

"We'll see them all tomorrow. I think we can just sneak on out of here without saying a word." I walked backward and reached for his hand.

"Someone's in a hurry to get out on the water, huh?" He chuckled as his fingers intertwined with mine, and he fell into stride beside me.

I tipped my head back to look up at the stars.

I didn't know how I'd gotten so lucky—but I wasn't questioning it.

I was just going to enjoy it.

For the rest of my life.

Exclusive Bonus Content

Charlotte

"Okay, so today is the day. You've got your ideas, and I've got mine, so we're going to compare notes and then move forward with the drawings," I said as we sat on a blanket in the middle of our lot. The picnic basket in front of us was filled with bread and wine, fruit, cheese and a few chocolate-covered strawberries, as we had a lot to hash out.

"You do know that I'm an architect, right?" he asked. His voice was all tease.

"Yes. And you know that I'm a kindergarten teacher and I like to draw, too."

He barked out a laugh. "I want all your ideas, Ladybug."

"Obviously I want all of yours, too. This is your field of expertise, but I want to share my vision with you, and then you can work your magic and turn it into a masterpiece."

"I like the sound of that," he said as he poured us each

a glass of wine. "Cheers to building a house that we love, where we grow old and raise our family and create a lifetime of memories."

"I will always drink to that." I clinked my glass with his, and we took a sip.

"So, tell me what you see."

"Well, I'd love if we built a dock down by the water, so we can get to the canoe easily."

"Yep. That's a must. We can build a large dock, so if we want to get a boat in the future, as well as other water toys, it'll be easy to access when everyone comes over."

"We're on the same page so far," I said.

"We usually are." He tore off a piece of bread and handed it to me, just as I pulled out the cheese and set it down for us to grab. "I was also thinking of a good-size patio off the back of the house, and a built-in barbecue and kitchen area."

"Oh, that's a great idea. I'll let you run with the outside, because I'm visualizing the inside more."

He pulled out his notepad and a pencil. "Tell me everything you are wanting inside, and my job will be to make it all fit."

"Okay. So one thing I was thinking about is a guest room for Nan, or we could build a separate casita in case she needs to move in with us at some point. To give her a space of her own."

His gaze softened, and he stopped drawing. "I love the sound of that. You know she's stubborn, so she'll never say she needs it, but it'll be nice to have that option if she does. Or if your father or anyone needs a place to stay but wants their own space, we'll have it. We can add a kitchenette and a bathroom so it will be fully functional."

"That's a great plan. Now for the kitchen." I rubbed my hands together. "I want a big open kitchen so we can have everyone over. Modern farmhouse style, and a big island in the center with white shaker cabinets and a cool hood made of wood and white quartz counters. Maybe some rustic beams above."

He barked out a laugh. "That's very specific. I love that you know what you want. Let me show you something."

He started sketching on the paper and quickly drew out a rough portrait of a kitchen. "One thing I've been seeing more lately is kitchens that have two islands in the center. You can walk between them, but they offer extra storage, and in a large kitchen, having two separate islands balances the space."

"I love that. Yes. Let's do it. I like the idea of two islands." I waggled my brows. "You know, being a twin, two is always better than one, right?"

A wide grin spread across his handsome face. "Yes, that's a good point."

He continued drawing some more and showing me the layout.

"What else do you see in this dream space?"

"I'd love a walk-in pantry, and a banquette in the nook area."

"We can do that. Those are great ideas. I know we discussed a large great room, with the floor-to-ceiling doors that open to the outside," he said, drawing faster now.

The man was ridiculously talented, and I knew he was going to design our dream house better than I could ever even imagine.

"Yes. And you need a home office."

He nodded. "And a craft room for you."

"I am so excited to have a space where I can have everything out and I don't have to shove all my glitter and glue into a closet." I chuckled.

"That'll be nice. And we can customize it with shelving and a workspace for you."

"I love that," I said.

He paused and set his notebook down as he grabbed a chocolate-covered strawberry, and I did the same. "How many bedrooms are you thinking?"

"That depends on how many kids we want," I said. My voice was laced with humor as I took another bite of my strawberry.

"I want as many kids as you do," he said, his gaze locked with mine.

"That was easy. Not much negotiating there."

He tipped me back, hovering above me. "I want all of it with you, Ladybug. The life we're building together. A family. A home. All of it."

"Good, because I want all of it, too." I ran my fingers through his hair and sighed. "I don't know what I did to deserve this life, but I'm not questioning it."

"You shouldn't. All you have to do to deserve all the good things is just exist. Just be you." He leaned down and kissed me.

We got lost in the moment, per usual, until a little gust of wind caused a pinecone to fall on his head, which made us both laugh.

"Okay, should we go over the rest of the house plan?"

"I basically covered everything I wanted to cover, at least until we get to the design stage. How about we just stay right here for a while, eating chocolate-covered strawberries and looking at the water?"

"Are you saying you trust me enough to take it from here?" He smirked as he sat forward, pulling me with him. He positioned me between his legs, my back to his chest, so we were both facing the water.

"I mean, you are an architect, right?" I teased. "I think if I can trust you with my heart, I can trust you to design our dream home."

"I promise to be worthy of both," he whispered against my ear.

You already are.

Acknowledgments

Greg, Chase & Hannah…You are my forever loves! Thank you for always supporting me, putting up with my crazy hours, my endless daydreams, my embarrassing TikToks and celebrating every achievement, big and small. You are the reason that I chase my dreams every day!

Willow, I could not begin to thank you for being such a bright light in my life! For making me dream about Taco Bell and happy hour with you. Thank you for reading my words, for sprinting with me, for making me laugh and for always being there. I am so grateful to be on this journey with you. Love you!

Catherine, I am so thankful for YOU! For the talks, the laughs, the encouragement, more laughs, the spiraling and the endless online shopping for dresses for book signings. Love you so!!

Nina, I am forever grateful to be on this journey with you! Your guidance, your encouragement and your friendship mean the world to me!! Love you!!

Kim Cermak, I mean, how did I exist without you? Thank you for ALWAYS figuring everything out that needs to be done and keeping me on track! Thank you for answering my emails no matter what time of day, and for always being so kind. I am so grateful for YOU!!

Christine Miller, I cannot thank you enough for all that you do for me. For figuring all the things out that completely confuse me, and never complaining about it! I am so thankful for YOU!

Valentine Grinstead, I absolutely adore you!! I love our Zoom calls and I truly appreciate all of your feedback! Thank you for catching SO MANY things that I miss! I am so happy to be on this journey with you! Cheers to many years of working together!

Sarah Norris, I get so excited every time you send new graphics!! Thank you for all that you do to make my releases extra special! It means the world to me!

Debra Akins, thank you so much for helping to get my books out there on TikTok and being so supportive and patient! I am so grateful!

Kelley Beckham, thank you so much for all that you do to help me get my books out there! I am truly so thankful!

Abi, Pathi, Natalie, Doo, Caroline, Jennifer, Lara and Annette, thank you for being the BEST beta readers EVER! Your feedback means the world to me. I am so thankful for you!!

Sue Grimshaw (Edits by Sue), I love being on this journey

with you. I would be completely lost without you. I love your feedback and talking through all the things with you!! Thank you for taking all the endless questions on this one and going back through it!! I am so grateful for your support and encouragement.

Ellie (My Brothers Editor), I am so thankful for you!! I love being on this journey with you, and I am beyond grateful for your friendship and for all of your encouragement and support. Thank you for always getting me in and making time to read my books! Love you!

Julie Deaton, I am so happy to be working with you and appreciate all that you do to help make my books even better! It means the world to me!

Jamie Ryter, I am so thankful for your feedback (and yes...your comments were the best part of my day and so entertaining!) and for your help in making this story the best it could be. I am so grateful for you and so happy to be working together!!

Christine Estevez, thank you for all that you do to support me! It truly means the world to me! Love you!

Jennifer, you saved the day on this one! Thank you for taking those panicked calls and dropping everything to do a read-through for me. I am endlessly thankful for you! From the gorgeous book bibles that help me keep it all straight to helping me with the Facebook group!! Thank you for talking through issues and always being there when I need you!! Your friendship means the world to me!! Love you! Xo

Mom, thank you for your love and support and for reading all of my words! Ride or die!! Love you!

Dad, you really are the reason that I keep chasing my

dreams!! Thank you for teaching me to never give up. Love you!

Sandy, thank you for reading and supporting me throughout this journey! Love you!

Pathi, I am so grateful to be on this journey with you! Thank you for believing in me and encouraging me to chase my dreams!! I love and appreciate you more than I can say!! Thank you for your friendship!! Love you FOREVER!

Natalie (Head in the Clouds, Nose in a Book), I don't know what I would do without you, Nat. I am so thankful for all that you do for me from beta reading to the newsletter to just absolutely being the most supportive friend!! I love you so much!

Sammi, I am so thankful for your support and your friendship!! Love you!

Marni, I love you forever, my little Stormi, and I am endlessly thankful for your friendship!! Xo

To the JKL WILLOWS... I am forever grateful to you for your support and encouragement! I treasure your friendship and love you all so much!! Xo

To all the bloggers and bookstagrammers who have posted, shared, and supported me—I can't begin to tell you how much it means to me. I love seeing the graphics that you make and the gorgeous posts that you share. I am forever grateful for your support!

To all the readers who take the time to pick up my books and take a chance on my words...THANK YOU for helping to make my dreams come true!!

Don't miss any of the sweet and sexy small-town romances of Honey Mountain!

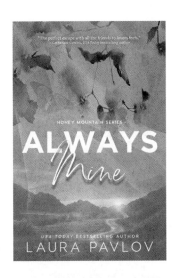

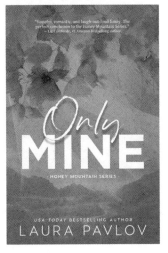

*Don't miss the exciting new books
Entangled has to offer.*

Follow us!

 @EntangledPublishing

 @Entangled_Publishing

 @EntangledPub

AMARA
an imprint of Entangled Publishing LLC